FIRST
DOWN

By Grace Reilly

FIRST DOWN

A NOVEL

Grace Reilly

AVON

An Imprint of HarperCollins*Publishers*

FIRST DOWN. Copyright © 2022 by Grace Reilly. Bonus Epilogue copyright © 2022 by Grace Reilly. All rights reserved. Printed in the United States of America. No part of this book may be used or reproduced in any manner whatsoever without written permission except in the case of brief quotations embodied in critical articles and reviews. For information, address HarperCollins Publishers, 195 Broadway, New York, NY 10007.

HarperCollins books may be purchased for educational, business, or sales promotional use. For information, please email the Special Markets Department at SPsales@harpercollins.com.

Originally published as *First Down* in USA in 2022 by Moonedge Press, LLC.

Bonus epilogue originally published online in 2022.

Designed by Diahann Sturge-Campbell

Library of Congress Cataloging-in-Publication Data has been applied for.

ISBN 978-0-06-338411-8

23 24 25 26 27 LBC 5 4 3 2 1

For Anna, whose support made this book possible.

Author's Note

While I have tried to stay truthful to the realities of college football and college sports in general throughout this book when possible, there will be inaccuracies within, both intentional and unintentional.

Please visit my website for full content warnings, as some heavy topics are discussed in this book.

FIRST
DOWN

CHAPTER 1

James

I've just arrived on campus when my phone starts ringing.

My asshole little brothers made their ringtones match, so whenever either one of them calls, vintage Britney Spears blares out of the speaker. I've got nothing against Britney, obviously, the woman's a goddess, but nothing about "Baby One More Time" screams number one nationally ranked college quarterback.

Of course, those fuckers know I don't know how to change it back to something normal. I may be twenty-one and grew up on my phone like everyone else, but technology has never been my strong suit. And I'd rather strangle myself with my jock strap than ask either of them to help me with it.

And fine, maybe I like it. Just a little. I get out of the car and hum along as I pick up the phone, grateful no one is around. It wouldn't do for McKee University's new QB to make a first impression as a 2000s pop lover. I have a reputation from Louisiana State University to uphold.

Cooper's voice fills my ear, rough and impatient like always, as I walk toward the administrative building. "You here yet?"

"Not near the house. I need to talk to the dean first, remember?"

He makes an agonized noise that sounds akin to a dying animal. "Dude. We've been waiting forever. If you don't hurry up, I'm taking the owner's suite."

"What if I want the owner's suite?" I hear my other little brother, Sebastian, say in the background.

"That should be for the guy who fucks the most, Sebby," Coop says. "And you never bring chicks home and James is sworn off the V until he's in the league, so that leaves me."

"Age trumps fuckboy status," I inform him.

"You're barely older."

"Irish twins," I say with a grin, even though Cooper can't see me. We're technically not, since we have about two years between us, but our last name's Callahan and we're super close, so it's a joke that's always stuck around. (Although never in front of our mother, who can make balls shrivel up with a single look.) "Right, baby bro?"

I pull open the door, flashing the receptionist a smile. On the line, Coop and Seb continue to argue. I have it on good authority that my smile makes panties melt away, and this time is no exception. I see the moment the girl—a student worker—flicks her gaze down from my face to my groin.

"Hey, I gotta go. See you soon." I hang up before Cooper has a chance to try and keep the conversation going. Despite his bluster, I know he won't pull a move like that without talking to me first. And maybe I will let him have it—he's right about the fact I'm not letting girls into my life right now. Not if I want to win the national championship and get drafted to the NFL in the first round.

"Hey," the girl says. "Can I help you?"

"I have an appointment with Dean Lionetti."

She leans over the appointment book in a way that very obviously lets me see the swell of her tits. She does have a fantastic pair of them. Maybe in another universe, I'd ask her out for a drink. Hook up with her. It's been ages since I've *seen* a pair of tits, much less got to play with them. But that would be the definition of distraction, especially if she turned out to be all drama.

No distractions. I didn't come to McKee for any reason except getting my football life back on track . . . and fine, yes, to get my degree. Which is why I'm in the Dean of Student Affairs's office instead of on my new field, scoping out the territory.

"Name?" she asks.

"James Callahan."

Her eyes widen in recognition. Maybe she's an NFL fan and thinks of my father first. Or maybe she read something about me transferring schools. Either way, she looks about ready to climb me like a tree.

"Um, you can go on in. She knows you're coming."

"Thanks." I'm proud that I manage to resist winking at her. If I do that, she'll just find me on campus somehow and insist we're soulmates.

I stride down the hallway and into Dean Lionetti's office, taking stock of the surroundings as I do. I can't help it; I notice everything. I'm used to taking in the other team's defensive line, looking for subtle shifts in their play calling, figuring out where they're going to try and crush our rush or passing game.

Dean Lionetti has a sweet setup. Fancy dark wood desk with a glass case of awards behind it. Books all along one wall, plus two velvet-covered chairs in front of the longer part of the desk's L-shape. Behind the desk sits Dean Lionetti. Her gray hair must be natural; it falls at her chin-line in a severe bob. Her eyes are slate gray too, and her '80s-style power suit? You guessed it, gray. She stands when she sees me, holding out her hand for a shake.

"Mr. Callahan."

"Hey," I say, then wince internally. Not that I seek this out, but usually people—women especially—are a bit warmer to me when they meet me. My mom calls it the Callahan charm, and it's foolproof . . . except for now. Dean Lionetti is looking at me like she can't believe I'm standing in her office. She must have some sort of immunity to all things dimples, because her gaze only sharpens as I take a seat.

"Thank you for coming in on short notice to talk," she says. "I have some updates about your classes this semester."

"Are there any problems?"

I only have a couple of major requirements left to fulfill in my senior year. My major is mathematics, so most of the classes I take deal in numbers alone, but I have space for an elective or two. This semester I signed up for marine biology, which is apparently easy and involves no essays, thank fuck. According to Seb, the professor is ancient and spends most of class showing *National Geographic* documentaries.

Dean Lionetti raises a gray eyebrow. "There is an issue with your writing class."

Fuck. I have a lot of regrets about last year and letting myself fall off the wagon with schoolwork is a major one. I'm terrible at writing, but it's still pathetic that I failed a writing class as a junior that I was supposed to take and pass freshman year anyway.

"I thought everything transferred."

"Primarily, yes. But when we reviewed your records more closely, it revealed that you failed the required writing course the first time around. Perhaps at your old university they made concessions for athletes"—she says *athletes* like we're all a fungal disease—"but here, we hold everyone to the same academic standards. The professor was kind enough to open a spot in his class, which you will retake this semester since it's only offered in the fall."

I feel that marine bio class slipping away by the second. Dean Lionetti's tone makes it clear she thinks I'm dumber than a sack of rocks. She probably feels the same about all athletes. Which is total bullshit. What happened last fall was the anomaly; I've worked hard for my degree. As Dad constantly reminds us, our athletic careers will only last so long. Even if I have a successful NFL career—which I fully intend—most of my life will take place after I retire.

"I see," I bite out.

"I've updated your schedule accordingly—the class will take your elective spot. If you have any questions, please take it up with my office or the registrar."

She stands. She's dismissing me without a discussion.

I swallow down my embarrassment, although my ears feel hot. Welcome to McKee University.

I take a deep breath and remind myself why I'm here. Degree, then the NFL.

I just have to find a way to get through this class first.

* * *

WHEN I ARRIVE at the house, Seb is sitting cross-legged on the floor, untangling a ball of wires. I give him a wave as I set my keys down on the foyer table, then look around the den. Aside from Seb and his mess, there's not much going on yet, just an L-shaped leather couch, a coffee table, and a TV mounted on the wall. When we decided to rent this place for the year, seeing as all three of us would be at the same university, the listing said it wasn't furnished. I have a sneaking suspicion about who made this happen.

"Sandra sent it all," Seb says, gesturing around the room with the ball of wires. "The delivery guys set it up like this, but we could move it if we need to."

Mom works scary-fast. I'm sure that the moment she heard her boys, the two she carried and the one she adopted, were sharing a house together, she went to Pottery Barn. Lucky for us she has nice taste.

There's a crash overhead, and we both glance up with a wince.

"He's doing some redecorating," Seb says. "How was the meeting?"

I wander into the kitchen. I doubt the fridge is stocked yet, but a guy can hope there's at least beer. I don't drink much during the season, but technically we still have a couple days before everything gets in full swing. Lo and behold, there's a six-pack sitting on one of the shelves next to a container of pineapple and a carton of eggs, and for some reason, a little jar of horseradish.

Seb appears in the doorway as I bring the heel of my hand down on the bottle cap to loosen it. It comes off with a pop. I take a long pull, and I must look as pissed as I feel, because Seb's brow knits together.

"What happened?"

"The dean decided to fuck me, that's what happened. She's making me retake that writing class."

"That sounds dumb."

"It is dumb," I grumble. "But they looked at my transcripts and saw I failed it at LSU. Back when . . ."

"Yeah," Seb says. "I know."

A twang of hurt runs through me. Last year was a disaster for many reasons, but I miss Sara anyway. I take another sip of my beer, looking around the room. There's a big dining room table, which reminds me of our home in Port Washington, and the kitchen isn't half bad. Plenty of space to cook some meals like the athletic trainers suggest. There's a door to the backyard, which has a firepit and a couple of Adirondack chairs set up around it. And once Seb has the den set up, we should be able to play some sweet games.

"This is nice," I say.

"Yeah," he says. "So, what did you say?"

"I mean, I couldn't argue it. I did fail the class."

"But it's your senior year. You came here to play football."

"And graduate."

Seb sighs. "Yeah. There's that."

My parents are amazingly supportive of my football ambitions, in part because Dad played. He knows the grind better than anyone. It was his dream at first, that one of his boys would follow in his footsteps, but it became mine too long ago. Without a shot at playing in the league, my life would feel incomplete. End of story. But we've been taught that education is important too, so as much as I'm focused on football, I know I need to get my degree. As talented as Cooper is at hockey, Dad didn't even let him enter the NHL draft because he was afraid that he'd leave college for the league and never graduate. Following Seb's dad's wishes, he entered the MLB draft after high school, but in the end, he committed to playing at McKee and re-entering the draft when he's eligible after junior year. "You can't ask your new coach to intervene? He practically stole you from LSU, he wants you here."

"And be the entitled athlete the dean thinks I am?"

Seb shrugs, running his fingers through the mop of blond hair on his head. "Maybe you won't fail this time. Maybe it'll be easier. Or you'll just know more since you've been taking college classes for a while now." He grimaces as we hear another crash from upstairs. "And there's always Cooper."

"The last time I asked him for help with school, I almost stabbed him. He's impossible."

"With a pen."

"I stand by my actions. It was an attempted stabbing and I'm not sorry."

Seb sighs. "Well, maybe someone else can tutor you. You can't fail this."

"No." I finish the beer in a few gulps and set it in the sink. The panicky feeling I've been fighting since the dean's is threatening to make a reappearance. I'm not good at writing. Never have been. Throwing a wrench this big into the year that's supposed to catapult me into a starting quarterback position is almost as bad as an injury. But an injury I could play through. Grit it out through the season. This? This is out of my depth.

Coop saunters into the kitchen, sweaty and wiping his face with his T-shirt. "Finally got the desk put together. Only took four fucking hours."

"Aw, look at you," Seb says sweetly. "Waylaid by a crappy desk."

He flips Seb the bird without wasting a beat. "So, I have a proposition."

He stops as he takes in our expressions. Whatever he's thinking, it probably involves a party, and I don't know if I have the energy for that right now.

Instead of launching into his speech, his eyes narrow. "Okay, who are we fighting?"

Bex

One of the benefits of being a senior in college is first dibs on the dorms, which is how Laura and I got this awesome two-bedroom suite. Kitchenette, living area, private bathroom, bedrooms that aren't closets . . . it's almost enough to make a girl forget that when this year is over, she'll be back to living over the family diner and spending her days wading through small business hell.

It's me. I'm the girl.

But currently I'm on the couch, arm dangling almost to the floor, sandals precariously close to falling off. My shift at the Purple Kettle, the on-campus coffee shop, ended a little while ago, and after being on my feet for the stampede of students back for the semester and ready to arm themselves with lattes and cold brew, I'm beat. I'd prefer to be in bed, but Laura insisted on a fashion show. Apparently, the lighting is better in the living room.

"Oh, and I got this cute mini dress," she calls from her bedroom. "I was thinking about it for tonight."

"What's tonight?" I say. I already sort of know the answer, because it has to be a party, but the question is where. A frat? Sorority? Frat-slash-sorority? An off-campus house that's full of frat bros anyway?

"A party!" Laura crows as she comes out of her room. She's in high heels that show off her tanned legs to perfection, and her little black dress clings to her curves like tape. For some reason, she has on devil ears and is carrying a little pitchfork. "And before you say you're not coming, you're coming."

Sometimes I think about the fact we're best friends and . . . it doesn't stun me, exactly, but it does leave me wondering. Laura is smart as hell, don't get me wrong, but college has been a series of social functions for her, and as for me, when I'm not working on school or at the Purple Kettle, I'm at Abby's Place, putting out fires and generally trying to contain the chaos. Laura's father is a fancy lawyer, and her mom is an equally fancy doctor, and she spent half the summer in Italy and the other half in St. Barts. I spent it nursing a broken heart, arguing with suppliers, and slinging hash browns for locals.

I love her, but our lives are totally different. She's been at McKee since freshman year, and this is only my second since I transferred in as a junior. Two years at McKee instead of the local community college is the absolute maximum amount of time I can be away from the business, sort of, and the money is the amount of loans, while still astronomical, that I feel comfortable taking out. Maybe one day I'll do something with this business degree and the port-folio of photography that quietly keeps growing, but for now, the plan is the same as ever. Home. Diner. Take over the business so my mother can quit pretending she's well enough to do it herself.

She hasn't been anywhere near that since the moment Dad walked out of our lives.

"Earth to Bex," Laura says. "Do you like it?"

She's holding out a dress, a shimmery white thing with a thigh slit and a plunging neckline.

"For me?"

"Yeah!" she says. "And don't worry, I got you angel wings and a halo."

"Um . . . why?"

"Because the party theme is Angels and Demons," she says. "Were you even listening?"

I scrub at my face with my palm. "No," I admit. "Sorry. I'm exhausted."

Her shoulders droop. "You told me you wanted to have more of a social life this year."

"A social life, not a spin as a Victoria's Secret model."

She rolls her eyes. "Just try it on. It'll look gorgeous on you and make your tits look fabulous. All the boys will drool over you."

I take the dress, knowing from experience that she won't drop it until I at least try it on. I have a different white dress in my closet that will have to do for this party. "And why do I want that?"

"Because you need to show everyone you've moved on from Darryl! It's perfect. Find some sexy guy to grind up against! Get drunk! Just try and enjoy yourself, Bex, please."

I did tell her, during one of our many FaceTime sessions over the summer, that I wanted to try having a social life before I effectively shut that down by moving back home. I don't think I'm capable of having a boyfriend again, but she's right, I could try to hook up with someone. It's been a long, lonely summer. I got plenty sweaty, but never for fun reasons.

I've never been a hookup sort of person, but there's a first time for everything, right?

"I'll try it on," I say as I stand.

She squeals, clapping her hands together.

"But I'm not promising I'm wearing it. Or that I'm going to the party."

She just smiles serenely. "Don't forget the halo."

As I shimmy into the dress in my room—and Laura was totally right, my boobs look amazing—I can't push away the part of me, however petty, that hopes Darryl is there tonight. Maybe Laura's right. If he sees me dancing with someone else, he'll get the message that we're over. It's not like anything else I've done has worked, even though he's the one who cheated.

As if on cue, my phone screen lights up. Darryl again. I can't believe that at one point in time I thought this was sweet. Supportive.

Now he makes me want to claw my hair out.

> You're coming tonight, right? I miss my angel.

For some reason, the most annoying part about the message is the way he knows I'm dressing up as an angel. I'll never be the devil, and maybe that's part of the problem. He doesn't believe we're truly over because he's used to getting exactly what he wants and I'm not forceful enough to get it through his thick skull that we're not a couple anymore. Just because he's an arrogant football player who believes he's going to marry his college girlfriend and have her follow him around his whole career like half the men in the NFL . . .

I put on the wings, looking at myself in the mirror over my bedroom door with a frown. They look ridiculous, big and fluffy and not something I'd normally want to wear in front of other people. I grab the halo and put it on too. Somehow, it ties everything together. With some winged eyeliner and matte lipstick for edge?

Darryl will be drawn to me like a moth to a lantern. But hopefully other guys will too.

CHAPTER 3

James

I tug at my collar as I follow my brothers up the drive to the frat house. Every lamp in the house must be on because light is spilling out like a jack-o-lantern, and I swear I can feel the bass of the music under my feet. As Cooper puts his hand on the door handle, about to pull it open, I stop him. I take a deep breath as I continue to adjust my collar.

I've had a lot of teammates over the years. It's important to start off on the right foot, especially with the leaders of each group of players. I met most of them through the minicamp earlier this month, but that was formal. Work. They all knew where I came from and what I've accomplished, so we put our heads down and got started on season prep. But a social situation like this? That matters more. They might follow my calls on the field because they want to play a good game of football, but for me to actually get to know them and earn their trust, we have to connect socially. I have to get to know each of them, both as individuals and in connection to the team. What are they studying? Who's going to join me in the league next season and who has other post-graduation plans? Who's a rookie, who's coming off an injury, who has a partner I need to remember the name of? I know I can prove myself to them on the field, I've been doing that my entire life, but this is a make-or-break moment. I don't do many parties during the season, so this is it.

And right now, I feel like an ass in my suit.

"We look like a couple of mafia dons," I say. "Are you sure this is the theme?"

If I go in there in a black suit with a black silk button-down, the top buttons undone and my hair slicked back, and everyone else is in shorts and t-shirts, I will murder my brother. He even convinced me to wear the gold chain I usually only bring out for special occasions. The one consolation I have is that he looks just as ridiculous.

Coop runs his hand through his hair and hits me with a grin. I have no idea how he manages that shaggy mess. He uses his status as McKee's star defenseman to get away with pretty much everything. "You look good, I promise. What's more devilish than a bunch of hitmen for the mob?"

"He's not lying," Seb says as he adjusts the heavy watch on his wrist. That clunker looks straight out of the '80s. "It is themed, like every other party this frat throws. It's mostly to get the girls to dress as skimpily as possible."

Coop claps Seb on the back. "And I for one am ready for some eye candy. Can we go in? Or do you need another moment to angst?"

I stand up straighter. "No, let's go."

As the door swings open, I'm hit by a wall of sound. There are people everywhere—and fortunately everyone is dressed as stupidly as we are. Beer pong, a dance floor, strip poker, a bunch of couples making out, a threesome getting going in the corner . . . seems standard, as far as frat parties go.

A bunch of dudes who must be from the baseball team wave to Seb, who heads over to the beer pong match. A girl wearing the tiniest skirt I've ever seen makes eyes at Cooper, who is more than happy to follow her onto the dance floor. If I had to bet, she's a puck bunny who came to this party hoping to hook up with him specifically. Which leaves me standing in the doorway, scanning for anyone I know from the football team.

The hair on the back of my neck prickles when I realize someone is staring.

Fuck, she's pretty. An angel in white, complete with feathery wings and a golden halo. She's leaning against the far wall, watching the mob of dancers, a red solo cup dangling from one delicate hand. Her hair, a strawberry blonde, falls in waves around her face, framing big, dark eyes. Her heels make her legs look long and supple. I almost take a step forward, magnetized by the way she's looking at me, but then I hear my name.

I turn to look for the source of the voice, and out of the corner of my eye, I see the girl shift and head for the dance floor.

"Callahan," the voice says again. I recognize it now; it belongs to Bo Sanders, one of the offensive tackles and a fellow senior heading into the league come fall. He's so tall he practically towers over the rest of the partygoers. Case in point: I'm six foot two, and I have to look up to meet his eyes. I can't wait until he's fucking squashing the opponents' defensive lines. With him in my corner, I'll have days to make my passes.

When he reaches me, he presses a beer into my hand and claps me on the back. "Nice to see you, man."

"Sanders," I say, clapping him back. "Fuck, you're rocking the suit better than half the boys here."

He's in a deep red suit, complete with a handkerchief folded into his pocket. The color looks great against his deep brown complexion.

"This is my pregame fit," he says. "Prime time, baby."

"Forget pregame, you look draft ready. Everyone else here?"

"We're in the next room playing poker."

I groan. "Not strip, I hope."

"Like you have anything to worry about," he practically shouts over his shoulder as I follow him through the crowd. The music is thrumming inside me, loosening me up.

I'd like to say I'm beyond noticing every look we get, but I'm not there yet. It comes with the territory, being the number one ranked college quarterback in the country, not to mention the fact I'm good-looking. Most everyone knows my face and my skillset. And the female attention isn't something to complain about. As we squeeze by a large group, a girl sticks a scrap of paper with what must be her number on it into my waistband.

Tempting, but the bigger part of me wants to go back to the dance floor, find that little strawberry-blonde angel, and ask her for a dance.

"Callahan!" someone else practically roars as Sanders nudges me forward. I recognize most of the guys in the room, which sets me at ease. There's our kicker Mike Jones, and Demarius Johnson, one of the best receivers in the college game. Darryl Lemieux, another key receiver in my weapon arsenal. Jackson Vetch, the rookie who will be my backup QB.

Not that I'm planning on giving him a minute of gametime. He can take over next year when I'm in the NFL.

I settle down next to Darryl on the couch. He's part of the poker game, but he's not paying attention; he's grouching about his girlfriend. Or wait—ex-girlfriend?

"You can't help if she doesn't want to be with your ugly ass anymore," Sanders says, which earns a laugh from the rest of the guys. I agree; what's the point in pining over someone who doesn't want you anymore?

But Darryl is my new teammate, which means I'm on his side.

"I'm sure she'll come around and realize what she's missing,"

I say, clapping him on the shoulder. "Don't even worry about it." I take a long sip of beer, relishing in the crispness. Even if everyone else gets shitfaced, this is the one drink I'm allowing myself tonight.

"You know what?" Darryl says. "Fuck her. She's no better than any of the other girls I've had."

"Her tits are nice," says Fletch, one of the D-men.

"She was stuck-up," Darryl declares. "Always so fucking busy. It's like she left me no choice but to look elsewhere."

I hide my displeasure behind another sip. I don't want to rock the boat, being the new guy here, but assholes like him raise my hackles. Bo catches my eye and shakes his head slightly.

Okay, so there's something deeper at play here. I take the cue to back off. "Anyone going to cut me in?"

Darryl grabs the deck of cards and shuffles them sloppily. "She's a stubborn whore bitch, Fletch. You don't want to fuck with that."

Shit. We're doing this.

"Hey," I say. The edge of seriousness in my tone must be evident, because Fletch freezes halfway to reaching for his beer, and Demarius looks up from his phone. "I don't know what things were like around here before me, but on my team, we respect women."

Darryl opens his mouth. I put up my hand to stop whatever stupid shit he's going to say next.

"Even if she's your ex and you think she did you wrong." I look him right in the eyes. "You got that?"

Darryl glances around the group, rolling his eyes. "Got what, exactly?"

"Need me to repeat myself?" I set my beer down, deliberately slow, and lean back in my seat. "You should know I don't like saying the same thing twice."

Darryl stands. His shoulders are set, his fair face flushed with anger. On the field, I'm going to have to watch to make sure our competitors don't bait him with the wrong taunt. He'll draw penalties with a temper like this. "You got something to say to me, you tell me to my face. Don't tip-toe around, Callahan, it's not cute."

I stand too. Maybe it's dumb, but I'm pleased I have at least two inches on the guy. I lean in close, until we're almost touching. "Fine. Call a girl—any girl—a name like whore or bitch again, and I'll fuck you up."

He scoffs. "Like you'd fight me."

"I won't fight you." I look around at our teammates, who are hanging on every word of this interaction like we're WWE heavyweights in the spotlight. "But I won't throw to you."

The threat practically echoes around the room. Sure, I won't punch him, even if he deserves it. But if I make him invisible on the field? That's worse than being sidelined. Darryl knows it, I know it, and so does every guy in this room.

"Oh shit," Demarius says. "He's serious."

"You can't do that," Darryl says. "I'm one of the best receivers on this team. You need me."

"You think I can't?" I tilt my head to the side. "Why do you think Coach recruited me? To be a good little soldier or to be a fucking leader?"

Darryl's mouth snaps shut.

I glance around at the rest of the boys. "What do you think? Why am I spending senior year here?"

"To win us a fucking national championship," Bo says.

"Yeah," says Fletch. "National champs or bust."

I snap my fingers as I point over to him. "Exactly. And if you want that, you play by my rules. You got that?"

My demand hangs in the air for a long moment. I can hear the music in the background, thumping the beat into the walls. This is the make-or-break moment. Not what I expected it to be, but here it is, and if I don't get the boys on board now, this season is going to be hell.

Then Bo says, "Hell yeah," and everyone else is nodding and voicing their assent. Someone claps my shoulder, but I don't tear my gaze away from Darryl, who is looking very much like he wishes he could take a swing at me.

"Got it," he says finally. He shoulders past me roughly, heading out of the room.

Christ, I feel bad for the girl that had the misfortune of dating him.

Bex

I stand in the corner, watching as Laura dances with her boyfriend, Barry. They're in the honeymoon stage again after yet another "maybe we're done" conversation, and honestly, there's a real possibility of frottage happening in front of half the party. As it is, they're grinding and making out like they can't see the other dancers, the spirted beer pong game taking place across the dance floor, or the game of strip poker spilling over from the next room.

I'm about three seconds from ripping off my stupid halo and bolting out into the humid August night.

Darryl arrived a while ago, accompanied by half of McKee's football team. He didn't spot me; fortunately, I was in the corner, chatting with some of the girls I'm friends with through Laura. But even though he made his way further into the house, into one of the other rooms filled to the brim, I can feel his presence.

Last year, feeling his closeness, even when we weren't right by each other, was one of the best parts of dating. I could look across the room and find his eyes on me, even when he was talking to his friends. Whenever I went to one of his games, there would be a moment where he looked back into the stands, somehow found me, and winked.

His attention set my skin on fire in a good way. Now? My skin is still on fire, but out of annoyance and embarrassment.

I shouldn't have come tonight.

I don't know which is worse, dreading the moment his drunken ass will try to sweet-talk me back into bed, or seeing him accept the flirtations of some football groupie sorority pledge. I know better than anyone how weak he is for a girl who promises him she's his biggest fan.

Across the room, the front door opens and three guys dressed in black suits walk in. Two of them have dark hair; the third's is blond. He heads into the party right away, and soon one of the dark-haired ones, the one with the beard and a roguish grin, heads to the dance floor with a girl. That leaves the third guy. The one who has my attention. Unlike the guy I'm assuming is his brother, he doesn't have a beard. I can't stop staring at his perfect jawline, the way his thick hair curls over his forehead. He's tall and obviously built, and the way he looks around . . . it's like he notices every detail.

Including me.

I swallow, trying to act casual as I feel his gaze on me. Then Bo Sanders, one of Darryl's teammates, goes over to say hi to him. Is he a football guy, then? He must be new, since I don't recognize him, and I spent a lot of time with the team last season.

I down the rest of my warm beer and make my way through the dance floor. Someone stomps on my foot, which knocks me back into Laura. She giggles, gripping me in a tight hug. "Bex! Aren't you having the best time!"

Barry presses another drink into my hands. "It's cold!" he shouts unnecessarily.

This beer is blessedly less lukewarm, so I take a gulp. Laura kisses me on the cheek, her arms still wrapped around me, swaying us in a circle. I can smell her signature orange blossom perfume along with the beer on her breath.

"Hey," I say. "I'm going to head out."

Her lips, still somehow perfectly black with matte lipstick, curve into a pout. "What? No way! We're just getting started!"

"Darryl's here."

"Darryl?" she says loudly. "Where?"

My stomach pinches in on itself. I pull her away from the dance floor, back into the shadows. "Stop, you'll summon him."

She roots her feet in place and refuses to go another step. Even though she's tipsy, her eyes are clear as she looks at me. "Bex, it's okay. Don't tip-toe around him, show him you're fine."

My voice cracks as I respond. "But what if I'm not?"

The pain in my words must register to Laura because she throws Barry an apologetic look and drags me off. We go upstairs, past a few different couples in various states of hooking up, and stop in front of one of the doors. Laura pounds on it. Someone shouts at us to go away, but she just jiggles the handle until it swings open, revealing a shirtless dude pulling up his pants and a girl adjusting her braless, backless dress.

"What is your problem?" she shrieks.

"Out!" Laura says with such ferocity they don't argue. She pulls me inside and makes me sit down on the edge of the tub, locking the door and leaning against it. She blows the hair out of her eyes and takes a deep breath.

"Do you want to get back together with him?" she says.

"No," I say immediately.

"Do you still love him?"

"God no."

"Good. Because he's a jerk. Hooking up with random cleat-chasing chicks."

I grimace. Last spring, I stumbled upon all the sexting, and then the story of his side pieces unraveled, and that had been the last blow in a rapidly unwinding relationship. I met Darryl at a party like this my first semester at McKee, and the prospect of having a real boyfriend for the first time since high school was too tempting to resist. During the football season, it was easy to be with him; he was so busy that he didn't mind me being busy as well, as long as I went to all the home games. But after the season imploded and the spring semester rolled around, he became clingy, overprotective, and downright annoying—while at the same time cheating on me with a couple of football groupies.

Despite me making it clear that I wanted to break up, he spent the summer texting and calling like he thought there was a chance I'd change my mind. Darryl Lemieux is not used to being told no, especially by women.

Now all the distance I built up over the summer, with him being home in Massachusetts and me still in New York, has vanished in one night, at one crummy party.

"I know," I say. "I'm not . . . I'm just dreading it, you know? He's going to try to rekindle things, and when he realizes I can't do that, he'll act like a baby. That's what he did the entire time we were together. Someone doesn't give him what he wants, he complains. It's like he thinks that just because he can catch a stupid football, he's some sort of god."

Laura sits down next to me on the edge of the tub. She glances back and makes a face. "Ugh. Someone needs to clean this bathroom, it's nasty. Nice showerhead though."

I laugh weakly. "Not regretting living with me instead of here, are you?"

"Definitely not. Like I'd choose having to guard my hair iron from vultures instead of living with my bestie."

I knock our shoulders together. "I'll go home. Have fun with Barry."

She frowns. "Are you sure you want to take a cab back alone? It'll be expensive."

"I'll figure it out," I say, even though inside I curse, because she's right. An overpriced cab, even only going back to the dorms about fifteen minutes away, will pretty much negate what I made from my shift at the Purple Kettle. On the way here, I was fortunate enough to tag along in the rideshare Barry paid for.

"Okay," she says, pulling me into a hug. "But call me once you get back to the suite. And maybe go around the back."

I kiss her cheek and disentangle myself. Winding my way through the crowds, I head to the back room, where there's an exit to the patio.

"Bex."

Like an idiot, I turn—and almost smack right into Darryl.

"Hey," he says, steadying me with his hands on my shoulders. He squeezes before stepping back. "Finally, I thought maybe you wouldn't show. What're you drinking, baby?"

I close my eyes briefly. The urge to flee is right there, pushing down on me, but I force myself to stay put. "I . . ."

"I know," he says, snapping his fingers. "Vodka soda."

That's not even remotely right—if I'm drinking something other than beer or wine, it's usually a rum and coke. I try to sidestep him, but he wraps his arm around my waist. He strokes the neckline of my dress, his fingers brushing my skin.

I grit my teeth. "Darryl."

"I knew you'd come back around," he says. "You're so pretty, baby. So glad you came tonight for me."

I push his hand away. "I didn't."

Out of the corner of my eye, I see him. The guy from before. He has a frown on his face. He takes a step forward.

"I'm here for him, actually."

I don't know what possesses me, but I shake myself free of Darryl and walk over, reach up to put my arms around this stranger's neck . . . and kiss him.

On the lips.

Holy hell, this is a good kiss.

Maybe I caught him by surprise, but he's kissing back, his arms coming around my waist to squeeze me, his warm body pressed right against mine. He deepens the kiss, his tongue darting out to drag over the seam of my lips, and I open for him, let him kiss me until I'm breathless and overheated. He smells woodsy, like his cologne has hints of pine in it, and those hands . . . they're big and set low on my body, almost brushing my ass. After half a second's breath, I kiss him again. Intending it to be a goodbye. To run away. But he tightens his grip, plundering my mouth with his as he steals my very breath.

This one kiss—from a stranger—is better than any kiss I shared with Darryl. He's ridiculously good at this, kissing like it's his job. I could happily stay here the whole night, offering my mouth to his.

He shifts a little, bending down to murmur against my ear, "What's your name, sweetheart?"

The spell shatters. Maybe Laura wants me to be the sort of person who can handle a hookup, but I can't. I'm not built for it. And I'm not letting myself get drawn into another destined-for-doom relationship, even if he kisses like sin and smells like a goddamn forest. I step back, untangling myself from him. My body immediately misses his touch. I feel cold, even in this crowded room. The music is still pounding, but I can barely hear it.

I turn on my heel and make a beeline for the door.

"Wait," I hear the guy say at the same time Darryl calls my name.

Shit. What the *hell* did I just do?

CHAPTER 5

Bex

I can't believe that out of every person I could have kissed, I chose McKee's new quarterback.

The so-called savior of our football program.

Darryl's teammate.

Shit.

Even though I need to get up and make myself presentable for class, I can't stop thinking about the kiss. Not the ugly expression on Darryl's face or the way half the party was staring as I fled, but the way the kiss felt. I've always been self-conscious when it comes to kissing, especially in front of others. But this guy . . . he made everyone and everything else disappear. The way he put his hands on me to pull me closer, the slight roughness of his lips, the reluctant way he broke it off . . . it was a kiss worth fantasizing over. I inch my hand under the waistband of my sleep shorts, just skimming the top of my sex. Maybe I can go fast and—

No.

I can't. Even if I can't stop imagining his lips right between my legs.

I glance at my phone. I have time.

I bite my lip, torn, and then slide my fingers downward. My fingers part my folds, and I bite back a gasp when I nudge my clit. I circle it with the tip of my finger. James had just a bit of stubble; if he put his mouth where my fingers are, it would scratch against my skin deliciously. Would he be gentle? Rough? I may have started the kiss, but he took it over with ease. Quarterbacks are in command of the whole show on the field, right? So, in bed . . .

"Bex!" Laura says, banging on my door.

My hand flies out of my shorts. I can't even be mad at her because it's for the best. No good would come from fantasizing about a guy I kissed out of panic, in front of my ex.

My face burns suddenly. He might've kissed me back, but with a couple days' distance, I'm sure he realizes I'm a freak. I can only hope I don't accidentally run into him on campus. It's a good thing we go to a big university. Maybe he's not much of a coffee drinker and he won't even stop by the Purple Kettle.

"Bex," Laura calls. "We have to go soon if we're going to grab breakfast before class."

"I'll be right there!" I roll out of bed and yank open the closet door. Throw on a pair of jean shorts and a faded Abby's Place T-shirt—when it comes to the diner, that's the one thing that's always in supply. I yank a comb through my hair and find my sandals. I guess I'm just going to have to forego makeup today.

After brushing my teeth and throwing my stuff into my back-pack, Laura and I head out. Our dorm has a dining hall attached to it, so it's blessedly easy to get that first cup of coffee and some toast without making it ourselves every time. That's the best part about college and one of the things I'll miss the most: food on demand. My hashbrowns are way better, though.

When we both have a plate, we find a booth in the back. Laura looks a lot more put together than me—full face of makeup, matching jewelry. I'll bet she got up to work out and everything. And what was I doing? Getting off to the thought of some dude's stubble?

Ugh. I just worked my way out of an all-consuming, soul-sucking relationship. I can't give myself any unnecessary distractions this semester, not with Mom and the diner and everything else I have going on.

"Are you going to tell me what happened?" she says finally.

I raise an eyebrow as I take a sip of coffee. "You know already."

"I know because Mackenzie told me, but that's not the same thing as *you* telling me."

"You did tell me to get with someone else."

"Not him!"

I scrub a hand over my face. "I know it was monumentally stupid. I hope Darryl hasn't been annoying about it to him."

It would be just like him to try and fight the guy, even though *I* kissed him and it's not his business anyway. That's another reason why I hope we never have to interact again. I would spontaneously combust if my body betrayed me in front of him, plus he might've had to fend off a pissed-off Darryl, which means he wouldn't be too pleased with *me*.

"You're blushing." Laura leans in, delight on her face. "Does that mean he's a good kisser? He looks like he kisses as a preview to what he's like during the deed."

"Laura!" I screech. I look around, but fortunately we're out of earshot of anyone else.

She just waves her piece of toast around. "What? He's hot as fuck."

I take a bite of my bagel. "It was good."

"Just good?"

"Really good," I admit.

She sighs. "It's too bad he's Darryl's teammate. Boys tend to have codes about that shit."

"I don't want him anyway," I say. My traitorous stomach flops as I think about the kiss again. "I'm not getting involved with anyone right now."

"So, if he came up to you and asked you on a date, you'd say no?"

"Like he would."

"You kissed him and ditched him. Guys like the chase."

"Well, I hope he doesn't waste his time." I check my phone. I'm going to have to hustle if I want to get to class on time, since the building is across campus, so I stand, grabbing a napkin for the rest of my bagel. "I'll see you later."

"Are you going to that writing class?"

I roll my eyes. "Unfortunately."

When I transferred to McKee, some of my credits didn't transfer over with me, so I've been working double-time to finish every requirement and graduate on time. This writing class—an introduction to college writing—is the most annoying of all of them. Insulting, too—I'm a business major, I've written plenty of papers over the course of my college career. I'd have preferred to be working on my photography this whole time, but that's life.

"You'll get through it. Text me what you want to do for dinner later," she says.

I wave goodbye and head out into the morning. It's still way more summer than fall in terms of the weather, so after a few minutes of fast walking, sweat starts to gather on my forehead and under my arms. I hitch my backpack further onto my shoulder, lengthening my stride as I hit one of the many hills on campus. We're only about an hour outside of New York City, so not in the mountains, but I swear it's like McKee terraformed the place to be extra hilly. I didn't need to bring my camera with me, but I like carrying it just in case I get inspired, and now I'm regretting it, because it keeps slapping against my hip.

I make it with a minute to spare, find a seat in the back, and take out my notebook, along with a gel pen. They're my one school-related luxury. Something about writing notes in sparkly purple instead of plain black makes studying business when I'd rather have been a visual arts major just a tiny bit more bearable.

The professor, who, no surprise, is an old white dude, starts to talk about the importance of taking this class seriously because it sets up everything you do in college. It's not bad advice, but definitely meant for the baby-faced seventeen- and eighteen-year-olds around me. Essay structure? Check. The importance of outlining your work? Double check. Peer feedback? Got it. The one thing I can say about this class is that it will be an easy A, and considering the five other classes I'm taking to stay on track with wrapping up my major requirements, I can't complain.

"Let's take a closer look at the syllabus," the professor says. "Make sure you get a copy."

Someone drops into the seat next to mine. I suppress a snort. Poor baby freshman. I'd bet five bucks it was an alarm malfunction.

Whoever it is, they smell *really* good. A bit like pine.

I look up, and my heart does a little surprised flop in my chest.

"Hey," says James freakin' Callahan. "Got an extra copy of that?"

CHAPTER 6

James

"Yo, Coop! Get your ass up if you want a ride!"

I keep pounding on the door as I shout. I have no idea how my brother manages to always be on time for hockey, but late for everything else. He's like a hurricane, but the eye of the storm is always hockey.

Seb walks out of the bathroom at the end of the hallway, a towel wrapped around his waist. He snorts as he takes in the scene. "Still not up?"

"You heard him last night, right? 'James, we have class at the same time, let me tag along with you?'"

"Yep."

"Jesus. Cooper, I'm not going to be late for the first meeting of this stupid-ass class!"

The door flings open, revealing my brother, who looks about ready to skin me alive. His eye is actually twitching. I give him a grin and say sweetly, "There's Sleeping Beauty."

"I hate you."

"You love me. I don't know how you've survived college without me."

"He barely has," Seb pipes up, which causes Coop to give him a death glare. He looks like he's considering violence, so I step between them swiftly. Seb might've been adopted after his parents passed when he was eleven, but he and Coop act like honest-to-god twins. Which means a lot of hitting.

"You have five minutes," I tell him. "I'm waiting in the car."

When Coop retreats to his room, Seb doubles over in laughter, shaking water droplets everywhere. "Hate living with us yet?"

"Nah, you know I love you both. I missed you when I was down in Louisiana."

In the week or so since I moved in—specifically into the owner's suite of this house, thank you very much—I've made myself at home when I haven't been busy with football practice. I missed living with my brothers. Even though we've always been busy with our season schedules, living together meant we'd see each other at least some of the time. Sometimes that meant saying hi to Coop as I arrived home from practice and he was just heading out to the rink, or catching the end of one of Seb's games after a training session. We've had breaks and summers since college began, but the past few years I've been lonelier than I'd be willing to admit aloud. I had friends at LSU, good teammates, but I've always been closest with my family. My parents, who are both amazing people. Coop and Seb, even when they're being terrors. And Izzy, the best little sister a guy could ask for. Getting to live with my brothers for one last year before I graduate and go off to some city, who knows which one, to play in the NFL, is a gift.

Seb smiles. He might not be a Callahan by blood, but he's got a smile that fits right in. A little bit of the Callahan charm. "I missed you too. Good luck today, kick butt with the class."

I scowl as I head downstairs. "If I survive, that is."

Coop dashes down the stairs, his Nike backpack slung over one shoulder. He shoves his feet into his sandals and follows me out the door to my car, rubbing his eyes all the while.

"What class do you have again?" I ask as I pull out of the driveway.

He steals a sip of my coffee. I throw him an outraged glance, but he just shrugs and says, "Hey, you didn't give me time to make a cup."

"Which brings me back to my question. Are you late to class every day?"

"Don't tell the folks. And the class is Russian lit."

I whistle. "That sounds hard."

He looks glum. "Tell me about it. I kick myself every day for choosing this stupid major."

When Dad talked Cooper out of entering the NHL draft at eighteen so he could have a guaranteed four seasons in the NCAA, Cooper tried to get back at him by picking the least practical major he could think of—English. He likes to read, so it makes sense, but he seriously underestimated all the work that would go into it, a fact that never fails to make Seb burst out laughing like a hyena.

"Maybe you'll have something in common with Nikolai, finally."

Nikolai Volkov is Coop's nemesis. The son of a Russian hockey powerhouse, he's the star of McKee hockey's biggest rival, UMass Amherst. Coop hates him, mostly for his dirty style of play, which is hilarious considering Coop spends time in the sin bin every game. I don't know the ins and outs of hockey the way he does, but I'm pretty sure avoiding penalties is a priority like it is in football.

"Ha ha. I don't think so."

Our off-campus house is in Moorbridge, the town that entwines around McKee's sprawling campus, so fortunately we get where we need to be quickly. I drop Cooper off at his building and make the short drive over to mine. I have five minutes before my butt needs to be in a chair, surrounded by freshmen.

Ugh.

I park in the nearest student lot and run over to the building. If I'm going to manage to wrangle a Pass out of this class, I need to make a good first impression.

I find the right room and ease the door open. Crap, this class is way smaller than I was expecting. McKee really does take the whole professor-to-student ratio seriously, I guess.

I sneak to the back, where a girl sits alone, head bent over what must be the syllabus.

When I'm about a foot from her, I freeze. That's her. Little Miss Angel. Fucking kissed me better than anyone in my life and then left like we hadn't just sparked like lightning.

Not to mention she's Darryl's ex. The very one I told him to treat with respect, oh, an hour before she kissed me. After she fled the party, Darryl got in my face about the kiss, but fortunately he believed me when I said I didn't know who the hell she was. I still don't, really, just that her name is Beckett, she's drop-dead gorgeous, and she kisses like the world is burning down around her.

Oh, and she's off-limits.

She can't possibly be a freshman, so what is she doing here?

I sit down next to her. She smells nice, like vanilla and maybe something floral. And she's very studiously highlighting parts of the syllabus. Since I don't have one, I say, "Got an extra copy of that?"

The professor, an older-looking man with gold-rimmed glasses, stops his droning. He clears his throat as he glances down at a stack of papers. "Mr. Callahan?"

"Yes. I'm here."

The professor keeps his gaze on me as he talks. "Students, please make note of the start time for this class once more. 8:30, not 9. It will benefit your academic career not to be late to class. Other professors may not be so . . . accommodating."

He punctuates that by passing a copy of the syllabus my way.

Fuck. I can feel my blush like a five-alarm fire. "Sir, I'm sorry. I was up early for practice and went home to get changed before coming here, and I must have mixed up the times with my other morning class."

A girl looking back at me shrugs, as if to say, *tough*. I resist the urge to make a face at her. Beside me, Beckett heaves a sigh.

"What?" I say.

"I just lost a bet with myself. I thought you were late because of an alarm malfunction."

"I'm an athlete. I don't have alarm malfunctions."

"Ah," she says. "Right, I forgot that you guys are gods who never need alarm clocks, whereas we mere mortals—"

Mr. Professor clears his throat again. He's still looking my way, although I'm gratified to see him raise his eyebrow at Beckett too. "As I was saying, the tenets of academic writing at the college level include . . ."

"What are you even doing here?" I whisper.

She taps her foot against mine under the table. "I'm wondering that about you."

"I failed this class when I first took it." I don't know what compels me to be totally honest with her. Maybe it's her big brown eyes or the way she's twirling a little sparkly gel pen or how I can't stop remembering how her lips felt on mine.

I shove that thought away. She's my teammate's ex. Even if she was interested, I couldn't.

"I transferred here last year," she murmurs. "Even though I

took classes like this at my community college, they didn't accept all my credits."

"That sucks."

She shrugs slightly. "It's not like it'll be hard, right? We've been in college for three years already."

I look at the syllabus. Twice-a-week seminar-style meetings. Weekly writing assignments. *Peer feedback.* My skin begins to crawl. Give me partial differential equations and I'm fine, but this? This is impossible.

And of course, a third of the grade is a final research paper on a topic of our choosing. Fuck. Me.

This class might not be difficult for her, but it's going to be hell for me.

I give her what I hope is a semi-normal smile and settle in for the rest of class. But despite my best efforts, I can't stop stealing glances at her. She looks just as pretty now as she did fancied up in that little white dress. My type, too; those full tits are distracting even in a T-shirt.

Did she choose me to kiss because I'm her type as well? I'm not dumb, I know she kissed me to get back at Darryl. But she could've approached any guy at that party, and I'm the one she landed on.

She bites her lip as she thinks. That's cute.

The professor wraps up his spiel with an in-class assignment. We're supposed to read an article about research into academic writing and distill it down to a paragraph explaining the thesis and main points.

I stare at my copy of the article for so long the words start to blur. All around me, the other students are highlighting keywords and scribbling notes in the margins; Bex seems to have a whole color-coded situation going on. I tug at the collar of my shirt, glancing at the clock. We have twenty minutes for this assignment, and five have already passed.

I force myself to read the first paragraph again. I pick up my pen, tapping it against the table before underlining a sentence with a bolded word in it. I remember that tip from one of the tutors I've had over the years, be it the one my parents hired in high school or the many I tried to work with at the writing center at LSU.

"If you're stuck, try reading the topic sentences first," Bex says.

I glance over at her. She taps my paper with her pen.

"Look," she says. "There are a couple of sections in the article, and each of them covers a different topic."

"But then it just talks about something else," I say.

"Not quite," she says. "I know it seems like it, because it starts out talking about research into academic writing and then switches into an anecdote, but that's just to humanize the topic a little. It's not important information."

I'm only about seventy percent certain I know what an anecdote is, but I don't want her to think I'm even more of an idiot than I already sound, so I just nod along. "Seems unnecessary."

She snorts, which makes a dude in front of us clear his throat pointedly.

"Skip down to the part where it discusses the study on formal writing education," she whispers.

She takes me through the article, showing me her own annotations as examples for what to focus on. I can't help but be a little distracted by the way she smells and how much I'm yearning to lean in closer, but in the end, I have a halfway decent paragraph to hand in. Something about the way she explained it made way more sense than in the past, which is weird, considering I've always had such a block when it comes to writing. If she was the professor, I'd probably get an A in this class.

I reach over and pluck her pen out of her hand. She gives me an outraged look, but I just grin and scrawl *thank you* on her syllabus. I have to resist the urge to include my phone number. That would definitely make her scowl even more adorable, but I don't want to come on too strong—because a plan is forming in my mind, and I need her on board for it to work.

After all, who would say no to a paid tutoring gig?

CHAPTER 7
Bex

H ey, Bexy."

I turn to James, a scowl already planted on my face. I figured he was going to follow me outside, but no one calls me Bexy. Darryl ruined that nickname completely.

I hike my bag over my shoulder and shade my eyes as I look up at him. He's even taller than Darryl. It's seriously unfair that he's up there and I'm all the way down here. "It's Bex."

"Sorry. Bex, can we talk?"

I thought he was attractive at the party, all dressed up in a black suit, but this is somehow better. He's wearing a tank top that shows off his drool-worthy shoulders, athletic shorts, and sandals, and I have no idea why it's working so well for me, but it is. The irrational part of my brain is chanting, *"Lick him!"* Pathetic.

But his eyes are *so* blue.

I mentally put my foot down. "I have work."

"Where do you work?"

I huff out a breath. "Just make it quick. I need to be back across campus in fifteen."

"Let's walk and talk, then."

He literally starts walking away, and I can't help it, I burst out laughing. He looks so confident—and if he headed that way, he'd end up in town.

He looks back at me, frustration in the set of his jaw. "What?"

"It's this way." I point in the opposite direction and start fast-walking. "And you can walk with me, but only because I have a feeling you're going to make this conversation happen one way or another."

He jogs to catch up to me. "What makes you think that?"

I look up at him. "We kissed."

"We did," he agrees. He lowers his voice. "It was a good kiss."

"I'm sorry I did it," I blurt as my cheeks heat up. "Darryl—" I stop walking abruptly and bump into him. He steadies me, his big hands on my shoulders, and for a hot second they feel like a brand going straight between my legs. What's with this guy? My body loves when he's close. The entire time I helped him with that assignment, I wanted to lean my head on his shoulder.

"Bex," he says. "Look at me."

If I look into those ocean eyes, I'm afraid he'll be able to see how much he's affecting me.

He hooks his finger under my chin and tilts up my head. My hands flutter around him for half a second before finding their way to his sides, resting lightly. Even through the shirt he's wearing, I can feel the power in his body. Stupid athletes with their stupidly sculpted bodies. Something about knowing the dedication that had to go into creating and maintaining it gets me every time.

"Hey," he says, still holding me in place. I'm frozen, looking up at him, torn between pulling away and staying put. "Don't worry about it. I know a jealousy kiss when I see one."

"I didn't realize you were his teammate."

He just shrugs. "Like I said, don't worry about it. We talked; we're cool."

"Oh. Good." I stop and pull away, giving us a couple feet of distance. "Um. Even besides that, we can't."

"I know," he says easily. "But I did want to talk about something else."

His lack of a fight hurts, which is stupid, because I just told him to back off. It would never work. Even if we just hooked up, that would make things more awkward for him and Darryl, and I'm still firmly in no-relationship land. I don't know him, but the intensity he radiates practically screams that he doesn't do anything halfway.

"Why do you know?" I say.

He smiles slightly. "Because a girl like you deserves more than I can give, Bex."

I risk a step closer in his direction. Angle my chin up as I look at him. "How do you know what kind of girl I am? We barely know each other."

"I saw how you looked after we kissed. Trust me, you're a relationship girl."

Annoyance pricks my skin. He's right, but the casual way he says it makes it feel like a negative. "And you don't do relationships?"

"I don't do anything but football." His hand curls and uncurls on the strap of his backpack. "Let's just move on, okay?"

"Fine," I say as we continue walking. I make sure there's a few feet between us, so I don't do something idiotic like try and kiss him again. Even though we decided to move on not two seconds ago, I still feel that tug in my belly. I never gave much thought to chemical attraction before, but how else can I explain this? "What did you want to ask me?"

"Thanks again for helping me out in class." He runs a hand through his hair, ducking his head. "Um . . . you know I failed the class the first time."

"Yeah."

"I really can't fail it this time. I need it to graduate, and it's only a fall class."

I sigh. "Yeah. I think that's shitty of them since they're so strict about it."

"You obviously know what you're doing. I need your help. I need you to tutor me."

"There's a TA. You can go to office hours."

"Can't."

"Can't?" I repeat.

"I have practice all of those times," he says. He looks genuinely frustrated, which almost makes me say yes, but I give myself a little mental shake. I really don't have time to be someone's tutor, even if he paid me. Not to mention the attraction to him that I can't seem to turn off. Being alone with the guy to tutor him? That sounds like heaven . . . I mean, torture.

He scuffs the pavement with his shoe. "I'll pay you for your time, of course."

"I have a full course load too. Six classes. Plus my job." *And running home whenever the diner needs help*, I think but don't say aloud. There's always something wrong at Abby's Place and it's never my mother who can fix it.

"There's nothing I can offer to convince you?"

"Nope."

He raises his eyebrows. "Everyone has a price."

"Everyone but me, apparently." I check my phone and curse softly at the time. I need to hustle to get to my shift on time. "Sorry, I need to go."

"I'll figure it out," he calls when I'm almost up the next hill.

I look over my shoulder at him. He has a smile on his face, but there's something else in his eyes. A challenge. I'm suddenly aware of one very important fact: he's an athlete. And athletes don't quit.

"Oh yeah?"

"Whatever your price is," he says, taking a deliberate stride forward, "I'll figure it out, Bex."

I try to swallow, but my throat is as dry as a desert. Some small, traitorous part of me wants to ask if that's a promise.

"I doubt that. See you around, Callahan," I manage to say, turning back on my heel.

I feel his gaze all the way to work, burning straight through me.

CHAPTER 8

James

I secure the football in my hands and step back, scanning the field up ahead. Even though this is just a scrimmage, the boys are playing hard; the defenders on the other side fighting to get past my blockers. I only have another second or two before someone breaks through and I'm sacked.

Twenty yards ahead, Darryl breaks free of his defender, hand raised. I fire in his direction. It's a little high, so I expect it to go over his head, but at the last minute he snags it and hauls it close to his chest. He runs with it tucked under his arm, diagonal to hustle away from the defense, and out of bounds. Coach Gomez blows the whistle to end the play.

I jog over to where the offensive line has grouped together, wiping the sweat away from my face with the hem of my practice jersey. Darryl walks over to our huddle slowly.

Since that party, I've seen Darryl entirely too much and Bex entirely too little. Despite us clearing up the kiss situation, it's never been more obvious that a guy hates my guts. On the field, he plays his hardest, but in the huddle, on the sideline, and in the locker room, he acts like I don't exist. After our win against West Virginia this past Saturday, in which he caught two of my touchdowns, I thought he'd chill out, but nope. You'd think he caught us fucking on top of the pool table, not kissing *once* when it was clear I didn't even know who she was.

I'm convinced he can read my mind and knows I can't stop thinking about her. I managed to get her number last class, and we've been texting, but no matter what I offer her in exchange for tutoring, she turns me down. Doesn't mean she's not on my mind all the fucking time. I was almost late to practice this morning because I got caught up jerking off in the shower to the thought of how her soft curves would feel against the hard planes of my chest.

"Great catch," I say when Darryl finally reaches us.

He chews on his mouth guard. "Thanks."

Okay then.

"Let's all come around, gentlemen," Coach Gomez says. He spits, hands on his hips, as we form a circle. He reaches out to slap Darryl on the back, and a genuine smile crosses the guy's face. "Good catch, buddy. So, boys. I think we're beating out some of that sloppy play that slowed us down last week."

We nod in agreement. Last week was a win, which is all that matters at the end of the day, but there were times where we could have taken a commanding lead of the game and didn't.

"We keep playing this crisp and we'll walk out of the home opener with a win. I want you all back bright and early tomorrow to go over film. Their new left tackle is a big fucker and we need to shut him down if we have any hope of getting to Notre Dame's QB."

From across the huddle, Darryl gives me a look. I meet it stone-cold, but inside, I'm rolling my eyes. I don't care if he hates me as long as he leaves Bex alone, but that doesn't mean it's not annoying.

Most of the team heads back into the showers, but I stay put. So does Darryl.

"You got something to say to me?" I ask. I cross my arms over my chest. Fuck, I'm sweaty as hell and want nothing more than to take a shower before heading home, but I'm tired of this shit. We're teammates, which means we're brothers, and if I have to tell him to his face that I'm not going to make a move on Bex, I guess that's what I'll do.

Even if saying that will hurt. Sitting next to her in class, even though it's only twice a week, is a special form of torture. Yesterday she wore a sundress and I nearly got hard looking at the way she crossed one tan leg over the other.

Darryl digs at the grass with the toe of his cleat. "Heard you've been talking to her."

"Says who?"

"Is it true?"

"I don't see how it's your business."

"She's my girl."

"Was your girl. And she can text whomever she wants, especially when it's about a class she's taking with someone."

He takes a slow step forward. "But you want her."

"Hey," Coach Gomez barks. "What're you still doing out here?"

I reply without taking my gaze off Darryl. "Just talking strategy, Coach."

"I need to talk to you, Callahan." Coach glances between us, as if he can literally see the tension sparking in the air. "Lemieux, go on in and shower before Ramirez uses up all the hot water."

Darryl keeps up the stare for a long moment before leaving.

"Is there a problem I ought to know about?"

I haven't known Coach Gomez very long, but I figured out quick that he likes to know about personnel problems on his team. He's serious, too, still nearly as fit as when he was a player and a straight talker. The silvery strands in his otherwise dark hair glint in the late afternoon light as he waits for my response.

"No. There was a little miscommunication, but I'm handling it."

He nods. "What kind of miscommunication?"

Damnit, I'd been hoping to leave it at that. He'll smell bullshit for sure if I try to lie.

"A girl." Embarrassment burns my throat at the admission. For half a second, I'm back with Coach Zimmerman, trying to explain why the administration had called to tell him to bench me because I was on academic probation. *A girl.*

Coach curses. "Callahan—"

"It's handled."

"That so?"

"Yes."

He gives me a look that feels like an X-ray. "When we agreed to bring you here, we spoke about distractions. You remember that?"

"Of course."

He leans in, knocking his fist against my chest twice. "Son, you're going to be a star in the league. And I want to help you get there. But remember—save the off-field distractions for after you've signed your first big contract. Once your future is set, you can start to think about who will be in it."

"Yes, sir," I say with a nod.

In the aftermath of everything that happened with Sara, my dad sat me down with Coach Gomez. That conversation ended with me agreeing to transfer to McKee, and he had the same advice then. I hadn't been lying to Bex when I said the only relationship in my life was football. Last time I tried to balance both, I nearly lost everything.

I don't think much about Sara anymore, but lately, she's come up more than I'm comfortable admitting.

"All right. And how are you adjusting to McKee?"

"It's been good, sir. I like living back with my brothers."

"Shame that Rich Callahan has three sons, but only one chose the right sport." He chuckles a bit, shifting his weight from one foot to the other. "And how are the classes? What about that writing one? Still sorry I couldn't get you out of it."

"It's okay. I failed it the first time, I deserve to take it again." I run a hand over my sweaty hair. "It's fine."

"You sure? Any help I can give you?"

In the locker room, stuffed at the bottom of my bag, is my first formal assignment for this stupid-ass class.

I got a D-. Who gives a D-? The guy should've just failed me. I still can't believe that's what I got; I spent longer on that one page of writing than any of the work for my other classes all last Sunday. The thought of all those red marks on that crumpled-up piece of paper, hidden like a child's report card, burns into my mind.

And maybe that's why I lie.

I already told Coach Gomez one truth. I'm not sure I can handle another today. He's giving me the chance of a lifetime, letting me come here and lead his team to hopefully a victorious season, resetting the view the NFL has of me before it's time for the draft next spring. He shouldn't have to worry about anything but the game. Not me getting distracted by a girl. Not me still being a crap writer.

"Yep," I say. "I, um, hired a tutor and everything."

His face relaxes. "Good. Who is it? Someone from the media center? TA?"

"She's in my class. She took it already and did well, at her old school, but McKee didn't accept the credit."

He shakes his head. "This academic policy, I swear. Well, happy to hear it, son. Let's keep your eyes on the prize. No distractions."

"No distractions," I repeat. "Got it, sir."

I don't know much about writing, but I do know I've had a lot of tutors in my life, and for whatever reason, Bex managed to get through to me in a way no one else has. If there's anyone who can help me with this class, it's her. I'm just going to have to put my attraction in a little box, not think about it, and focus . . .

But first, I need to get Bex on board.

CHAPTER 9

Bex

There you go, Sam. Need anything else?"

"No, ma'am, that looks perfect." Sam, one of Abby's Place's regulars, smiles at me from where he sits on his counter stool. He unwraps his silverware with shaking fingers. I resist the urge to offer him the salt before he knocks it over again. Like small town diners everywhere, the same people come into ours almost every day for breakfast and lunch, and a lot of them are older people who don't want to, or can't, cook anymore. Sam's a widower. His wife used to take care of the cooking, but now that she's passed, he comes here for his morning eggs.

I smile before clearing the place setting next to him. I scoop up the tip, but instead of tucking it into my own pocket, I stuff it into the communal jar. Stacy and Christina need the money more than me right now. Christina catches me doing it and shakes her head, but I don't miss the grateful look in her eye. She's a single mom and her son's dad is an asshole. She's taken him to court over child support, but it's not resolved yet.

I grab my mug of coffee and take a deep sip. The morning rush has emptied, leaving behind a couple of older folks like Sam. Lunches are busy, thanks to our location in downtown Pine Ridge, and we keep things open a couple evenings a week because we sell pie and ice cream to the teenagers hanging out in town at night. Since I started at McKee, I haven't been able to take every weekend shift, but I try when I can, since the weekdays are harder for me.

Maybe someone coming in here casually wouldn't see what I see. They'd see the photography I took and carefully framed on the walls, or the polished metal buffer that wraps around the counter, or the shiplap over the booths that I painted white two summers ago. I have a deal with the florist two doors down to keep fresh flowers out front and on all the tables. But all I can focus on is the stains on the ceiling, the hole in the wall we're covering up with a photograph, and the finicky refrigerator in the back. Abby's Place is a popular spot, but like all restaurants, it bleeds money. Just getting the food to cook costs an astronomical amount, especially with my mother changing the menu every other week. People like Sam just want their eggs the way they always have them. They don't need avocado crema on the side, even if it's delicious.

The bell over the door rings, and a couple walks in. They're young, probably just a couple years older than me, and honestly, they look a lot like my classmates at McKee. She's wearing Lululemon and a gold necklace that could probably pay to replace all the appliances in the kitchen, and the guy looks just as put together in a button-down and slacks. I don't know the brand, but I'm sure it's expensive. It's probably the sort of thing James would wear out to a restaurant.

The thought of James runs through me like a bolt of lightning.

I still can't believe that he hasn't given up on trying to convince me to tutor him. It's been a week, and his offers are getting more and more ridiculous. Last night, he told me he'd do my laundry for a year. That just made me think about him seeing my underwear, which wasn't helpful in the slightest.

I need to get him out of my mind.

"Table for two?" I say, coming over with menus tucked under my arm.

"Can we sit at that booth back there?" the woman says. "This place is so charming."

I smile as I lead them to the back, by the picture window. "Thank you. It's my mother's."

"I told Jackson that we had to check out the local flavor before moving here." She sits, accepting the menus for them both. "Well, not quite here, of course."

My smile stiffens. "Of course."

Pine Ridge isn't a bad area by any means, but I'm sure someone like her, with money, is looking in one of Hudson Valley's more expensive areas. I'd bet that he works in finance or something in the city, and she wants a nice big McMansion for him to come home to in the evenings.

"Can I grab you some coffees?"

"Yes," the guy says. "Waters too. But only if it's purified."

As I'm fetching the coffees, the door opens again. I look up automatically . . . and immediately wish I hadn't.

"What the hell are you doing here?" I hiss as I meet Darryl at the door.

He leans down and kisses me on the cheek. "What a way to greet me, babe."

I back up two big steps. My hands are trembling, so I shove them into my apron's pockets, hoping my glare helps him get the goddamn message. "Babe? I'm not your babe anymore, Darryl. What's going on?"

The door behind the counter opens. It's built right into the wall, so most of the time it blends in; if you go through, you're immediately met with a cramped flight of stairs that leads to an upstairs apartment. That's where I grew up. First with both my parents, then just with my mother.

I sense the moment Mom walks into the diner. She smells like smoke and flowery perfume. When I arrived early this morning to open, she was still asleep. I'd been hoping against hope she'd just stay upstairs for the day so that we wouldn't have to talk, but she's always had impeccable timing.

"Darryl!" she says warmly, pulling him into a hug. "I thought I saw your car out front. Bexy hasn't brought you home in ages."

"That's because we're not dating anymore."

She tuts at me. "Don't be rude to the nice boy. He drove all this way on game day just to see you, isn't that sweet?"

"I have tables." I put the coffees on a tray along with cream and sugar and head over to the couple. Maybe if I keep ignoring Darryl, he'll get the message and go away.

Wasn't me kissing James in front of him enough?

Mom's right, it's Saturday, they have a home game. Darryl should be with James, getting ready to go. For all his other faults, he's a good player, that should be his focus today. Not . . . whatever this is. Embarrassing me in front of a room full of people. Drawing my mother downstairs so she can add fuel to the inevitable fire.

"Sorry for the wait," I tell the couple. "What can I get you?"

"Is that your boyfriend?" the woman says, leaning in with a conspiratorial smile. "He's handsome."

"He's familiar," the man says. "McKee?"

"Football," I admit.

"Hey, man! Kill it today!"

Darryl raises his hand in a wave. I grit my teeth and smile, hoping like hell the heat I'm feeling isn't showing on my face. "Um, your orders?"

I don't need to scribble it down, I've been holding orders in my head for as long as I can remember, but I make a show of doing it anyway. Anything's better than having to talk to Darryl.

In the kitchen, I hand the ticket to Tony, the head cook. He peers around me, a worried look on his lined face. "Do I need to get him out of here for you?"

"Nah." I give him a smile. "Thanks, though. I can handle it."

"Damn straight you can." He barks out the order to the line cooks. I stand there for a long moment, just watching them move around the cramped kitchen with fluidity.

Darryl obviously took the kiss as flirtation, not a goodbye. He's not just ignoring what I'm saying—he's ignoring what he's seeing, too.

As I walk back out, I pull Stacy aside. "Can you handle my table in the back? I need to deal with this."

"Sure." Stacy is my mother's age. She traded off with my Aunt Nicole, Mom's sister, when it came to spending time with me when I was younger, after my dad left and my mom ceased to function. She tugs on my ponytail, giving me a sad sort of smile. "I'll try and get her upstairs, too."

"Thanks."

My mom has Darryl at the counter and is plying him with coffee and a slice of pie. I watch as she lights a cigarette, blowing out the smoke expertly. She laughs at something he says, her hand on his forearm, squeezing.

Jesus.

"Darryl, let's talk."

He leans back. "Finally. Bexy, don't worry, I forgive you for kissing Callahan."

"Outside." I yank the front door open, trying to ignore the interested look Mom gives me. I'm sure she's just dying to know who "Callahan" is.

Darryl doesn't protest when I drag him around to the back of the building. "You look pretty playing waitress, baby."

"I'm not playing," I mutter. "That's the reason you cheated on me, remember? I was always here."

"Those girls didn't mean shit to me."

"So? That doesn't make it not cheating."

"Says who?"

"Says me!" I burst out. I bite the inside of my cheek to stave off the tears that are threatening to make an appearance. "Darryl, come on. You know what you did. We're over. Just leave me alone."

"I don't think so." He takes a step closer, reaching out to entwine our hands together. "Sweetheart, come on. I don't know what you were playing at, kissing Callahan, but he told me he's not interested in you, so there's no problem. We can go back to the way things were."

He told Darryl he's not interested? That stings more than it should. "You talked about me?"

He drags me even closer. "Sure we did. I had to know if I needed to fight him for making a move on my girl, after all."

He slides his hand up, circling my wrist, and does the same with my other arm too. I freeze.

"Bex," he says, "just give in and let yourself be happy. Being with me can open so many doors for you. Once I'm in the league, we'll sell this shitty place, and you can just take care of me. That's what you wanted last year, so why ruin things now? Not like your life would amount to much otherwise."

His grip tightens as he leans in to kiss me. I'm still frozen, too stunned to move as his lips graze mine. I always knew he was possessive, but this is a whole different level. This scares me.

"Darryl," I whisper.

"Yeah, baby?"

"Fuck off." I yank myself out of his grip, rubbing my wrists, and shove past him. "Go play your game. And if you bother me again, especially here, I'll call the cops."

He clenches his fists. I stare at him, terrified for the moment the swing connects with my face. My father hit my mother exactly once, shortly before he left for good, and she had a black eye for weeks. Not that it mattered much, because she was in bed mourning her marriage and the miscarriage triggered by heartbreak, but eleven-year-old me saw it every day when I crawled into bed beside her.

If you asked me while we were dating, I'd have said Darryl would never truly hurt me.

But then again, I never thought my father would hurt my mother, and he destroyed her.

He steps so close my heart jumps into my throat, a flat look in his eyes I absolutely hate to see, and pulls me in again, his fingers gripping my wrists so tightly I cry out. "You're going to wish you didn't say that, sweetheart."

I swallow hard, trying to ignore the burning of my eyes.

After a handful of seconds that stretch out into what feels like an eternity, he shoves me backward. I stumble, watching as he stalks away. I clasp a shaking hand over my mouth, trying to swallow down the shock and hurt.

I should go back inside, get back to work, but I can't make myself move. A tear makes its way down my cheek, and I wipe it away roughly.

No crying, even though my wrists are aching.

Two things are clear. One, I can't believe I ever had feelings for that asshole. And two, I need a new plan, because obviously he's not going away.

I need James.

James

Winning is always fun, but the first home win of the season is something else. The turnout was incredible; every seat in McKee's massive stadium was filled. Between the marching band and the shouting from the student section, I could barely hear the referees. I'm still hopped up on adrenaline an hour later, ready to celebrate with the team.

"There's a bar in town," Bo says as we gather up our duffels and head outside. "McNamara's. You coming?"

"I won't drink, but yeah, I'm coming."

"Sweet." He hollers the same question to Demarius, who gives us a thumbs-up from across the parking lot. "There's always a ton of girls there after a win, so if you're looking to hook up, you won't have any trouble."

"Good to know."

Not that I plan on it. One, because I don't want to create false expectations for some poor girl, and two, because the only one I've been fantasizing about lately is Bex. I've tried not to—it's not like anything is going to happen—but whenever I rub one out, she's who I picture. Her fantastic tits. The way her nose scrunches up when she's frustrated. The pouty curve of her lips.

Fuck. I need to figure out a way to put a stop to this, especially if she's going to be my tutor.

"There he is," Coop says as he walks toward me. He hugs me, then steps back so Seb can do the same. "Great game, bro."

I smile. "Didn't know you came."

"The perks of having an afternoon scrimmage. Which I crushed, by the way. I'm ready to relax."

"I'm heading to a bar, want to come?"

"McNamara's?"

"Yeah, I guess."

"Sweet," says Seb. "That place is great. I'm down."

"Same," says Cooper. "Maybe I'll see Elle."

"That girl from the sorority party? I thought you didn't do more than one hookup." Seb knocks his shoulder into Cooper's.

"I don't." He grins. "But that doesn't mean she can't try."

I roll my eyes as I get into my car. "Show me where to go." I wrestle my phone out of my jeans pocket, unlock it, and toss it to Coop. "Do I have any messages? Didn't get a chance to check. ESPN wanted to do a live interview right after the game ended."

He snorts. "Only you could make that sound casual. And yeah, Mom and Dad texted. Ooh, and someone else."

"Who?" I try to sneak a peek while we're at a red light, but Coop holds the phone to his chest.

"Look, Seb." He hands the phone over to Seb, who whistles.

"I regret this," I mutter. "Who is it?"

"It's that girl," says Seb. "Beckett."

My heart thumps extra hard in my chest. "Beckett Wood?"

"Do you know more than one Beckett?"

"What's it say?"

"She wants to talk."

"That's it?"

Seb and Coop exchange a glance. "Should there be more?" Coop asks.

"I mean, no." I make a right at Coop's direction. "But since she wouldn't let me just hire her, I've been trying to figure out her price."

"Oh, good," says Seb. "Especially since you went ahead and lied about her being your tutor."

"Don't remind me."

"Maybe she wants you to hook up with her," Coop muses. "As payment, I mean."

I think back to our conversation after that first class. I pretty much stomped on any chances of that happening. "Dude, I'm not going to sleep with my tutor."

"What? She's hot."

"And my teammate's ex."

Coop waves his hand. "Doesn't count because they broke up before you got here."

"I'm sure he wouldn't see it that way."

"Well, he's an idiot anyway."

I park the car in a lot down the street from McNamara's and heave out a sigh. "Won't argue that point."

Outside the bar, which looks packed with college kids and town regulars alike, I hold up my phone. "I'll be there in a minute. Order me a non-alcoholic beer, okay?"

Bex's text is three simple words.

Can we talk?

I call her instead of texting back. This feels too important for a text, and fine, maybe I want to hear her voice.

"Callahan," she says when she picks up.

"Bex. What's up?"

"Where are you?"

I glance around. A bunch of girls in jerseys—some in seemingly nothing but the jersey, their shorts are so short—wave to me as they cross the street and head into McNamara's.

"Downtown Moorbridge, at McNamara's. You can't talk over the phone?"

"Not about this."

My grip on the phone tightens. "Are you okay?"

I hear keys and a beep; presumably she's unlocking her car. "I'm fine. I just think if we're going to discuss the terms of this . . . arrangement, it should be in person."

"Arrangement, huh?"

"I'll come to McNamara's."

"Where are you? I'm sober, I can pick you up."

"Pine Ridge."

"Where's that?"

She laughs. The sweet, throaty sound makes my heart beat a bit faster. "Not too far. I'll see you soon, Callahan."

"You can call me James, you know."

There's a pause, then I hear her car turn on. "I know."

I search for Pine Ridge as soon as she hangs up. It's not too far from here, about thirty minutes or so. What was she doing there?

Maybe she's got a new boyfriend, my mind taunts.

I force myself to head inside, although all I really want is to wait out here. I should celebrate the win, after all. We crushed Notre Dame tonight. As soon as I enter the bar, I see my brothers and teammates waving to me, so I head over to the pool tables in the back. Coop hands me my non-alcoholic beer—which tastes almost the same as a regular beer, even though he never believes me—and nudges my shoulder.

"What's going on?"

I lean back against the wall, getting comfortable. "She's coming here to talk." I feel more relaxed already. Whatever Bex wants in exchange for tutoring, I'll give her. A ridiculous hourly rate, whatever. I can afford it. And the fact it means I'll be seeing a lot more of her? Not complaining about that either.

"About the . . . thing?"

I roll my eyes. "Yes. The thing."

"Fucking A," he says. "That's great, man."

I watch as Seb lines up for his next shot in the game of pool he's playing against Demarius. One of the things I like best about him is that he can fit in anywhere. He's never spent time with these teammates of mine, yet he looks perfectly at home. His attempt goes wide, and he laughs at himself, accepting another shot from Demarius.

"Every missed turn is a shot," Coop murmurs. "We're going to be wiping him off the floor at the end of the night."

"Is he your brother?" someone asks. I turn; there's a girl at my elbow, giving me doe-eyes as she sips her beer. She's pretty, with bleach-blonde hair tucked back over one shoulder and pouty lips. Her V-neck shirt shows off the top of a lacy pink bralette. Seeing that she has my attention, she leans in a bit, her hand grazing my bare arm.

I smile at her. "Yeah, baby. Want an introduction?"

"Tempting," she says. "But something tells me you have more . . . experience."

This time, the tips of her fingers touch my jeans. She bites her lip a little, one perfectly manicured finger rubbing over the inside seam. "Don't you want to ask my name?"

I play along. "What's your name?"

"Kathleen," she says. "But you can call me Kitty."

Cooper, the asshole, tries to turn his snort into a sneeze. I know I should disentangle myself from her, point her in the direction of any of my more willing teammates if fucking a football player is what she's after, but her touch does feel good. I'm not so desperate that she's actively turning me on, but it's been a while since this has happened.

Besides the kiss Bex and I shared.

Damnit, now I'm thinking about Bex again. As if she can tell my mind is in the gutter, Kitty leans in even further, until her lips are grazing my ear. "Can I put you down on the guest list for Kappa Alpha Theta's party tomorrow? I'm a pledge."

"Sorry, but I don't do parties during the season," I tell Kitty.

"Just come for a little while. The theme is ABC." She kisses my neck, punctuating each word with a nip of her lips. "Anything. But. Clothes."

I slowly extricate myself from her grasp. I'll bet she's a clinger when she's drunk. If I say yes to this party, she'll consider us dates and refuse to leave my side the whole night. Plus, on a Sunday? I haven't gone to a party on a Sunday since freshman year. I'd much rather do homework while NFL games play on the television.

And I'd much rather it was Bex asking.

"As much as I'd love to see you make a paper bag sexy, sweetheart, it's not personal. It's about football."

She pouts playfully. "So serious."

Across the room, the door to the bar opens. Bex isn't particularly tall, but I think I catch sight of that strawberry-blonde hair. I glance at Darryl, but he's deep in conversation with a couple of guys from the team. "Maybe you'll have better luck with him," I say, pointing him out to Kitty as I head to the front.

Bex is wearing a McKee sweatshirt and a pair of jean shorts, plus sandals, and these dangly earrings that I realize are little sculpted pieces of pie. Adorable. Her eyes light up when she sees me, and she stands on her tiptoes to get close to my ear as she says,

"Want to talk outside? I swear half of the McKee student body is in here."

Hell, I'd follow her into the bathrooms if that's where she wanted to go. I let her lead the way.

She steps around the side of the bar once we're outside, away from the windows. "Darryl's all the way in the back," I tell her. "I sent a girl his way."

"And I'm sure he's flirting with her." She sighs. "Never mind that he came to the diner today and demanded we get back together."

I push down the possessive streak threatening to run through me. I have no claim to her. A kiss doesn't mean anything, and with luck, she's about to be my tutor. Good guys don't sleep with their tutors. Or their teammate's exes.

"Diner? I thought you worked at the Purple Kettle."

"I do. The diner is my mother's. It's in Pine Ridge, hence the drive from there. Thanks for waiting."

I offer my beer to her. "I should have asked if you wanted a drink. Want a sip? It's non-alcoholic."

She curls her hand over mine and tilts the neck of the bottle into her mouth. I shouldn't be staring, but I can't help it, especially when she looks up at me through her lashes as she steps back. "Thanks. Do you not drink?"

I clear my throat. "Um, I drink, but not much during the season."

She nods. "Smart of you. I remember Darryl complaining about being hungover at practice."

I take another sip of the drink. "So, does this mean you reconsidered my proposal? Name your price, I'll pay it."

A smile curves over her lips. "I know. You've texted me some truly ridiculous offers over the past few days."

"So, which is it? Basket of puppies? Lifetime season tickets to the team of your choosing? Me doing your laundry personally for the rest of the year?"

That makes her laugh, and fuck, it's a gorgeous sound. Not at all dainty, but full-throated, almost like a rumble. I like that I know this about her. She's not fussy about taking a sip of someone else's drink, her laugh is infectious, and she wears earrings shaped like goddamn pieces of pie.

"No," she says, looking down at the pavement. "Although that was tempting."

I wait for more, but she's silent, still looking down like if she tries hard enough, she can burn a hole into the asphalt. My stomach does a flip. Something is off; the rapport I thought we were building disappears like smoke in the night.

"Bex?"

She finally looks up at me, her teeth digging into her lower lip.

"I'll tutor you," she says. "But only if you agree to pretend to date me."

CHAPTER 11

Bex

The instant the words leave my lips, I blush. I can feel it all the way to the tips of my ears. There's asking for help—for a deal—and then there's humiliating yourself.

But my wrists are aching where Darryl grabbed them. He won't leave me alone unless he knows, or at least thinks he knows, that I belong to someone else. Breaking things off with him politely hasn't worked. Getting direct hasn't worked. I know him well enough to know the only thing that will keep him away is if he gets it through his caveman-brain that I'm with another man.

It's embarrassing. But he's a distraction that needs to go away, and this is the best way I can think to get that to happen.

Now I just need James to agree to help.

"Callahan?" I say. "Did you hear me?"

"I heard you." He looks at me until I'm forced to meet his gaze. "Why?"

"Because he won't leave me alone."

His voice is sharp as he says, "Won't leave you alone how?"

"It's fine—"

"Like hell it's fine." The grip on his beer tightens. "Has he been harassing you?"

My face feels like it's on fire. "Not . . . really. He's just not listening to me. He keeps ignoring what I'm saying, and even what I tried to show him when I . . . when we . . ."

His lip darts out to lick his lip. "Yeah."

"If he sees I'm with someone else, he'll back off. I know him. It sucks, but it's true. And you need a tutor, so I thought we could work something out."

For a terrifying second, I think he's about to walk away. He's working his jaw like he wants to bolt. "He's my teammate."

My stomach sinks. Of course, he wouldn't want to ruin his relationship with a teammate, even if it's Darryl. "He said you talked through things."

"And this would take a match to it."

I shake my head. "You're right. I'm sorry, it was stupid. I'll see you around."

I turn, taking a deep breath as I throw my shoulders back. I can manage walking away with dignity, even though I just laid myself bare in front of the guy and he shut me down. But before I get two steps, I feel his hand encircle my sore, bruised wrist, tugging me backward.

I can't help it. I flinch.

His gaze is dark as he looks down at where he's touching me. "Bex—"

I shake my head, lips pressed tightly together. Like hell am I admitting aloud that I let Darryl hurt me.

"Fuck it. I don't like the guy anyway." He drops his hand, shoving both into his pockets. "You really don't mind tutoring me?"

I can tell he wants to press. To ask more about Darryl. But I jump on the topic change gratefully. "This is a deal, right? Quid pro quo. You take me on a few dates he'll hear about, and I'll make sure you pass this class."

He nods. "Okay. I can do that."

"You're not worried about him trying to fight you?"

He laughs. "Why would I be afraid? Let him try. I can take him, baby."

I raise an eyebrow in a way that I hope covers up the jolt of arousal that runs through me at the term of endearment . . . and the casual way he's talking about fighting Darryl. "Baby?"

"If we were really dating, we'd use pet names, right?" He leans in, brushing a lock of my hair behind my ear. "Do you prefer something else? Sweetheart? Honey? Sugar?"

"Definitely not sugar."

"Princess?"

"James . . ."

He gives me a half-smile. "There we go."

"Just to be clear, none of this is real."

He cups my jaw with his big hand. I fight the urge to turn my head slightly to nuzzle it. Focus. I need to focus. Going on a few dates together so everyone—and most especially Darryl—think we're dating is not the same thing as actually dating. This will work well because we're obviously attracted to each other, but people have sexual chemistry all the time and nothing comes of it.

"I know," he says. "Football, remember? But if you want people to buy it, you need to sell it, princess."

I nod. He has football. I have the diner and everything else. This is a mutually beneficial arrangement, like . . . like clownfish and sea anemones. If Darryl doesn't believe that I've moved on, he won't leave me alone, and this is the way to ensure that happens.

That's enough motivation to kiss James again.

He smiles against my lips, winding his arms around my lower back. "You know," he murmurs, "you can call me anything you want, but I do like the way you say James."

I crowd closer, wrapping my arms around his neck. This kiss is just as heady as the first one, inexplicably addictive. He has some stubble right now, and as we kiss, the friction against my cheeks and jaw makes me shiver.

Then his hands go lower, lifting me up against him. He maneuvers me so I have my back against the rough brick exterior of the bar. My legs go around his waist automatically, seeking purchase, and my arms must be tight around his neck, because he laughs and says, "Easy, Bex."

My insides turn to goo. How is it that Darryl saying my name never lit a fire like this inside me, but James tries it once and I'm halfway to abandoning my morals? James kisses me like he's hungry; I can taste the beer on his lips and feel his hands holding me in place like a brand. Even though this is for show, he's obviously into it.

Then he kisses down my throat, and I freeze.

Kissing is one thing. But that's not just kissing. If he goes any farther, I'm going to soak my panties in this parking lot.

I turn my head to the side, shoving at his chest until he puts me down. He complies, but not before dragging his thumb over my lower lip.

Fuck. I straighten my sweatshirt as I glare at him. "What was that for?"

He shrugs. "You looked like you wanted to be kissed. We need to practice so it's believable."

"That wasn't kissing, that was . . ."

He grins. "Never been kissed like that?"

I hit his chest lightly. "Not outside a bar!"

He takes my hand, entwining our fingers together. "Let's go inside."

"Now?"

"Why not? I'll introduce you as my date. We can play pool, talk for a while."

"He's there."

"I know."

"What if he . . ." I trail off as I feel my cheeks get warm. "You know?"

"Then I'll handle it."

"Just like that?"

"You're supposed to be my girl, right?"

I nod. "But not really."

"I know," he says again, patiently. "But he needs to believe it, and if I was really dating you, I would defend you every time someone so much as looked at you the wrong way."

Warmth blooms through me. "You're a sweet talker, James Callahan."

I let him lead me into the bar.

CHAPTER 12

James

As soon as we're back inside, Bex is mobbed by a girl with dark curly hair and the most earsplitting scream I've heard outside of the movies. She hugs her tightly, smacking her cheek with a lipstick-covered kiss. "I thought you had work!"

"I convinced her to come spend some time with her boyfriend," I say, holding up my hand.

Bex blushes scarlet. That makes me want to kiss her. Instead, I squeeze her hand. "Well . . ."

"No way," the girl says. Her eyes light up as she takes in the fact Bex and I are holding hands. "Seriously?"

"It's . . . complicated," Bex says. "Right, babe?"

I shrug. "Not that complicated. She kissed me, I asked her out, she said no, then she reconsidered."

Bex rolls her eyes, clearly fighting a smile at my recollection of how we struck this arrangement. "This is Laura, James. She's my best friend, so she knows everything about me, don't you, Laura?"

"I didn't know this," Laura says with a pout. "I can't believe you didn't mention you traded up to a good football boyfriend."

But I get Bex's drift; she's about to tell Laura that we're not dating for real. "Can I get you ladies something to drink?" I ask. "If you want to drink, princess, I can always drive you home later."

Laura's jaw drops. "You're my new favorite person," she says, looking at the guy standing at her shoulder. "Barry? Take notes, do whatever James does."

Bex shakes her head fondly. "I guess I'll take a rum and coke, if you don't mind," she says.

"Lime?"

"Of course."

"Me too," Laura pipes up.

"Coming right up." I head to the bar, slowed by a couple guys who recognize me and want to chat about the game. By the time I look over my shoulder, Bex has dragged Laura into the far corner.

Hopefully Laura will still like me after she knows the truth. She seems like a firecracker; that Barry guy has his hands full.

At the bar I order the drinks and another non-alcoholic beer for myself. I continue to watch her as I lean against the bar to wait. Fuck, she's pretty. If I had to pretend to date anyone, I'd choose her a hundred times over. Kissing her again, finally, set my skin on fire. I haven't gotten stiff like that from a kiss in ages; the second I got her legs around my waist, I had to keep myself from deliberately pushing us both over the edge. She tasted like my beer and fruity lip balm and her cute, curvy body was so warm against my chest, even through her thick sweatshirt. It's going to be a struggle not to take this thing too far.

It's not like I have any other options, though; I need her help to pass the class. If this is what she wants in exchange for that, I'll do it, and do it well. Darryl won't know what hit him, other than the fact Bex has someone in her corner who will fuck up anyone who hurts her.

The bartender sets the drinks down at the exact moment I see Bex lift her sleeves, holding out her wrists to Laura.

Fuck. She did flinch when I grabbed her wrist. I wasn't sure if I'd been imagining it.

I practically throw some cash down on the bar top, then gather up the drinks. But I'm not in the mood to kick back and relax anymore, knowing Darryl hurt Bex. I shove through the crowd, glad that my size makes it easy. The moment I reach the girls, I say, "How badly?"

Bex flicks her gaze up to look at me. "Not too bad. James—"

"He fucking hurt you."

"And he won't again once he knows we're together. He's a coward. He talks a big game, but—"

I cut her off again; I can't help it. "He won't again because I'm about to break his fucking face."

She shakes her head as she reaches out for my hand and squeezes our palms together. "You can't."

"Watch me."

"Don't," Laura says.

I turn to her. "No offense, but I didn't ask for your opinion."

She puts her hands on her hips, glaring right back at me, clearly not the slightest bit intimidated by the energy I'm radiating. "If you start anything, you'll be blamed. You could be suspended, and that's the least of it."

I grit my teeth. "He hurt her."

"And this wouldn't be helping her."

"She's right," Bex says. "You can't risk it."

I take a deep breath. Now that the immediate wave of emotion is receding, I feel a little calmer. "You're right."

I can't believe how close I came to sending myself right over the edge again. The second I decided Bex was mine—even if it's just for show—I was ready to throw it all away for her. This is exactly what Coach Gomez warned me against. Sara proved that I can't let myself get drawn in completely. I jump right off the cliff without a second thought.

Her eyes search mine. "Promise me you'll leave him alone. Act like everything is normal. Just tell him that it's not his business who I decide to date. I promise that he'll get the message."

"You're sure?"

"Yeah." She leans up, kissing my cheek. "But thank you."

I have no choice but to believe her. "Fine. But let me know if he tries anything."

She takes her drink from the table and sips it. "You know, I think girlfriends usually get introduced to the team."

"You sure? He's right back there."

She takes my hand and leads me through the crowd. "I know."

When we reach the back, we're still holding hands. Seb chokes on his beer, and Bo gives me a pointed look. Cooper even pulls himself away from the girl he's making out with to stare.

And Darryl looks like he's about to tackle me into the pool table. For half a second, everyone is frozen, waiting to see how he'll react. Beside me, Bex squeezes my hand, hard. She's smiling, but she's putting up a front. She's scared of what Darryl will do.

If I need to throw myself in front of her, I will.

"Hey, Bo," she says. "Good game earlier."

"Uh, thanks." Bo looks at me as he adds, "Wasn't expecting to see you here."

"I know, right?" she says with a little laugh. "Because it's been so long since Darryl and I broke up."

Darryl sets his beer down so hard the table rattles. "Baby, I know what game you're playing, and you need to cut the shit now."

"No games. I've just moved on." She gives him a grin. "Haven't you?"

He works his jaw, trying to force a smile that doesn't quite work. "Watch out," he tells me. "She'll leave you high and dry, she's such a—"

"A what?" I say pleasantly. "Can't hear you."

Darryl thinks about saying it, he really does. I can see the gears working in his slimy little brain, wondering if the satisfaction of calling Bex a nasty word will be worth the pain of my threat. I stand my ground, well aware of how our teammates are staring. Out of the corner of my eye, I see Seb slide over to Cooper. The two of them are ready to jump into action to defend me if this turns into a fight.

"Let's go," Darryl eventually mutters to a couple of his buddies.

One of them—a safety I haven't interacted with much yet— gives me a sneer as he goes, "Watch it, Callahan. Coach Gomez might've gone out of his way to bring you here, but you're not untouchable."

"Aw," I say. "Is that your crappy attempt at shit talking? No wonder Notre Dame ran all over you today."

He scoffs, but at Darryl's look, leaves instead of retaliating.

The tension seeps out of me once they're gone. Bex's hand goes limp in mine, too; I hadn't even noticed how tightly she was holding on until I rub the blood back into it.

"Sorry," she says. "I didn't mean to make things even more awkward."

"It's fine."

"Is it, though?" She's whispering now, glancing over her shoulder at everyone who stayed. "I can't fuck up the team for you."

"I already told him that if he disrespected a woman—you included—I'd stop throwing to him. They know that." I lead her over to the table Darryl just left, sitting down. It takes her a moment, but she decides to perch on my lap. I steady her with a hand on her knee, fighting the smile that threatens to overwhelm my face. I have a feeling that being around Bex means always being surprised.

"When?" she asks.

"Before I even knew who you were. He was talking shit about you at that party."

Her eyes widen. "Before I kissed you?"

Coop and Seb settle into the two other chairs at the table. I raise an eyebrow at them, but they just share a grim glance.

"Bro," Seb says. "What the fuck is going on?"

CHAPTER 13

James

When I walk into the classroom—a full fifteen minutes early, thank you very much, Mr. Professor—I see immediately that I managed to get there before Bex. Score. Every other class meeting so far, she's been there ahead of time, her laptop already open, scribbling in her planner with one of her cute gel pens. But today, I get to have a moment alone at our table before facing her.

Pretending to date her has made this class easier and harder all at once. On the one hand, it's easier, since she's holding up her end of the deal with tutoring. But on the other hand, it's way more difficult, since I'm drawn to her like a candle to a box of fucking matches, apparently, and sitting next to her for over an hour while being expected to pay attention to something boring like essay writing is cruel and unusual punishment. I've given up fighting my attraction to her. Attraction is fine; it's safe. So what if I acknowledge she's gorgeous and I'd love nothing more than to sleep with her? It's the feelings I need to watch out for. That's what got me in trouble with Sara.

I set the two coffees down on the table and slide my backpack off my shoulder. I've been to the Purple Kettle a bunch of times, mostly to see if I can catch a few moments of conversation with Bex, and I figured out that she likes her coffee iced with two pumps of caramel syrup, so I got that along with a black iced coffee for myself. On impulse, I went ahead and bought her a pumpkin muffin, too. Something tells me she's the sort of girl who gets excited about all the pumpkin-related products that pop up during the fall.

The class starts to filter in. A bunch of girls stare at me, but they always do, so I ignore them. They've been straight up glaring at Bex—I guess the news of our "relationship" is making the rounds—but she doesn't seem to mind. Maybe if this was real, I'd want her to be more possessive, but as it stands, I'm relieved. If anything, I'm more worried about this snowballing into something I'm not ready for emotionally for *me* than for her.

She walks in with just a couple minutes to go, and she's on the phone with someone. Her mouth is taut as she whispers into the phone. She gives our professor an apologetic look as she slips past him to her seat.

"Yeah," she's saying. "Just tell him I'll figure out a way to pay for it later. I'll move some money around."

Her eyes widen adorably as she takes in the surprise I left on her side of the table. *Thank you*, she mouths as she sits down. I hide my smile as I sip my coffee.

"Got you. Yep. Thanks." She slides her phone into her bag, then takes a sip of coffee. "You know my coffee order?"

I shrug. "I just picked up on it."

She leans in and smacks my cheek with a kiss. "Thank you. I haven't had breakfast yet, so this is perfect."

"Everything okay?"

She groans as she takes out her laptop. "It's just the diner. Something happened with an appliance, and I need to move money around to pay for the part the repair guy needs."

"That sucks."

She breaks off some of the muffin and offers it to me, but I shake my head regretfully. "No thanks. Unfortunately, pumpkin muffins don't fit in with the football diet."

"That's tragic," she says around a bite of muffin. "Sucks even worse than a broken refrigerator."

I want to reply, but the professor starts class, so I open a blank document for notes and take another sip of my coffee. Not for the first time, I'm left wondering why Bex is the one who handles all the headaches of her mother's business when she's supposed to be in college. Not to say she's not capable, because she clearly is, but why does she have to? Doesn't her mother own it? It doesn't sound like her dad is in the picture, but good luck talking to her about that. I asked her about her family a few days ago while we were at the campus library for a tutoring session, and she shut down in a way I absolutely hated to see.

I'm attempting to type some notes as the professor drones on when Bex pokes my arm. I look over; she's pointing to her notebook, where she wrote down something in sparkly blue ink.

We should plan that date.

We were going to make an appearance at a party together last weekend, but Bex was hit with an unexpected assignment for one of her classes, so that didn't happen. But she's right, we should have a proper date. Even though we've met up for tutoring in public places so people see us, it's not the same as going out like a couple would.

Bowling? I write back.

She makes a face and writes back, *No way.*

Arcade? Mini golf?

"Are all your suggestions this boyish?" she whispers.

"Hey, don't let my sister hear you say that. She's the mini golf queen," I reply just as quietly, keeping my eyes on the front of the room. "What were you thinking?"

"Antiquing?"

"Hell no."

"Bookstore?"

"Maybe."

She huffs out a breath. "Fine. The arcade isn't a bad idea, there's one right in town."

"Really?" I can't keep the hopeful note out of my voice.

"Are you free tonight?"

* * *

THE BASKETBALL IN my hands feels way different from the curves of a football, but when I jump shot, it lands in the net without hitting the rim. I grin, bumping my hip against Bex's side. "And that's how a master does it."

She rolls her eyes as she picks up a basketball. We've been wandering around the arcade for half an hour, trying out the different games. On a weeknight, it's not too crowded here, which is how I prefer it. According to Bex, this arcade, Galactic Games, is a popular destination for teenagers and college students alike, so sometimes it can get overwhelming. So far, she beat me at Pac-Man, which was surprisingly satisfying to see—she's a little trash-talker when she's doing well at a game, something that reminds me of my sister—and I cleaned up in our game of air hockey. Hoops aren't my favorite, but she seems into it, so I let her drag me over. It's fun to see her relaxed like this. When we arrived, I bought her a blue raspberry slushy, and I've been stealing sips even though my nutritionist wouldn't be pleased. I haven't had one since a memorable weekend at a state fair with my brothers and sister a couple years ago, and the taste reminds me of sunshine and my siblings' laughter.

I take another slurp as she sets up. With her hips popped forward, her ass sticks out adorably, and the dark skinny jeans she's wearing make it look extra fantastic. I want to palm the curve, slip my hand into her back pocket, but that'd make her stomp on my foot for sure. Real boyfriends can get away with stuff like that, and that's not me. I need to remember that, however much fun I'm having.

Her shot goes straight into the net. She bounces on the tips of her toes, her grin wide and infectious. I slap her palm with a high-five. "Atta girl. Want to do a speed race?"

"I'm gonna wipe the floor with you when we're done," she says, a glint in her eyes that lets me know she's serious. I love it. I wasn't expecting this side of her, but as an athlete in a family of athletes, a competitive spirit is sexy as hell. Anyone looking over right now probably sees the desire in the way I'm looking at her, and I don't give a damn.

It's good for the image we're trying to promote, right?

She sets the buzzer for one minute, and the second it starts counting down, we're off to the races. I'm grabbing basketballs and putting them through the hoop as fast as I can, but she's almost as fast, biting her lip in concentration. When the buzzer goes off, I've beaten her by only five points, which is way less than I was expecting.

"Aw, nice try, princess."

She scrunches up her nose as she takes a sip of the slushy. "Let's go again."

I steal the slushy from her. "You know how many completed passes I made today during practice alone?"

This time, she goes for the same basketballs I do, bumping into me and trying to mess up my stance. What a little sabotager. I still beat her, but only by two points this time, and we're both laughing by the end. She leans into me and I wrap my arm around her automatically, squeezing her hip.

"Let's bet this time," she says. "If I win, you cash in your tickets and get me one of those stuffed animals."

I rub her hip, resisting the urge to tuck my hand underneath her tank top. "And if I win?"

She pretends to think, tapping her finger against her chin. "I'll give you a kiss."

That piques my interest. We've been affectionate with each other when we're in public, but we haven't truly kissed since outside McNamara's, and I've been thinking about doing it again an unfair amount. The relationship might be fake, but the kisses sure as hell haven't been. I *know* how much I affect her.

"Deal, princess."

Fifteen minutes later, she's clutching a stuffed bear to her chest, and I'm still sulking.

She giggles as she takes in my expression. "Aw, babe. You look like you need cheering up."

"A kiss would help."

She reaches up and kisses me on the cheek. "Better?"

I hold her in place before she can slide away, crushing the poor stuffed animal between us. She named it as soon as I put it in her arms—Albert. Why, I have no idea, but it was almost worth losing to see her smile.

Almost.

I give her a proper kiss, running my tongue over the seam of her lips. She gasps, opening her mouth, letting our tongues meet. By the time I pull away, my heart is pounding, and if her blush is any indication, she's feeling the same way.

I wink. "Now I'm better."

CHAPTER 14

Bex

I adjust my ponytail as I wait for James to answer his front door. Before him, I never worked as a tutor, but I'm pretty sure the job usually doesn't involve dinner reservations after. But here I am, laptop and writing handbook nestled into my tote bag alongside a dress and change of shoes.

My life is *so* weird now.

It turns out that even when you're fake dating, it leads to a lot of texting and hanging out. In the past couple of weeks, James has sent me Snaps of himself at practice, FaceTimed me while his brothers battled it out on Super Smash Bros, and texted me an unfair amount of cute animal videos. He calls the latter "happiness hits," which is more adorable than it has any right to be. Last week we went to an arcade together, where I totally owned his ass in Pac-Man, and he's developed a habit of showing up to the Purple Kettle when I'm working to say hi and buy a coffee.

And honestly? As much as it scares me, I kind of love it.

The first time he texted me out of the blue, I assumed it was to ask a question about our latest writing assignment for class. And that was part of it—but not before he asked me how I was doing. I'd been at the diner, so I told him all about the latest drama about a supplier falling through, and he shared about how practice went for him.

It was almost enough to feel real, which is why I shut it down.

Now, we just chat for a bit before he asks me something class related.

The door opens, but it's not James who greets me. Cooper gives me a grin. "Hey, Bex. James is upstairs."

I eye him. "Why are you shirtless?"

He shuts the door behind me as I step inside. "Why not?"

I haven't known James's brothers for very long, but ten minutes in Cooper's presence was enough to tell me he's cocky as hell and knows he has the looks to back it up. He has a similar build to his brother, cut to perfection like each of his abs is made of diamonds. Tonight, he's wearing nothing but a low-slung pair of sweatpants, and his hair is damp, like he just came out of the shower. Objectively speaking, he's gorgeous. But his hair doesn't fall over his forehead the way James's does. His eyes aren't quite as blue. His beard is attractive, but I prefer James's clean-shaven, razor-sharp jawline better. Is the happy trail leading down similar, or—

I force my gaze down to the floor once I realize I'm staring. I'm here to help James, not ogle his brother and fantasize about his pecs.

"Now that you're done checking me out," Cooper says cheerfully, "I want to thank you. James told us his last assignment didn't suck quite as bad. What was it, a C-?"

"I got a C+, dickhead." James bounds down the stairs to our left. When he reaches my side, he pulls me into a sideways hug and kisses me on the temple. His brothers know we're not actually together, so there's no need to pretend, but if there's a word James Callahan doesn't have in his vocabulary, it's "halfway." He gives my waist a squeeze. "Coop, we'll be in the kitchen. Are you going out?"

Cooper groans. "I wish, but I have to finish reading *Crime and Punishment*."

James leans in to whisper in my ear, "Is that really the name?"

"Yes," I whisper back, feeling goose bumps where his breath brushes against my skin. "Wait, please tell me you knew that."

His laughter is adorable. "You're fun to tease, you know."

We settle at the big dining room–style table in the kitchen. This is the safest place for us to study—if we're in his room, I'm afraid I'll do something stupid, like ask for a kiss when no one is around. Even if we're alone here, it's a common area. I take out my things and settle into a chair, waiting for James to do the same.

He pokes around in the fridge first. "Want something to drink?"

"I have my water bottle." I hold up the battered reusable bottle. It's covered in stickers, a guilty pleasure of mine. I don't have a ton of money to spend on impulse purchases, but when they happen, I'm either buying stickers or cute pairs of earrings.

Tonight, though, I'm wearing the one good piece of jewelry I own: a pair of small gold earrings that belonged to my mother's mother. And the dress in my bag is borrowed from Laura. James told me we're going somewhere fancy, which I told *him* wasn't necessary for a fake date, but he insisted.

He gets himself a glass of iced tea and settles down across from me. "I finished my draft."

"Yeah? Can I see?"

"I tried writing it by hand like you suggested, and it worked, I think. I finished it faster than when I was trying to type and kept deleting things."

He flips through his notebook and passes it across the table to me. His fingers brush mine accidentally, and it makes me bite the inside of my cheek. Focus. I need to focus on helping him, on upholding my end of our deal. Aside from a few annoying texts, Darryl's been leaving me alone, just like I knew he would if he thought I was off the market. That's allowed me to focus on school and work.

We're working on implementing research in our writing. As a business major, I do this all the time, but it's a skill that takes time to develop, and I don't blame James for still needing practice. I scan over his work with my pen in hand as he waits.

"You have such messy handwriting."

He shrugs. "Eventually I'll only need to be able to write one thing."

"Which is?"

"My autograph."

I break into a smile as I shake my head. "Ego much?"

"Not ego. Manifestation." He takes a sip of his drink, wagging his eyebrows at me when I kick at him under the table.

"Wouldn't have taken you for that type."

"There's a lot you don't know about me," he says. "Yet, of course. You're my fake girlfriend, you'll have to know everything eventually."

I set down the notebook and give him my sternest look. It works whenever I need to be firm with a customer. "Are we going to study or not?"

He holds up his hands. "You're right. I'll save the date talk for the date."

"Thank you." His words sink in after half a second. "Not the date. The dinner."

"No one just goes to dinner at Vesuvio's. It's a date place."

"That's where we're going?" Thank goodness I packed my good heels. That restaurant is the fanciest a small college town like Moorbridge has to offer. I'm surprised he would spring for it, and fine, a little flattered. No one will think we're faking it if he takes me there. It's so clearly a date place that for a couple months last year, there was an Instagram account run by some gossip at McKee that accepted photo submissions of every couple spotted there.

"Like I would take my girlfriend to get bad pasta."

"Fake girlfriend."

He grins. "Isn't that what I just said?"

I pick up the notebook and pointedly bury my nose in it. Even though his handwriting is messy, I can read it, and I do a little happy dance in my seat when I see he nailed the transitions. That was the sticking point with last assignment, and we didn't have time to revise it because of his schedule, so it ended up being a C+ instead of the B it should have gotten.

When I finish, I jot down some revision feedback for him and get to work on my own assignment while he edits. He switches to the computer so he can start typing it out, and more than once, I have to remind myself that I can't just stare at his long, precise fingers as they move on the keyboard. He's surprisingly graceful, like with everything else—it must be the athlete in him. There's an effortlessness that I can't help but be drawn to.

I bite the inside of my cheek as I stare down at my own laptop. I knew it would be hard, getting close to him. I don't operate logically where attraction is involved, which is why it's best not to be involved at all. But he's taking me to the fanciest place in town and I just know he's going to want to kiss at the table in case any busybodies are watching.

I need to set better ground rules. A peck on the cheek, not a kiss like the one he gave me outside McNamara's or at Galactic Games. This isn't real, and it's not like he'd actually want a relationship. Or that I want a relationship. I don't want anything at all except escaping this semester—this whole year, really—unscathed and as ready as I'll be for the future.

"Bex?"

"Hmm?" I glance up like I hadn't just been staring at the way his fingers looked drumming on the table as he thought about what to type next.

"You're thinking so loud, I can hear it from over here."

Heat erupts on my cheeks. "Sorry."

"Is something wrong?"

I look at him. Which doesn't help at all. He's looking at me with genuine concern in his blue eyes, and for one horrible second, I imagine myself leaning over the table, shoving our work aside, and kissing him.

He's *such* a good kisser, it's criminal.

"No." I swallow, tucking my hair behind my ear. "How are the revisions going?"

"Good, I think." He frowns, glancing back down at his screen. "Can you look at this citation? I think I did it right but I'm not sure."

I find myself getting up and walking around the table so I can peer over his shoulder. He stiffens slightly when I get close. Too close, probably. In a weird way, I'm grateful for the reminder that he doesn't truly want me. He might be cocky and a bit of a flirt, but that's just how he's playing the part of boyfriend. And even if he doesn't do relationships, he definitely does hookups—every popular guy like him does. The way he kissed me is the way I'm sure he kisses every girl.

The citation looks good to me, so I tell him and turn to hightail it back to the safety of the other side of the table, but he stops me by gently cradling my hand. I swallow again, trying to ignore the stupid little flutter in my stomach.

This deal is getting more ridiculous by the second.

"I'm hungry," he says, looking up at me. "Want to get ready?"

"What about the reservation?"

"I can get us in early."

"Just like that? It's so popular."

He shrugs. "My family knows the owner, so yeah. Just like that."

We could never work for a lot of reasons, but one of them is that James and his family are in a totally different stratosphere. My mom and I live in a shitty apartment with a dryer on the fritz. He probably had nannies and whatever he wanted growing up— his father is still one of the most famous athletes in the country, after all. During the football season, everyone can watch him on network television, because he provides game commentary.

I force a smile. "Sounds great. Can I change in your bathroom?"

James

This girl is going to kill me.

I've hooked up with a couple of girls since Sara, but none of them made me feel half what I felt with her. I haven't even slept with Bex—not that I will—and the way my body responds to her feels just like how it was with Sara. Like a fucking forest fire, threatening to burn me alive if I get too close.

Sara did burn me. I can't let the same thing happen with Bex. But what the fuck am I supposed to do when just her hair brushing my shoulder makes my cock stiffen? It was a good thing she walked right back around the table, because I was close to pulling her into my lap. We're going to dinner early so I don't do something completely stupid like that while we're alone. The restaurant will have witnesses. It'll remind me that this is all an act.

What makes it worse is the fact I know she's into me. I can see it in the way she looks at me, the way her breath hitches when I get too close. I know she doesn't want to complicate things either, and I appreciate that, because if she was even just a bit more willing, I might throw away the playbook entirely. I want more of her touch. More of her soft noises. More of her, smelling like vanilla, skin like velvet.

Just like how it was with Sara.

That thought makes my jaw tighten as I finish buttoning my shirt. Bex has commandeered my bathroom, so I'm in the bedroom to get ready for dinner. For half a second after she shut the door, it felt domestic, like we're truly a couple and this is something we do every week, but fortunately that feeling has passed.

Cufflinks next. I pick up the steel "C" set, a gift from my father, and pin them in place. Sara was an abyss. Every crying phone call, every dramatic fight, every desperate fuck dragged me in further, until it was missed assignments, missed classes, missed practices. How could I go to practice when my girlfriend was begging me not to, that if I went, she might do something dangerous? I missed my life for her.

Bex is not Sara. I know that. But if I let myself get too close, I'll do anything for her. No matter how ridiculous, outlandish, or damaging.

The bathroom door opens. Bex steps out slowly, her hand over her eyes. "Are you decent?"

I laugh. "You just made it."

She looks me over. "Okay, I'm glad I brought this dress."

The dress in question is a beautiful lilac with a fitted bodice that shows off her curves and a full skirt that sways as she walks closer. She's wearing black heels that make her legs seem even longer. Her earrings are the same little gold stars that sparkle as she runs a brush through her hair.

"You look so pretty."

She smiles. "Thanks. And look, I'm not as short anymore." She does a twirl, which makes the skirt rise a few inches.

I swallow, focusing on a spot on the wall so I don't think about something indecent, like putting my hand up that pretty fabric to see what kind of panties she's wearing.

"Will you do up the back?"

"Hmm?"

"The back zipper." She turns so I can see that the dress is only partially zipped. She's wearing a purple bra with some sort of lace situation on the straps. Maybe her panties match. This is clearly her fancy date outfit. Did she wear it to the very restaurant we're going to when she dated Darryl? Somehow, I doubt he sprung for it. But she could've worn this sexy outfit anyway at some point, taking it off for him piece by piece after they went home.

Bex glances back at me. "Um, James?"

"Sorry." I clear my throat as I zip up the dress, trying to touch as little of her skin as possible. She has an adorable birth mark on her back, right between her shoulder blades. I could kiss it, and then kiss lower, and take the whole dress off.

But I don't. Instead, I let her turn. She smiles at me. "You look nice too. Good to know you can clean up well."

"It's a requirement for us Callahans. You don't want to guess how many charity events I've been to."

She puts her hairbrush into her tote bag and takes out a little clutch. "I know."

"Oh yeah?" I say as I shut the door behind us.

She glances at me as she heads down the stairs. "I may have, um . . ."

"Oh," I say as it clicks. I holler to Cooper that we're about to leave, then lead the way to my car. "You googled me?"

"More specifically, I googled your father. Your family. But you came up." She buckles into the passenger seat, biting her lip as she looks at me. "Is that a problem? I'm sorry."

"It's not like you were snooping. It's right there on the internet." It does feel strange, though. I don't have any big secrets, the real reason behind the mess of last fall aside, but knowing she did research on me, like I'm some news story, hits me wrong, and I'm not sure why.

"Yeah." She smooths her skirt down. "The Callahan Family Foundation, right?"

"My parents' pride and joy. They're very serious about it."

At a red light, I glance over at her. Something about her expression unsettles me. I've worked hard on making her feel comfortable, texting her, talking to her, getting to know her. Just because we can't date for real doesn't mean we can't be friends. I like her, and I appreciate that she's taking time out of her busy life to help me with this class. Suddenly, it feels like all the progress we made disappeared, and now we're not even friends.

At the restaurant, I lean in and speak quietly to the manager, who is more than happy to set us up with a table an hour early. He leads us to the back, where there's a small circular table tucked into an alcove.

Bex sits down before I can pull her chair out for her. "You weren't lying, you really do know the owner."

"He has a catering business too; we've used him for a bunch of events."

She nods as she unrolls her napkin, carefully placing it on her lap. I do the same, absolutely hating the awkwardness. She takes a sip of water, looking at the ceiling like it's fascinating.

"Is something wrong?"

She looks at me. "No."

"Something's wrong."

"I'm fine. Really." She opens her menu. But something clearly isn't fine because her jaw is all tight.

"Is it my family?"

She doesn't look at me.

"Bex," I say, "tell me what's up."

She bites her lip, stalling as she traces over the typography on the menu. "It's just weird, okay? The reminder," she says. "Your family is famous and you're going to be too."

"And that's a problem?"

"I'm just some random person who happens to be eating dinner with you."

"You're not some random person."

She finally looks at me. I exhale at the glimpse of her pretty brown eyes. "But I am. I'm not really with you, and I'm not saying I should be, or that . . . I want that, but we're just not the same kind of person." She sets down the menu, gesturing to the restaurant. "I'm not the kind of person who goes to places like this."

"I don't see the difference."

"Of course you don't, you have everything." She reaches out to touch my wrist, turning my arm to show off the cufflinks. "And you're going to keep having everything. I'm not saying you don't deserve it, because you do. You're talented at what you love. But that's never going to be me, and I just remembered that."

She retreats, but I softly take her hand, tracing over the lines on her palm. "What do you love?"

She shakes her head. "Fake boyfriends don't get to know that."

"So there is something."

"Photography," she says, flicking her gaze up to mine. "I'm a photographer. If I could do something else, it would be that."

"But—"

"But I can't, okay?" she interrupts. "Don't. I know my future already."

"Which is what?"

"The diner."

"You could sell it. You're majoring in business. You can do whatever you want."

She laughs shortly. "Did I ask for your advice?"

I let her hand drop. "No."

"Let's just have dinner, okay?"

There's a tired note in her voice that I hate, but I'm afraid if I continue to push, she'll just get up and leave, which wouldn't be good for the image we're portraying to the world, so I drop it.

It's for the best, anyway. If we're too vulnerable with each other, it'll just be that much harder to say goodbye whenever Bex decides Darryl isn't a concern anymore.

I'm dreading the moment that comes.

CHAPTER 16

Bex

I'm an idiot.

James saw that there was something wrong and tried to help, and I shut him down at every turn. If we were actually dating, I'd be a frontrunner for the worst girlfriend ever award. As it stands, I'm a shitty friend.

Is that what we are? Friends?

That doesn't sit right with me. But what's the alternative? He isn't interested in dating, and I shouldn't be, either. We can be friends while we're pretending to date, but I'm delusional if I think for a second it could go further. Even if I wanted it—and I don't—it wouldn't work out. Rich quarterbacks with Hall of Fame fathers don't go out with barely-scraping-by, hash-slinging wannabe photographers like me.

And even if we tried, eventually he'd realize I'm not worth it and leave. Just like . . . Dad.

His future is in a different city. Mine is half an hour away.

We're not the same, and I need to stop this line of thought, because this dinner is getting more awkward by the second and at the table closest to us another couple our age just sat down, and the way the girl is looking at us makes it clear she knows who James is and would absolutely love to eavesdrop. Even worse than pretending to have a boyfriend in the first place would be Darryl finding out I've been lying about this whole "new relationship" thing.

"This looks great," I tell the server as she sets my ravioli in front of me. It's lobster with a tomato cream sauce, something I love but almost never get to eat. She smiles at me, but that shifts into something way flirtier as she sets down James's steak.

I need to ramp things up if this fake date is going to be successful. Eyes on the prize. I lay a possessive hand on James's arm. "That looks delicious, honey. Make sure you let me try a bite."

If he's surprised, he does me the courtesy of hiding it. "Sure, princess, but only if you share yours."

I giggle as I make eye contact with the girl at the other table. "So generous of you."

His hand curls over my arm, dragging me close so he can whisper in my ear, "What the fuck is going on? Two seconds ago, I thought you were going to walk all the way back home."

I keep up my smile as I whisper back, "That girl over there is staring. I'm making the date believable. Play along."

To my relief, he settles back in his chair. "You haven't told me about your day yet," he says as he cuts into his steak.

I seize on the opportunity, feeling the tightness in my stomach ease. "It was good. I gave a presentation in my management class."

"How did that go?"

I tear my gaze away from the girl—who really needs to get a life of her own—and look at him as I reply, "Fantastic. I wasn't that nervous; the professor is very chill. Which, considering the major, is rare. Most of my professors have been seriously intense."

"I took a couple of business classes before I decided to major in math," he says. "That's definitely true."

"I still can't believe you do that, by the way."

"What?"

"Study math." I make a face as I pop a piece of ravioli into my mouth.

He suppresses a smile. "I like it."

"I do the books for the diner, and I always mix something up, without fail."

"Like, by hand?"

I sigh. "Unfortunately. I know there's software that will do it, but there's only so much I can do with a cash business."

"Cash only still? Wow."

"There's a lot my mother won't change." Whatever my father set in place before he left, you'd think was etched in stone on the ceiling. Making improvements has been a slow, painful process.

Before I can get too far down that road, I change the subject. "How was practice? Who are you playing again this week?"

"It was good. But we're playing LSU."

"Your old team."

He nods, a grim look on his face. "It's going to be an interesting matchup. They know me well, but I know them well too." He nudges my shoulder. "You should come on Saturday. Do you have work? It's at noon."

Part of me wants to say no right away, but wouldn't a girlfriend go to her boyfriend's games, especially when he's playing his old team? It would probably be weirder if I wasn't there. "Sure, that sounds nice."

"Awesome." He smiles widely, transforming his face from simply handsome to stunning. My breath catches in my throat half a second before I remember I'm not supposed to let this attraction root any deeper. "Feel free to bring Laura or anyone else, I have plenty of tickets."

"Will your brothers be there?"

"Not Cooper, unfortunately. He has a game in Vermont. But Seb will be there, and my parents."

I nearly choke on my drink. "James."

"What? You'll like them." He leans in a bit, dropping his voice even lower. "Even fake girlfriends can meet the folks."

"What about friends?" I whisper back.

For some reason, that makes him brush his lips against my forehead. "Definitely."

His kiss unleashes a cloud of butterflies in my belly. I've been trying to ignore it—especially when he crossed over the line—but it's useless. Something about my body reacts to his in a way it does for no one else. I want to feel his lips on mine. His hands. When he brushed my skin as he zipped up my dress earlier, I had to press my legs together to relieve the ache his touch inspired.

If his kisses are anything to go by, he would be amazing in bed. If only I'd be capable of keeping it casual, I'd be all over him. We'd never work as a couple, but as a hookup?

"You're staring," I tell him.

He grins. "Sweetheart, you stared first."

Crap. That was probably true.

He puts his hand on my thigh. It's underneath the table, so no one can see; it's not for the benefit of the server or the nosy couple. It's very clearly for one person—me.

I swallow. His gaze flickers down to my throat and lower before settling back on my face. His hand, which covers my thigh easily, squeezes lightly. "Don't try to make this any more or less than it can be," he says.

I nod.

"Don't leave me tonight, baby. Stay."

I shouldn't say yes. I should keep the boundary between us as airtight as possible. Because this scares me. This could so easily lead to deeper feelings, and I'll be the one looking foolish again the second James finds someone he truly wants to be with or decides he doesn't need our deal anymore.

Before him, I had no trouble doing the smart thing. Now? I make decisions I shouldn't left and right. Like asking someone my body aches for to pretend to date me.

Yet the streak continues; I nod. I lean in. I press a lingering kiss to his mouth, promising him—and myself—something I have no business offering.

But in this moment, with candlelight shining on the table and James's ocean eyes on mine, I don't care.

CHAPTER 17

Bex

The second we get in the house, James hauls me over his shoulder. I shriek at him to mind the dress, which just makes him laugh. Thrown unceremoniously over his shoulder, I'm aware of every single one of his muscles. This is why athletes are the best; their bodies are toned to perfection. He steadies me by cupping his hand on my ass, making me shiver as he climbs the stairs.

Hopefully Cooper is super into *Crime and Punishment*. It would be just my luck if he came out just in time to see James drag me, caveman-style, to his lair. I knew he was working up to something; he kept his hand on my upper thigh the whole ride home.

I might be a *teeny* bit thrilled I'm affecting someone so much. This is going to blow up in my face, but I'm resigned and determined to have fun first.

"You're being barbaric, you know."

He laughs. "Don't pretend you don't like it."

"You don't know what I like." I punctuate that by pinching his back. I'd think it didn't bother him at all, if not for the way he tightens his grip on my butt. "We're only fake dating, remember?"

"Vividly." He practically kicks open the door. My tote bag is in the exact same place it had been when we went to dinner. I'd expected to change out of the dress, grab it, and book it home to watch a couple episodes of *New Girl* before falling asleep. This is . . . different.

I could stop it all right now. Tell him that we can't.

But I don't. Instead, I let him set me down on the edge of the bed, a surprisingly gentle juxtaposition to the whole carrying situation. He shrugs out of his suit jacket, draping it over the back of his desk chair, and to my surprise, kneels before me.

My hands find his shoulders, smoothing over the fabric of his shirt. "James?"

He runs his hand down my leg, all the way to my ankle, and undoes the strap of my heel. I moan a bit as he takes off the shoe; they've been pinching my toes all evening. He does the same for the other shoe, setting them both aside gently.

"And just like that, you're fun-size again."

I hit his shoulder lightly. "Rude."

"What if I told you I prefer you this way?"

"Do you?"

He presses a kiss to the inside of my thigh, right at the hemline of the dress. "You ought to know by now that I'm not big on lying."

I can't stop the smile from crossing my lips.

He keeps his mouth right where it is, speaking against my skin. "We can do this. We're obviously attracted to one another."

"Once to get it out of our systems, and then we can just be friends."

He looks up at me. "Exactly."

My body is already aching for him. In the position we're in, he could so easily slide his head up my skirt and taste me.

If he did, I wouldn't push him away. Not right now. Now, I refuse to think about the future. I meant what I said earlier—we're not the same—but attraction doesn't care about that.

My body wants his, pure and simple. I've only tried to have sex a couple times since Darryl and it was never good, but I have a feeling that James won't disappoint. He's so talented with his body in other ways, after all.

He pulls me into a kiss that makes my heart do a somersault. "You sure about this?"

"Yes," I whisper against his lips. "As long as you are."

He slowly pulls down the zipper on the back of my dress. It falls, pooling around my waist, showing off my lacy bra. The heat in his gaze nearly burns as he looks down at me. Without a word, he lifts me up, carefully pulling the dress the rest of the way off, and goes to drape it over the chair like his jacket.

I swipe my tongue over my lower lip as he undresses. Holy fuck, his chest is incredible. Each muscle is perfectly defined, showing off the power in them with ease. He has a tattoo over his heart, some sort of swirling pattern designed in thick lines of black. My eyes zero in on the trail of dark hair that leads down to his crotch, where he's clearly half-hard already, his cock straining against the fabric of his black boxer-briefs.

I know I'm staring, but of course that just makes him huff out a laugh. "Like what you see, princess?"

"Come here." I start to unhook my bra, but he does it for me, flinging the whole thing to the floor. I gasp as he takes one of my breasts in each hand, kneading gently. Then he leans down to lick at my nipples, and my mind short-circuits. I moan as he pinches one, sucking on the other to get it hard.

"You're sensitive here," he says. "I bet if I played with them long enough, you'd soak your panties through."

I shake my head, whimpering all the while. "Don't. I want you inside me."

"I'll get there, sweetheart. I've been dreaming about this, let me enjoy it."

He continues to tease me, scraping his teeth against the extra-sensitive undersides of my tits, sucking a hickey into the top of one. I clench my core at the dizzying sensations. At this rate I will completely ruin these panties. I've never come just from this kind of stimulation, but something tells me James could get me there if he tried hard enough. I drag my nails down his back, digging in accidentally when he drags a rough hand down my soft belly. When his fingers find the waistband of my panties, I whimper aloud.

He pulls back, his mouth wet with his own spit, and gives me a cocky grin that makes my pussy clench. "You're easy to rile up, you know."

I press forward. "Keep touching me."

He tears the panties down my thighs. "Next time, I'm going to see if I can make you come just like this, Bex. My mouth on those gorgeous full tits, teasing until you cream yourself."

I freeze, even though his hand is right at the top of my sex, and I desperately want it lower. "There won't be another time."

The smile drops from his face. "Right."

"This is just sex." I can't keep the waver out of my voice. But that's exactly what this is, and the clearer we are on that, the better.

"I know." He leans in, kissing the corner of my mouth. "But that doesn't mean we can't enjoy ourselves."

"Just—don't talk about a future that can't happen."

"Okay." He strokes the top of my folds, bringing his other hand up to tweak my nipple again. "But I'm tasting you."

"You don't have—"

He cuts me off by spreading my legs and burying his head between my thighs.

CHAPTER 18

Bex

I choke out a moan, my hands gripping his hair tightly as his tongue explores my cunt. My legs are shaking, wanting to close, but he holds them open with ease. When his tongue finds my clit, he sucks on it until I cry out, arching my hips off the bed. He groans in response, dragging his mouth down, licking over and inside my hole.

My brain short-circuits when he presses a finger into me alongside his tongue. He uses his other hand to continue to play with my clit as he laps up my wetness, leaving me clenching around his finger. I sob with relief when he adds another, scissoring them, stretching me.

"That's it, princess." He speaks right against my skin, and the rumble of his voice just heightens the sensations running through me. He brings his mouth back to my clit, kissing it in an oddly sweet gesture before licking it, and pushes a third finger into me. I'm shaking, barely able to hold myself back from the edge as he teases me with his tongue. I grip his hair so tightly it must hurt, but he doesn't try to get me to stop.

He turns his head and kisses my inner thigh. "Be a good girl and come for me."

He punctuates that by pressing his thumb against my asshole.

My hips shoot off the bed as I come with a shout. He keeps fingering me, teasing me, *tormenting* me as I come down from my climax. By the time he finally removes his fingers, kissing my belly instead of my pussy, I'm so oversensitive every movement makes me gasp.

He brushes the hair from my forehead. His lips and chin shine with my slick, and when he kisses me, I taste myself.

"Fuck, James."

"We're getting to that," he says. He sits on the bed, pulling me into his lap, his hands finding my ass as he grinds me down against his crotch. This close, all I can focus on is his cologne and the way his hard cock feels against my folds. He's so thick I find myself aching as we move together. His fingers were good, but ultimately, they were a tease. I can come again, and I want to do it while he's inside me, fucking into me with all the power in his body.

I throw my arms around his neck and kiss him, rubbing myself against his cock until his breath hitches. He's been having his way with me and I'm loving it, but there's no way I'm letting him have all the fun. I reach down and grip his cock, pumping it slowly. He groans, burying his face in the crook of my neck as I work him over, my thumb swiping over the head.

He presses a kiss against my ear. "Fuck, you feel good, baby."

"You have condoms, right?"

He reaches over, grabbing one from the nightstand. I take it from him, impatient now, and try to rip it open with my teeth. No such luck. He laughs as he takes it from me, opening it with ease and rolling it on his cock. "I got you."

I trace over his tattoo. Does it mean something, or did he just get it for fun? Now that I think about it, his brother has a tattoo in the same place. Maybe he got it with him. The thought is unfairly adorable.

If we were really dating, I'd ask. But that's the kind of question that comes from a girlfriend, not a hookup. And if there's anything I need to remember, it's that this is not for real. This is just to scratch an itch we're both feeling. Even if he calls me princess and makes me see stars when I come.

He rolls us over so I'm on my back, and nudges my legs apart with his knee. I oblige him, gripping his arms to steady myself as he lines up. A muscle in his arm jumps as I squeeze. He rubs his cock against my entrance, getting the tip wet with my slick.

"James." I gasp as his hand brushes my still-sensitive clit. "Don't tease."

He looks down at me, something unidentifiable in his gaze. "I won't, Beckett."

He pushes in. A little at a time, his face taut with concentration, leaving me rapt as I watch the intensity in his eyes. Beckett. He called me by my full name. Not Bex, not "princess."

Beckett.

It makes my toes curl, even though it shouldn't.

By the time he finally settles all the way inside me, I'm arching my back, legs wrapped tight around his hips. He stays still for just a moment, but true to his word, he doesn't tease. He's thick as fuck; his fingers helped, but I still feel a delicious stretch. He pulls out almost all the way, the drag of his cock exquisitely slow, before thrusting his hips forward.

"Is this good?" he asks as he builds up a rhythm. "Tell me if I need to do something different."

I nod, my grip on him tightening.

"Use your words, baby."

"Yes," I say, the word intermingled with a cry as he hits the spot inside me that makes me want to melt. "Keep going. Please, just don't stop."

"Good girl," he praises as he snaps his hips forward. His hand finds my clit again, rubbing in time with his thrusts. "What a good fucking girl."

I close my eyes, lost in the tsunami of pleasure that's hitting me from all angles—his huge cock inside me, his talented fingers, the power with which he's pleasuring us both. When he lowers his head to my breasts again, I come, the orgasm and my voice ripped from me all at once. He holds me to his chest tightly as his rhythm gets erratic, finally finishing inside me with a low groan.

For a few minutes, we don't say a word. I can feel his heart pounding, just like my own is, and it's comforting, knowing he needs a minute to breathe as much as I do. He makes to move off me, but I shake my head, digging my nails into his skin.

"I like it," I mumble. "You're like a sexy blanket."

He laughs against my neck. "I don't want to squish you."

"Mm. You *are* pure muscle."

"Don't you know it." He stays put, his hand stroking through my sweaty hair.

Eventually, though, he does move. I sit up as he goes to take care of the condom. As much as I hate the thought of getting dressed and driving back to campus, I know I need to do it.

He comes out of the bathroom, running his hand through his hair, and smiles when he catches sight of me curled up against the headboard. That smile has no right to be that charming. "Hey. It's pretty late."

"I know," I say quickly. "Thanks, I'll go change and be out of your hair soon. Text me about the game, okay?"

He walks over to his dresser and takes out a t-shirt. Instead of putting it on, he tosses it to me. "Stay. It's late, I don't want you on the road right now."

"It's a ten-minute drive to campus."

"A lot can happen in ten minutes." He crosses his arms over his chest. "I have to get up early for my workout and morning practice tomorrow, so you'll have plenty of time to get where you need to be. Stay, okay? We can watch something together, or just sleep if you're ready for that."

It's so tempting to say yes. I don't have an early class tomorrow, so I could take it easy. And what girl says no to a guy asking her to spend the night? Usually, the complaint is that guys *won't* offer cuddle time.

But it's dangerously couple-like. Domestic. And as much as I want it, I know I can't have it, even if it's just a night of pretending.

I reach up and kiss him softly before I slip out of the bed. "I can't."

He watches as I gather up my clothes, slipping back into what I wore when I first arrived at his place and then tucking my dress and shoes into my bag. I know I probably look all rumpled—I don't even want to think about what a mess my hair is—but I can't bring myself to care. With a bit of luck, Laura will be asleep already or spending the night with Barry.

"Call me when you get to your dorm room," James says eventually. He throws on a pair of sweatpants and walks to the door with me. "Okay?"

"I can just text you."

"Call."

His voice holds a surprisingly serious note, so I look up at him. "I don't want to bother you."

"You won't be. I want to make sure you get home safe."

I wait for him to open the door and send me out into the night, but he doesn't. He just keeps looking at me, clearly waiting for an answer.

"Okay," I say. "I'll call you."

"Good." He leans in, hesitating for half a second before kissing me on the cheek. "We can talk about the game tomorrow."

As I drive home, only one thought echoes in my mind: *I just slept with my fake boyfriend.*

James

Sweetie!" my mother calls.

She's still halfway across the parking lot, but her arms are open, ready to pull me into a hug. I jog over, letting her wrap me up in her arms. We FaceTime every week, but nothing beats seeing her for real. I hug her back, breathing in the familiar floral scent of her perfume, as she smacks my cheek with a kiss. A Sandra Callahan hug is like nothing else in the world. I'm halfway in game mode already, but can't help relaxing a bit. I know not everyone has a good relationship with their parents, but I'm fortunate to have two awesomely supportive people in my corner, and in my siblings' corners. I still feel bad that Bex was intimidated by the thought of them. Yes, we have a lot of privilege, but my parents are good people, and they use their money for good, too. If I'm half as successful as them in my career and my life, I'll consider that a job well done.

Dad reaches us as Mom steps back. He holds out his hand to shake mine before pulling me into a hug too, slapping my back. "How are you, son? Feeling good?"

"A little nervous," I admit. The game isn't until later today, but I've been thinking of it since I woke up for my workout. I don't have many game day rituals—the simpler things are, the better—but I can't help feeling the nerves in my gut. If we win today, we keep the perfect record we've been carrying this season. Beyond that, a win will help prove to everyone that I made the right decision, leaving LSU for McKee as a senior.

Every single game I play this season is an audition for two things: the Heisman Trophy and the NFL draft. While the draft won't be until the spring, leaving me the full course of the season to impress my potential future bosses, the Heisman is awarded in December, before the college bowl games. I haven't allowed myself to think about it too much, but nominations will be coming soon, and I know I'm part of the conversation. Another Heisman winner? My father, who is looking at me with pride in his serious eyes. Cooper, Izzy, and I all have his blue eyes and dark hair. My mother always teases that if a girl ever wants to know what Cooper and I will look like when we're older, she should just check out Dad.

I've always been close with my parents, but my dad especially. Cooper, Sebastian, and Izzy all play their sports with talent and grit, but I'm the one who chose to follow in Dad's footsteps. He had the fortune of a full career in the NFL with the Cardinals and the Giants, several Super Bowl wins, and since retirement, a flourishing post-sports career in broadcasting. I've looked up to him since I was a little kid, and the closer I've come to reaching the league, the more pressure I feel to become him. Hell, they started writing articles about my potential for professional football when I was in middle school. Anything less than success as an NFL quarterback will be a disappointment for everyone, but especially me and my father.

"You'll do great," he says, voice gruff. "Gomez keeps texting me about your progress."

I feel my face redden. "Has he? Dad—"

He holds up his hands. "I know, I know. You want to do your own thing. I'm just proud, son."

Suddenly, a blur of long, dark hair and a purple McKee jersey engulfs me. I play along, pretending to stagger backward as Izzy hugs me, her lean arms squeezing so tightly it hurts. She rubs her cheek against mine, and I drop a kiss to the top of her head.

"Hey," she says breathlessly as she steps back. "Sorry about that, Chance called me."

I raise an eyebrow at her. "Oh, you're still with Chase?"

She flushes, tucking her hair behind her ear. "We've been dating for almost a year now; you know his name."

"I know Chance is a dumb name," I say cheerfully. "How's it going, Iz? Glad you could make it."

"I wanted to go to Vermont to see Coop's game, but Mom and Dad wouldn't let me go on my own," she says.

"And let Cooper take you to a college party?" I say, filled with horror at the mere thought. I love my sister, but she's a social butterfly, and has caused more than one headache for our parents at her prep school. On the one hand, it's a good thing she's a senior and finally about to graduate, but on the other, I'm not sure McKee is ready for her. "Absolutely not."

"Exactly!" Mom says.

Izzy huffs out a sigh. "Anyway, this can count as my McKee campus visit. I'm sending in my application as soon as I finish working on my personal statement."

"That's great," I tell her. "It still sucks we won't overlap at all."

She shrugs. "I'll just take your room."

I bark out a laugh at the thought of Cooper letting our baby sister have the owner's suite. She's got all of us wrapped around her finger in one way or another—being the little sister of three protective older brothers will do that—but I'd bet that that will be a bridge too far. "Good luck with that."

"Seb's coming, right?" she asks as we head into the restaurant.

Coming up from Long Island, they decided to make a day of it, so we're in Moorbridge for breakfast. After this, I need to go into true game prep, so they'll be on their own, but I'm excited to know they'll be watching the game. And an even bigger part of me is excited by the fact Bex will be watching, too.

"Yeah," I tell Izzy. "Actually, he's here already, look."

Seb stands up from his table in the back, a grin on his face. "Izzy!"

"Sebby!" she cries, launching herself forward for another bone-crushing hug.

Dad gives me an exhausted smile as we wind our way to the back. "I wish you were going to be around to keep an eye on her."

"I'll make sure Coop and Seb do," I say. "Even if I'm out in San Francisco."

"You'll go there for sure if you're the first pick," he agrees. "But I wouldn't count out Philadelphia."

Before we reach the table, he pulls me aside. "How are things really?" he says. "What about that one class you're taking?"

His voice is serious, shifting into coach mode. He never coached me in an official capacity growing up, but he's been my football mentor as much as my father, and when we're talking like this, there's a certain unspoken set of rules in place. I stand up straighter as I reply, "It's going well, sir. I'm working with a tutor."

Bex is not just a tutor; the second she's in my mind, I'm thinking about how fucking good it felt to finally give in to our mutual attraction. I know we agreed there wouldn't be a repeat, but in the couple of days since, I've been itching to kiss her again. To hear the pretty sounds that she makes when she's turned on. To make her feel so good she's clenched tight around my cock, panting, showing off her beautiful tits as she arches her back.

It's a problem, but it's not one I'm about to tell my father about.

After Sara, we got clear pretty fucking quick about my priorities. When he meets Bex later, he'll just be hearing about how she's tutoring me, and we've become friends. Hopefully the whole fake relationship we're weaving doesn't even come up.

He nods. "Good. What about the team? Any issues?"

Darryl's smug face comes to mind. Bex was right about him; aside from annoying texts from time to time, he's left her alone now that he thinks she's taken by another guy. That shit is stupid, but as long as he's out of her life, I don't care. Still, that doesn't mean I like the guy.

"Nothing major."

He just keeps looking at me. I swear, sometimes his gaze is so intense, it's an X-ray.

"Really, sir. No issues."

"Good." He claps my shoulder. "Remember your goals, son. You'll have time for everything else once you're settled where you need to be. This season is important, it's setting the building blocks for everything that will come after."

He couldn't have made things clearer if he told me explicitly not to fuck up. Even though I know it, I appreciate the reminder. I might be thinking a hell of a lot about Bex lately, but that doesn't mean it's leading anywhere. I've never tried to be just friends with a girl I've slept with, but there's a first time for everything, right?

The most important thing right now is to win this game.

CHAPTER 20

Bex

When I stumble into the kitchenette on Saturday morning, there's a package waiting for me on the table.

Laura, who is still in her pajamas—a gray t-shirt that must be Barry's—takes a sip from the mug she's clutching with both hands. She just shrugs when I raise an eyebrow. "It was leaning against the door when I came back from Barry's. Oh, and I brought bagels."

"Ooh, you went out for bagels?" I put a fresh coffee pod into the machine on our tiny countertop and set it to brew while I poke around in the brown paper bag next to it. There's a still-warm sesame seed bagel waiting for me, plus scallion cream cheese, the true undefeated combination. "You're awesome."

"I know." She smiles, tapping on the mug with her long nails. When she heard I had tickets to the game and wanted her to come with me, she went to get a fresh manicure, so now her nails are silver and purple, McKee's colors. I had work, so I couldn't tag along, but last night she painted my nails purple too. Hopefully James won't think it's silly.

I put creamer in my coffee and toast my bagel, then plop down at the table across from Laura. The package is staring me in the face, and I can't help the flutter of my heart at the sight of it. I haven't seen James since we slept together; we've both been too busy for a tutoring session, but we've been texting, and every time his name flashes across my phone screen, I smile.

"Let's hope it's from James, not Darryl," I say as I pull the package closer. A couple days ago, Darryl cornered me in the library to try to chat me up, so I wouldn't put it past him to try something.

"I still can't believe you slept with him," Laura says. "And that you haven't given me details!"

I blush. "You know it was good."

"*Obviously* it was good, but what's he like in bed? Sweet? Dominant?"

I just roll my eyes. "I'm going to go ahead and open this now."

There's a note on the top, and when I see my name written in James's handwriting on the envelope, I try and fail to bite back my smile. Inside, there's a single piece of notebook paper with just one line on it, signed with a J.

Figured you'd need the right jersey princess.

-J

Laura snatches the note from my hand as I tear into the package. "Princess? He calls you *princess*?"

"Kind of."

"That's *so* romantic." She gasps as I unfold the jersey. It's his, of course; the number 9 stitched on both sides and CALLAHAN across the back in block letters. I used to have Darryl's jersey, but I got rid of it along with a bunch of other things back in the spring, after I discovered that he was cheating.

"It's the perfect size," I say.

Laura nods sagely. "It'll show off your boobs. I'm sure he picked it out with that in mind."

I kick her under the table, but she just laughs, and after a moment I start laughing too. I have a presentation to work on for class, plus an essay to write, but later today, I'm going to see James play football.

* * *

THANK GOD WE'RE not trying to fool James's parents with our fake relationship, because I'm pretty sure Richard Callahan hates me.

When Laura and I arrived at the box with Sebastian, he introduced me as James's friend. Sandra immediately pulled me into a hug and asked how I knew her son, so I explained the tutoring, leaving out the other half of the deal. Richard greeted me politely, but the game is almost over now, and he's been glaring at me nonstop.

Maybe it's the jersey—girlfriends wear their guys' jerseys, everyone knows that. But honestly, why would he care if his son is dating someone? Maybe he can tell that even if I was with his son for real, we wouldn't be a good match. The Callahans are rich and famous. I'm just a diner rat. When James ends up with someone for real, she'll be like him and will make the perfect NFL wife.

The thought makes me tighten my grip on my drink.

Sebastian nudges me. "James is back on the field. LSU only got a field goal."

I look to the big television screen across from us, which is currently showing a close-up of James's face as he surveys the field. He has a cut on his nose from a sack back in the second quarter, and his jersey, which had been pristine at the start of the game, is covered in dirt and grass stains. He points and shouts as he adjusts the offensive line. As I watch, he takes the snap and immediately hands it off to one of the other guys, who darts through a hole in the defense and gains twenty yards. The crowd erupts into cheers. Out of the corner of my eye, I see Richard nod, his face serious as he leans forward in his seat.

It's been a back-and-forth sort of game, with McKee getting plenty of offensive opportunities, but LSU getting them as well. McKee is leading, but barely, so a touchdown on this possession is important. I didn't pay much attention to football before Darryl, but last fall I got really into it, and now I know what's going on. James sets up again and throws a pass this time, but it goes wide, so they drop to a second down.

Sebastian leans in. "You're going to hang out with us after, right?"

"Yes, she is," Laura says before I can reply.

I roll my eyes. "Of course. Izzy pretty much threatened me with pain of death if I didn't."

"You'll get used to it," he says. "She can be very persuasive."

For a moment, I wish what he just said was true; that I'll get used to it because as his girlfriend, I'll be seeing a lot more of his family. But I shake my head slightly, banishing that thought. If anything, I can let myself get comfortable with being his friend. But that's it.

McKee inches down the field for the next few plays, and a penalty gives them a fresh set of downs. Richard claps his hands together in celebration, laughing and replying to something the guy sitting next to him says. Sebastian gives a whoop, standing to get a better view of the field. I follow suit, even though it makes me feel dizzy to be up this high. McKee's football stadium is huge, and it's rocking right now, lights flashing in the overcast late afternoon.

James escapes a sack and throws the ball while he's falling backward; somehow it finds one of the receivers, who catches it on the tips of his fingers and hauls it in right at the edge of the red zone.

"Go James!" I shout. Then I blush because half the box is looking at me. But my heart is beating in time with the crowd, and James is so close to putting this game away for good that I can't help the excitement running through my veins. They set up again, and he fakes a pass before spinning around and airing it out into the end zone. It sails over the receiver's head.

They try again. Same result.

"Come on," I whisper, my stomach clenched tight as I see the close-ups of him as he runs over to Coach Gomez for a time-out regrouping. It's third down. If they don't get the touchdown here, or a penalty for new downs, then they'll probably try for the field goal, and that leaves the door open for LSU to try and win it on a touchdown in the last minute.

He looks so serious as he sets up the line, yet somehow relaxed as well. I've never been an athlete, so I can't understand it, but something tells me he's got this.

This time, the pass connects in the end zone. I scream, bouncing up and down on the tips of my toes as Laura grabs my hand tightly, cheering in my ear. Izzy calls out her brother's name, and Richard and Sandra meet eyes and smile, which is an unexpectedly sweet gesture. Down on the field, James pumps his fist in a quiet celebration, then jogs over to his teammates.

They're going to win this game. I can feel it, and the rest of the crowd can too, because everyone is going nuts. LSU has a minute, but they need a touchdown and a two-point conversion to tie it, and the McKee defense shuts them down before that can happen.

McKee still has a perfect season. *James* still has a perfect season. His old team came to his new house, and he showed them right to the door.

I'm so freakin' proud I can't stop smiling.

CHAPTER 21

James

It takes an agonizingly long amount of time to get to Bex and my family. First the media crew at ABC, which televised the game, wants to interview me, so I put on the headset and try to answer the reporter's questions with charm, even though I'm still out of breath and my teammates keep coming over to congratulate me. Then there's the locker room celebration, where Coach Gomez makes me give a speech. I'm terrible at these big speeches, so I say something to the effect of, "Good game, boys," which gets everyone laughing. Then I finally get into the showers, where I make quick work of getting off the dirt and sweat, but as soon as I'm dressed, Coach pulls me over for a private talk. He finally lets me go, slapping my back hard, and only then do I manage to scoop up my duffle and make a beeline for the lobby.

I see my father; he's talking to someone away from the rest of the crowd. My stomach drops down low as I realize I'm staring at Pete Thomas, the most respected scout in the NFL. He was a player for the Dolphins for years before getting into coaching and finally scouting, and although we've met before, I'm still intimidated by him. He pays attention to every little thing with eyes better than a hawk's. In his reports, he strips a player down to his most basic skills. Fancy stats don't mean anything when there are fundamentals to work on. I'm sure that however well I played tonight—and I know I did, interception in the second quarter aside—he has plenty to critique.

He's the sort of man who is whispering in the ears of my future potential bosses, telling them who is worth their time and who won't make the cut in the NFL. The fact he's friends with my father doesn't mean shit.

"Sir," I say as I walk over to them. "Didn't realize you'd be here."

My father has a hard expression on his face, which is weird—shouldn't he be happy I pulled off the win? But then he smiles, reaching out with one arm to pull me into a half-hug.

It's just not the sort of smile that reaches his eyes. I've seen enough of the two to know the difference.

"James," Pete says, reaching out his hand to shake mine. There's genuine respect in his deep brown eyes, which makes me relax somewhat. "I've just been talking to your father about the game. It was a pleasure to watch you perform, son. Pleased you got out with the W."

"Thank you, sir."

"We've no doubt that if you continue to put together wins like this, you'll end up the Heisman winner. Keep it between us, but I have it on good authority that you're going to be nominated for the award."

The back of my neck burns. Hopefully they can't see any evidence of my blush on my face. Winning the award would be incredible, which is exactly why I've tried not to think about it.

"It would be an honor, but this was a team win. This whole season has come together because the guys are playing up to their true potentials."

"Spoken like a team player," Pete says approvingly. "Rich, you did a good job with him."

I duck my head, pride swelling in my chest, as my father murmurs in agreement.

"Of course, that misread on third down in the second quarter was a big misstep," Pete continues.

I snap my head up. "Yes, sir. I looked over the tape during halftime." I'm still kicking myself for that one. Interceptions suck under any circumstances, but especially when I know for a fact it's my own fault. Ball security is the number one priority, always.

He nods. "Being willing to acknowledge your mistakes is big, too. I look forward to seeing more from you, James."

He shakes my father's hand, then mine again, and walks off, cutting through the crowd easily because of his broad frame.

I turn to my father, expecting him to have something to say about that interception, but before he can talk, Bex appears at my side. She grabs my arm, leaning up to kiss my cheek. "Hey."

"Hey, princess," I say automatically. I give my dad a quick glance; he's frowning in a way I don't like. Shit. "Did you enjoy the game?"

She turns my face with her finger and kisses me on the lips. It's clear why the moment I see Darryl walking by. He glowers at me, but doesn't come over, thank fuck.

"You were amazing," she says, her pretty brown eyes sparkling with excitement. There's glitter in her hair and scattered over her cheeks, and the jersey I sent over this morning looks amazing on her. My stomach tightens pleasantly at the thought of her wearing my name and number on her back. "I had a lot of fun. Plus, your sister is hilarious."

"Beckett," my father says, "would you mind if you gave us a moment alone?"

Bex looks between us with a frown. "Sure. Sorry."

I don't want her to go, but I don't protest when she does, either. My father is pissed.

He walks away from the crowd, heading further into the stadium, and I follow without a word. I knew asking Bex to watch the game from the box was a risk, but I expected to have a chance to explain everything first. I don't blame her for kissing me—that's the deal, after all, we act like a couple, especially in front of Darryl—but that doesn't mean the timing doesn't suck.

When we're alone, he turns around, arms crossed tightly over his chest. "When were you going to mention the fact you're screwing your tutor?"

His tone is clipped, impatient. I take a deep breath. My father is wonderful, but ever since Sara, he's been wary every time I even *look* at a girl for more than half a second. Seeing me kiss someone who is wearing my jersey probably raised alarm bells in his head. But it's not what he thinks.

"We hooked up once," I say. "We're not actually dating."

"Sure as hell seems like she thinks you are."

"We're pretending to date," I amend. "In exchange for tutoring."

He works his jaw. "Pretending."

"Her ex . . . he won't leave her alone. He's a piece of shit who was threatening her." I don't mention he's also on the team because that would just add in another complication. Another reason for my father to doubt my commitment, when in reality, I'm doing this because I'm as committed as ever. "I needed a tutor for the writing class, and she's getting through to me in a way other tutors haven't. She didn't want money, but she said if I pretended to be her boyfriend in public, she'd help me out. It's keeping her ex away from her."

He grunts. "And then you slept with her."

"Once." I run my hand through my still-damp hair. "We're friends, Dad. I asked her to the game because she's my friend. And us hooking up has nothing to do with my game."

He shakes his head. "I don't like it."

"Noted." I turn to go because he's starting to piss me off, but then he says my name. I turn back around.

There's genuine concern in his eyes. That's the thing about my father. He's hard on me sometimes, but it always comes from a place of love. I've never doubted that. When the whole situation went down with Sara, he acted like my dad first and a coach second.

"I love you," he says. "And I want the best for you. And a relationship is not the best thing for you right now."

"I already said we're not dating."

"She's wearing your jersey, son."

"Hundreds of people in this stadium wore my jersey tonight. Maybe thousands." Although he does have a point, even if he doesn't realize it. Bex is wearing my jersey because I gave it to her. I went to the bookstore on campus and picked out the one I liked best, and then I wrapped it up like a present and left it at her door. It's the one I wanted Darryl to see her in. The one *I* wanted to see her in.

He sighs, rubbing at his jaw. "You said her ex was threatening her?"

"He's an asshole." I remember the way she flinched, the bruises on her wrists, and feel my stomach tighten. "But you don't have to worry about me."

He studies my face. I meet his eyes, even though part of me wants to look away. He must like what he sees in my expression, because eventually, he nods. "As long as you don't let yourself get caught up in her."

"I won't. It was a one-time thing."

"Good." He pulls me into a hug, slapping my back so hard it stings.

I might have convinced him, but in my heart, I'm not so sure I'm going to be able to keep this casual.

* * *

LATER, BACK ON McKee's campus, Sebastian stops his car in front of one of the many beautiful old brick buildings. He glances over his shoulder at Bex and Laura. "This is it, right?"

"Yep, thanks," Laura says, opening the car door. She looks back at Bex with a teasing curve to her smile. "It was nice hanging out with you guys. I'll see you inside, Bex."

Bex waits until Laura disappears inside the dorm building before undoing her seat belt. "Walk me to the door?"

"Like you have to ask."

She smiles. "Bye, Seb. It was fun spending time with you and your sister today."

Seb gives me a look as I get out of the car, which I ignore. So what if I sound like I'm actually her boyfriend? It's not real. I told Dad the same thing. It's just the polite thing to do since she was my guest to the game today.

According to Seb, she had a good time. It would have been fun to see her react to the plays on the field, since everyone has a different style when they're into it. Some people scream and clap, and others stay silent, pleading with the football gods for each play to go in their favor. As soon as the game ended, I wanted to see her and drink in her reaction.

She must have looked so pretty, her eyes lit up with excitement.

I take her hand as we walk in the direction of the dorm building. "Hey, you painted your nails purple. That's cute."

"Laura insisted."

"Did you actually have fun?"

She smiles. "Yeah. I knew you were talented, but this was next level. You're incredible on the field."

Pleasure sings through me. "Thank you."

She ducks her head, blushing. "I'm sure you get that all the time."

"It means more coming from you."

"Really?"

"Really. You look good in my jersey." I brush a lock of her hair back behind her ear. "Pretty girl."

"James," she whispers.

I kiss her.

She makes a hungry little sound, running her tongue over the seam of my lips. My hands find her hips, pulling her close. My father's voice echoes in my head, and I know he's right, I know I shouldn't. There's no one around but my brother. No one to fool.

But I can't help myself.

"Come inside," she says.

I can't say no.

CHAPTER 22

James

After texting Seb to tell him to go home, I let Bex walk me to her building. She's up on the third floor, and every time we reach a new landing, she pulls me into a kiss. I'm still pumped up from the game, and my blood is flowing hotly. By the time we reach her door, I'm halfway to hard. If she told me to get on my knees and eat her out right here, I'd do it without hesitation.

I want her in that jersey and nothing else, stat.

She stops with the key in the doorknob. "This is still just sex."

"Definitely."

"We're just exploring our attraction."

I nod against her neck as I kiss it. "Show me inside."

She has a shy look on her face as she opens the door, revealing a little living-area-slash-kitchenette. The couch has a pink throw over one of the arms, and it's covered in pillows. I'm not sure how anyone manages to sit on it, but finding out isn't the goal. I want to know which of the doors leads to Bex's bedroom.

She stands on her tiptoes to kiss me. I wind my arms around her, urging her up; she jumps into my arms and wraps her legs around my waist. Holding her in my arms like this, smelling her vanilla perfume, has me so desperate to be skin-to-skin with her again that I shudder. "Which bedroom is yours?"

"Right." She kisses me deeply, nipping at my bottom lip.

I open the door, fumbling for the light switch. The overhead light comes on, revealing a neat little bedroom. There's a bed in the corner, made perfectly with a floral-patterned quilt, Albert the stuffed bear plopped down against the pillows. In the opposite corner, there's a desk covered in books and papers, plus lots of photography on the walls. I want to look at them more closely, because I'm sure it's her own art and she hasn't let me see any of it yet, but right now, I'm too turned on to stop and ask.

A thick area rug on the floor softens my footsteps as I walk us over to the bed. I set her down, but instead of settling back against the bed, she kneels, hanging onto my belt loops.

She licks her lips.

Her eyes are bright as she undoes my pants.

"Bex," I say hoarsely.

"I've been thinking about this ever since you got to taste me," she says as she pulls out my cock. Her hand strokes my length, and I gasp. "This is okay, right?"

"Fuck yeah it's okay."

She runs her nail down my shaft delicately. "Good."

When she puts her mouth on me, she does so experimentally. I push my fingers into her hair, tugging her closer. It takes all my self-control not to pull her onto my dick. I don't want to choke her, but fuck, I don't think I've ever seen a sexier sight than her on her knees, mouthing at me.

She swirls her tongue over the head, then takes me into her mouth properly, massaging my balls with her hand. They're tight, aching; already I'm on the edge of blowing my load. When I tighten my grip on her hair, she moans around my cock, and I squeeze my eyes shut, seeing stars.

She takes me in deeper. When she hollows out her cheeks, I stroke her cheek with a trembling finger. Feeling the outline of my cock in her mouth nearly makes me come, but I manage to control myself. I want to ride this out for as long as she's willing to give me.

"Fuck, princess. You look so gorgeous on your knees for me," I tell her. She looks up, and I see tears in her eyes, but she doesn't pull away. I wipe my thumb at the corner of her eye, then lick away the saltiness. Her eyes widen, and she hums around my cock. When I tighten my grip in her hair, she just responds by firming her grasp on my balls. I moan, clenching my ass to keep from coming.

I'm not exaggerating when I say I've never seen anything more beautiful in my life. Her hair wrapped around my hand, her fluttering eyelashes, spit running down her chin. She continues like this, moving on my cock with agonizing slowness, until she has every inch in her gorgeous mouth. Her throat is so tight, wet and warm and welcoming, but what makes me lose my mind is when I notice she has a hand down her leggings. She's fucking touching herself as she sucks me, too turned on to wait.

"I'm coming," I grunt a second before it happens. She pulls off, but not all the way; I come in her mouth and all over her lips rather than down her throat.

And this little minx just smiles, licking at her lips. The hand between her legs is still moving. I practically growl as I haul her up onto the bed, sweeping the poor stuffed animal onto the floor. I kiss her, tasting myself on her tongue, as I rip down her leggings and panties in one go. I lick into her mouth, relishing in her breathy moan, and sink two fingers into her. My thumb finds her clit, rubbing in tight, rapid circles.

She comes on my fingers before long, soaking them in her slick. When I pull them out of her warm cunt, I tap my fingers against her lips; she opens her mouth, licking her own wetness. I replace my fingers with my lips, kissing her until we're both breathless, and finally we curl up on the bed together.

I kick off my jeans and pull my t-shirt over my head, and she does the same with her leggings. She's about to take off the jersey, but I stop her. "I love seeing you in this."

She presses her face against my bare chest, kissing my tattoo. "Oh yeah?"

"Sexy as hell, babe."

"You're the sexy one. I was thinking about sucking you off the whole game."

I play with the hem of the jersey. "Seriously?"

"You're in command on the field. It's hot, trust me."

After a few minutes, our breathing evens out. I like having my legs tangled with hers. Her bed is a twin, so my feet are nearly hanging over the edge, but I'm making it work. The exertion from the game, not to mention the orgasm, is catching up to me. I stifle a yawn with my hand as I pat the floor, looking for Albert.

She sits up a bit, looking down at me. "James?"

I set Albert on the bed next to us. "Yeah?"

"I'm sorry if I messed up anything with your dad."

I'm shaking my head before she can say anything else. "Don't. I handled it."

"I don't think he liked me being there."

"He was just surprised."

Her brow knits together. "Does he know we're not really dating?"

"Now he does," I say, even though that makes my chest hurt. "He was just concerned about it, but I explained."

"But why would he be concerned if you're with someone? I mean, if it was real, wouldn't he be happy for you?"

"You know I don't date."

"Because of football."

I nod. "He helped me make that decision."

Part of me wants to explain further, but I'm coming off a high, and the thought of getting that real, even if it's with Bex, makes me nervous.

She continues to trace the lines of my tattoo. "Your brother has the same one."

"Yeah. Seb too. We got them together a couple summers ago."

"It looks familiar," she says. "What is it?"

"It's the Celtic knot. You know, Callahan. Irish roots."

"It looks good on you." She kisses it softly. "I know I didn't want to stay over last time. But you will, right?"

I kiss her cheek before saying, "Show me your photography."

She blinks, eyes widening. "If you really want?"

I hold her gaze. "I do. I was going to ask before, but full disclosure, I was too fucking hard."

She bursts out laughing, slipping out of bed, and grabs a folder from the desk. She settles back against me, and I wrap my arm around her middle. I'm grinning; I love making her laugh.

"I've been taking some portraits of the diner patrons, that's always good practice. And I've been looking at angles in architecture," she says.

I stroke her arm. "Let me see them."

She opens the folder, which I see now is filled with proofs. "I have more on my computer, obviously," she says. "Printing is expensive. But it's helpful to see what the vibe of the physical photo is like, you know?"

"No," I admit, which makes her laugh. "But I love hearing you talk about it."

We flip through the stack slowly. She explains how she took each one, and I think I ask semi-intelligent questions, because I get her rambling about stuff like aperture and white balance and bokeh. It's adorable, even when she gets overly excited and accidentally elbows me in the face.

"Crap," she says, turning my face from side to side. "Are you okay?"

"Just fine," I lie, kissing her. In truth, she's stronger than she looks, because my cheek is stinging. "Tell me about this one."

I point to a photograph of somewhere I recognize; it's the great hall in McKee's library. The table looks familiar, because it's the one we sit at when we go there to study. My laptop is open on the table next to hers; our jackets hang on the backs of two chairs.

She blushes, tracing over the photograph. "I took it when you went to go call your sister."

I snort as the memory comes back to me. "She was afraid she accidentally ate a pot brownie."

"Did she?"

"Honestly, I'm still not sure. Coop thinks she did." I hold up the photograph. Seeing evidence of our time together makes me feel warm inside, like I just drank a huge gulp of hot cider. "You're seriously talented."

"Do you want it?" She ducks her gaze down. "I mean, if you want it, you can have it."

"Not like this."

She looks up, hurt flashing on her face momentarily.

I kiss it away quickly. "Princess, you need to sign it for me first."

She practically throws the photography on her nightstand, climbing into my lap. My hands grip the backs of her thighs automatically, groaning when she presses open-mouthed kisses to my throat.

"Can you go again?" she says breathlessly, rubbing her cheek against mine as she grinds down in my lap. "Want to ride your cock."

And again, I can't say no. Not to her. There's nowhere I'd rather be right now than in her bed, watching her bounce on my dick in my jersey. I bring my hands up, massaging her firm ass. "As long as you let me eat your pretty pussy after."

CHAPTER 23

Bex

Several weeks later, I wake up in James's bed. Again. After Darryl, I thought I wouldn't wake up in a bed other than my own dorm room the whole rest of the time I was at McKee.

Yet here I am, buried comfortably in James Callahan's bed, fighting the sinking feeling in my stomach that comes with waking up alone.

I'm not worried he left because he ended up not wanting me to stay; he said last night that he needed to wake up early for his workout. But that doesn't mean I don't wish he was here so we could wake up together in a much more pleasant way.

I rub the sleep out of my eyes, sitting up with a yawn. Before we went to sleep last night, he shut the curtains—which he admitted his mother made him put up, insisting the room needed more homey touches—so even though the sun is up, the light inside the bedroom is still soft and gray. On the wall opposite, I see the photograph I gifted him. I signed it for him like he wanted, and he had it framed. It looks good over his desk, like a real piece of art.

There's a note on the pillow, written in his messy handwriting. I bite the inside of my cheek as I read it. Trace my fingernail over the letters that make up my name.

Bev,

Hate to leave you. Stay, so I see you when I come back?

-J

I hate how I need to remind myself yet again that we're not dating.

Not. Dating.

After the game against LSU, something shifted. I invited him home, to my suite, and he spent the night. We fucked three times before finally falling asleep. When I woke up in the morning, he was curled around me almost comically, his feet hanging over the edge of the bed, one hand palming my bare bottom, the other tucked around Albert. I'd stared down at him, panic curling through me like smoke, and the intensity of my gaze woke him up.

He'd smiled at me, gaze soft, the corners of his eyes crinkled adorably.

And then I'd tried to kick him out.

I blush now as I remember it.

"I have work," I'd told him, even though that was a lie. I scrambled out of the bed, pulling the jersey over my head and tossing it into the hamper before crossing my arms over my bare chest. He'd sat up, looking at me calmly, and my voice ran ragged as I told him he had to go.

Instead, he pulled me back into his arms. Kissed the top of my head.

"Don't panic," he told me. "This doesn't have to change anything."

"How?" I whispered.

"We're friends," he said, stroking my tangled hair. "Friends who are attracted to each other. We can keep doing this without complicating it."

"Sounds like a recipe for disaster."

"Do you want to stop? Say you want to stop, and we will."

"Our deal?"

"Not the deal. Just this."

I shook my head. In the end, I couldn't lie. "I don't want to stop."

"Then we won't."

He kissed me properly, then, and I hit his arm because our breath smelled horrible, and he'd just smiled and pulled me closer. That's where we left it. Texting, tutoring, dates to keep up the fake relationship. I'm doing things like waking up in his bed and wishing he was around so I could sit on his dick.

A couple days ago, he officially received his nomination for this fancy football award, and where was I? In the background, doing a silent happy dance as he called his parents to share the news.

I slide out of the bed, making it up so it will be nice for him later, and use his shower. Having the private bathroom is a seriously nice perk. His brothers have been good to me, but it's still nice to not have to see them before I'm put together. I dress in the change of clothes I brought along, throw on some makeup and my favorite pie slice earrings, and tuck my phone into my back pocket before heading downstairs.

The air smells like coffee; my stomach growls. I have a little while before I need to drive over to the diner—it's been a few days since I saw my mother, thanks to a double shift at the Purple Kettle and working with James on our midterm paper—and maybe if I'm lucky, I can scrounge up a proper breakfast. Last night Sebastian made a roast chicken, which was delicious. Maybe there are some leftover potatoes that I can fry up with eggs.

As I walk through the living room, I smile, remembering how intense James and Cooper got about their game of Mario Kart last night. After we wrapped up tutoring, I had readings to do, so I plopped on the couch with my textbook, but I kept getting drawn into the trash talking. I wish I had siblings to hang out with the way that James does.

If not for the miscarriage, I would have a sibling. There must be an alternate universe where my mother ended up having that baby. I used to wonder more often about what life would be like if my dad hadn't left the way he did. If my mother managed to overcome her heartbreak. But ultimately, it's useless to linger over. It just makes me sad. I try to avoid thinking about the what-ifs as much as possible.

I blink away the sudden tears that threaten to slip down my cheeks and open the fridge. Although there's a pot of coffee on the counter, I'm the only one in the room. I pour myself a cup and add in some half and half.

There are eggs, which is a good start. Leftover potatoes. A slab of bacon. I scrounge up an onion and half a bell pepper, too, which means I can make a hash. If there's one thing I can cook confidently thanks to the diner, it's breakfast. Breakfast and pie.

I turn on one of my playlists, a pop mix that has me rocking my hips, and poke around until I find a frying pan. Within half an hour, I have a delicious hash steaming in the pan, crispy bacon draining on a paper towel, and eggs ready for frying. I'm cutting up some fruit I found in the crisper when I hear the front door open and shut.

"Yeah, I feel good," Cooper is saying. "It was a nasty bruise for a few days, though."

"If I got hit like that, I wouldn't be able to walk straight," Sebastian replies.

"That's what she said."

"You're such a child."

"Remember when you got hit with that wild pitch last season?"

"I swear my hip still aches."

"Bro, you'd make a terrible hockey player."

"Or football," I hear James say. My stomach flips over pleasantly as he appears in the doorway, giving me a grin. "Hey. What's all this?"

I tuck my hair behind my ear. "Thought you might want some breakfast."

"It smells incredible," Cooper declares as he brushes past his brother. He grabs a mug and fills it with coffee from the fresh pot I made, then pokes at the hash browns, stealing a bite.

"Hey," I say. "Let me make you a plate. I still need to fry the eggs."

"You really didn't have to do any of this," James says. He pours a cup of coffee too, kissing the top of my head before grabbing a piece of bacon.

Sebastian and Cooper give each other a look. I hide my blush by turning back to the stove and cracking the first batch of eggs into the skillet I've been warming slowly.

"I grew up in a diner," I say. "I can do this in my sleep. Besides, I didn't want Sebastian's potatoes to go to waste."

"How can I help?" he says.

"You can set the table, if you want?"

James does that while I crumble the bacon into the hash. Sebastian takes four plates down for me, and I put a big spoonful of the hash on each plate. When the eggs are perfect, I slide one atop each scoop of hash, finishing with salt and pepper and a dash of paprika. I don't photograph food that often, but now I'm wishing I had my camera. It's at the apartment, though, left there by accident when I had to rush back to campus for a last-minute study group. I'll grab it when I get to the diner for the lunch shift.

"Holy crap," Cooper says as he picks up two of the plates and brings them to the table. "Bex, you've been hiding some serious skills."

I shrug, biting back the smile that threatens to engulf my face. "Wait until you taste it."

James sits at the table next to me, leaning in so our arms brush. "I'm sorry I had to go this morning. Although less sorry now."

"Did all three of you go to the gym?"

"Yeah," he says as he breaks the yolk of his egg. "Probably sounds silly to you, but it's a fun thing for us to do together. Hey, Coop, show her the bruise you got at that game."

Cooper lifts his t-shirt, showing off a deep blue and purple mess on his ribcage. I gasp. "What happened?"

"Chirped at the wrong guy."

I tilt my head to the side. "Like, smack talk?"

He grins as he takes a bite of hash. "Exactly. I'm sure he's got a matching shiner; we went pretty rough against the boards."

Sebastian rolls his eyes. "And then you went into the penalty box for slashing."

Cooper shrugs at Sebastian's chiding tone. "So did he."

"And it's going to catch up with you, racking up all those penalties."

"Who are you, Dad?"

"He does have a point," James says. "You don't want to give your agent a reason to be pissed at you."

My eyes widen. "You already have an agent?"

"It's not official," says Cooper. "She's a friend of our father's, I'll actually sign with her after graduation."

"Coop's still salty that Dad didn't let him go into the draft," James teases.

"How?" I ask. "You haven't been drafted yet."

"Hockey is different. A lot of guys get drafted way before they end up signing with a team, but our parents would've killed him if he left college early."

"Ugh, don't remind me," Cooper grumbles.

"But the NFL does things differently?"

"Yeah. Most guys don't enter the draft until they're seniors. I'll get drafted in the spring and go straight into the NFL after graduation."

I lean back in my chair, coffee mug in hand. "And then baseball?"

"Different again," Sebastian says. "Even if you're drafted out of high school, guys play in the minors for a while anyway."

My phone buzzes in my back pocket. I almost don't pick it up, but it's my mom.

The first thing I hear is sirens.

My heart forces its way into my throat. I stand up, my chair scraping against the floor. James glances over at me.

I think he says my name, but I can't hear him, not over the sirens, my heartbeat, and worst of all, my mother's frantic sobs.

"Mom," I say. "Slow down, I can't understand you."

"It happened so fast!" she says. "Bex, I don't know what to do!"

I hurry around the table, making a beeline for the stairs. I burst into James's room, grab my bag, and shove all my crap into it. I can barely understand her, but the word *fire* comes through.

As I turn, I run smack into James. He steadies me, looking down at me with concern in his expression. "Bex, what's going on?"

"Who's that?" I hear my mother say from the phone.

"No one," I say. "I'm on my way right now." I don't have time for this. And I don't have time for the hurt way James is looking at me. I brush past him, rummaging in my bag for my car keys.

"Bex!" I hear him call from the landing. He thunders down the stairs, reaching the front door half a beat behind me. I unlock my car with shaking fingers and slide into the driver's seat.

James appears at the window and knocks on it. "Bex, stop. Tell me what's going on."

"I have to go."

"Like hell you are." He opens the car door, covering his hand with mine to prevent me from shoving the key into the ignition. "You're panicking, you'll get into an accident. Let me drive."

"No. Just leave me—"

"Goddamnit, Bex, no! You'll get hurt."

I roughly wipe away the tears streaming down my face. From somewhere in the haze of panic, I recognize he's right. I don't want him to go to my hometown with me; I don't want him to see the diner like this—*if* there's a diner to see—and most of all, I don't want him to see my mother. But I need to get there as quickly as possible, and he's my best option.

"Fine," I mumble.

He relaxes visibly. "Good. Get in the car, baby. Let me just grab the keys."

Cooper and Sebastian approach, Cooper holding out a set of keys. He tosses them to James, who catches them with ease. "Got them. Let's go."

In this moment, I'm too strung out to argue, so I just climb into the passenger seat as James starts the car. His brothers get into the backseat. I type the diner's address into the map app on my phone, and in the silent car, the slightly robotic voice of the directions starts to talk.

With each mile, the pit in my stomach tightens.

CHAPTER 24

James

After a tense drive, I finally slow the car. We're in a downtown area; to our left is a post office, and to the right, a coffee shop. I've never been to this town before, but it reminds me of Moorbridge, minus McKee's influence.

As I pull into an open spot, Bex gasps. The sound frays my already-tense nerves, and I hit the brake a little too hard. There's a thud in the backseat, and Cooper mutters, "Ouch, asshole."

Out of the corner of my eye, I can see the red and blue flash of sirens.

Bex flings the door open before I can put the car in park. After we got on the road, I managed to wrangle exactly one piece of information from her: there was a fire at the diner. She's lost in her own world of panic, refusing to let me in. I tried holding her hand on the drive, and she looked at me like I just dropped my pants in public. I tried to push her for more details, and she snapped at me. At this point, I'm just glad she let me drive her here.

But I'm not leaving her alone. Not now. She needs someone to support her, whether she likes it or not.

I run after her, vaguely aware of my brothers following close behind. She's in the middle of the street. Jesus, she's lucky she hasn't gotten run over. I hustle her to the sidewalk, and she must be stunned, looking at the fire trucks, because she doesn't protest.

The air is hazy with smoke, but it doesn't seem like anything is still on fire.

When we get to the end of the street—safely, on the sidewalk—Bex approaches a group of firefighters who are rolling up a hose. One of them lights up when he spots her; he's about our age, maybe a couple years older, with a buzz-cut and sweat dripping down his face. "Bex, hey. Your mom said you were on your way."

She knows this guy? I know I shouldn't care, but I do. I inch closer to Bex.

"Kyle," Bex says. "How bad is it?"

How does she know this guy? Did she go to high school with him?

He grimaces. "It could be worse. The fire was upstairs, mostly."

Bex glances at the building, her teeth digging into her lower lip. "Upstairs? The apartment?"

"Your mom will need to stay somewhere else while the damage is fixed. Smoke ruins more than you'd think."

"Was there any damage to the diner?" I ask.

Kyle glances over at me. "Who's this?"

"I'm James." I hold out my hand. "Her boyfriend."

Behind me, either Seb or Coop coughs. I ignore them. The last thing Bex needs right now is this dude hitting on her.

Kyle shakes my hand, but he keeps looking at Bex. "The diner is pretty much fine, maybe needs some repairs. The building needs to be inspected, of course. Your mom was upstairs when it happened, but she's okay."

She gets a funny look on her face, like she's not sure whether she's going to burst into tears or start screaming, and strides over to the diner.

"I wouldn't get too close yet," Kyle calls.

She doesn't stop. I hurry after her, reaching her the moment she stops, looking up at the building. The front of the diner looks good; the door is propped open, revealing a long row of booths, and the neon sign over it, while unlit, is intact. But above it, there are two smashed in windows, and scorch-marks on the whitewashed brick. I reach out, tangling my hand in hers, and follow her into the diner.

She walks us around the counter. I catch sight of framed photographs on the walls, red stools, shiplap made into a feature over the booths. She pushes open a little door behind the counter. It leads to a cramped set of stairs. The air still smells acrid, not yet cleared from the smoke. I suppress a cough, my eyes watering.

Kyle reaches us. "Bex," he says. "You need to have someone come in and inspect the damage done to the building. Don't go upstairs, it's not safe."

"He's right," I tell her, even though I'm reluctant to side with Kyle on anything. I don't want her breathing in this shitty air or trying to see the apartment and getting hurt.

She steps forward anyway, touching the scorched banister. My hand twitches in hers. If I need to haul her out of the building to keep her from hurting herself, I will, but I'd much rather it not come to that.

"How bad is it?" she asks.

Kyle hesitates. "Maybe you should talk to the police about it. Chief Alton is here talking to your mom."

Her eyes flash as she looks over her shoulder. "How. Bad?"

He swallows, his Adam's apple bobbing. "Like I said, it's mostly smoke damage. Insurance can help you replace any belongings you lost. It's good you have most of your stuff at your school, right?"

Her expression shutters. "Not everything."

She shoves past me and Kyle, pressing her sleeve against her nose. As I watch, she makes a beeline for the police car parked next to the firetrucks. An older white man in uniform stands talking to a woman wearing leggings and a ragged old sweatshirt. A cigarette dangles from her long, thin fingers. She has the same hair as Bex, that strawberry blonde, and the heart-shaped face. She must be Bex's mother, Abby.

"This is a mess," Cooper says quietly. "You're creating expectations, man."

Bex approaches Abby, who turns to her and pulls her into a tight hug. Who the hell lights a cigarette five feet away from an actual fire? I don't like the guilt in her expression, the way she's looking at Bex like she's sorry. Something doesn't feel right here.

What did she lose in the fire?

"She needs support," I say.

"Sure," Seb says. "But you just introduced yourself as her boyfriend."

"And you look like you're about to commit murder for her," says Coop. "I know she's cool, but—"

I turn on him. "Watch your mouth."

"James, come on. She's going to think this means something."

My heart thuds. "And maybe it does. It's not your fucking business."

I walk away before I do something I'll regret, like decking my brother. I love Cooper, but he doesn't understand. Something shifted the moment I saw her take that phone call. I can't examine it right now, but I can't push it away, either.

"It *was* your fault!" Bex is saying as I approach.

My jaw tightens. I'd figured as much, once I saw her mother, but I'd hoped that maybe Bex found out differently.

"I'm going to give you a moment alone," Chief Alton says. When we cross paths, he gives me a heavy look. "You're with Beckett?"

I nod. "Yes, sir."

"Damn mess," he says, shaking his head. "At least the diner's in good shape."

"Honey," Abby says, "it was just a little fire."

Bex crosses her arms over her chest tightly. I wind my arm around her waist, bracing myself for her to move away, but instead she leans into my grip. It's subtle, but enough to loosen the knot in my chest somewhat.

"Little?" she says. "Kyle just told me you need to go live somewhere else while they fix the damage. Everything's gone, even . . . That's not little, Mom. You're lucky you're not dead."

Abby takes a drag from her cigarette. "Who's the hunk? You cheating on Darryl now?"

"He cheated on me," Bex says with exaggerated patience. "We haven't been together since last spring. This is James."

"And the other two?" Abby looks over to my brothers, who are lingering like they're not sure whether to come over. "What about the blond. He's cute."

Bex glares at her mother. "I have to call Aunt Nicole and see if you can stay with her. And then call the insurance company and file a claim. What the hell were you thinking, falling asleep like that?"

Abby has the decency to look embarrassed. "Let's not talk about it in front of your friend, Bexy."

"Don't Bexy me. And he's my boyfriend, so he stays."

I bite the inside of my cheek to keep from smiling. Even though the situation is serious, and I want to shake Bex's mother, that word on her lips in relation to me makes me feel a certain kind of way.

"You've always lost your head for jocks," Abby says with a sniff. "Why do you care about this? You're never around anymore."

"That's not true. I come back to the diner all the time."

"What, to work a shift and collect tips?"

My hand tightens on Bex's hip.

"That's not fair," she says softly.

"I'll tell you what's not fair," Abby says. "A man leaving his wife and daughter isn't fair. A daughter leaving her mother isn't fair."

"Mom." Bex is trembling. "I'm going to McKee to help us, you know that."

"Right up until you aren't."

"My old photography was up there. My *camera*." Bex takes a step forward, tears streaming down her cheeks. "And because of you, that's all gone, because you fucking fell asleep in the middle of the day when you're supposed to be managing the goddamn diner!"

Her words are loud; they carry through the air in a way that makes certain everyone within the vicinity hears her. My brothers. The firefighters. The police. Some random onlookers, still lingering despite the fact the show is fucking over. I move around, trying to shield Bex with my body. She doesn't deserve this. I want to gather her up into my arms and hug her so tightly she knows I'm never letting go.

Abby's face crumples. "You know how hard it is, baby."

"I don't care." She fists her hands in her hair, taking in a ragged breath. "You're supposed to be my mother. You take care of me, not the other way around." She sobs. "I made you a promise and you promised me back."

Abby doesn't say anything. The cigarette slips from her fingers, and I step forward before she can, grinding it underneath my heel.

"Mom," Bex whispers. "Tell me you remember. You made me promise."

But Abby doesn't say a word.

Bex

You're sure about this?" Laura asks.

She's on my bed, watching as I pack the suitcase. Jeans, a pretty dress, James's jersey. Fancy lingerie I splurged on during a trip to the mall with Laura earlier today. That's where I got the little suitcase, too. I've never owned one because I never had anywhere to go. Even though it's only Pennsylvania, I can't help but be excited.

Anything to take my mind off the shitstorm at the diner. That's how James pitched it to me when he invited me to tag along with him for the away game at Penn State. I've been busy arguing with the insurance company, trying to line up rehab work for the apartment, and keeping the diner running amid a period where my mother has disappeared into her grief, not to mention keeping up with my job and schoolwork. Aunt Nicole calls every day to update me. Mom hasn't been this bad since the last time my father sniffed around.

I wish I could bring myself to feel worse about it, but I don't. Her accusations of abandonment stung, but even worse was realizing that the fire ruined my camera and tons of photography. I keep some of it in my dorm room, and a couple of pieces were framed in the diner, but all the work from middle and high school had been in my room. The fire and resulting smoke damaged everything. The fancy camera that Aunt Nicole bought me as a sixteenth birthday present was ruined beyond use.

I'd never abandon my mother or the diner, but a small, selfish part of me wishes that the fire had ruined the diner too.

I add pajamas to the top of the suitcase and zip it shut. "It's just one weekend."

"Alone with him in a hotel room." Laura frowns. "It's not something you do when it's casual. Or when you're pretending."

"I don't think we're pretending anymore," I admit. The confession makes Laura's jaw drop. I try to laugh, to make light of the confession, but it's scary to say aloud. If I'm being totally serious, James Callahan has worked his way into my life and is refusing to let go.

When he introduced himself as my boyfriend, it felt right. True, not part of the lie. Maybe somewhere between study sessions and texting, the fake dates and kisses, something changed. When I look at him, I instantly feel a little safer. Not just around Darryl. All the time, even if we're just at his dining room table, doing schoolwork while Seb cooks dinner and Cooper reads.

He had my back at the diner. Now he wants me to have his at this game.

"You *have* been spending a ton of time with him. Which you totally deserve," Laura says. She pulls me into a hug, planting a kiss on my cheek. "Have fun banging him after the win. You still haven't given me the deets about his dick, you know."

"Laura!" I hit her shoulder, laughing as I pull away.

She arches a perfectly plucked eyebrow. "You can't tell me a guy like him doesn't have a huge package. I've seen how tight his football pants are."

She's not wrong, of course. But I'm not about to give her the satisfaction of confirming it.

"I always wondered what girls talk about alone," I hear James say. "Now I know you're just as dirty as the guys."

I spin around. He's in the doorway of my bedroom, wearing a leather jacket and a McKee football T-shirt. A grin breaks out on my face; before I can register what's happening, I'm in his arms, planting a kiss on his lips. I feel his hand come up to stroke through my hair.

"How did you get in here?" I demand.

"You left the door open." He makes a chiding noise. "You're lucky it was me who walked in, you know. You could have been murdered by the next Ted Bundy."

"You can murder me any time," says Laura with a grin.

I roll my eyes. "You're still cool with me coming?"

"Of course. Real question is if you're cool with my off-key car singing."

"As long as it's the classics."

He grabs my suitcase before I can and wheels it into the main area. "Which are?"

"Britney Spears, mostly. Vintage Beyoncé. Spice Girls," Laura says. I glare at her, but she just holds up her hands. "What! Babe, you know I'm with you on this."

James groans. "I change my mind. I'll meet you there."

I smile at him innocently. "No, you don't."

"Have fun and make good choices!" Laura calls as we head downstairs.

When we get on the road, I settle back in the stupid-comfy passenger seat of James's car and scroll through my Spotify play-lists. I'm still not over the fact he drives a Range Rover. It's only going to take us a couple hours to reach Penn State, but I want to make the most of my time in his fancy car. There are butt warmers and everything, a fact I appreciate in the chilly weather.

"Are you actually going to flip when I put on this playlist?"

James glances over for half a second before settling his gaze back on the road. "Put on whatever you want, baby."

"It won't mess up your pre-game routine or whatever?"

"My routine doesn't start until game day." He drums his fingers on the steering wheel, giving me another look. There's a light pink flush on his cheeks. "And I'm hoping to add new routines, anyway."

My heart does a somersault; I can't help smiling. "Oh yeah?"

"Waking up next to my girl can't hurt."

My girl. The words fill the air, the car. Part of me wants to ask about it, but I don't want to ruin the magic, not now. It's good enough to know I'm his girl.

I pick out the pop playlist I use when I work out, and Rihanna's voice starts to play from the fancy speakers.

And almost immediately, James starts to sing along.

I turn to him with delight. Apparently, he knows every word to "Umbrella," and doesn't seem at all bothered by that. His voice is awful, but he sings with such conviction I can't help but join in, wiggling my body to the beat. When the song ends, we're both breathless with laughter, and his hand is on my thigh, squeezing lightly. Possessively. I look over at him, but he's busy checking the mirrors before merging into the next lane.

I never gave much thought before to whether driving is sexy, but you know what? I'm loving this.

* * *

BEFORE JAMES, I liked football, but honestly, I didn't care enough to learn all the intricacies. I watch football on Thanksgiving at Aunt Nicole's like the rest of the country, and thanks to Darryl, I came into this knowing the basics. But watching James play has gotten me into it on a whole different level. He's faster than you'd expect him to be, and his passes are like bullets arcing through the air. I wince whenever he hits the ground, cheer whenever he escapes a tackle, and screech like a banshee during each touchdown.

Still, McKee barely makes it out with the win.

"My heart's still racing!" Debra Sanders says as we head down the stairs after both teams leave the field. James got me a seat next to Bo's mom, and we hit it off over the course of the game. I know way more about Bo now than he probably wants the girlfriend of his teammate to know, like how his nickname throughout middle and high school was "Stinky."

"Bo made an awesome block right at the end," I say. "He saved the game."

"Don't you know it. My baby's going to fit right in with the big guys in the league."

She gives me a hug before we part ways, patting my cheek fondly. She's about my height, with this awesome pink streak in her braids that I complimented her on the moment I saw her. "It was nice to meet you, Bex. I don't know James too well, but he seems like a good boy. Darryl wasn't good enough for you."

That makes me tear up unexpectedly. "Thank you."

"Now, if only Bo would find himself a nice girl. I told him to bring someone home for the holidays, but something tells me he's been ignoring that."

I laugh as she heads off. "Bye, Mrs. Sanders!"

Instead of hanging around waiting for James postgame, I call a cab to take me back to the cute little inn he booked for us this weekend. He had to get permission from Coach Gomez to stay somewhere other than with the team. He'll be all pumped up from the close win. Hungry. This morning, I asked if he wanted to go out somewhere with the team, but he said he didn't want to have to make nice with the guys when all he'd be thinking about was getting me alone. When I get back to the room, I'll order in from a restaurant we picked out that does delivery.

I move outside to wait, watching as the Penn State fans head back to campus or their cars.

"Going to all his games now like some kind of cleat chaser?"

I stiffen, trying to keep a neutral expression as I look at Darryl. He's still in half his gear, his Under Armor shirt plastered to his skin, hair damp on his forehead.

He's standing too close, but I refuse to give him the satisfaction of backing up. "Is that what you called me when we were dating? A cleat chaser?"

His expression tightens. "You made your point with him, Bexy. Give up the act."

"It's not an act."

He scoffs. "Come on. The guy's a douche."

"Oh yeah? What brought you to that earth-shattering conclusion? Is it the way he's been leading your team to wins all season? His nomination for the Heisman? How he told you off when you hurt me?"

He works his jaw. "I never meant—"

"Stop. Just stop." I lower my voice since we're in public. At least he didn't try to get me alone. "Go back to the locker room, Darryl."

He hustles me against the wall, underneath a memorial plaque. I'm caught by surprise, so I don't fight it, but my heart hammers wildly as I look up at him. He settles a hand on the side of my head, flat on the wall, like he's just trying to chat me up. Casual. No one glances at us as they pass by.

"Stop."

"You might think he cares about you, but he's just as selfish as you think I am," he says. "Did he tell you the real reason he left LSU?"

I stay silent. He takes my lack of an answer as confirmation, chuckling softly. "I didn't think so."

"Shut the hell up, Darryl."

"Ask him about Sara Wittman, babe. His ex-girlfriend."

"Don't call me that." I try to wriggle away, but he uses his height and weight to his advantage to pin me in place. "And get the fuck off me, or I'll call him."

"You won't." Darryl's eyes pierce mine. "If he fights me, he'll get kicked off the team. That already happened once."

His words catch me off guard, and I can't help replying. "What do you mean?"

"Of course, his daddy cleaned up the problem. Tried to make it disappear. But that doesn't change the fact that Sara nearly killed herself."

I dig my teeth into my lower lip, wiping my sweaty palms on my jacket. "You're lying."

"And when he realizes you're just another slut, he'll dump your ass like he did her. You think he's going to save you? Babe, the second you get in the way, you're gone. And I'll be waiting."

"Fuck off," I say, unable to keep the tremble out of my voice. I shove at him.

He goes this time, laughing. It takes a minute for my mind to stop spinning. By the time I think to check my phone, I see that my cab has come and left, so I need to call for another.

But when the panic quiets, I'm left with one thought: Who is Sara Wittman, and what happened when she dated James?

CHAPTER 26

Bex

When I get back to the inn, there's a bottle of champagne on ice sitting on the table, plus two crystal flutes and a box of chocolates. There's also a present wrapped in silver paper sitting in the middle of the fluffy white bedspread.

My heart skips a beat. He's so sweet.

But I can't get the conversation with Darryl out of my mind.

I shrug out of my jacket and peel off my jeans, sitting in his jersey on the edge of the bed. I pull out my phone to see that he texted that he's on the way. I reply, then search the web for Sara Wittman.

Maybe Darryl is lying to me. He's obviously jealous; he can't let me go. He'd say anything to make James seem shitty in my eyes.

There isn't much I can find. A private Instagram. A page from LSU featuring a picture of Athletic Director Peter Wittman and his family—a wife and a daughter, Sara.

So, she's a real person. That I didn't doubt. The question is, if James dated her, what happened? Did she try to hurt herself? Even if that's true, how was James involved?

I didn't search his name again after the first time, before our dinner at Vesuvio's. He didn't seem to like it, and I didn't want to make him uncomfortable. That was back before I thought I had any real claim to him, anyway.

Wouldn't he tell me if something that horrible had happened?

I thought he left LSU because he couldn't win a championship with that program. He'd made it sound cut-and-dried. But Darryl talked about it like he left in disgrace. Threatened with getting kicked off the team? My heart twinges with sympathy. That would be devastating for him.

I'm typing his name into my phone when the door opens.

I exit out of the window and set my phone aside. He comes into the room with all the energy you'd expect after that kind of close win; he sweeps me up into a hug and kiss immediately.

"I missed you," he murmurs. "Couldn't think of anything the second the game ended except coming back here to you."

I force myself to smile. Even though I'm dying for some real answers, I can't do that to him now. Not after a win to keep their perfect season intact. Not while he's looking at me like I'm the only person in the world and holding me like he wishes we could meld into one.

"It was an amazing game," I say, instead of any of the questions echoing in my mind. "I was worried you wouldn't pull it out."

"Sanders saved it for us." He rubs his hand down my back. "Did you talk to his mom?"

"She's really sweet."

"Definitely."

"Did you order dinner yet?"

Shit. I'd forgotten about that. "Nope. I just got back a couple minutes ago."

"No problem." He walks over to the champagne and pops the cork, then pours us each a glass. "Want to do that, or should I? I'm starving."

"Um, no, I've got it." I force another smile as I accept the glass of champagne. "What's the occasion?"

He joins me on the bed. "First time we've gone away together. I thought we'd like to make a nice memory, instead of it being, you know, that time we went to the Holiday Inn and my teammates tried to drag us to a party."

I smile for real this time. "You're sweet. Do you still want that pork dish?"

"Sounds great."

I call the restaurant and order, which is way harder than it needs to be because he keeps touching me, kissing my neck and dragging up the hem of the jersey to palm at my ass. I glare at him over my shoulder, but he just ducks in for a kiss.

When I hang up, he brushes my hair back. "Are you wondering about the present?"

"It's big."

"Not the only big thing you'll be getting tonight."

"James!" I stage-whisper, widening my eyes like I'm scandalized.

He just grins as he grabs the present and passes it over to me. "Want to open it now?"

"I'm surprised you don't want to give me the other big thing first," I say dryly.

"This is worth the wait."

I give him a look as I tear at the wrapping paper. There are actually two things wrapped together. I see the photo album first, and then the box registers.

A camera.

"James," I whisper.

He leans in a bit, an anxious look on his face. "Is it okay? I did some research into it, but if it's not the right kind, I'll return it and get you exactly what you need."

I take it out of the box slowly, marveling at the clean lines and the pristine lens. A Nikon Z9 with all the bells and whistles. Cameras like these cost several thousand dollars, easy, and now I'm holding one in my hands. I set it aside gently, then launch myself into his arms.

He catches me with ease. "Hey, princess. Did I do good?"

"It's perfect." I kiss him deeply, squeezing my arms around his neck. His hands settle underneath my thighs, holding me close. "You didn't have to, though, it's not cheap and I can always—"

"No." He cuts me off firmly. "This is a gift. Make new art with it, honey, okay?"

Instead of responding with thank you like a normal person, I let out a sniffle. I can't even find a way to respond because my throat feels like it's blocked up. I bury my face in the crook of his shoulder instead, breathing in his cologne and relishing in the sturdy way he's holding me. It doesn't replace what the fire destroyed, but it gives me the ability to get started again.

"Thank you," I finally whisper. I kiss him again, moving my hands to his face, framing his jaw. He looks right at me with those eyes I've come to love before kissing me back, settling me down on the bed.

I spread my legs so he can dip his body between them, his hands exploring underneath the jersey. He drags his lips down from my face to my neck and lower, then takes the jersey off entirely, leaving me with messy hair. He doesn't seem to mind, though; he's still looking at me in a way that triggers heat in my belly and lower. It's like I'm a prize he just won. Like I'm some-thing precious.

"God, Bex," he says. "You're so fucking beautiful."

He splays his hand on my soft belly, pulling me into another kiss. I stroke my hand through his hair as I kiss him back. "You are too," I say with total honesty.

And because he's confident in his masculinity, he doesn't make a face. He just breaks away to look at me, a tender expression on his face.

"This lingerie is so pretty," he says as he traces over the lace on one of the blush pink bra cups. My breath hitches at the promise of contact where I want it. "Did you get this just for me?"

I nod, digging my teeth into my lower lip. He pulls off his sweater and jeans and makes short work of my bra, nuzzling at my breasts, rolling one nipple between his thumb and forefinger, and sucking on the other until I'm arching my back. I can feel myself getting wet, my clit tingling and begging for attention. I try to wriggle my hand between us, but he catches it.

"Keep your hands over your head, pretty girl," he says.

I whimper, toes curling, as I fist my hands in the sheets. He rewards me by sliding my panties down my legs. Still, he doesn't pay me any attention there yet, continuing to just focus on my tits until I'm shamelessly begging him for more contact. When he finally drags his hand down, I spread my legs wider, eliciting a soft laugh from him. He finds my clit, stroking around it in a tantalizing circle, before dragging his fingers down and pressing two into me at once. I'm so wet that his fingers go in easily. He groans as I clench my pussy. He scissors his fingers as he continues to play with my clit, and with every movement, every breath, I come closer to reaching my peak. He lowers his head to my tits again, mouthing at them, and the added contact makes me cry out. "James—I'm gonna—"

"Come, princess," he tells me roughly as he presses a third finger into me. "Come on my fingers and I'll give you my dick."

I sob as I do, pressing myself against him as tightly as I can, even though the sensitivity that comes with climaxing makes me want to curl up and catch my breath. He continues to finger me for a moment before withdrawing his fingers; I shudder, hating the feeling of emptiness.

He reaches for his wallet, taking out a condom and rolling it on quickly. "Tell me what you want, Bex."

I blink wetly at him, trying to form words and utterly failing. He's gorgeous, handsome as sin as he wraps his fist around his cock and pumps. Fuck, his muscles are incredible. I want to lick the grooves between each one of his perfect abs. I struggle to sit up so I can kiss him. He obliges me, gasping as I bite his lip. When I pull away, he has a dark look in his eyes, like he's struggling not to throw me down and fuck into me.

Fuck, I want it. I want him to fill me up so completely I can't help but come again, this time all over his cock.

"Bex," he says, his voice still so low and rough it makes me shiver.

"I want you," I say. "I want . . ."

"Keep going."

"I want you to fuck me," I say in a rush.

"Good girl," he praises. He drags his thumb over my lips, dipping into my mouth in a tender gesture before pulling back. Before I can ask again, he flips me over, so I'm on my belly, and he spreads my legs like this, digging his hands into my ass as he pulls me up onto my knees and elbows. He presses the head of his cock against me, rubbing until I moan and buck my hips. He presses into me all at once, filling me so completely I can't feel anything but him.

This position has my pussy clenching around him, my breasts swaying as he thrusts experimentally. He presses his mouth to the back of my neck, breathing against my hair as he fucks into me. He tangles one of his hands in mine, pressing it flat against the bed.

"I'm close already," he whispers against my skin. "I can't help myself when it comes to you."

"Come," I whisper back. "Fill me up."

He snaps his hips forward, coming inside me with a moan. I squeeze around him, helping him through it, loving the way his breath hitches and he tightens his grip on my hand. He rolls us onto our sides and rubs my clit until I come again with a weak cry.

We both catch our breath, panting, for a long moment. There's a strange feeling inside my chest, a balloon of pressure that I can't make go away. Maybe it's because of how he looks at me as he comes back from discarding the condom with a washcloth in hand to clean me up. Or maybe it's how he kisses me, his hand cradling my jaw. Or how he pulls his sweater over my head the moment I begin to shiver. The food is here, and I watch as he sets up everything, pouring us each more champagne.

I'm feeling something I don't want to name, even in my mind, because it scares me too badly. Especially after what Darryl told me.

James Callahan has infiltrated my heart.

CHAPTER 27

James

When I wake up, Bex is staring down at me.

She's holding her new camera, and she has a cute look of concentration on her face, teeth digging into her lower lip. She's still wearing my sweater and her hair is messy, and my heart clenches at the sight.

Last night, something shifted. It's been shifting ever since the diner, drawing me closer to her with inexorable sureness. I looked down at her, saw her flushed cheeks and the desire in her gorgeous eyes, and I almost said something I promised my father I wouldn't tell a girl again for a long time.

And now I have the urge to say it again, so instead I grin, winding my hand around her calf. "Hope you got my good side."

She tucks her hair behind her ear. "The natural light is so good right now."

I kiss her knee. "And?"

"And you're a handsome subject," she says. "But James, this camera!"

I sit up on one elbow. "It's good?"

"It's *amazing.*" She looks down at it with a cute little smile. "Thank you. I still can't believe you did this for me."

"Bex?"

"Yeah?"

"I'm no photography judge, but I know you're talented. You should be pursuing this, not resigning yourself to the diner."

I know the moment the words leave my mouth that I pushed when I shouldn't have. She sets down the camera, a faraway look in her eyes. I brace myself for her to rebuke me—because even though my girl is starting to accept my help, the diner is a sore subject for her—but instead, she asks something that floors me.

"Who's Sara Wittman?"

I sit up, heart jackhammering in my chest. "What did you say?"

"Sara Wittman," she says. "Was she your girlfriend?"

"Yeah," I say. "Babe, how did you . . ."

She presses her lips together. "Tell me what happened with her. Tell me the real reason why you came to McKee."

I know that she's asking me something reasonable—she's my girlfriend, she deserves to know about my past—but the part of me that still wants to protect Sara rebels against it. I haven't spoken to her since that day in the hospital, but she still echoes in my mind from time to time. I loved her. I thought I was going to marry her one day.

"James," Bex says, a note of urgency in her voice.

I scrub my hand through my hair. "We met last year," I say. "She was a freshman, and her father was involved with the team, so I met her at a function at the beginning of the season. I asked her out, and I'd dated other girls before, but this was different."

I don't like the way Bex curls in on herself, but she keeps looking at me, so I force myself to keep going.

"Sara is an intense person," I say. "Pretty soon we were spending all our time together. She didn't like to be alone, and I sort of became her person, you know? She came to all my practices. We practically lived together; I had an apartment off-campus that she stayed in. And it worked, for a while. Maybe it was stupid, but I assumed we were going to get married, so why wouldn't I want to spend all my time with her?"

Bex plays with my fingers. "And then?"

I swallow. "And then she didn't want me hanging out with the guys from the team. Whenever I went to an away game she couldn't go to, she called me until I picked up. I kept blowing off assignments to be with her, and eventually practices. Whenever I tried to give us some distance, she clung tighter. She said she had to come first."

Bex's eyes widen slightly, but she doesn't say anything.

"Coach gave me some leeway at first, because of the goodwill I'd built up over my first two years there. But I was failing two of my classes after mid-semester, including the writing one, and according to school policy, that meant I had to be benched."

"Were you?"

I shut my eyes briefly. "No. We worked out a deal that I would make up the work I missed and come in for extra practices to prep for the postseason. And to make that work, I told Sara that we needed to cool things down for a while. Just until the end of the season." I look at Bex, tracing my thumb over her knuckles. "I didn't break up with her, but she took it that way. And I hadn't realized how fragile she was. She kept saying she was fine with it, but she spiraled."

"Spiraled how?"

"She stopped going to class. She blew off her job working at the student center. She'd always been a bit of a party girl, but she started drinking during the day and taking pills."

Bex's eyes widen further. "What?"

"I tried to ignore her calls because I wanted to set boundaries.

I had no idea she was hurting so badly. Not until she called me the night before the last game of the season and told me she was going to—"

I break off, my voice cracking. I'd never been as terrified as the moment I heard her voice. The panic in it still turned my stomach over.

"No," Bex says softly.

"She cut herself." I swallow hard. "By the time I got there, she'd already done it. She was passed out, and I couldn't wake her up. I tried the whole time I was waiting for the ambulance."

My eyes are burning. I blink, trying to prevent the tears from coming. Bex crowds closer, winding her arms around me. I hook my chin over her shoulder. It's easier to talk like this.

"I missed the game. I didn't want to be away from her, not for a second and not for an entire football game. But the team lost, of course, the backup quarterback hadn't played at all." I squeeze Bex, shuddering in a breath. "And I didn't want the news about Sara to become public because of me. So, when the media asked why I missed the game, I made it seem like I blew it off. Like I was irresponsible, and it had nothing to do with her."

Bex pulls back to look at me. "Oh, James."

"She's okay now. Her parents put her in a program so she could get the help she needed." My voice cracks again. "Her father was grateful that I protected her when I could have used her as an excuse to make myself look good, so when all was said and done, he helped me wipe the slate clean and transfer to McKee, for a shot at a championship and maintaining my position in the draft. I fucking hurt his daughter, and he still . . ."

Bex's eyes are shining. She blinks, and a tear slips down her cheek. She kisses my cheek gently. "It wasn't your fault."

I shake my head. "You don't have to pretend."

"I'm not." She cups my cheek, her eyes searching mine. "When I was eleven, my father left my mother. One day he just packed up and left. It turned out he had another family, and everything he built with my mother, the diner, their marriage—he threw it away in an instant."

I stare at her. "What a fucking dick."

She laughs shortly. "It destroyed my mother. She was pregnant, and the news shocked her so much that she miscarried. She turned into someone I didn't even recognize, and even now, years later, she's not the same." Color floods her face. "She turned into someone who takes a valium with wine at noon and accidentally sets apartments on fire."

"Bex—"

She shakes her head. "Even though I hate my father, I don't blame him for how my mother still acts a decade later. What happened with Sara wasn't your fault. You couldn't have known that's how she would react. She was sick, and she needed help."

"She could have died."

"And she didn't. You helped her. You did a lot more than most people would." She strokes through my hair, then presses our foreheads together.

We stay like that for a while, breathing in tandem.

After all was said and done, my father and I agreed: no girlfriends until I got into the league. No distractions.

But being able to hold Bex, just like this? I'm willing to take the risk.

CHAPTER 28

James

I don't want to impose on your family though

Wouldn't be imposing. I want you there

Is this bc I can't make the Heisman?

Nope. Ideally I'd want you at both, but
if I had to pick, I'd choose Christmas

Us Callahans have some kickass traditions ;)

Anything would be better than
being alone w/ my mom

I set down my phone, even though Bex just sent another text, and try to focus on my homework. Getting her to agree to come home with me for Christmas will take a lot of coaxing. I knew this going into it, but if I'm anything, it's persistent. Bex had to spend Thanksgiving with just her mother; her aunt and uncle went to Florida to visit other relatives. They haven't been talking much since the fire, according to Bex, so the whole thing was awkward.

The post-season hasn't started yet, but with the season winding down, I've been working around the clock to prepare. Press for the Heisman ceremony is happening too, and I haven't even *seen* Bex in a couple days, which feels criminal.

Almost the second I get back into the groove with the problem I'm solving, however, Cooper bursts into my room. I scrub my hand through my hair.

"Hey," he says as he shuts the door behind him.

I don't even get into the whole not-knocking thing. "What's up?"

Both of us have been so busy with our respective seasons that I've barely seen him either. McKee's men's hockey team isn't doing nearly as well as its football team is this season, but Coop's still been playing his heart out. He has a deep purple bruise on his cheek, thanks to a puck to the face last game.

He lets out a sigh as he sits on the edge of the bed. "You and Bex are getting pretty serious."

I keep my grin in check by burying my nose in my textbook. "Yep."

"Even though you said you weren't going to date anyone the rest of your college career."

"She's different, man."

Coop flops back against the bed. "Seb told me you want her to come over at Christmas."

"Yep."

"Christmas."

"Isn't that what I just said?"

Lately, it's all I've been thinking about. Bex would fit right in with our traditions. I want to show her my parents' house in Port Washington. My parents always go all-out for decorations, with a towering tree in the entryway that my mother has professionally decorated, plus the little one in the den with all our homemade ornaments. I want to take her downtown for the town tree lighting. Kiss her underneath the ball of mistletoe Mom always puts over the kitchen entryway. Drag her into the cutthroat game of Monopoly my siblings and I play every Christmas Eve.

Maybe it's silly, but I want to fall asleep next to her in my child-hood bedroom. I want to see if she has any cute Christmas ear-rings, and if she doesn't, buy her a pair or ten. I want my family to see how special she is.

Cooper draws me out of my daydream with a frustrated noise. "James. I love you. But this is a bad idea. Dad already doesn't like her."

"I can handle Dad. She's not Sara."

"At least Sara would have followed you anywhere you went in the league."

"What?"

"She's committed to the diner, right? Which means she'll be here. You're probably going to be across the country."

I set down my notebook. I love my brother, but this is irritat-ing. Sometimes his overprotectiveness, a quality I usually admire in him, can be a bit much. When it comes to our baby sister, sure. But I can handle myself, and he doesn't know Bex the way I do. "It's complicated. Her mother is still attached to the diner."

"Her mother the accidental arsonist?"

"Jesus, Coop."

He sits up. "What, am I wrong? You started out pretending to date her, which was doomed from the fucking start because you get like this, man. You romanticize things. You're letting yourself get in too deep with a girl who isn't going to be able to give herself to you the way you're giving yourself to her."

"Because you're some great expert on relationships? Have you ever even tried to be in one?" I pretend to think for a moment. "Right, you haven't."

"I know you. I know how you get when you think you're in love."

"I'm not in love with her," I reply. But my heart jumps into my throat.

I'm not lying, exactly. But I'm not telling the whole truth, and damnit, Cooper can tell.

"I think she's cool," he says. "I'm not saying she isn't."
"But?"
"But she's going to hurt you. It's just a matter of when."
Anger rolls through me. "Noted."

He scoots up the bed until he's sitting next to me. "Just make sure you're thinking this through."

"Did you come in here just to insult my girlfriend?" I say shortly. I'm officially done with this conversation.

He rubs his beard, looking me over. He must sense my resistance because he shakes his head slightly. "No, I wanted to talk about Izzy. Does she still want to go into the city for a shopping spree? Dinner after at Le Bernardin?"

I stifle a sigh. Arguing with him about Bex won't lead anywhere good, so instead I say, "I was hoping she wanted to go to see that Harry Styles concert or something."

He huffs. "Same. But you have to admit, this is the most her Izzy Day she's ever come up with. Fifth Avenue shopping? She'll love it."

When we were younger, our parents turned our birthdays into fun, exclusive excursions, dubbed "James Day" or "Sebastian Day." That's how Cooper got to skate in Madison Square Garden during a Rangers practice for his sixteenth birthday, and how when I turned fourteen, we had the most kickass arcade day ever. When Izzy had her Sweet Sixteen, our parents took her and her friends to St. Barts for a long weekend. This year? All she's wanted lately is to be in the city, so this isn't surprising, but it's going to be brutal to watch her try on dresses for six hours straight.

"Maybe she can help me pick out my suit for the Heisman ceremony. That would be productive, at least."

"It'll be good to spend time with her," Coop says. "Mom was telling me that she broke up with that weird guy."

I do a little fist pump. "Finally."

"I know, right? He sucked."

My excitement fades as it occurs to me that she might be heartbroken. "Did he hurt her? Do we need to go kick his ass? Shit, that was her first real boyfriend."

"I think he was flirting with other girls, like an idiot."

"What a prick."

"I'd offer to go find him and beat him up, but I'm sure she has that handled."

"She's scrappy, I'll give her that. I don't envy you and Seb having to keep an eye on her next year." I laugh. "Wait, so tell me what's up with you. I thought I'd see you more often since we're living together right now, but this is like when you had ice time right after I got back from practice."

"That season sucked," he says with a groan. "And I've been buried in readings. I haven't scored a chick in weeks. It's *terrible*. I've forgotten what pussy feels like."

I laugh so hard I snort.

Bex

Is it cool?" I say into my phone from the entryway of Aunt Nicole's house. The December chill cuts through me, even wearing a thick sweater I stole from James, so I move away from the window. It's flurrying outside. "Are you nervous?"

"Very cool," James replies. Even over the line, I can't help the little smile that crosses my face at the low tenor of his voice. "Lincoln Center is gorgeous. Joe Burrow just congratulated me, and I think I pissed myself a bit."

I smirk, even though he can't see me. "He is very attractive."

"Hey," he says.

"Of course, not as attractive as you," I amend. "Or Aaron Rodgers."

"Babe, no," he says, a horrified note in his voice.

"I don't know, I feel like the whole Nicolas Cage dirty mountain man thing works for me. Don't act like you don't have celebrity crushes too. I saw that photo of Jennifer Lopez on your phone."

"I'm hanging up."

I giggle. "Sorry. But really, are you nervous?"

"Nope. I don't get nervous about performing."

"I feel like there's a dirty joke in there," I say. "Seriously? I'd be melting into the floor."

"I mean, I hope I win," he says. "But even if I don't, it's an honor just to be recognized."

"Such a diplomat already."

"Don't you know it." He says something to someone off the line, then comes back to say goodbye.

"Good luck," I tell him.

His voice is soft as he replies, "Thanks, princess."

I'm grinning like an idiot at my phone when Aunt Nicole pokes her head in to look for me. "It looks like the ceremony is going to start soon. Do you want me to heat up some queso?"

"That would be awesome."

She squeezes my arm, leaning in a bit. "For what it's worth, I think he's loads cuter than Darryl."

I wander back into the living room and settle on the couch next to my mother. She glances over at me as she takes a sip of her wine. "Which one is yours again?"

I force a smile. When James invited me to come with him and his family to the ceremony, I wanted to, of course, but ditching my mother on the anniversary of my father's leaving was unthinkable. "You know who he is. He came to the diner after you set it on fire."

I shouldn't feel a grim sense of satisfaction at the way her face twists, but I can't help myself. I'm still pissed about the fire, even though James bought me a new camera.

Aunt Nicole sets a plate of chips and dip on the table, patting Uncle Brian's thigh as she sits down next to him on the other couch. "Isn't it exciting that Bex's guy might win, Bri?"

Uncle Brian grunts out an affirmative. My uncle isn't much of a talker, but now that I know more about football than before, we've been able to relate to each other. "Seen some of McKee's games this season. He's talented, I'll give him that."

I smile as I reach for a chip. "He deserves this. He's so talented. Watching him live has been incredible, Uncle Brian, really."

"Of course, I prefer the NFL," he says. "College play can be very different than professional. But I think he has what it takes. Where are they saying he'll end up, most likely? Philadelphia or San Francisco?"

"Even Philadelphia is pretty far," Mom says. "Have you thought about that at all?"

"No," I say, which is the truth. I've been trying to keep next April out of my mind as much as possible. If I think about the fact that this time next year, he'll be living in a different city, playing on the professional level every Sunday, my stomach ties itself into knots and I can barely swallow. It's not that I'm not excited or happy or proud. I'm all those things at once.

It's just that it's a future I know I don't fit into.

Aunt Nicole turns up the television to fill in the silence. I angle myself away from my mother and focus on the show.

James keeps telling me the other three finalists are equally, if not more, talented, and that the nomination is honor enough, but I know he wants it. The Heisman is given annually to the most outstanding college football player. It's an affirmation to the world that even what happened with Sara—even if the story that is out there isn't the real story—isn't slowing him down as a player. That he's ready for this career. I can't stop smiling every time the camera cuts to him. He looks so self-assured and confident.

I wish I was there with him now. I wish I was in the audience, waiting to cheer his name.

My phone buzzes, and I check it automatically. Ugh. Another text from Darryl. Something tells me he's watching the same thing as me. At least when he's reaching out digitally, I can just ignore it. When he came to the Purple Kettle during a slow moment the other day, I only managed to escape his conversation because my coworker took pity on me.

"He looks a bit flashy," Mom says as she leans back, balancing her wineglass on her knee. "What's that, a designer suit?"

"I think he looks nice," Aunt Nicole says diplomatically.

Mom takes a deep sip of wine as she watches the camera pan over James and the other finalists. "Not exactly our kind, Nicole."

James is wearing a deep blue suit with a white shirt and a slim purple tie. It is designer—I know because Izzy told me, matter of fact, over FaceTime—but he wears it so naturally it doesn't feel out of place. I suppose to him it is natural; he always grew up with plenty of money. The cost of a suit like that would keep my mom and I afloat for months.

Mom glances at me. "Of course, he can buy whatever he wants. Got you that fancy new camera."

I don't point out it was to replace the one she ruined because it would just make this evening more tense. This night is terrible every single year, but ever since the last time my dad tried to sniff around, back in my freshman year of college, it's been extra shitty. I can't help if Mom's hoping against hope that something will change, or just wallowing in the fact it never will. Regardless, it marks the date we became a family of two, and at the end of the day, this is where I need to be.

By the time they introduce James, I'm shaking a little. They show a highlight reel of his best plays so far—some from LSU, but a fair amount from McKee, too. They compare him to his father and other quarterbacks who have won the award. They do the same for the other finalists too, the quarterback from Alabama, a defensive end from Michigan, and a wide receiver from Auburn.

And then they finally announce the winner.

It's James.

I distantly hear Aunt Nicole's whoop and Uncle Brian's clapping. I definitely hear Mom's snort as she gets up. My eyes blur with tears as I clap my hand over my mouth to cover my gasp. He walks onstage, the biggest smile I've ever seen from him on his face, and accepts the trophy with a handshake. He looks perfect. Handsome and confident and every bit the prodigal son the football world is expecting. When the clapping quiets, he just stares down at the trophy for a long moment before clearing his throat.

"I don't know where to begin," he admits, and the crowd indulges him with kind laughter.

From the kitchen, I hear a smash. Broken glass.

I shoot to my feet before Aunt Nicole can. Mom is in the kitchen, leaning over the sink. Shards of glass litter it, still dripping with red wine, but I zero in instantly on the blood running down her palm.

"Mom?" I can't keep the crack of fear out of my voice.

She looks at me with tears running down her cheeks. Her mascara, which was messy to begin with, is smudged. She winces as she pulls a piece of glass out of her palm.

"Jesus." I hurry over and grab a dishcloth, wrapping her hand in it and pressing down. She surprises me by pulling me into a fierce hug.

She hasn't hugged me like this, cheek to cheek, in a while.

"Bex," she whispers. "Sweetheart."

"Mom," I murmur back, rubbing my cheek against hers. "What did you do?"

"I slipped."

I'm sure that's a lie, but I don't call her out on it. I pull back instead and start to pick the pieces of glass out of the sink. She crowds close. "Sweetie. Look at me."

I pick out a couple more pieces, setting them on a paper towel.

"He's going to leave you."

I blink hard, keeping my attention on the sink. "That so? What, you have a crystal ball?"

"No, but he's a man, and men leave."

"Uncle Brian is right outside with his wife. Your sister."

"Men like the ones we want," she says, her voice low and insistent. "Look at him, baby girl. Do you really think you'll be able to compete with all the women he'll meet the second he steps out in his new uniform? There's a reason men like him marry models. Who do you think you are, Gisele fucking Bündchen?" She laughs, a bitter sound that echoes in the quiet kitchen. "You might have his attention now, but you're just another slut to him. He'll cheat just like the rest of them. Like Darryl. Like your father."

I grit my teeth. "You don't know him."

She glances back in the direction of the living room. The television is still going, but it sounds like my aunt and uncle are watching a game show now.

"I know enough," she says. "A man with a smile like that? He's a shark, and you're a convenient bit of prey. I'm just trying to protect you for when he chews you up and spits you back out, honey."

I've never hated my mother. I've resented her inability to move on, and whatever sickness keeps her in a cycle of unhealthy coping mechanisms. I've felt sorry for her. I've wanted to shake her, scream in her face, do whatever it took to bring back the version of her I remember from when I was a little girl. The Abby Wood she used to be, back when she experimented with pie flavors for the diner and danced in the living room for no reason at all and walked me back and forth from school every single day. The Abby Wood who encouraged me to take pictures of everything I saw with the cheap disposables she bought me from the drug store.

But in this moment, I think those three words for the first time.

I hate you.

I hate her and who she's become. I hate having to clean up her messes. I hate the promise she roped me into at fifteen that I would always protect the business she built with Dad. I hate watching her wither into a shell of a person who can say such shitty things to her daughter's face and call it caring.

But most of all, I hate that she's right.

It doesn't matter what city James ends up in. He could be in San Francisco or Philadelphia or anywhere else, and the outcome will be the same. He'll meet a girl, he'll fall in love with her, and he'll forget that he ever had anything to do with me. And me? I'll be here, living the same life I always have.

Right now, he's exactly where he's meant to be. And the problem is, I am too.

CHAPTER 30

James

I jump in place, my cleats hitting the frozen ground with a little more force each time. My breath comes out like the steam escaping from the top of my coffee mug. We had snow last night, and because football doesn't stop for anything short of an electrical storm, we're out like usual, warming up for practice. The only thing that dragged me out of bed this morning was the thought of seeing Bex, who promised she'd stop by the practice to work on her live action photography.

"Bit different from the Bayou!" Demarius calls to me as he runs by, a shit-eating grin on his face. "You're looking like a popsicle, man!"

Fletch jogs over and hits him in the arm. "He's not actually from Louisiana, dumbass."

"No, he's right," I say glumly. "I forgot how much it sucks to play in the snow."

"Why the hell aren't you running laps?" Coach Gomez calls as he walks over to the field. "Hustle, gentlemen! You're not going to warm up just standing there with your thumbs up your asses!"

I peel off my coat, setting it down on a bench. I don't wear gloves when I throw, I've always preferred the grip I get with my fingertips, but today has me wishing I did, just for the excuse to wear an extra layer. At least I have on leggings underneath my shorts, and a long-sleeved compression shirt on underneath my T-shirt. What the fuck kind of temperature is this? Long Island gets cold, and sure, it snows, but with water on all sides, it's usually not as frigid as other parts of the Northeast.

I take off jogging, setting a pace I can maintain for a long time if necessary, and one by one, the team peels off to follow me. Demarius sprints ahead, doing a backflip into the end zone and landing his way into a snow-angel. I roll my eyes as I hold out a hand to help him up. He has a gleam in his eyes that I don't like, and I'm proven right when I duck and avoid a snowball to the face. It hits Bo instead, who goes fucking nuts, chasing Demarius around the end zone. Demarius is tall and lanky and fast as hell, but Bo catches up to him and throws him down at the exact moment Coach's whistle splinters the air.

"I told you to run, not have a fucking snowball fight! Callahan, do you call that a run?"

"No, sir."

"Fucking run. Get your blood pumping. Ten laps. Fifteen for the dumbasses over there," he adds, pointing to Demarius and Bo. If looks could kill, Demarius would already be six feet under the frozen ground. The guys around me burst out laughing, even Darryl. I bite my lip, giving Bo a "what can you do" shrug before taking off running again.

I lead everyone in a real run this time, feeling the wind sting my cheeks and make my nose run. By the time we're done, I feel a lot more comfortable, although I'm halfway convinced the tips of my ears are going to fall off. I spot Bex on the sidelines and peel off to say hi before Coach notices.

"Hey," she says as I walk over. "It's so cold!"

I bend down and kiss her. She has on a thick knit cap that covers her ears—lucky—and a puffy white coat that makes her look like a marshmallow. A very cute marshmallow, mind you. I tuck her scarf into her jacket and tut when I see her bare hands.

"Can't operate this baby as well with gloves," she says with a sigh, holding up her camera. "Why aren't you wearing a hat, at least?"

"It'll fall off the moment I run a play. Did you see Bo and Demarius?"

"James!" Coach calls. "I told your girlfriend she could take pictures of the practice, and practice doesn't start until you have a football in your hands. Get over here."

I kiss her cheek quickly. "See you. Get my good side."

"That's his butt," Fletch says with a wink. "Make sure you get plenty of butt shots."

"He does have a nice butt," she says, which of course makes half the squad hoot and holler.

"You're gonna be in trouble later!" I call as I grab a football from one of the assistants and jog back onto the slushy field.

"What are you going to do, throw a snowball at me?" she calls back.

Not a bad idea. "With my aim, princess? Don't give me ideas you're not prepared to handle."

It's not the best practice I've ever had, but fortunately, it's not the worst either. I like knowing Bex is close, looking so cute and squishy in her coat, her eyes narrowed in concentration as she walks the sideline, taking shots with her camera. It's distracting, don't get me wrong—I want nothing more than to challenge her to the snowball fight for real, and when she's finally admitted defeat, kiss her senseless, maybe do something cheesy like call her my own snow angel—but I show off, too, even though we're just running drills. I warned her before she came that practices are usually kind of boring, but she insisted she wouldn't mind.

I glance over in between reps to find her chatting with someone on the staff. I've been keeping an eye on Darryl, making sure he doesn't try to talk to her, and fortunately, he's stayed away, although I've caught him looking. She holds up her camera, eyes lit up with that passion I love seeing on her. She doesn't let herself have that enough. I've seen her at the diner, and sure, she likes it. She likes talking to the regulars and being in charge. Even now, with the fire damage limiting operations and the insurance company trying to undercut her, she isn't complaining. But why would she want a future like that if she knows that when she has a camera in her hands, she comes alive in a whole different way?

I know better than to bring it up. The last time I tried, she chewed me out. The insurance company, the business—she doesn't want my help with it, and I have to respect that.

Doesn't mean I have to be happy about it.

When practice finally wraps up, I head over to her. She smiles, accepting my kiss. An older woman with light brown skin and dark curls spilling out from underneath her cap stands next to her.

"This is Angelica, do you know her? She handles team operations."

I shake her hand. Of course, she's wearing a nice pair of leather gloves. "I think we met once, right when I first came here," I say. "Thank you for all you do for the team."

She smiles at me. "I was just telling your girlfriend that she ought to get in touch with someone from the athletics publicity department. They like submissions from student photographers, it ties together the arts and athletics nicely for the university."

My eyes widen as I look at Bex. "That sounds incredible."

Her cheeks are already pink from the cold, so they're covering up the blush I know must be there. She fiddles with her camera lens. "Maybe. You know I'm already so busy."

"But you're so talented."

"Maybe," she repeats.

"Maybe that's what you should do after graduation," I say, glancing over at Angelica. "You could be a sports photographer."

She laughs. "James, come on."

"I'm serious."

"And I am too." She smiles at Angelica. "Thanks for the information. It was nice meeting you."

There's something hard in her tone, a clear dismissal. She busies herself with putting away her camera in its case. I give Angelica an apologetic look.

She presses a card into my hand. "Have her call my office," she says quietly before she goes. "I'll put her in touch with Doug."

"Bex," I say, looking down at the card.

"I'm not taking it."

"Come on. I'm sure the photographs you took of practice are amazing. You could do this for a career."

"I already have a career."

"Oh yeah?" I say. "Making pie is a career? Arguing with suppliers because they brought you the wrong kind of bacon is a career?"

"Yes." She slings her camera over her shoulder with way more force than necessary. "Don't be a snob."

"A career you're excited about, I mean."

She looks up at me with fire in her eyes. "We've been over this."

"It's not you, Bex," I say, setting my jaw in frustration. "This? This is you. And forget the sports part, fine, don't do sports. But you deserve to have a camera in your hands. You could have a photography studio. Or do weddings. Or—"

She snatches the card out of my hand and stuffs it into my pocket, effectively shutting me up. "It's a hobby. I love it, but it's just a hobby."

"Would you say the same thing to me about football? 'Hey, babe, I know you're super talented at it, but it's a hobby, you ought to go get that real job now.'"

"It's not the same and you know it."

"Why?"

"Because it is!" she cries. "I don't have a choice."

"You could sell it. Just sell it and take the money and open a business you actually want to run. You'll have the business degree."

"Don't tell me what to do."

"I'm not telling—I just want you to be happy."

She turns on her heel and walks away.

"Beckett, come on."

She doesn't stop.

I catch up to her, ignoring the looks I'm getting from the couple of guys from the team who are still out on the field. I really ought to go inside, warm up and debrief about the practice with Coach, but like hell am I letting Bex walk away mad.

"You deserve everything you want," I say. "Okay? That's all I meant. If the diner is really what you want . . ."

"It is."

"Okay." I reach out and take her hand. Her fingers are like little icicles. "I'm sorry. But call her, please. Even if it's just a hobby, if it interests you, you should do it. I watched you way more than I should have during practice, and I could tell how much fun you were having. Even in the snow."

She looks up at me. I don't like the guarded edge to her expression, like she's afraid of revealing too much. We've gotten seriously honest with each other lately, and now I'm terrified that I fucked that up. As much as I want to just handle it all for her, I know I can't. Not if I want her in my life.

I hope that by graduation, she figures out that she shouldn't feel obligated to continue a business she never asked for in the first place. She's loyal to her mother and that's admirable, but if her mother really cared, she'd be helping her set up her own life, not guilting her into wasting it running the business she began with the husband who left her.

"I'll see you later," she says. "Tutoring session?"

"Sure. Definitely."

She walks off to her car. I stand there for a moment, rooted in place, before the reality of the moment hits me.

I don't want her walking away mad, and I don't want her walking away without a kiss.

I run over to her and pull her into my arms. She makes a surprised noise as I kiss her, our cold lips slotting together perfectly. I knocked off her hat in my eagerness; my hand comes up to cup the back of her head and she shivers. To my relief, she kisses back, her hands fisting in my shirt.

"What's this for?" she whispers when I finally break away.

"Wanted to do that all practice."

She snorts. "I know what I look like in this coat. I'm a marshmallow."

"Cutest marshmallow ever." I kiss her again. "Sexiest, too."

The knot in my chest loosens when I feel her smile against my lips. I pull away, moving my hands to her face so she's looking at me. "I'm sorry. I'll back off. But only if you promise two things."

She looks at me warily. "What two things?"

"Call Angelica."

She presses her lips together tightly.

"Just think about it," I urge.

Finally, she nods. "What's the second thing?"

"Say yes to spending Christmas with me and my family."

CHAPTER 31

Bex

Laura thrusts the flyer into my hand with a flourish. "You're welcome."

I barely glance at it before setting it down on my desk. As soon as I finish the last paper I'm writing, I'll be done with the semester. *Finally.* Taking six classes is not for the weak. As finals season has winded down, the tension has leeched from me bit by bit.

It's being replaced by the panic I feel every time I remember I agreed to spend Christmas with James's family, but you know. Variety is the spice of life, and all that. It was easier to agree to it and let him get excited about that, rather than argue more about what he thinks I should do with my future.

Laura drops down on my bed, making the mattress bounce. "Really? I'm about to leave, you know. I'm not going to see you for a month. The least you could do is say goodbye, if you're not going to even look at my super-awesome parting gift."

"And I'm still green with envy," I say, spinning the desk chair around so I can look at her. "Is Barry really coming to Naples?"

"Yep. It took some convincing, but he's in." She grins. "My brother is going to eat him alive. Are you still going to Port Washington?"

I play with a bit of fuzz on my sweater. Port Washington. Even the name sounds fancy. "Yeah. And every time I think about it, I feel like I'm getting an ulcer."

"You have to take some sneaky pics, I'll bet the house is *spectacular*. If his parents don't hire someone to professionally decorate for Christmas, I'll eat my hat."

"I thought you never wear hats because they make your head look big."

"Well, if I had a hat, I would eat it. His mother is so glamorous. You better get ready for glam Christmas."

I raise an eyebrow. "Is this supposed to make me feel better? I'm already freaking out, so thanks."

She bounces on the bed a few times. "Look at the flyer. I'm sending your real Christmas present to James's house, but this is like a mini present."

I sigh as I turn to grab the flyer. The second I start scanning it, heat erupts on my cheeks. "Laura—"

"You don't have to be a visual arts major to enter," she says quickly. Of course, she preempted all my arguments. "It's for anyone who wants to try. And it'd get your work in an actual gallery in the Village!"

I force myself to read the flyer. It's a contest sponsored by McKee's Visual Arts Department, offering prizes in various categories . . . including photography. All the finalists will win a thousand dollars and have their work displayed at the Close Gallery in the West Village, and there's a grand prize for the set of pieces the department deems most exceptional. The amount nearly makes my jaw drop. Five *thousand* dollars. That could be a huge help with the apartment rehab.

"Wow," I whisper.

"You could use the pieces from the diner," she says. "Or those new ones you showed me from the football practice, those were amazing. I still don't know how you made a bunch of cold dudes running around in the snow look so good. Tell me you'll at least try?"

I fold the flyer carefully and stick it into my planner. "Yeah. But don't expect anything. It's probably one of those things where they really prefer someone from the department to win it."

"You've taken some classes. That one professor tried to convince you to double major!"

"It's not the same."

"Don't count yourself out."

"I won't. I'm just—being realistic."

I haven't told Laura about the offer from Angelica. After I called her, which I did because I promised James I would, she called this guy named Doug Gilbert, who handles media across all McKee athletics, and he looked at the photographs I took of the practice. He was impressed, and now I have a student press badge to use if I want, provided I give any photographs to him to look over and possibly use—with payment—in promotional material for the teams.

It felt weird, like I was there because I'm James's girlfriend, but he assured me that it wasn't because of that. Looking at my work was a favor to Angelica, who apparently likes me a lot, but offering me the access badge was something he did because he thinks I'll deliver good photography.

I haven't told James yet, either; I'm planning to spill the beans on the drive down to his parents' place. I've never had a secret like this to keep before, and honestly, it's pretty fun.

But even if I do this, even if I sell some photographs to the university or enter the contest Laura just told me about, it doesn't replace the reality of my situation.

Laura looks like she's going to push, but I shake my head incrementally, so she backs off. "Show me what you're going to wear to Christmas dinner. Do they cook? You know what, they probably have a chef. That's what my parents do, especially for holidays."

* * *

"James! Beckett!"

Sandra pulls both of us into a tight hug the moment she opens the door, even though we're still bundled up in our coats on the front porch. My knit cap—the same one James knocked right off my head when he kissed me after his practice—goes askew thanks to the force of her embrace.

"Sandra," I reply with genuine fondness. I haven't really had a chance to speak with James's mother, so the enthusiasm is puzzling, but welcome anyway.

Three whole days of this before we head down to Atlanta for the championship game. Despite Laura's best efforts, I'm not at all calm about this. Christmas for me usually means pie for dinner on Christmas Eve and opening presents while *Elf* plays on the television, then dinner at Aunt Nicole's. This Christmas, I may as well have gone to the moon to celebrate.

She helps me get the hat back on properly before giving Cooper and Sebastian the same treatment. "I'm glad you got down all right—was the traffic rough?"

"It's Long Island, the traffic's always rough," Cooper says, his voice muffled against his mother's hair. When she pulls back and sees his face, she gasps. The remnants of a bruise linger on his cheekbone.

"Cooper Blake Callahan," she chides, rubbing her thumb over the bruise.

"You should see the other guy," he says, trying for a grin.

I sneak a glance at James because we both know that's not from hockey. Cooper and Sebastian got into a bar fight with some dudes at McNamara's a week ago, and as far as I know, it's on the list of things Richard Callahan is hopefully never going to find out about.

She sighs. "Do you need help bringing in your things? Richard, the kids are here!"

As we walk into the entryway of James's parents' house, I have to make a conscious effort not to let my jaw drop. We left McKee mid-afternoon, so it's evening now, and it didn't sink in, when we first pulled up to the house, just how much of a mansion it is. I'm pretty sure the entirety of Abby's Place would fit into the entryway alone. It has one of those towering cathedral ceilings with a double staircase leading to the upper level and a chandelier overhead; in between the staircases, there's a tree that's at least twelve feet tall and decorated to perfection with gold and silver trinkets and lights. Sandra takes my coat and scarf. I hear her complimenting my sweater dress, but I'm too busy staring at Richard.

Even though I've seen him a few times now, it's still jarring to realize that James and Cooper look so much like him. For half a second, I feel like I'm looking at my boyfriend twenty years into the future. He smiles as he takes in the sight of his wife fussing with Sebastian's collar, but then his gaze finds mine, and his smile doesn't quite reach his eyes anymore.

"Beckett," he says, nodding at me as he accepts a hug from James. "How wonderful that you'll be joining us for the holiday."

I try to keep my smile relaxed, even though inside, I feel like bolting. That intensity that James radiates out on the field? Richard has that all the time, apparently.

"Isn't it great?" James says, winding his arm around my waist. "It took some convincing, but I think what really sealed it was the promise of the annual Monopoly game."

"Which I'm winning," Cooper declares. "Three years in a row."

"One year and two years of cheating," Sebastian retorts.

"I hope you don't mind traditions like this," Sandra says with a fond eye roll. "We'd love to do a family football match, but no one wants to risk the injury. Anyway, I had Shelley set up snacks and drinks in the den. Izzy's back there picking out tonight's movie."

Sebastian and Cooper give each other a look before dashing down the hallway.

"Cooper thinks it's not Christmas until we watch *Christmas Vacation*," James murmurs in my ear. "Sebastian prefers *Elf.* Izzy is a wildcard who can easily be bought with the promise of more presents."

"And what about you?"

He grins. "You first."

"I'm siding with Sebastian."

His jaw drops. "No way. Here I was thinking my girlfriend had taste."

Instead of leading me down the same hallway, though, James pulls me into the next room. "I figure I'll give her the tour now," he tells his parents.

"Sure, honey," Sandra says. "But don't take too long, there's hot cider."

"We want to hear more about what you've been up to," Richard says. His tone is light, but I hear the question in it, and James must as well, because his jaw tightens slightly.

He turns on the lights in the room, revealing a formal sitting room with a massive fireplace. There are bookshelves all along one wall, and a piano in the corner.

"Izzy was really into it one summer," he explains.

"It's nice," I say. The room doesn't feel all that personal, though. Hopefully the rest of the house looks like someone actually lives in it.

He takes me through his father's office, kisses me underneath a bunch of mistletoe in an entryway, and shows me the hallway that leads to his parents' wing of the house. In the kitchen, an older woman with a spiky blue hairdo chides James as he steals a cookie from a plate.

"Thanks, Shelley," he says as he breaks it in half and hands me a piece. "This is Bex, my girlfriend."

Shelley holds out her hand for a shake, her eyes crinkling when James drops a kiss to the top of my head. I'm blushing, but I don't mind much. I can't stop staring at the incredible marble countertops and the industrial-sized refrigerator.

He takes me upstairs, walking past a series of doors. Sebastian's room, Cooper's room, Izzy's room. Two guest bedrooms. I peer into one of them. It looks cozy enough to spend a few nights in, piled with throw pillows and a thick quilt. For some reason, there's a painting of a cow on the wall opposite the bed. I'd gotten more of a coastal-chic vibe from the rest of the decor, which feels fitting for a house only minutes from the beach.

James reaches around me to shut the door. "You're not sleeping there."

I raise an eyebrow. "What about your parents?"

"We're adults. They know we're sleeping together." He entwines his fingers in mine and tugs me down to the end of the hallway. "No point in pretending."

He opens the door to his own bedroom, revealing a neat space with light blue walls and tons of football posters on the walls. I smile, looking around at every inch. There are trophies on a shelf above the bed and a bookcase filled to the brim with novels. The sheets and bedspread are a creamy white, but there's a threadbare plaid throw laid over the end of the bed.

"This is nice," I say. "Did they change anything after you left for college?"

"It's definitely missing something," he says.

I suppose I should be expecting it, but I still squeak when he pushes me back onto the bed.

He looks down at me, eyes dancing, and swipes my hair away from my face. "Ah, that's better."

I shove at his stomach. "Your parents want us downstairs."

"In a minute." He pushes me back gently, covering my body with his as he kisses me. "I didn't get a chance to kiss you congratulations for getting the press pass."

I can't help myself; I kiss back. His lips are chapped from the cold, and he has a tiny bit of stubble that he needs to shave; the friction has me swallowing back a moan. We stay like that for a few minutes, pressed tightly together, kissing until we're breathless and have to break apart for air before going at it again. His hands don't wander, but I can feel his growing hard-on, and I'm on the verge of giving in to a quick blowjob if he wants it when the door opens.

"Found them!"

Izzy walks into the room with a shit-eating grin on her face. "You two are *such* dorks."

James

In the morning, it's torture getting up. I'm forced to leave a stunning, gorgeous, naked Bex in my childhood bed to go run in the cold. On the morning of Christmas Eve.

And I'm not even the first one downstairs.

My father looks up from his stretching as I sit down on the last step to put on my sneakers. "Nice of you to join us, son."

"Slug," Izzy says, poking my cheek as she walks by. "Were you up late getting frisky with Bexy?"

I roll my eyes. "One, she doesn't like to be called that. Her name is Bex. And two, on the list of things I'm not discussing with my little sister, my sex life is in the top three."

Seb stifles a laugh as he stretches out into a lunge. "Getting frisky. Nice one, Iz."

"We were just about to leave without you," Coop says, shaking his head solemnly. "The Heisman winner is getting sloppy."

Dad straightens up and claps his hands. "Troops! Your mother insisted on sleeping in because of the holiday. Coop, Seb, Izzy, you start on Amberly, James and I will tackle Greenwich. First ones back get to pick the first movie of the day."

I race my brothers out of the house.

Even as a much older man who hasn't laced up his cleats in years, my dad nearly smokes me for the first couple of blocks.

With the cold morning air stinging my cheeks, I pick up the pace, weaving in between cars parked on the side of the street.

"So," he says eventually. "You brought her home for Christmas."

I swipe at my forehead. "Yep."

"After we agreed no girlfriends."

"I didn't mean for it to happen. It just . . . evolved."

"After you pretended to be with her. I could have told you how well that was going to go."

"She's not like Sara." I sidestep a pothole. "She's nothing like her, actually. And I really care about her."

He stops suddenly, and I nearly bump into him. He eyes me, chest heaving. "Christ. You're in love with her."

I've been trying to avoid saying it, even to myself, but there's no point in denying it. It may have started out as a fake relationship, but Bex has worked her way into my life so thoroughly that I can't imagine a version of it without her being mine. She's the first thing I think about when I wake up and the last thing I think about before I go to sleep. I dream about her. If I thought I could convince her, I'd move her into my house, so I don't have to spend even one night without her in my arms.

And my father can see those thoughts running through my mind, as clear as if they were written on my forehead in fucking Sharpie.

"James," he says heavily.

"It's different this time."

"Until she gets in the way."

"Sara didn't—" I pause, scrubbing a hand over my face. "She didn't get in the way. She was sick. I made the choices I did because I cared about her."

"Exactly." He reaches out, squeezing my shoulder. "Beckett

seems like a nice girl. I'm not saying she isn't. But we talked about needing to choose the game. I thought you understood that."

"I've been choosing the game all season."

"And what happens when she wants you to choose her, but it gets in the way of the game?"

I swallow hard. I've thought about it myself, not that I'm about to admit that to my father. If the diner fire had happened during game day? I'd have gone with Bex no matter where I was supposed to be right then. All I knew was that the moment I saw the panic on her face, I was going to be by her side through whatever she was facing. "It's almost the end of the season."

"What about when this becomes your full-time job? Would she be willing to move with you?"

"Mom moved with you."

"Your mother and I had a unique understanding," he says. "It's very hard for most people to understand and accept the sacrifices necessary to succeed in this world."

"And despite not knowing Bex, you think she's like that?"

I want to look away, but his eyes search mine, keeping me in place with the force of his gaze. "I'm just reminding you to be careful. If you play the way you've been playing, in a few days you'll be a national champ. But then comes the draft. Graduating. Reporting to your first training camp. Your first season, likely in Philly or San Francisco."

"And I see Bex by my side for all of that. Just like I'll be at her side for everything she needs and wants to do."

"Does she?"

I don't say anything. I think so, but I don't know. Bex should be a visual arts major; I know she's lukewarm at best about her business degree. She should be looking at careers that utilize photography. If I asked her to come with me to San Francisco right now, I don't know what her answer would be; she's been steadfast about sticking with her mother's diner. Long distance? I've never tried it and I'm not sure I could make myself. There's a hell of a difference between away games or a couple weeks of training camp and living across the country from your girlfriend.

"I know you love her," Dad says into the silence. "I know you think you're going to be with her forever. But you thought that about Sara too, son, and look how that turned out."

He rubs my shoulder. I blink, swallowing even though my throat is dry. I should tell him off, but the words don't come.

"Let's keep going," I finally say. "Izzy's going to pick *The Family Stone* and I can't put myself through that shit again."

Bex

I'm kind of in love with James's mother.

When I walked downstairs half an hour ago, the house was quiet. Even in such a big space, I could tell that James and his siblings weren't around. I tiptoed to the kitchen anyway, hoping to find some coffee, and ran into Sandra instead.

She made me pour-over and insisted on us eating cookies for breakfast. What an icon.

Now she leans back in her chair, bare feet tucked underneath her, and takes another sip of coffee as she looks at me. I have the sense some sort of interrogation is coming. The first and only time I met Darryl's parents, his mother immediately asked how many children I was planning to have. Sandra could say practically anything and would instantly be better than her.

"You're wearing my son's sweater," she says.

I flush, looking down at myself. It's just a gray McKee sweatshirt, but on me, it's baggy and the sleeves flop over my hands. I roll them up, picking at a random thread. "His is cozy."

She smiles. She has a kind face, natural in its age, with crow's feet around her eyes that add extra softness to her smile. There's nothing artificial about her. Even now, she's just wearing a T-shirt that occurs to me might be Richard's, and soft cotton pajama pants. Her tongue is stained blue from the frosting on the cookies. Her tortoiseshell glasses frame her face like a character from a Nora Ephron movie. This is the woman who has loved James throughout his whole life. Every win and every loss, every triumph and crisis. She was by his side through everything that went down with Sara.

"James has told me so much about you," she says. "He was afraid of telling his father, but I make us have regular phone calls, and lately, they've been all about you."

"You're not making him," I say honestly. "He's always happier after you call."

"You've been spending a lot of time together."

I nod. Even though I have my dorm room, I've been spending more and more nights at James's lately. As the semester was wrapping up, it just made sense—we had work to do for the writing class, and it's not like I could go to the apartment to get a break from the dorm. Plus, he has a hang-up about me driving home alone late at night. I suspect it's an excuse to keep me in his bed, but I don't intend to ever call him out on it. It makes me too happy.

"I was worried, after Sara—he told me you know about Sara—that he would punish himself. What happened was horrible, but it wasn't his fault. That's not how a healthy person responds to a breakup."

"No," I agree softly. "She's doing okay now though, right?"

"Yes. I still talk to her mother from time to time. She's safe and finishing up her degree at a different school, close to her cousins."

"That's good." I pick up my coffee mug, even though it's nearly empty, and take a small sip.

"But tell me more about you. He says you're a photographer?"

I tuck my hair behind my ear, looking at the Christmas tree instead of her. The den has another tree, one that I can recognize; it's decorated with rainbow strings of lights and homemade ornaments from when James and his siblings were little. Last night, Sandra explained that they always do a formal family portrait with the tree in the foyer—it's ended up in magazines before, usually alongside press for the foundation—but she likes the silly pictures they take in the den way better.

"Yeah," I say. "I mean, it's my hobby."

"Oh," she says. "That's not what you're studying?"

"Um, no. I'm going to be taking over my mother's diner when I graduate." I force myself to look at Sandra and smile. "It's a cute little place not too far from McKee. We've got the best pie in the Hudson Valley."

She considers that. "What's the best flavor?"

It's not the question I'm expecting. I smile for real. "Well, it's famous for the cherry pie, but I'm partial to the lemon meringue."

"You love it?"

"It's where I grew up."

"And it's your dream?" She shakes her head as soon as she says that. "I'm sorry, I'm prying. It just fascinates me, what passions people have. Of course, in my family, my boys all have the same passion."

"You must be so excited for James to go into the NFL," I say, grasping at the weak opportunity for a conversation change.

"Excited? Yes. Terrified? Also yes. I watched my husband get knocked down routinely by men built like freight trains for seventeen years. It's not for the faint of heart, Bex."

"At least they don't usually fight like they do in NHL hockey."

"Don't even get me started," she says, shaking her head. "This is why Izzy is my favorite. Volleyball doesn't usually involve flying fists, thank goodness." She winks. "Don't tell the kids I said that."

"I'm sure Izzy would rub it in their faces for years to come."

"You're starting to get how our family works." She sets her coffee cup aside. "I can see my son cares about you. A lot. And I know you're probably going to think this is weird, but thank you for that. He deserves to have someone in his corner. He's so serious all the time—he was that way even as a boy. Always following the rules, always giving everything his all. But when he looks at you . . . his whole face lights up and he just relaxes. It's beautiful."

She stands up, gathering up her mug and mine, and cups my cheek. "And I may not know you all that well yet, but that's what I see when you look at him."

She goes into the kitchen, leaving me alone with the Christmas tree, presents overflowing from underneath. The fireplace crackles; she lit a fire as soon as we walked in earlier. Can she really see that when she looks at me, or is she just imagining it?

My feelings for James have gotten so deep. It's like I was swimming in the shallows for a long time, and now suddenly I'm realizing I'm nowhere near the shoreline. He leaves me breathless. Every time he calls me "princess," my heart does a silly little somersault. He's cheesy, he's romantic. Maybe he is the kind of person who follows the rules, but he bent them when we made our deal, and I have the sense he never looked back.

I hear James's laughter. He bursts into the den along with his brothers, his eyes lighting up as soon as he spots me. When he ducks to kiss me, I push him away; he's sweaty and cold all at once. He manages to press a kiss to the top of my head, grinning as I swat at him.

"Sorry I had to leave you," he says.

"You know I don't mind. Unless you make me tag along. Then we'd have a problem."

He crouches, so we're eye to eye, and raises one of his eyebrows. "Oh yeah?"

"Yeah," I say, voice breathier than I intend. Before him, I'd tell you sweat was gross, but now? I kind of want to lick the bead that's trailing down the side of his face.

And by the way he's looking at me, he knows what I'm thinking. Clearly, I'm nowhere near as cool and collected as I'd like to be.

"What would you do to me?" he teases.

A million thoughts are racing through my head, but before I have a chance to tease back—or maybe just push him back onto the floor and kiss him, sweat be damned—we're interrupted. Aside from when Cooper accidentally walked in on us hooking up, and the time Laura almost burst in on us taking a shower together, we've had pretty good luck with privacy. Less than twenty-four hours at James's house and his little sister has interrupted *twice*.

"I'm putting on *The Family Stone*," she declares, flicking James on the cheek as she walks by.

"Please, no," James groans. "I'll do anything, Iz. Anything to avoid sitting through that pain."

"Rachel McAdams's incapable of making a bad movie." She glances back at me. "Right, Bex?"

I look between my boyfriend and his sister. If I agree, I'll win some points with Izzy, but James will pout.

Eh, he can take it. It's not a sack delivered by a freight train of a linebacker, to use Sandra's phrasing.

"You know what, Izzy? You're totally right."

* * *

JAMES OPENS THE taped-together Monopoly box with the same reverence afforded to historical artifacts. The board looks like I remember from the couple of times I've played this, as do the cards, but the little silver game pieces? Instead of those, he sets out a strange assortment of objects. A button, a toy soldier, a locket with a broken hinge, what looks like a shoe for a Barbie, a sparkly pom-pom, and a dented bottle cap.

"Bex is the guest, she should pick first," Sebastian says from across the coffee table. We're all on the floor by the Christmas tree, mugs of spiked hot chocolate (except for Izzy) in hand. I thought I'd have some girlfriend privileges here, maybe be able to be on a team with James, but that went out into the chilly December night the moment I saw the gleam in his eyes. I might be snuggled into his side now, but once the cards are drawn, he's The Enemy.

Fine. I may need to admit defeat whenever we go to the arcade to play hoops, but I can beat him in a board game for sure.

Cooper looks at me with intensity in his deep blue eyes. "If you take that button from me, I will lose my shit."

"The button?" I glance down at it. "I figured that would be the one no one wants."

"The button is luckiest," James says. "Then the shoe."

Izzy cracks her knuckles. "I'm getting that shoe. You *ruined* me last year, James."

"Which is the unluckiest?" I ask.

"The toy soldier."

I shake my head. "Three guys and no one wants the toy soldier?"

"He's the soldier of death," Richard says dryly from his spot on the couch. Sandra is tucked into his side; they're the only ones paying attention to the movie playing. *It's a Wonderful Life.*

I swallow back a sudden swell of emotion as the memory of watching that movie on the diner television with my mom hits me. When I was little, she loved it, the way she liked other classic things—music and art and fashion. After my father left, the movie made her too sad, and I've never pushed us to watch it. I haven't seen it in years.

"The only fair thing is to dump them all in the middle," Sandra says. "Everyone makes a grab for it."

"Do you really want Seb to get Coop into a headlock again?" says James.

She raises her eyebrows at her son. "All's fair in love and games."

"Well said, darling," says Richard, punctuating that with a kiss.

James wrinkles his nose, but I smile. The bittersweet ache in my chest won't go away tonight. We had breakfast for dinner—apparently a Callahan family tradition on Christmas Eve—and that reminded me of the diner. A big, cozy family event like this? I never had that; even when I had both of my parents in my life, it was just the three of us. No older siblings to tease or younger siblings to torture.

"Okay," James says, shoving all the pieces into the center of the board. "On three. Three, tw—*Cooper*!"

James

After midnight hits, I carry Bex to bed.

She's a little tipsy, her breath smelling like Irish cream, cheeks flushed, mouth slack. I am too; the longer we played the game, the more Bailey's we added to our hot chocolates. Cooper pulled out a completely improbable win after the back-to-back bankruptcies of Seb and Bex, and that came hours after my parents bid us goodnight.

She fits right in with my family, just like I thought she would. My mom loves her. And the more time Dad spends with her, the more he'll love her too. I'm totally biased, sure, but she's impossible to resist.

I set her down on the bed gently, pulling off her sweater so she won't get hot in her sleep. She whines, reaching for me when I move away to fold it and set it on my desk. Her fuzzy socks have little Santa hat-wearing penguins on them. Almost as adorable as the light-up Christmas tree earrings she wore earlier today.

"Let's go to sleep," I murmur, stroking my hand through her tangled hair. "Otherwise, Santa won't come."

She cups my jaw. "One day you'll tell our kids that."

"Bex," I say helplessly. Fuck, she's so pretty it makes my chest ache. Those beautiful brown eyes look at me in my dreams, and every day I wake up grateful I get to see them for real.

"I love you," she whispers, so quietly I think for a moment I imagined it.

But she keeps looking up at me with confidence shining in her eyes, and I know she really said it.

"Fuck, I love you." I gather her up into a hug, fisting my hand in her hair. She digs her nails into my back. We stay like that for a long moment, breathing each other in. When I pull away, she has a tear tracking down her cheek. I brush it aside tenderly and kiss her.

"Show me how much," she says. "Please, James. Show me."

She peels her shirt off and flings it aside, shivering immediately. I pull her up the bed, settling us underneath the covers. I can't stop kissing her; every time my lips brush her skin, she whispers encouragement.

I love you. The words are on a loop in my mind and on my lips as we move against each other. *I love you. I love you.* I say it so many times I get breathless. She's laughing against my neck, smiling as she kisses me, moving with me in the cool quiet of my bedroom. I'm distantly aware that we're not the only two people around; that even though it feels like it, we're not alone in the world. But in this moment, it absolutely does. I'm in the house I grew up in, surrounded by the family I would protect with my life, but never has it felt so real and perfect and like *home.* Not until now. Not until Beckett.

If I could only pick one person to be around, one person to know, one person to love, for the rest of my life—I'd choose her.

We're still pressed tightly together when I hear her breathing begin to even out. Pressing a kiss to her forehead, I slip out of her. She turns into my chest, yawning, nestling her head against me.

No, we're not alone in the world, but right now, underneath the covers—it does feel like we're in a world of our own.

"One day I will tell our kids that," I whisper. My heartbeat quickens at the thought. "Because I'm yours, forever."

Bex

It turns out that Christmas morning is a lot more fun when you're in a houseful of people, and when the guy by your side told you he loves you . . . and that he's yours. I think James thought I was asleep last night for that part, but I caught it in between waking and dreaming. I've spent the morning curled up on the couch with him, watching his family unwrap presents while instrumental Christmas music plays in the background, and between the teasing and laughter, I haven't stopped smiling. James's siblings surprised me with a very thoughtful mini tripod and a book of Annie Leibovitz's photography. James loved the monogrammed leather duffel I got him; I texted Laura immediately to thank her for helping me pick it out.

James presses a little blue box into my hands. "Here, princess."

I look up at him, blushing like I do every time other people are around to hear the nickname. He has a gleam in his eyes that instantly makes me wary that he spent too much money on me. I recognize the particular shade of blue; I doubt there's a woman in America who wouldn't. When I open the box, a pair of cheesy football-shaped earrings fall into my lap. Which is adorable, but I'm too focused on the gorgeous pair of diamond hoops nestled into the velvet underneath.

"James, this is . . . this is too much."

"Do you love them?"

I nod, touching one of the hoops with my fingernail. It's so delicate. Pretty and perfect—just big enough to show off, but not too flashy. I don't even want to think about how much he spent on them, especially after the camera.

"Then that's all that matters."

"You're too sweet." I lift one of the hoops from the velvet and put it on. "Did you help him pick them out, Izzy?"

"Nope," she says. "That was all him. He disappeared into Tiffany's for like, an hour. *On* Izzy Day."

I kiss his cheek as I put on the other one. "Thank you. Although this means you don't need to buy me another present possibly ever."

My phone buzzes in my lap. I pick it up distractedly; I tried calling my mother earlier to wish her Merry Christmas, and she didn't pick up. "Hey, Mom, Merry Christ—"

"Bexy. I knew you'd pick up."

Darryl's voice stops me cold. I get up, murmuring an apology to James, his family, the room at large—I don't know. I can barely swallow. My heart is in my throat.

"Yeah, their house is beautiful," I say loudly, so James won't follow. "James got me the prettiest pair of earrings; I'll text you a picture."

Somehow, I make it to the bathroom. I lock the door and slump against it. "Darryl. What the fuck are you doing?"

"You're with him?" He snorts. "Should have guessed. You're still riding his dick for all it's worth."

"What do you want?"

"Is that all it takes, babe? A mansion and fancy earrings? I thought you had more substance than that."

"I'm going to hang up."

"Wait." There's a genuine note of emotion in his voice, so I don't. Damnit, why is he calling me on Christmas? "I want to know."

"Know what?"

"Why him?" He pauses, breathing heavily on the line. "Why'd you pick that asshole?"

"You don't know what you're talking about." I barely resist the urge to correct him about Sara; he doesn't have the right to that information, plus I don't want him to know I caved and confronted James about it. "And he's not an asshole, he's my boyfriend and your teammate and you need to back the hell up."

"You never wanted to meet my family. Go to my parents' house. I had to drag you to dinner with them. The one time I tried to do something fucking nice for you and buy your stupid photography, you wouldn't let me."

I shut my eyes. "Who cares, Darryl? It was a year ago."

"I know I fucked up when I cheated," he says. "But I'm not letting you go."

"You need to."

"No."

"Saying no won't—"

"No," he snaps. His voice cracks over the line like lightning. "Don't fucking tell me no."

I take a deep breath. I'm trembling, but it's not like he's actually here. He's in Boston with his family. I'm on Long Island. We're hours away from each other; the freakin' Long Island Sound is between us. But his voice feels so forceful that for half a second, I have to resist the urge to look over my shoulder.

"Bexy," he says, his voice breaking, softer now. "I miss you. I still . . ."

I'm quiet for a moment. "Darryl, we're not together anymore."

"You're the only one I've ever—"

"Stop calling me," I interrupt, terrified of whatever he's about to say. I can't hear those words come out of his mouth. Not now, not ever. Especially not so soon after James said it to me.

"You don't even want to hear what I have to say?"

I hang up. He calls again immediately, and when that goes to voicemail, he just calls again. I block his number, shaking so badly I miss the button the first couple of tries. I flush the toilet, in case anyone is waiting in the hallway, and run the sink to splash some water on my face.

I look normal enough to re-join the party, I think. I tweak one of the earrings. James will be wondering where I went.

But when I exit, Richard is waiting for me.

"Bex," he says. "How is your mother?"

"Oh, um, fine." I stand up straighter. I haven't been alone with Richard, and after the conversation with Darryl, I'm jumpy as hell. He doesn't love me, but if he really thinks he does, that makes me more uncomfortable than I'd like to admit. "Thanks for asking. Should we . . ."

"You love my son," Richard says.

It's not a question. I nod.

"And you agree that he's destined for greatness."

I've never heard someone use that expression seriously. But it's not like he's lying, so I nod again. "He's so talented."

My response makes Richard relax slightly. He puts his hands in his pockets, leaning back against the wall. He came down this morning in a sweater with a fuzzy Christmas tree on it, and his outfit juxtaposed with the serious expression on his face is making me feel slightly hysterical. "I like you, Beckett. I think you have a good head on your shoulders. I admire practicality."

"Thank you?"

"I want to talk to you about a matter of practicality." His eyes, so like James's, look me over. I shiver. How James and his siblings handled having that look directed at them growing up is beyond me. "I have no problem with you dating him. In fact, I think you've been good for him. In an ideal world, you'll be in his life for a long time. But we agree that the most important thing is for him to fulfill his destiny, right? He should have the chance to become the legend he has the talent and potential to be."

I nod; that's easy. "Yes. It's all I want for him."

"Good. We're in agreement." He cocks his head to the side slightly. "All I'm asking is for you not to threaten that. If my son cares for you, he'll put you first. He'll never put himself first. And that's exactly what he needs to do right now." He takes a step closer. "Whatever problems you're dealing with, whatever leads to phone conversations like *that*—don't tell him. Don't make it his problem. Not now. Do you understand?"

He's right. There was a problem at the diner, and James practically fought to come with me. If he knew about Darryl, he'd do something he'd just regret later. "I understand."

"Good." He reaches out and squeezes my shoulder. "And Bex? A word of advice."

I look up at him. He has a serious expression on his face, but there's softness in there, too. It's almost fatherly. I haven't had a look like that directed at me in years.

I hate how much it affects me.

"This goes for the diner, too. Think long and hard before tying yourself to it. Because he won't choose the team he ends up on."

"I know."

"He'd be faithful, but would it be the best thing for you both? Think about it."

He gives my shoulder another squeeze before smiling and walking back to the den, leaving me alone in the hallway.

I wipe at my eyes, taking a deep breath, and tell myself to move.

Instead, I stare down at my phone. Since I blocked Darryl's number, I have no idea if the calls have stopped. I take a chance and unblock it, sending a text that does nothing to slow my heart rate or ease the tension in my shoulders.

Let's talk before the game.

Bex

If someone told me back before the semester started that on January 2nd, I'd be in Atlanta to watch my boyfriend play in the college football national championship, I'd have demanded to know how I got back together with Darryl.

Instead, I have James.

When I kissed him at that party, I couldn't have imagined a future where we'd be together. In love with each other. Where I'd be supporting him in the biggest moment of his life so far, my camera slung over my neck because I'm using my student press pass to take photographs during the game.

It might be the biggest moment of my life so far, too.

I just need to get this talk with Darryl out of the way.

It's probably pointless to try and reason with him, but I can't help myself. We do have history, even if all he's been doing is working to sour it at every turn. Maybe there's something I can say to get through to him once and for all that I don't want him texting me, or calling, or seeking me out on campus, and I definitely have no plans to get back together with him.

I find him in the hallway near the locker room. There's still some time before the game, so he's not in his uniform yet, and he hasn't put any eyeblack on his cheeks. He runs his hand through his hair, which is shorter than the last time I saw him, and gives me a smile that doesn't quite reach his eyes. Did he smile differently when he thought he liked me, or did I just see it in a different light?

"Bexy."

I sigh. There's no point in trying to correct him. "Darryl. Are you ready for the game?"

He reaches out and tugs at my press pass. "Oh, shit, look at you."

I lean back slightly. "You have to stop doing this."

"Doing what?" he says. "Trying to get back my girlfriend?"

"Yes." I cross my arms over my chest. I'm wearing James's jersey, and I know it's not productive right now, but I hope it annoys him. "You gave that up when you cheated on me."

"And I told you, that was a mistake. Worst mistake I ever made."

"Good. Tell that to whomever you date next."

I go to leave, because the longer I stand here the more uncomfortable I get, but like at the Penn State game, he boxes me in. I peer around him nervously to see if anyone is around. It's a risk, meeting him somewhere James is too, but I wanted to keep it semi-public.

I'm not scared of him; besides that time at the diner, he hasn't tried to touch me. He's just not used to losing something he wants, and unfortunately that thing is still me. I give him what I hope is a placating smile, putting my hand on his arm. "Darryl. You don't want me anymore. Even before I met James, we were broken up."

"Cut the shit," he says, that cold, angry note back in his tone. "You dump me and then turn around and immediately start dating him? I love you, Bex. You know how much it hurts to see you together?"

"If you really did, you wouldn't have cheated on me!" I can't help my rising voice. "I moved on, and you need to move on too. Stop finding me on campus. Stop coming to where I work. Stop calling me. Just stop."

"I know you were lying about dating him," he says.

I force myself not to react, even though his words make me break out in a sweat. The deal James and I made feels so long ago now, but it *is* how this whole thing started. "What?"

"Maybe you're not lying now, but you lied to begin with, and you made me look like a fucking idiot."

I swallow. "I cared about you a lot. I still want you to be happy. But you're not going to be happy with me."

He shakes his head. "No. Stop telling me no."

"Darryl—"

"Break up with him."

I laugh incredulously. "You're not seriously asking me that."

"Break up with him, or I'll tell everyone the real reason why he left LSU." He leans in, making my heart jump in my throat. I remind myself that we're not really alone, that any moment someone will walk by, and that I don't have to give in to his ridiculous demands just because he thinks he still wants me. I don't think he ever truly wanted me—just some version of me, a version of the good, supportive girlfriend who loves her football-playing boyfriend. I couldn't give that to him, but I've been giving it to James all season, and now that's finally catching up to me. "You miss me, baby, I know you do."

He leans in and kisses me. I don't move away fast enough, numbly standing there as his words echo around my mind. He deepens it, his hand fisting in my hair, forcing my lips to part for him. Too late, my hands come up to push at his chest, but he's so much stronger that I can't make him budge. I stomp my foot down on his instead, as hard as I can, and he breaks away, cursing.

"Fuck, Bex!"

"You're an asshole!" I cry, trying to keep my voice as quiet as possible in case anyone else is around. "I'm not breaking up with him. You need to back the *fuck* up."

He stares at me, working his jaw. The moment he moves—whether that's to hit me or kiss me again, I don't know and don't want to find out—I bolt for the open door across the hallway. I lock myself inside; it looks like some sort of supply closet. I slump against it, blood rushing in my ears, and wipe my mouth.

"Hey, Darryl."

Fuck. I'd know that voice anywhere.

"Callahan," I hear him say. "Ready for the game?"

I stop breathing. He sounds totally unaffected by what just happened. At least he's not about to fight James. But if James realizes what he just did . . . I can't even finish that thought. I cross my arms tightly, resisting the urge to throw open the door and burrow into James's chest. This is exactly the sort of thing I told Richard I wouldn't bother him with, and if he sees me now, he'll instantly know that something is wrong.

A sob works its way out of my throat. I cover my hand with my mouth. I'm trembling, tears streaking down my cheeks.

"Yeah," James says. "Coach is having a talk down in the locker room. It's almost time to suit up."

"Let's go then."

I listen, body tense, until their footsteps fade.

Then I carefully wipe away the tears and check to see if my mascara still looks okay. It's nearly game time, after all. I can't afford to break down now, and I'm not about to give Darryl that satisfaction. And even more importantly, I can't ruin this game for James.

James

Talk to any football player about the big games in his career, and he'll say something about every game being big. That philosophy holds true, to a certain extent—I'm never not going to give my all to a game—but the fact remains that some are more important than others.

Sometimes it's a highly anticipated early season game, or a conference matchup that's been blooming into an intense rivalry. Other times it's the championship.

Today is one of those times.

Right after Christmas, I left for Atlanta to prep with the team. Coach Gomez is wound tight, and I don't blame him; it's the first time McKee has gotten this far since his tenure as head coach began. The other seniors on the team have been as quiet as I am these past couple of days, meditating on what will be our last college game, win or lose. Some of these guys will end up in the NFL like me and Sanders, but a lot of them won't. For some of them, this is the last football game they'll play, period.

And I need to lead them to a victory.

I uncross my legs and stand up, wiping my hands together. The floor of the gym isn't the nicest meditation space I've ever used, but it's been working fine for my purposes when I add on the noise-cancelling headphones. There are a million thoughts going around my mind right now, begging for my attention, and I can't give the time of day to anything that isn't related to the game plan. It's just the truth.

I check my watch. T-minus an hour to game time.

In addition to being in Atlanta, the game is Monday night, prime time. We're playing against Alabama, but that doesn't scare me.

I can do this. The team is good, and we've been clicking on all levels the last couple of games in particular. I could recite the plays in my sleep. I've watched so much film of Alabama's season I can spot their defensive moves in half a second. And I'm going to need to do exactly that to win.

Bo glances over at me as I walk by, rolled-up yoga mat tucked under my arm. "Coach came in while you had your headphones on. We're having a talk in a few minutes."

I nod, clapping his shoulder. "Thanks."

We look at each other for a long moment.

"I appreciate you, man," I say. "You've been incredible this whole season."

"You're not too bad yourself," he says with a lopsided grin. "We're taking this fucking trophy home."

"We are." The words ignite the fire in my belly. I take a deep breath. "Sixty more minutes."

"Sixty more minutes."

As I head down the hallway, I check my phone. My family texted wishing me good luck; they're all at the game, of course. ESPN did a special interview segment on Dad and me a couple of days ago as part of their pre-championship game coverage, and the pride in his voice had me choked up. They got footage from when I was little, throwing around a football at seven, ten, twelve years old, and Mom gave them photos of me in my various uniforms over the years to use in a montage. Some of it was a little embarrassing, but it was mostly fun. The only awkward moment came when the interviewer asked about my dating life and brought up Sara. I steered the conversation to Bex and got to say that she'll be on the sidelines taking photographs of the game, so that was awesome.

But I do wonder if Sara will be watching tonight. I haven't contacted her; her parents asked me not to, and I've respected that. But I wish I could send her a message and make sure for myself that she's okay.

Darryl walks around the corner, whistling. "Hey, Darryl."

"Callahan," he says. "Ready for the game?"

"Yeah. Coach is having a talk down in the locker room. Almost time to suit up."

"Let's go then." He leads the way down the hallway. "Bex is here?"

"She is," I say warily. "She's actually one of the student photographers. She'll be on the sideline."

"Is she?" He pushes open the door to the right room. "Good for her."

I narrow my eyes. He sounds too flippant for my liking. Hopefully this means he's just focused on the upcoming game, and with a little luck, finally realizing that Bex is off the market and won't be back on it anytime soon.

"Yeah," I say as we join the rest of the guys gathered in the middle of the locker room. "I can't wait to celebrate with her later."

I can't wait to get out onto the field and play this fucking game, but seeing Bex post-game will be incredible. The second we secure the win, I'm finding her on the sideline and kissing her senseless. Just the thought is enough to make me want to run out onto the field.

Coach claps his hands together once we're all in one place.

"Gentlemen. You traveled the road, and you made it here. Let's take a moment to let that sink in."

Most of the guys drop their heads down, thinking or praying, some swaying in place, others shutting their eyes. I do that, visualizing the exact moment the referee will blow the whistle to end the game. The stadium will go nuts and my teammates will mob me, but I won't celebrate until I find my stubborn, perfect girlfriend. Having her on the sideline as a student photographer, besides being cool as hell for her, is a bonus for me. I'll see her way sooner than any of the other guys will see their partners.

I imagine the whole scene—the confetti, the press running around, Bex chiming in when I talk to the interviewer from ESPN. My teammates pulling me into hugs. The guys from Alabama congratulating me as I tell them they played hard. The moment my family comes down onto the field to congratulate me; the way my father shakes my hand before hugging me. I even imagine the way the championship cap will fit on my head and the weight of the trophy in my hands as I hold it up. This visualization technique is one I use often, but I've never gone this in-depth with it before.

I want to leave nothing to chance. I'm going to win this game, come hell or high water.

After a minute or so, Coach clears his throat, and I open my eyes.

"I'm proud of you all," he says, making eye contact with us one by one. His gaze lingers on me, his lips quirking up in a half-smile. I know I've exceeded his expectations this season. He took a chance, taking me on after everything that went down at LSU, and it paid off for him and for me. "And I'll be proud of you win or lose, don't get me wrong. You've played a hell of a season, undefeated, and no one can take that away from you. No matter the outcome of this game, no matter what you do in the future—you did *this*. You dug deep and played your hearts out. You've made my job damn easy, gentlemen."

We all laugh a bit. I can sense the energy in the room, the nervous anticipation, the excitement. We've played on a big stage all season, but even the other postseason games can't hold a candle to this.

"Let's go out there and get one last win," he says. "We know our game; we know our opponent—we have a plan and we're going to stick to it. Callahan?"

I step forward.

"Fucking Heisman champ!" Demarius says as Fletch whistles.

"That's our guy," someone in the back calls out.

I grin, shaking my head. "Men. Let's fucking do this."

The team explodes into cheers. Coach shakes my shoulder, starting a chant that quickly grows to echo throughout the room. It's so loud you'd think we won already; I can barely hear Coach when he shouts that it's time to get into our gear.

I stick my fingers in my mouth and whistle to shut everyone up.

"Coach said to suit up!" I shout. "Let's rock and roll!"

"Like you're not about to blast Lady Gaga," says Bo, earning him a hearty laugh from the guys. I flip him the bird as I walk over to my locker. Someone does turn on the team mix, which includes a healthy mix of pop, rap, and hip hop, and we're laughing, shouting across the room over the music, as we get ready to go.

I take off my watch and store it in my locker, then pick up my helmet. Tap twice against the locker door, the same way I've done since I was in ninth grade.

I'm ready.

Only thing left to do is play a good game.

James

I bark out orders as we line up again, glancing at the clock. Less than a minute left before halftime. We've been clawing our way through long drives all game, grinding out first downs, and we've been rewarded with several touchdowns and a field goal. Alabama isn't far behind, however, and another score here would mean it's a two-score game heading into the second half. Alabama will have the ball first when the third quarter opens, so scoring here is essential.

We're on third down, however, and need to make a first to keep the chance of a touchdown on this drive going.

I scan the field, adjusting a couple of my men quickly, then get into position for the snap. I make it seem like we we're going for a rush up the middle, but that leaves a lane open for me to the right. I fake passing the ball off, then tuck it under my arm and take off running into the first down.

I swipe my tongue over my lip as I watch Coach give me the signal for the next play. With a fresh set of downs, we have more options.

Next, a rush up the middle. Then a short pass that nets a couple yards. We try for the end zone, but it goes wide. I glance at the clock again; see Coach telling me to go for it. We have time for one more passing attempt before we need to drop down to the field goal.

I see Darryl fan out in the end zone, shaking the man-to-man coverage, and throw to him. It's a little high; he leaps and catches it one-handed, hauling it down to his chest before tumbling to the ground.

"Fuck yes!" I shout, pumping my fist as I jog over to him. Now I can breathe easier heading into halftime. He comes up grinning, mobbed by a couple of the guys, and does a little endzone dance. I reach out and pull him into a one-armed hug, slapping his back.

There's only a couple of seconds before halftime, so Alabama chooses to let the clock run down, counting, I'm sure, on that first possession next half. But I'm not worried. I trust my defense.

I haven't looked for Bex on the sideline, wanting to avoid the distraction during the game, but now I see her waving to me. I wave back, grinning. I'm sure she's gotten some amazing shots of the game so far, but really, all I hope is that she's loved doing it. If this helps her realize that this is a future she can have, that she deserves to pursue photography seriously, I'll be thrilled.

Darryl leans in as we jog to the tunnel that leads to the locker room. "Throwing a little high, C."

"That was a great catch," I say, totally sincere. It was. "You came up big."

"Yeah," he says. "I'm sure Bex loved it."

I almost stumble. What the hell is he doing, talking about my girl again? First the press pass and now this. Bex hasn't brought him up in ages, so I've followed her lead, not wanting to bring up bad memories. Darryl and I have been mostly good—or at least I thought that, up until two seconds ago. Even though I'm soaked in sweat, the back of my neck prickles like I'm cold.

"Hey," I say, pulling him away from the crowd before he goes into the locker room. "You trying to say something to me?"

"That depends," he says. "What do you think I should be saying?"

"Nothing," I say shortly. "Not where Bex is concerned. She's not yours, asshole. Hasn't been in months."

He shrugs, an infuriating little smile playing on his lips. "Okay, man. Whatever you say."

I'm not sure what the fuck that's supposed to mean, but Coach calls me over, and I can't disobey, so I reluctantly glare at Darryl for a moment before leaving. Something about his smirk isn't sitting right. If he even so much as *looks* at Bex, we're going to have a problem.

I wipe at my sweaty forehead with a towel as I listen to Coach break down the game so far, working over the plan for the second half. This is an important moment, and I need to be 100% focused. But I can't help looking over to Darryl from time to time.

He has no reason to try to throw me off my game; we're on the same side. Unless he hates me that much? But I didn't steal Bex from him. He lost her all on his own.

I tense when I hear him say Bex's name, but don't turn around. Even when I hear the word *kiss*.

"Yeah," he continues. "She's just as good as I remember. One kiss and she was begging for more."

I feel my fists curl at my sides. Blood pounds in my ears, but I still hear his next words, clear as fucking day.

"Was always a slut for it. She's been a little whore with Callahan all semester, but I'm getting her back."

My whole world narrows to a tiny point, the ugly words echoing in my head.

He kissed her. He fucking kissed her. When? How? And if it's true, why am I hearing about this from him?

"James?" Coach Gomez says. He clasps my shoulder, a gesture that usually grounds me, but right now, I want to rip his hand away. "You all right, son?"

"Excuse me," I say tightly. "Give me a second."

I want to throw Darryl against the bank of lockers and smash his fucking nose into his skull, but somehow, I manage to walk past him, out of the locker room. Bex is standing by the door, right where I saw her when I went in, and I hate how the cute, excited expression on her face dies the moment she sees me.

"James?" she says. "What's wrong?"

"He kissed you?"

Her silence would be answer enough, but her lip wobbles too, and my veins feel like they're filled with ice as I realize she's about to cry. I shut my eyes for a long moment, trying to stop the way my heart is pounding. "I'm going to fucking kill him."

"Wait," she says, grabbing my hand. "Just calm down."

"Did he do it?"

"Yes, but—"

"But what?" I interrupt. The anger that's coursing through me hits a fever pitch as the truth sinks in. "But what? He fucking touched you without your consent because I know no matter how he was bragging about it in there, you didn't give it. Did he hurt you?"

She turns away. "Let's not do this now. You still have to play the second half."

"Fuck the game." I turn her face so she's looking at me. I need to see in her eyes that she's not lying, that she's okay. That he didn't do worse than kiss her. She blinks, her eyes spilling over with tears. I pull her into a tight hug, cupping the back of her head with one hand. "Tell me what he did."

She sobs into my shoulder, a sound that strikes me right between the ribs like a bullet. "I'm sorry, I just—he's been trying to talk to me, and we met up before the game started, and when I tried to tell him to leave me alone, he kissed me." She pulls back, looking up as she hugs herself around her middle. Her eyes are wide, and as she swallows down another sob, I realize she's not just upset, she's scared. That fucker *scared* her. "That's it. I'm fine."

"Like hell you're fine," I practically growl. I hug her again, even tighter this time, pressing my face against her hair. She sobs again; I can feel her trembling against me. "You don't have to pretend you're fucking fine."

The second I get Darryl alone, he's going to wish he never even thought about touching my girl.

"You have to finish the game," she whispers.

I know she's right, but there's no way in hell I'm leaving her like this. "You're shaking like a leaf, baby."

She rubs her cheek against my shoulder pad. I can feel her fight to control her breathing, but she can't quite manage it; she sucks in a breath that turns into another quiet sob. A couple of people walk by, and I wave them along, gritting my teeth. We stay like that for a minute or so, pressed together tightly. I shield her body with mine so whenever someone else comes by, they don't see her while she's crying, even though each little noise she makes hurts me deep.

"I love you," I whisper.

"I'm sorry," she says eventually, so quiet I almost miss it. "I'm so sorry."

"It's not your fault."

She shakes her head. "You need to go. It's almost time, right?"

"Probably." I pull back, stroking my hand down her face. "Are you okay to go back out there?"

She wipes at her eyes carefully, nodding. "Yeah," she says, voice thick with emotion that makes my heart squeeze. "James?"

"Yeah, princess?"

She hesitates for a moment, like she's not quite sure what to say. "I love you too."

Bex

I step back as a couple guys come barreling in my direction, clicking away all the while. The hardest part of this whole gig has been avoiding the players, who can't help where they end up out of bounds sometimes. An errant throw by the Alabama quarterback almost ended up hitting me smack in the face back in the first quarter, before I learned I needed to move seriously fast to keep up. One of the ESPN cameramen, Harold, has helped me throughout the game, offering me pointers on anticipating the next moves. Even though he's an older dude and skinny as a pole, he runs fast and always has his camera in position to get the shot. He's a total pro.

I love watching the games, but this? This is incredible. My heart hasn't stopped pounding since the moment the game began, and most of that is from the adrenaline rushing through me. I'm excited and nervous for James, yes, but I've been so focused on my work I sometimes forget to even cheer when he makes a particularly good throw.

Of course, I liked this game a lot more before James found out that Darryl kissed me.

The teams line up again. I glance up at the scoreboard. Third down, so James needs to work some magic to keep the drive going.

He takes the snap, fakes a pass, and holds the football tight, taking it to the down marker himself, running out of bounds. He sees me and winks as he tosses the ball back to the referee. I flush, biting my lip as I take a couple of shots of him in the huddle.

After he went back into the locker room, I found the nearest bathroom and pulled myself together. By the time I left, I looked totally normal. I can usually put on a mask when necessary, and this isn't any different . . . not that it stops the ache in my chest. I've been on edge since then, holding my breath every time I see James and Darryl interact. I promised I wouldn't distract him, and then I went and gave him the biggest distraction possible halfway through the game.

I just have to hope he's able to put it out of his mind for the rest of the game.

I still can't believe I broke down like that. Whenever I think about it, my skin feels itchy, my throat thick with emotion. It was one thing spending the first half of this game trying to forget what Darryl did. Now that I know James knows? The panic threatens to turn into a wildfire.

I look up at the scoreboard again. Seeing the big numbers announce that McKee is still leading, 33–30, makes me calmer. We're deep into the fourth quarter now, and if James leads another scoring drive here, they'll be that much closer to putting the game away.

Only when James attempts another pass, it slips out of the receiver's fingers . . . and lands right into the hands of one of the Alabama players.

"Shit," I murmur under my breath. I take a couple of pictures anyway, but my stomach is in knots. They will have a chance at another possession, but the game might be tied then, or beyond that, if Alabama scores a touchdown. I sneak a peek at the McKee sideline as the guys switch with the defense. James rips off his helmet, practically hurling himself onto the bench. He doesn't throw a lot of interceptions, and while that one was barely his fault, I'm sure he feels awful.

Maybe he can't concentrate because he's thinking about Darryl kissing me instead of the game. If his father was right, if my issues lead to them losing . . .

My stomach turns over at the mere thought.

And it just gets worse when Alabama takes that interception and turns it into a touchdown.

37–33, with under a minute to go. James has plenty of time, but a field goal won't do; they need the touchdown. I keep reminding myself of that as I watch the team huddle together for a time out, James's coach talking with his hands as much as his voice. Plenty of time. James is completely capable of leading a touchdown drive under pressure like this; the previous game, they needed to come back from a deficit to tie before ultimately winning.

They start the drive with good field position, but quickly drop down to a third down when two rushing attempts don't lead anywhere. James throws a pass, then, and they manage to claw out a first down to keep the momentum going. I move along the sideline with them, ducking past players and staff and other members of the press. The roar of the crowd behind me is so intense it's like a solid wall of sound. I manage to get an awesome shot of Demarius the moment he catches a pass, and another of one of the Alabama defensemen diving to try and sack James, who runs out of the way just in time.

They set up in good position to send the ball into the endzone, but then a stupid holding penalty drops them back ten yards. I let my camera hang freely around my neck, digging my fingernails into my forearms as I watch James shout for the guys to get into position. It's only a second down, so they have a couple of chances, but they barely have time to make it happen. A handful of seconds in football means they have time for two, maybe three plays.

Rather than try the rush, which hasn't been all that successful this game, they opt for a pass, but it's broken up in the endzone thanks to good man-to-man coverage.

Third down.

They try again. Same result.

My stomach, which has been in a tight knot all game, gets so taut it almost hurts. I can feel myself sweating everywhere, under my arms, on my forehead, down my back. I shove my hands underneath my armpits, inching as close to the field as I dare. The crowd is as loud as ever; Alabama fans dying to begin celebrating, McKee fans collectively as anxious as I am. I wonder where James's family is sitting—probably up in one of the boxes. All of them traveled here for this—we had dinner the night before at a fancy restaurant—and yet all I can imagine is Richard Callahan's face, as intense as ever, as he leans in to watch this one final play.

Fourth down.

Two seconds to go.

Either they score a touchdown and win the game, or they lose.

"Go James!" I shout. My voice doesn't carry at all, but somehow, he hears me. He looks right at me; I can barely see his face with his helmet and face guard on, but I know he sees me.

He sees *me*.

Before him, I don't know if I believed in love—not really. I believed in the idea of it, the way it could hurt people, but I didn't believe I would truly feel it, or that I deserved it anyway. Every step of the way, James has shown me I do deserve it, that I deserve someone like him, someone good and devoted who makes my heart sing whenever I see him. Someone who makes me feel like I'm worth something more than the life I resigned myself to when

I was a teenager. Someone who pushes me and protects me and holds me when I cry.

The moment we locked eyes at that party, he saw the cracks in my armor, and he hasn't stopped prying it away since.

James drops back, scanning the field. The receivers fan out, but the only one who shakes coverage is Darryl. He has a clear shot to the endzone this way; all James has to do is deliver.

I don't even bring the camera up to photograph the moment. I want to see the exact second James realizes he just secured the win, that he accomplished the goal he's been chasing all season.

He slings the pass—but it sails right over Darryl's head.

The clock runs down to zero.

Cameramen rush past me onto the field to capture the moment. The stunned McKee players, still on the field, and the way the Alabama sideline has exploded with cheers. The stadium, which had been a healthy mix of red and purple before, looks pure crimson now, Alabama fans going nuts as the win sinks in. I look for James, but I can't see him in the crowd.

"I'm sorry he lost. Tough time to lose his accuracy," Harold says, giving me a sympathetic frown before jogging past me.

I know I should move—I don't want to see this moment. I don't want to see James congratulate the other team on a job well done. I know he can make that pass; I've seen him do it all season in spots like this. Darryl was wide open. It wasn't like he made the throw under pressure; his offensive line kept the Alabama defense away from him.

No, it wasn't a mistake.

He threw high on purpose.

He threw the pass high because he didn't want Darryl to catch it—even if it meant losing the game.

And I know he did it for me.

James

The moment the pass goes over Darryl's head, I expect the regret to kick in, but I can't feel anything but satisfaction, savage and biting. The whole half, I tried to keep my cool, to detach and let my instincts for the game take over. It worked—mostly. Then I'd see Darryl's face or catch sight of Bex on the sideline with her camera in hand, and the slow-simmering rage working its way through me threatened to explode. I'd see her crying face in my mind, hear the fear in her voice, and had to work at not punching his sorry ass then and there and getting ejected from the game.

All around me, my teammates look stunned. They were fully expecting me to make that pass, and I let them down. I ought to feel bad about that, especially for my fellow seniors. But I don't care. Not now. Not when rage is coursing through me like fire and Darryl's been put in his place.

The Alabama quarterback jogs onto the field, heading in my direction. He shakes my hand, congratulates me on a season well done. I congratulate him on the win and tell him he played hard, which is the truth. Alabama played a good game. The fact it was so close heading into the end, and that we needed a wild play to win it—that's on me too. I should have led more touchdown drives early in the game. If I had, then we wouldn't have been in this position in the first place.

I get caught up in the congratulations, the condolences. I shake so many hands I can't count, but the faces are blurred; I barely recognize anyone right now. I want to find Bex, to scoop her up into my arms and hug her tightly, but I can't leave now. This, like everything else—like the pass I fucked up on purpose—is part of the job interview I've been working on since I was in high school. Can I be graceful in defeat? Do I give credit where it's due? This wasn't the first big loss in my life, and it won't be the last. Rookie quarterbacks in the NFL don't tend to do well; it takes a year or two to get used to the pace of the professional level. My future employers are watching this moment right now, making sure I'm not about to fly off the handle.

Of course, they don't know that I messed up that pass because I couldn't stand the thought of Darryl winning the game when a couple hours before, he kissed my girl without her fucking consent.

Finally, we shuffle off the field, back into the tunnel. No one speaks. I see Bex lingering outside the locker room, but I don't go to her, not now. I need a shower first, and a clean change of clothes, before I face her reaction to what I did for her.

She's going to be mad, but I don't give a shit. I'd do it again in a heartbeat. I'd burn down the whole goddamn stadium if it meant keeping her safe.

Coach Gomez gathers us together in the locker room, looking around at all of us. A lot of the guys are still breathing heavily. A couple of them are crying. I bite my lip, shutting my eyes briefly.

"You played a tough game," he begins.

"Bullshit," someone says under his breath.

Coach turns and glares in the direction of the voice. "You played your hearts out until the end. I saw that. It takes fucking grit to get this far, and you acted like men just now, giving the other side the credit they're owed. This isn't just on the last play. Our opponent was—"

"Fuck you," Darryl snarls, shoving his way to the front, past Coach, so he gets right in my face. He has dirt streaked on his face, mixing with sweat; his eyes are wild right now, dark and filled with hate. "Fuck you, Callahan! You fucked me!"

He lunges at me, knocking me back into the lockers. His fist connects with my mouth; pain explodes across my face and I taste coppery blood immediately. I bring my knee up into his groin; when he doubles over, I grab him by the shoulders and knock him down onto the floor. He flails under me, but I press my knee into his stomach, making him gasp, and take a swing at his face. Pain explodes along my hand and up my arm as my fist connects with his stupid, cocky mouth. He grabs at my face with his hand, trying to push me away; I knock back his hand and dodge the next fist he tries to swing at me. "I fucking warned you," I say, digging my knee down until he gasps. "I warned you not to use those words, asshole. I warned you to leave her the *fuck* alone."

"James!" I hear Bex scream. "Stop it!"

Someone grabs at me from behind, but before I'm hauled away, Darryl works his way out from underneath me and takes another swing. He catches my cheek this time, and by the way it stings I know I'm going to have a hell of a bruise. I scramble to my feet. Everything is a blur around me except for Darryl, dragging himself to his feet as well. I can't even hear over the ringing in my ears. He grabs at me, pulling me in so close I can smell the sour sweat on his skin.

"You fucking warned me, huh? Think you're all that? She was fucking moaning into my mouth. I had her first and she's still my little bitch."

I slam my fist into his stomach. He staggers backward,

coughing up spit and blood, and has the nerve to grin at me. I launch myself at him, but before I can smash his face into the floor, two strong arms grab me around the middle and haul me away.

"Callahan!" Bo shouts as he drags me to the other end of the room. "Fucking stop it!"

I struggle against him, trying to get back to Darryl, but when I see someone has him wrapped up too, the fight goes out of me. I lick my lips, tasting my own blood. My head is aching so badly I'm worried I split it open somehow. Where the hell is Bex?

"Get your hands off me," I say. "Where's Bex? Bex!"

I spot her across the room, her hand clasped over her mouth. I try to go over to her, but Bo doesn't let me, even when I start struggling.

"What the *fuck* was that?" Coach roars, looking between me and Darryl. I've never seen him look so pissed. I straighten up as best I can while still held back by Bo, glaring at Darryl. His chin and mouth are covered in blood, and I'm not in the least bit sorry. I hope he swallowed a fucking tooth.

"Into the office," Coach says, stalking over to the office and ripping the door open so intensely the hinges rattle. "Now."

He slams the door shut behind us when we're both inside. "Want to tell me what just happened? Two of my seniors getting into a knockout fight two seconds after a loss? I thought I was coaching men, not fucking children!"

His voice rises with his last words. I look down at my dirty cleats, swallowing down a mouthful of blood, before looking up and meeting his eyes. He's right. I'm a man, I can handle the consequences of my choices as a man. But he deserves to know why I did it. Darryl, for his part, doesn't say anything. He's glaring at me like he wants to shove his thumbs into my eyeballs, so I just stare back. I imagine throwing a football right at his crotch. I can be plenty violent with a football.

"He kissed my girl and then bragged about it. Called her a slut and a whore, sir."

Coach rounds on Darryl. "This true?"

"He stole her first," Darryl retorts.

"I didn't steal her," I snap. "She's not an object. She broke up with your sorry ass and found someone better."

"Jesus fucking Christ," Coach says, pinching his nose with his fingers.

"He should have made that pass," Darryl says. "He sabotaged us all on purpose."

I turn to look at him. "I'd do it again. I warned you what would happen if you didn't back up, you slimy fuck."

Coach crosses his arms over his chest. I hate the surprise on his face, but even if he hates me forever, I'm sticking by what I did. If he recommends that the university suspend me for the fight, I don't care. Let it come.

"Darryl, go wait outside," he says.

"Sir," he protests. "He lost us the fucking game!"

"Out. Now."

After he goes, Coach just stares at me. I resist the urge to fidget. I'm sure he's expecting me to start apologizing, but I'm not going to. If he wants to punish me for defending myself and my girlfriend, he can go right ahead.

Eventually, he sighs. "You did throw wide on purpose, didn't you?"

"Yes."

"Goddamnit, James!" He slams his fist down on the desk, making it rattle. "You can't do that, even when you're upset. Even if your personal life is going to shit. When you're being paid to do this—paid millions of dollars—you're not going to have the luxury of choosing when to perform! You can't bring your issues onto the field. We've spoken about this. You might hate all your teammates, but they're your teammates, so you stick by them."

"I know that, sir."

"So why didn't you do it?"

I wipe my bloody mouth. "Because he scared my girlfriend. He forced himself on her. And as much as I love football, I love her more."

The moment I say it, I feel lighter. It's the truth, and while I'm not looking forward to telling my father that, telling Coach eases some of the tension inside me. If the price to have Bex and make sure she's safe is my football career, then I'm willing to let it go. I can always do something else with my life. What matters, at the end of the day, is the future I know I can have with her.

"You didn't just hurt him," he says, his voice softer. "You hurt the whole team. Men who have worked hard beside you for an entire season. They trusted you, and you let them down."

"Yes, sir."

He leans back, cupping his jaw. "I don't agree, but I respect why you did it." He drags his hand over his mouth, thinking. "James. You might get suspended for this, even though he started the fight. The university almost always punishes both parties in these situations. You were still in uniform, representing the school, and if McKee doesn't act, the NCAA could."

I just nod. I expected as much.

"I'll explain that you were defending yourself," he says. "I don't think either of you will get expelled, although if Bex chooses to report Darryl's actions, then that's a possibility. Sexual misconduct is a serious offense."

"Good. He should."

"And I don't disagree. But that's not for you to decide. You can't act like this, no matter how you feel. I thought you learned this lesson at LSU, but apparently not. You can't make a bad pass on purpose because you don't like the guy."

"With all due respect, this is different."

"How?"

"I'm going to marry Bex one day," I say. "This is my present, but she's my future. There's nothing I wouldn't do for her. Maybe it's wrong, but I'm going to defend her. I couldn't just give the ball to him."

He sighs. "And what good did that do? We lost."

"Even if I did throw it right, there's no guarantee he would catch it."

"No, but he deserved the opportunity to try. Even if you'd have hated it, he deserved that."

"And I disagree." I meet his eyes. "Sir."

He presses his lips together tightly. "I hope you're willing to explain that to all the guys out there."

He rubs at his temples, making his way around the desk to clasp my shoulder. He looks me in the eyes. Seeing the disappointment in them hurts, but I don't back down. I'm willing to stick by every word. "And to her."

CHAPTER 41

Bex

The longer I stand outside the locker room, the worse I feel. People are starting to recognize me—James Callahan's girlfriend, the photographer—and the looks of sympathy sting. They assume that the tears I can't quite hide are because my boyfriend lost and I'm sad for him, which is true—but only I know the real reason it happened in the first place.

Even if he tries to deny it, he lost the game for me. He was so close to making it happen, and at the last minute he sabotaged himself. The exact thing Richard warned me not to let happen played out, beat for beat, because I couldn't hold it together long enough to lie. He would have been pissed that I lied about the kiss, but at least he would have won. I could deal with his anger after that, but this? This is unbearable.

What if it ruins his career in the NFL before it can begin? What if he gets suspended or even expelled because of the fight? I ran into the locker room as soon as I heard shouting, and my heart nearly dropped out of my body when I saw James's face covered in blood as he wrestled on the floor with Darryl. If Darryl did worse than kiss me, I'm not sure that James wouldn't have committed actual murder.

My stomach rolls at the thought. I bend over slightly, fighting back a sob.

A pair of arms wrap around me.

"James?"

"Hey." He sounds so tired. I turn to look at him. The ache in my chest cuts like a hot knife. He cleaned up and he's in regular clothes now, but the cut on his lip and bruise on his cheek look painful. "Did my family come down?"

"I haven't seen them."

He nods, running his hand through his damp hair. "How are you?"

"How am I? I should be asking you that."

"I haven't seen Darryl in a few. Did he try to talk to you?"

"No."

"Good."

"We need to talk," I say. "I don't understand—why did you—"

"Come here." He ushers me down the hallway. We end up in a weight room, deserted now but still filled with evidence of warm-ups from before the game. He doesn't let go of me, pulling me into a tight hug instead. Even though his face must hurt, he buries it into my hair.

I hug back, tentatively. Now that I'm with him again, I'm surprised by the itch of anger working its way through me. I want to shake him. Yell in his face as I demand answers for why he did what he did. A moment of weakness on my part led to this, and I wish more than anything that I could take it back.

"James," I say eventually, pulling away. I wind my arms around myself, taking a step back. "What were you thinking? You can make that play in your sleep."

"I know."

"Then why—"

"Because I keep my word." He reaches out, but I lean back. Maybe it's stupid, but I want to see his face right now. I don't want to get distracted by him in any physical kind of way. Hurt crosses his face, but only briefly. "You know that I told him that if he used derogatory language to talk about you, I wouldn't throw to him. I said that at the beginning of the season, and it only became truer the moment I found out he actually . . ."

He stops, shaking his head. "He's a fucking asshole and he needed to be put in his place. I'm not sorry I did it."

"But I didn't ask you to."

"You didn't have to. You deserved to have someone stick up for you."

"Not like this." My voice rises a little. "You could have won the game! You should be celebrating right now! How could you do this to yourself?"

"Because every time I saw him, I just saw you!" he says. "I saw you crying. I heard the fucking fear in your voice. I didn't want to reward that. I couldn't live with myself if I did."

I bite my lip, hard, to stave off the tears that are threatening once more. Breaking down led to this; I can't do it twice. "He didn't matter. You should have won the game for yourself. For the rest of your teammates."

"You still don't get it," he says with frustration, working his jaw. "Bex. You're more important than a football game. Your safety is more important. Your happiness is more important. If you're not okay, then I don't give a shit about the game. All I care about is you."

I blink, wiping away a rogue tear roughly. "I'm sorry I fucked things up for you."

"You don't have anything to apologize for." He takes my hand, squeezing, as I choke down a sob. "You didn't make me do this."

"I did." My heart hammers in my chest. "I'm so sorry I broke down; I shouldn't have told you then. It threw everything off."

He shakes his head. "If anything, you should have told me the moment it happened."

I pull my hand away. "No. I ruined this for you. I took you out of the zone."

"And I keep telling you, I don't care!" He doesn't yell, exactly, but the exclamation echoes around the big room. I work hard to hold back a flinch. "I don't want you to keep things from me, I don't want you to feel like you have to hold things back. Nothing matters but you."

"And I didn't ask you to feel this way!" A sob works its way out of my throat without permission. I press the heels of my hands into my eyes, trying to avoid the onslaught of tears. "I'm sorry."

"Why do you keep saying that? You have nothing to apologize for. Tell me you know that, honey. Tell me you know that what he did wasn't your fault."

I shake my head. "It's just . . . your dad . . ."

"What about my dad?"

I press my lips together tightly. I don't trust myself to speak right now. If I ruin things between James and his father on top of everything else, I won't be able to forgive myself. "I need to go."

I head for the door, but he steps in front of me. "Don't."

I risk a look up at him. He looks stricken, scared. As much as I want to bury myself in his embrace, I know the best thing to do right now is to go. I should have left the moment the game ended. All I do is get in the way, and even if he keeps saying that's how he wants it, it's not what he deserves. He deserves someone who can truly support him, someone who isn't going to make him self-sabotage. Until I can figure out how to be that person, my presence is doing nothing but hurting him.

"I just need some space." My lip wobbles, but I stick to my guns. "I'll see you back in New York, okay?"

"No," he whispers. "Don't do this."

I shake my head. "We need to think. I know we keep avoiding the conversation, but we're heading in different directions. You're going to be living somewhere else soon, and you can't do things like this when it's your job. I have the diner, and I can't—I can't watch you sabotage yourself like this for me. What happens the next time I'm upset, but you have to play? What if I have an emergency, but it's the playoffs and you can't get away?"

"We'll figure it out," he says. "Trust me, Bex, please."

I want to, desperately, but I can't, not now. I'm too mixed up to think clearly, especially where James is concerned. I shake my head, darting past him. I hear him call my name, but I escape before he can say anything to convince me to break my resolve. I know that if I hear him beg me to stay, I will, and that won't do any good for either of us.

But that doesn't mean I don't feel like I'm letting go of the one person I can't live without.

James

"Last question, James," the reporter says. She leans in a bit, a grimace on her face. "Again, sorry for the loss. I was wondering, have you spoken to your father yet? I'm sure he was here tonight."

When I used to imagine my future, I only thought of football. I thought of the routine I'd have. The long practices. The Sunday games. The grind, day in and day out, in pursuit of a Super Bowl win. When I was twelve, just starting to realize how I could one day have what my father had, I snuck into his office where he kept his two—although soon it would be three—Super Bowl rings in a case on the desk. I took them out and put one on each hand, admiring the weight.

I loved football before then, but it wasn't until that moment that I knew what I wanted for my career. Anything less than the NFL became unacceptable to me. I wanted to follow in my father's footsteps. We've always been in this together, working toward the same goal. When he saw me with those rings on my fingers, he understood.

I look to the back of the room, where my dad is standing. He came in during the press conference, and since the moment I noticed him, I haven't been able to focus. I haven't gotten into the situation with Darryl to the reporters; Coach Gomez's official story about the loss is that we simply fell short at the last moment, but I know that my dad isn't going to buy that. He knows me, he knows I should have made that throw. He'll want answers.

But I want answers too. What the hell did he say to Bex? Before she left, she mentioned my father. He had something to do with her leaving, and I need to find out what, exactly, he said to her.

"Yes," I say, looking at him instead of the reporter. "He came to the game."

"Have you gotten a chance to talk about the loss?"

"Not yet." I sit back, trying for a smile and failing. My lip hurts like hell, even with the ice pack I used on it before the press conference started. "I'm sure we'll break it down, though. He talks about all my games with me, win or lose. It helps me improve."

"I'm sure he's still very proud of you," the reporter says sincerely.

The press conference wraps up, and I'm free to go back to the hotel. I could call a cab and go back on my own, but I wait for my dad to come find me. We're going to talk eventually, so it may as well be now.

When he finds me, he just nods. He wore a suit to the game, like usual, so he's still in a tie and jacket, looking as unruffled as when he dropped by before the game to wish me good luck. "I have a car waiting."

I follow him, duffel bag slung over my shoulder. "Where is everyone?"

"They went back earlier." He glances over at me. "No point in staying."

"Right."

Out on a side street, a black SUV is waiting. I go in first, throwing the duffel into the back, and tense up as my father slides in beside me. I know how he looks when he's pissed, and even in the dark of the car past midnight, the set of his jaw isn't promising.

But when the car starts moving, he's silent.

"Dad?" I expected him to have a lot to say, so the silence is nerve-wracking.

He looks over at me. The streetlamps outside make it so his face is bathed in yellow light. "Explain what happened."

I run my tongue over my busted lip, wincing slightly from the sting. "I threw high."

"Why?"

"The receiver hurt Bex. He's her ex, the one I told you about."

He breathes in sharply, his nostrils flaring. "How?"

"He—fuck, he forced her into a kiss. And then bragged about it while calling her a slut." I look down at my hands. "I found out during halftime."

"So you lost the fucking game? On purpose?"

"He terrified her."

"And what does that have to do with the game?"

"Everything," I grind out. "I didn't give a shit about the game when she was hurting."

He looks out the window. "You know I had a terrible rookie season."

"Yeah."

"So, I came into my second year determined to do better. I wanted to win, to prove I deserved to be there as a starting quarterback. But the third week of the season, your mother got into a car accident. T-boned at an intersection."

I'm so taken aback by his words that it takes me a moment to respond. "How come I don't know this?"

He looks back at me, working his jaw. "It happened so long ago, before you were born. I suppose we don't think about it much anymore. But it was a bad accident, and she needed a lot of support in the aftermath. Spent a couple weeks in the hospital. All I wanted to do was be by her side, helping her however I could."

"Of course."

"And I didn't do that."

"Dad," I say. "What—"

"The best thing I could do, then, was my job," he says, stopping me mid-sentence. "If I was focused on doing well, I was helping build the future we were going to have when she got better. I was building stability for her. Wealth. The team was paying me a hell of a lot of money, and I had a responsibility to them as well as her. The game isn't everything, but it's the key to your future." He huffs out a breath. "I thought you understood what you needed to do. I'm sorry he hurt her, and I hope she's okay, but James, look at yourself. Losing your head again over a girl."

I swallow hard. "She's not just a girl. You know how I feel about her."

"I do. And you ought to have handled this issue off the field, after, instead of bringing it into the game. When you're being paid millions of dollars to perform, you can't just shut that off, no matter what's going on in your personal life. What did you accomplish, besides making the guy hate you forever and lose the game for your teammates?"

His words feel like a strike to the face, and it hurts worse than Darryl's actual punches or my conversation with Coach Gomez. "You said something to her."

"Excuse me?"

"We talked after the game, and she mentioned you. What did you tell her?"

He sighs. "I reminded her that you have this tendency and told her not to create a situation where you'd choose her to the detriment of everything else."

"She thought she had to keep this from me because of you."

"Clearly she didn't," he says dryly.

"Only because I overheard him bragging about it and went to find her!" I make a fist, hitting my thigh. "What the hell, Dad? You can't go behind my back like that!"

"And clearly the better thing would have been for you to find out about it later."

The car slows as we approach the hotel. As soon as it stops, I jump out, grabbing my duffel before the driver can and hurrying inside. My brothers are in the lobby, clearly waiting for me because they look up as soon as the doors slide open.

"Is she gone?" I ask.

"She left a little while ago," Seb says. He has a concerned look on his face that makes my stomach somersault.

"What happened with you two?" asks Cooper.

I press my lips together. "Fuck."

Dad walks through the doors. He looks a lot more tired than I realized earlier. Older, too, than how I usually see him. When he sees the three of us standing together, he walks over. His hand settles on my shoulder, squeezing, and I feel my eyes burning, so I look down at the floor.

"The point is, your mother didn't want me there," he says. "If I'd tried to blow off a game to be with her, she'd have told me to get lost and go play. Her sister took care of her when I couldn't be there. She understood that I had responsibilities I couldn't ignore, even where my wife was concerned. She knew that we had to arrange our lives around the sport as long as I played it, and not everyone can handle that. I loved her for it then, and I love her for it now."

"Um," Cooper says, "what's going on?"

I ignore him, shaking Dad's hand off my shoulder. "Is that what you told Bex?"

"Not in as many words."

"But you told her that she has to shut herself away for me."

"Not shut herself away," he says. "I just told her the reality. It takes a lot of compromise, son, making something like this work. I wanted to make sure she knew."

I raise my eyes to meet his. "You didn't have the right."

"Someone had to know, because clearly you forget."

"No. Screw that." I clench my jaw, trying to swallow down the pain in my tone. "You knew how I feel about her, and you put that in jeopardy. You had no goddamn right to do that. If I lose her because of this, I'm never forgiving you."

"If you lose her because of this, she wasn't meant to be yours in the first place."

"Jesus, Dad," Coop says.

"Richard," says Seb.

If there's one thing I'm not about to do, it's start crying in front of my father and brothers. I turn on my heel and stride to the elevator, pulling my phone out of my pocket. I call Bex, but the phone goes straight to voicemail. I try again and get the same result.

After the third time, I throw the phone against the elevator doors.

CHAPTER 43

Bex

You're not going to report him? Are you serious? He was such a creep to you," Laura says as she settles back on her lounge chair. She's still in Florida for winter break. I'm so jealous that she gets to wear a bikini right now, whereas I just came in from shoveling snow in front of the diner, but I'm trying hard not to show it because knowing her, she'd just offer to buy me a plane ticket to Naples. Before the game, I probably would have pretty much lived at James's place during the winter break, but now I'm on Aunt Nicole's couch. The only upside? The apartment rehab is almost finished, so soon, Mom and I will be able to move back in. We've been hunting for some used furniture for the place since everything was smoke damaged and had to be thrown out.

I pick at my sweater. The diner is open, but with the snow, I'm not expecting very many customers, so right now I'm curled up in a booth in the back, laptop on the table. The real story about why James didn't make the throw to Darryl hasn't come out, and I don't think it will. But even though James and I are on a break, the issue with Darryl hasn't gone away. At the very least, both are facing suspensions, and that could get worse for Darryl if I report his sexual misconduct.

In the week and a half since the game, the diner has been just the dose of reality I needed. My life isn't fancy football games and playing around with photography. It's waking up early to meet suppliers and staying long after the diner closes to go over the books.

Only now it's missing James, too. If I'm not focused every single second of the day, I just revert to wishing I was with him. The urge to call him comes up about ten times every hour. I know I'm being unfair, pretty much ignoring him, but whenever I pick up the phone, I just think of the moment he gave up the game for me and want to cry.

Even if we stayed together, eventually he would realize that I'm not worth those kinds of sacrifices. And if he never figures it out, then he might end up doing something that will mess up his career.

I love him, and I have no fucking idea what to do without him in my life. But if it's between preserving his future and being selfish, I'd rather watch him from afar than ruin things for him by his side.

"I know," I tell Laura, mentally shaking myself out of my train of thought. "But they might expel him."

"Good."

"Is it though?" I look at Laura. While I appreciate the steadfast support, I'm not sure it's what I need to hear right now. "I don't want to completely ruin his life."

"He tried to ruin yours. He kissed you without your consent and tried to make you break up with your boyfriend! He's an asshole."

"Yeah, well." I bite my lip to keep it from wobbling. "We have history. He's not all bad."

"If you tell them, they might not suspend James." She shades her eyes, leaning in a bit. "He didn't start the fight, so he shouldn't even be suspended in the first place, but if they know the whole context, how could they? He didn't break any official rules by messing up that throw. Darryl's the one who hurt you and then fought him, that's breaking the rules."

"I guess."

"Even if you're on a break or whatever—which you know I think is stupid—"

I sigh. "Yes."

"—you owe it to James and to yourself to report it. You can't just let Darryl get away with that kind of shitty behavior. He shouldn't get suspended and then be able to make up the credits over the summer, come on."

"I know you're right," I admit.

"So what's the problem?"

"I don't know!" I burst out. "I feel like he already got punished, I guess. James took care of that."

"That's not the same as a real consequence. Who's to say he wouldn't do the same thing to someone else? Or worse? Maybe getting expelled would be the wake-up call he needs."

"You're right." I pull my sleeves over my hands. It's cold in the diner; that's something I should investigate. Maybe there's something wrong with the heater. I hope not, because that would mean spending money we don't have to fix it.

"You don't know he'll get expelled," she adds. "You'd report it and the student discipline council or whatever would figure it out."

I know Laura's right. Even though Darryl only kissed me, in that moment, I was afraid he'd do something worse. Maybe if we had been truly alone, he would have tried it. But the thought of reporting the whole incident feels . . . embarrassing, I guess.

"I fell for his shit and put myself in a position to let him do this."

Laura shakes her head. "Tell me you're not saying you think this is your fault."

"I shouldn't have agreed to talk to him."

"You're not in control of his actions. *He* chose to kiss you without your say-so. *He* chose to punch James. He chose to do all of this, Bex! Let him deal with the consequences!"

"If I didn't meet with him, then James wouldn't have had a reason to miss that throw." I sniffle. Tears seem to come so easily lately. "I let myself get drawn into his orbit again, and then I couldn't keep it quiet throughout one fucking football game." I swipe my hand over my eyes roughly. "I was a fucking idiot."

"I wish I could hug you right now," Laura says. "I would hug you so hard."

I smile, hiccupping. "I'd like that."

"You could come down to Florida for a couple days. Maybe it would help you clear your head."

I shake my head. "Thanks, but I can't. There's so much to do here."

"Okay," she says, reluctance clear on her face. "I have to go in a minute, but let me know what you decide, okay? If you want me to be there when you report it, I will be."

When she hangs up, I sit back, bringing my legs up to my chest. The bell at the front door rings, but it's just Christina, bringing in snow on her boots.

"Hey, Bex!" she calls.

I wave to her. "Thanks for coming in."

"There's a boy waiting outside," she says. "He asked if you were in here."

My heart skips a beat. "What did he look like?"

"He's blond." She grins, a little slyly. "Really cute, too."

So not James . . . but not Darryl, either. "Thanks. I'll go talk to him."

* * *

I BRING SEBASTIAN into the diner for a slice of pie and cup of coffee. He carefully wipes his boots on the mat at the front door, looking around the diner as he does.

"It's pretty in here."

"Thanks." I smile at him. "There are some hooks over there, you can hang up your coat. Want some coffee?"

"Only if you have a cup with me."

I look back at the empty diner. "I think I can squeeze in a break."

Sebastian settles in across from me in the booth, cupping his mug in his hand. I just look at him for a moment, nervous to talk to him alone. I've spent a lot of time with him over the past couple of months, and I'd say we're friends—we've cooked together a couple times, which has resulted in a lot of laughter and scolding Cooper and James for stealing bites mid-cook—but I've never been alone with him. He taps one long finger against the ceramic of the mug.

"James told us what happened," he says, finally.

I just nod. "How is he doing?"

"Terribly." Sebastian makes a face as he takes a sip of coffee. "I've never seen him go so long without talking to Richard."

My stomach pinches. "He's not talking to him?"

"He knows Richard talked to you." Sebastian sighs. "I love my adoptive dad, but he can be demanding. I know what it's like, being an outsider when it comes to him, and the family. That's why I wanted to talk to you."

I haven't seen this side of Sebastian before, and it's interesting. I knew he was adopted, of course; James filled me in on the story, but I never thought about him coming into an already close-knit family and needing to find a way to fit in. I certainly felt it at Christmastime, but I was the girlfriend, an outsider by design.

Even though I feel terrible that James hasn't been talking to his father, it eases some of the tension in my belly, hearing that Sebastian understands what I'm going through.

"The thing is," I say, "I don't disagree with him. James is meant to play football. I don't want to stand in the way of that."

"Still," he says. "He shouldn't have gone behind his back like that. James is terrified he's going to lose you because of him."

"Not because of him." I bite my lip. "I just don't know if I could live with myself if he does something like that again, only with an entire career on the line. If he ruined things for himself, because of me, *for* me . . . it's just . . ."

Sebastian reaches across the table and takes my hand. He squeezes it tightly. I look up at him with surprise. "You think you don't deserve him."

I feel myself flush. "Maybe."

"You know that my father played for the Reds."

"Yeah."

"So I had a lot of privilege, growing up. It wasn't like I came from nothing. But when I first moved in with the Callahans . . . I felt like I didn't deserve any of it. My parents had just died, I thought the whole world was over. And suddenly I had this whole new life, with brothers and a little sister and a new set of parents." He withdraws his hand, settling back into the booth, and huffs out a quiet laugh. "I was angry at everything in the whole fucking world. It didn't matter to me that my dad had been best friends with Richard. I wanted out. The first week at my new school, I provoked an eighth grader into a fight. I was a tiny sixth grader, mind you. He was twice my size. Two punches and I lost whatever element of surprise I went into the brawl with."

I smile at the thought of a little eleven-year-old Sebastian in his private school uniform, throwing a punch. "What happened?"

"James saw it and jumped in. Cooper was right on his heels. It didn't matter to them that I was this new kid, taking up their parents' attention. Their parents told them I was their brother, so they were ready to defend me no matter what. I'd been nothing but shitty to them since the funeral, and they didn't care. Not then. Not when I needed their help."

I blink, and a tear streaks down my face. "That sounds like James."

"Sandra picked us all up after—we got suspended, the three of us, mind you—and I broke down. I hadn't cried at all at the funeral, and suddenly I was bawling with a paper towel up my nose because it was still bleeding." He laughs again, shaking his head. "James put his arm around me, and I don't think he even said anything, but I got what he meant. We were best friends after that. It took me a lot longer to truly get comfortable calling them my brothers, but from that point on, we were inseparable. I didn't ask James or Coop to help me. They would've done in even if two seconds before, I'd told them I hated them.

"James is going to put the people he loves before anything else whether you want him to or not, Bex. I'm not saying there shouldn't be balance, I guess, but you shouldn't feel bad about what he did. He did it because he loves you, and I think he'd do it again. Don't push him away for being who he is. How he's always been, even if Richard would wish he wasn't, sometimes."

"How did you realize you're worth it?" I blurt. The moment the words leave my mouth, I wish I could take them back. Talk about pathetic. But it's been running through my mind ever since the game. James might love me, he might do anything for me, but am I worth it? Am I worth losing a football game? Risking a suspension?

Sebastian looks thoughtful; he doesn't laugh. "You really think you're not?"

"I don't know." I drop my gaze to the table. My cooling coffee hasn't been touched since we sat down. "Maybe."

"I don't know what to tell you to make you realize what you deserve," he says slowly. "What I do know is that you're smart, you're wicked talented, and one day, I'd love to call you my sister-in-law. If you decide that's what you want too, then I hope you find a way to work things out with him."

I wipe at my eyes. "Thanks, Seb."

"Believe in him," he says. "He wouldn't have done it if he thought you weren't."

CHAPTER 44

James

Cooper comes into my bedroom without knocking, flopping himself on my bed. I suppress an eye roll.

"Hey," he says, poking my thigh.

"Hey." I don't look up from my computer. "Didn't we talk about knocking after that time you walked in on me and Bex?"

"It's not like she's around right now."

That makes me look at him. "Seriously, man?"

"You've been moping for a week. Why haven't you gone to talk to her?"

"Because she won't listen." I scrub my hand over my face. I've had this exact conversation with myself a million times since Atlanta, so repeating it with Cooper isn't high on the list of things I want to do right now. "She said she wanted space, so I'm trying to give her space."

He peers over at my computer. "Um, what the hell is that?"

I shove at his shoulder. "Stop being so fucking nosy."

"A master's program? To become a teacher?" He looks at me with emotion blazing in his blue eyes. "Tell me you're not about to fucking do what I think you're about to do."

"If I have to pick, I'd pick her. So maybe instead of football, I can teach and coach somewhere around here. If she really wants to stick with the diner, I'd rather be there with her than off somewhere else alone. Playing football isn't worth losing her. It just isn't."

Cooper starts shaking his head before I finish speaking. "No. Come on." He shuts my computer and walks over to my closet, taking out my coat and tossing it at me. "Let's go."

"Go where?"

"Home."

I scramble to my feet. "I'm not talking to Dad right now."

"Maybe not, but you should talk to Mom."

"What?"

"Let's go talk to Mom." He checks his phone. "If we leave now, we'll get there in time for lunch. Come on. You're not becoming a fucking teacher or working at a diner or whatever the fuck you think you're going to be happy doing."

Part of me—a big fucking part of me—wants to resist further, but I know Mom likes Bex. Maybe there's something she can say that will help me get her back. And honestly, I miss her. I haven't seen her since Atlanta.

"Fine. But I'm doing this because she always wants us to visit more."

"Uh-huh. Whatever you say."

We roll up to the house in time for lunch, just like Cooper predicted. Dad is actually away—a fact Cooper knew but neglected to mention, the ass—playing a charity golf tournament in Arizona, so it's just Mom in the house. She opens the door with surprise written all over her face, pulling us into one gigantic hug, and ushers us to the kitchen.

"Do you want soup?" she says. "It feels like a soup kind of day. Shelley made these delicious little rolls, too." She pats Cooper's beard, tutting. "You should cut this, honey."

"I'm a hockey player," Cooper protests. "This is my natural state."

"At least trim it."

I raise an eyebrow when he turns to me for support. "You know how I feel about it."

"You're no help at all," he grouses. "What kind of soup is it?"

A couple minutes later, we settle at the table with bowls of potato leek soup and sourdough rolls. Mom leans over and squeezes my forearm, a sympathetic set to her mouth. "How are you? How's Bex?"

"I don't know," I admit. "We haven't spoken."

She sighs as she leans back, busying herself with her soup. "I was afraid you'd say that. Do you know if she's going to report that—pardon my language—scumbag?"

I suppress a smile as I take a sip of soup. "I don't know. I hope she does. She wanted space, so I've been giving her space."

"He's not just giving her space," Cooper interjects. "He's moping in his room and researching how to become a math teacher."

"Why?" Her eyes widen. "Oh, sweetie. No."

I set down my spoon, looking her in the eyes. Of the three of her children, not one of us got her brown eyes, but hers remind me of Bex's, just as warm and comforting. Fuck, a week and a half without her has been torture. "If this is what I need to do to keep her, then it's what I'm going to do."

"Did she ask you to stop playing?"

"No, but—"

"Then that's not the answer."

"Thank you," Coop mutters into his soup.

"But I don't know if I can do both." Admitting this hurts, but I force myself through it. "I know Dad has always wanted me to just focus on football, but I love her, and I choose her. If I can't be there for her when I need to be because of my job—if I can't focus on both at once, or let myself get distracted when I'm supposed to be playing—"

"James," she interrupts. "What do you remember about your childhood?"

"What?"

"What's something you remember about growing up? Anything you can think of."

I shake my head slightly as I think. "Um, going to the Outer Banks for vacation? That time we went fishing and cooked what we caught on the beach, when we made that bonfire?"

Cooper laughs. "Izzy was so grossed out by the fish."

She smiles; remembering, probably, how Izzy took one look at it and declared that she was going to eat ice cream for dinner. "What else?"

"Practicing football with Dad? The Christmas the power went out and we all slept in the living room? The James Day we went go-karting?"

"That was awesome," Cooper agrees.

"Why do you think these memories come up first?" Mom says.

I answer immediately; there's no question about why. "They make me happy."

"Yeah," she says, her voice softer. "Those are all good memories, honey. Why do you think you thought of them instead of the times Dad was playing away games? Or when he had to go to training camp every August and we didn't see him for a couple weeks? What about when he missed that big game of yours in ninth grade because he had to leave early to prepare for the wild-card game?"

"I barely remember that," I admit.

"When I think about my marriage, I think about all the good memories first, too," she says. "I think about all the wonderful moments I've gotten to share with your father. I don't think about the times I was alone, or when I had to parent alone. I don't think about the times he was away because he wasn't, sweetie, not really. We made compromises for us to have a life together. I'm not saying it was easy, but looking back, I wouldn't change anything."

I blink hard, swallowing down a sudden rush of emotion. "But how? He always seemed to be able to put everything else out of his mind, and I can't do that."

"A lot of trust." She rubs her finger over her wedding ring. "He knew that I supported him, and I expected him to put his work first when he needed to. When he was at work, he gave it his all, and when he was home, he gave that his all. You're not going to be able to do everything, and the sooner you accept that, the sooner you'll be able to sort out what's important. You *can* focus on both. It's not about one or the other, it's about prioritizing."

"But if she needs me—"

"She won't be alone. She'll have all of us. She'll have other people in her life who are important to her. But until you let yourself focus fully on the game when that's what you need to do, you'll never be able to make it work."

I'm quiet for a moment, letting her words sink in. It makes sense, but I'm pretty sure Dad never fucked up like I did. "I don't want her to think she has to keep things from me, or not tell me when she's struggling. I don't want her to feel like she's constantly coming in second."

"The fact you know that is a good start," she says. "But even if you do need to prioritize your job sometimes, that doesn't mean she's coming in second. What will playing football professionally give you? Beyond love for the game, because I've seen you play your whole life and I know you have that."

There's only one answer that comes to mind. "Money."

"Stability," she says, nodding. "Whenever things got hard between me and your father, I reminded myself that he was doing all he could to create a future for us, for our family. So that we could have all of this, long after he retired from playing." She gestures around the room. "Don't you want to take care of her? Think about how lucky you are to be able to do that while doing something you love. So many people don't have that option."

"I know you're right," I say. She is. The best way to take care of Bex—materially, at least—is to play football. "But she has the diner, and she's committed to it. If she's there and I'm across the country . . ."

"Talk to her about it," she says. "You can figure something out. Compromise, honey."

"Easier said than done."

She rises from her chair and comes around the table to pat my cheek. "I never said it was easy. Just that you can do it."

Bex

O rder up," I tell Sam as I set a plate of eggs and toast in front of him. "I added in some homemade apple jam for the toast, let me know how you like it."

Mom looks up from where she's wiping down a nearby table. "I made it, Sam. Rosa would have been proud."

"She would have been for sure." He smiles at me as I walk back around the counter. "Thanks, Bex."

"You got it." I redo my hair clips, then grab my notepad and pencil to go and take another order. It's been a relatively slow morning at Abby's Place, which is unfortunate, because I can use whatever distractions I can get, between mulling over what to do about Darryl and replaying my conversation with Sebastian. Sometimes I get caught up thinking about little kid James, defending his brother, and I smile. But mostly, I can't stop thinking about the mess of everything I helped make.

"You're all pensive again," Mom says, squeezing my waist as she walks by. "Are you going to take that order, or should I?"

"Right. Sorry." I paste on a smile and make my way over to the couple sitting at the table, two older women with matching tote bags and simple silver wedding bands.

"This is such a pretty photograph," one of the women says, pointing to the framed piece on the wall in the middle of their booth. "Do you know the photographer?"

I look over at it. It's a photograph I took of one of the farm-stands here in town that sells fruits and vegetables and cute little clay pots that the owner's daughter makes. In the spring and summer, they sell bundles of flowers, and in the fall, they sell pumpkins, then Christmas trees. I loved the way the flowers looked in their metal bins and focused on those. It was last spring when Laura and I visited; we bought a bouquet for our room and a bag of cherries to split.

"I took it," I say. "It's from Henderson Farms, right at the edge of town. They're closed in January, but they have really nice produce."

"Is it for sale?"

I blink. "The farm? I don't think so."

The woman glances over at me. Her wife laughs softly, putting her hand on top of hers. "The photograph, I mean. Is it for sale? I'd just love it for our kitchen. Reminds me of why we moved up here from the city."

"You'd really buy it?"

"Of course." She opens her tote bag and rummages through it. "I have cash if that's easiest for you. What do you normally charge for a piece that's already framed?"

I need to work hard to make sure my jaw doesn't fall on the floor. "Um, fifty?"

Her wife tuts. "Please tell me you're not undervaluing yourself like this. Two hundred."

My mouth really does fall open then, as the first woman counts out a whole bunch of twenties and passes them across the table.

"Unless the piece is particularly special to you?" she says.

"No, it's not that." I swallow, picking up the cash and tucking it into my apron. "Please take it and enjoy it, that's why I put it up in the diner in the first place. I'm just . . . surprised. I don't sell a lot of my photography."

I don't sell any photography, actually, but I'm not about to tell them that.

"You should," the second woman urges. "People will always pay for good art."

"Thank you," I say. "Um, do you want to order some food, too?"

They both laugh, then, and order two egg sandwich specials, so I take that back to the kitchen. Then I duck into the walk-in pantry, pulling my phone out of my apron to text Laura.

There's a new email alert from my McKee account. I shoot off a text to Laura about the women, then open the app.

It's from the visual arts department.

I hover over the email, not wanting to click down. I'm riding a high; the thought of smashing that to pieces with the contest rejection already hurts. But I'm not the kind of person who can put something off, good or bad, so I do click it, skimming for the telltale "we regret to inform you," or however they chose to phrase it.

I have to read it three times before it actually sinks in.

Dear Ms. Wood,

Thank you for submitting your work to the Doris McKinney Visual Arts Contest. We are pleased to inform you that your photography series, "Beyond the Play," has been chosen as the finalist in the Photography category and will be displayed at the Close Gallery in New York City this February 10th-13th. In addition, you have been awarded the $1,000 category prize, and your work will be considered for the

$5,000 grand prize. The judges were impressed by the level of range
and skills you brought to such a unique subject. We look forward to
seeing you and your invited guests at the prize ceremony on February
10th. Further details can be found below.

Congratulations on this achievement!

Best,
Professor Donald Marks
Visual Arts Department Chair
McKee University

I stare down at my phone, re-reading the email half a dozen
more times. I submitted a series of photographs of James for the
contest—some of him at work on the football field, and others
of him off the field, including one of the photographs I took of
him that morning in Pennsylvania. I hadn't expected anything to
come of it, not when there are plenty of actual visual arts majors
at McKee.

But they liked my work. No—they loved it. They loved my
range and my skillset.

Holy fuck.

I clasp my hand over my mouth as I scream, doing a little
happy dance. I know they probably intend the prize money to be
used for tuition, but screw that, I'm using it to buy myself new
furniture.

I want nothing more in the world than to call James. He'd be
so excited. If we were on good terms, he'd insist on going out to
celebrate, probably at the arcade or to get milkshakes or something equally sweet. I almost do call him; I bring up his contact
and everything. He's the one who bought me the new camera,

after all, and without it, I wouldn't have been able to get those photographs in the first place.

Before I can decide, someone knocks on the door to the pantry. "Bex, honey?"

I open the door. Mom raises an eyebrow at me. "Why are you hiding in here?"

"I won a contest."

"What contest?"

"I entered a photography contest, and I won." My voice wobbles; I'm on the verge of tears, but at least they're happy ones. "They said they loved my range and skillset."

Mom pulls me into a hug. "Oh, sweetie. That's wonderful."

"I won a prize, and I might win a bigger one." I pull back, adjusting my apron. "I was thinking we can use it to buy more furniture for the apartment."

Mom shakes her head. "I've been meaning to talk to you about that. Nicole and Brian are going to help us. They have some stuff they wanted to get rid of anyway, and Nicole knows someone who refurbishes furniture who would be willing to give us a few pieces at a discount. Keep the money and use it for tuition."

"You're sure?"

She cups my cheek, rubbing her thumb over my skin. "It's the least I can do. I know it's not much, to make up for what happened, but . . ."

"No, that's perfect."

"Bex?" Christina pokes her head into the pantry. "There's another boy here to see you. Not the same as last time." She winks. "I think this one is the football player."

My heart drops down to my belly. I have no idea if I'm ready for this conversation, but it's not like I can ignore him, either. He knows where to find me. I push past my mother and walk back out into the dining area, stepping around the counter. James is waiting near the door, taking off a cap; his ears and cheeks are bright red from the cold. He looks around the room, and when he spots me, his whole face transforms, his smile a mixture of relief and happiness.

"Bex," he says, "can we talk?"

CHAPTER 46

James

I hadn't imagined having this conversation out in the cold, but Bex bundles herself in her coat and leads the way out back, and I don't argue. At least she hasn't kicked me to the curb. I was afraid that would happen, since I got in touch with her even though she's the one who said she wanted space.

She crosses her arms over her chest, shivering slightly. I take my cap and stick it on her head. It's flurrying lightly, adding to the snow that's been on the ground since last month.

"James," she says. "Your ears look frozen."

"I'll live." I pat my chest before sticking my hands into my jacket pockets. The photograph is still tucked against my chest. Good. "How have you been?"

"Shitty," she admits.

"Same."

She gives me a half-smile. "I won that photography contest, though. My work is going to be in a gallery in the West Village."

My mouth drops open. "That's incredible!"

She bites her lip, probably to keep her smile from getting any bigger. "Yeah. It's really awesome. I just found out before you got here, actually."

I desperately want to pull her into a hug and kiss her silly, but I hold back. As much as I'd rather avoid it, we do need to talk.

I can't make her change her mind about thinking she's not right for me, but I want to do my best to try and nudge her in the right direction.

"I'm so happy for you." I can't help reaching out to clap my hand over the cap on her head, relieved when that makes her laugh a little.

"James."

"I forgot how short you are."

"Fun-size," she says.

I try to swallow. "Yeah. That's you, baby."

The amusement bleeds away from her expression. "I'm going to report Darryl."

"Good."

She takes in a deep breath, hugging her arms around herself. "Did you hear anything yet? Are you getting suspended?"

"I don't know. Coach vouched for me. Told them I didn't start the fight."

It's her turn to say, "Good."

We stand there for a moment, looking at each other. It's never been awkward between us; even when we didn't know each other very well, the conversation flowed, so I'm taken aback by the tension in the air.

"I love you," I can't help but say.

"I love you too," she whispers.

"I'm so sorry my dad made you feel like you couldn't tell me what happened." I take in a deep breath. Since the talk with my mom, I've been a little calmer about the whole thing, but I haven't tried talking to my dad again yet, and I'm not sure when that will happen. Getting Bex back comes first. "I want you to know that I'm always going to choose you."

Her expression shutters. "James."

"I know it's going to be hard," I continue. "I know I need to prioritize things better. I know that when I'm on the field, I need to focus on it completely—but when I'm off the field? When I'm with you? I'm choosing you, no matter what."

She looks up at me, her cheeks ruddy, eyes shining with unshed tears.

"I love you, Bex. I love the way you scrunch up your nose when you're concentrating. I love your laughter. Your talent with a camera. I love your passion and your loyalty and how fucking smart you are. You're everything to me. If you asked me to stop playing football, I'd do it in a heartbeat."

She sniffles, shaking her head. "Don't do that."

"Good. Because I thought about becoming a math teacher, and I don't know if I'm capable of that."

She laughs wetly. "Probably not, babe."

"If you need to stay here for the diner and we have to be long-distance, I'll hustle every single day to make it work. I promise. It doesn't scare me anymore, because I know that everything will be worthwhile if I get to call you mine."

She looks away, rocking in place as she shivers. Quiet so long I start to get a little worried. "What if I'm not . . . enough?"

"What?"

She meets my eyes. Her lip is wobbling. "What if it's two years in and I'm here and you're wherever and you realize it's not worth it? That I'm not worth it?"

I take a step forward, pulling her into my arms. I don't care that I'm supposed to be giving her space to think, she's cold and upset and I can't stand that. "You really think that?" I say. "You're my princess, you're worth the whole world."

She presses her lips together. "I'm nobody special."

"And I'm just some guy who's good at throwing a ball." I laugh softly, the sound caught in the cold wind. "Maybe neither of us are special, but that's not the point. The point is you're the best person I've ever met, and I wish more than anything that that's how you saw yourself too."

I reach into my jacket, pulling out the photograph. "I took this a couple of weeks ago. I know it's shit, but I love how happy you look."

She takes the photograph, looking down at it. It's a simple picture I took with my phone, and I liked it so much I printed it out. Put it in my wallet. It's of Bex taking a photograph in Mc-Namara's. She's wearing a fuzzy pink sweater and those pie-slice earrings, her eyes lit up adorably as she fiddles with the camera.

"I remember this," she says softly.

"That's how I see you. When I close my eyes before I go to sleep, when I daydream—I imagine you just like that, making beautiful art. Being you." I reach out, tweaking her earring; she's wearing the hoops I got her for Christmas. "You're worth everything, and you can do whatever you want to do, but don't sell yourself short, either. This is what you deserve to be doing."

She leans up and kisses me.

I accept the kiss gladly; some of the tension literally leeches away from my body at the feeling of her lips on mine, her hands clutching the front of my jacket. This is what I needed to feel right again, my girl in my arms.

When she breaks away, she cups my jaw with her cold hand. I just crowd closer. "I need to think," she says. "Not about us, but about me. About the diner. I made my mom a promise that I would take care of it, and I can't just . . . does that make sense?"

I nod. "I'll be ready when you are."

She presses her forehead to mine. "Thank you."

I kiss her again, hungry for more of her kisses after nearly two weeks of missing them. "Whatever you need to do, we can handle it. Together."

CHAPTER 47

Bex

I hang the last photograph on the wall, then take a step back, looking nervously at the whole set. When I arrived, the gallery owner, a woman named Janet who is quite possibly the most glamorous woman I've ever met, gave me an entire wall to work with.

Laura, who came early to help me set up everything, looks at me. "What do you think?"

"I think it looks okay." I wipe my sweaty palms on my dress. I'm wearing a little black dress with sheer tights, despite the bitter February weather outside, but I've been so anxious the whole time that I'm not even feeling chilly. "I mean, I guess?"

"Don't sell yourself short," she says, pulling me into a sideways hug. "This looks amazing."

"Great use of white space," Janet says as she floats by, her shawl fluttering slightly.

Laura bites back a giggle. "See? Great use of white space. Fabulous."

I release a shaky breath. "Well, it's how I want it."

"Good." She takes a few steps back and whips her phone out. "Smile, let me take your picture."

I flush, looking around the gallery. The other contest finalists are working on their own displays, and it's clear that most of them know each other, because they keep socializing, walking over to each other's spaces to offer feedback and compliments. They've been ignoring me, which is fine, but it doesn't mean I'm not a little self-conscious.

The semester is in full swing again, which means wrapping up my major requirements, enjoying one more semester of living with Laura, spending time with James, who wasn't suspended for the fight once the school heard my report about Darryl, and scaling back my shifts at the Purple Kettle so I can photograph some of the McKee hockey games.

This gallery show, the opportunity to work more on my sports photography—it's bumping up against the diner in uncomfortable ways, and despite telling James I'm thinking about it, I'm not sure what to do. Before this year, even the thought of leaving my mother alone to deal with the diner was impossible. I promised her I wouldn't, and I always intended to stick to my word. Now? I come closer to wanting to leave every day, but I don't know if I can trust her with the business. She's been more involved lately, but I'm still there most days of the week, putting out (metaphorical) fires and making sure things run smoothly. I wouldn't be able to do that from San Francisco, which is where James will end up, if the latest rumors coming out of the NFL are to be believed.

"You look so pretty," Laura gushes. She shows me the photograph. Honestly, I think I look super stressed, but maybe that's just because it's how I feel. In less than an hour, a whole bunch of people are going to be looking at my photography while I'm standing right next to the display. I'm going to hear their opinions. And with a little luck, I'll win five thousand dollars, although the painter across the room from me is seriously talented, so if I had to give the prize to someone, I would choose them.

"I guess so," I say.

"James is coming, right?"

"Yep. And probably his brothers, too."

Laura sighs. "Cooper is so hot."

I make a face. "You like the beard?"

"Definitely. Not that James isn't cute with his whole clean-cut serious quarterback vibe, but Coop's the one I'd tap."

"Good to know," I say dryly. "Considering James is mine."

"He is cute," someone agrees.

I turn, my eyes widening as I take in the fact my mother is standing in front of me, a bouquet of flowers in her arms. She kisses my cheek. "I know I'm early," she says. "But I had something I wanted to talk to you about."

I glance back at the display, wondering if maybe I should do some more rearranging, but my gut tells me no, it's perfect. "I guess I'm done. I have a couple minutes before the gallery opens."

She cradles the bouquet in the crook of her arm, holding out her hand. "There's a little cafe next door, Nicole got us a table."

"We can't be long," I warn.

"We won't be," she promises. "We'll see you in a few minutes, Laura."

I grab my coat and throw it on as I follow her out of the gallery. It's weird enough to be in New York City, but seeing my mother here? I can't remember the last time she left town, much less did something like this. Fortunately, the cafe is quite literally next door; I see Aunt Nicole in the window, sitting with a mug of tea in front of her.

"Bex!" she says, standing to hug me when we meet her at the table. "I can't wait to see your photographs!"

"Thanks," I say, sitting down across from her with my coat in my lap. My mom chooses to sit next to Aunt Nicole instead of me, which is a little weird. I'm irrationally worried I'm about to get a lecture, but there's no reason for that. I tap my ankle boot against the floor. "What's up?"

They look at each other for a long moment. My mother takes a deep breath. I dig my fingernails into my palms.

"Is something wrong?"

"No," she says. "Not at all, honey, this is a good thing. I want to sell the diner."

I just stare at her. "What?"

"Nicole and I talked about it, and she helped me realize what we need to do. I should have sold it way back when, but I didn't let myself move on." She blinks; when she continues talking, her voice is thick. "I've held you back for too long. It wasn't fair of me to try and tie you to it. I kept thinking maybe your father would come back to it, but he hasn't. It's time."

As she talks, my heart starts sprinting in my chest, and by the time she finishes, I'm a little worried it's about to explode. I realize with a start that I'm shaking. "Mom?" I manage to croak out.

"I listened in, the day James came to talk to you," she adds, blush coloring her cheeks. "He's right, you deserve more. You deserve to pursue your passion. You deserve to go be with him, no matter where he's drafted." She laughs a little, shaking her head. "Did I use that word right?"

"I think so," Aunt Nicole says, leaning in with a little nod. "Right, Bex?"

"Right," I say weakly. My mind is spinning so fast that I'm not even upset with my mother for eavesdropping on me.

"When your father and I bought the diner, we thought it would be something we could share, something we could build a life around. I didn't want to give up that dream, even when it was gone. I need to move on, and I need to let you go."

"Mom," I say again, my voice strangled, half a sob. "What are you going to do?"

"We'll sell it," she says firmly. "The whole building. You can use some of the money to help with your student loans, and I'll work on finding a place. There's an apartment near Nicole that I might rent. And I'm thinking . . ."

She trails off, blinking back tears. Aunt Nicole pats her hand.

"She's going to put herself in a program," Aunt Nicole says.

Mom nods. "I need therapy. I need to get my head right. I never coped with your father's leaving, with everything that happened after, and if I'm going to be a good mother to you moving forward, I need to find a way to make that happen."

"I can't believe it," I whisper.

"I know," she says. "But I'm going to prove it to you, honey. I want to be there for you, and I want you to have the chance to do whatever makes you happy. Truly happy."

I practically launch myself across the table in my rush to hug her. She laughs against my shoulder, hugging tightly as she rubs my back. "I love you," she whispers. "And I'm sorry."

"I love you too." I breathe in the smell of her perfume. A million memories rush through my mind; a movie of my childhood, the good parts. I'm not naive, I know if she's serious about this, she has a lot of work ahead of her, but the fact she's doing it at all is enough to rock my world. "Thank you."

* * *

THE GALLERY HOURS have just begun when I see James walk through the door . . . along with his entire family, Izzy included. Sandra I was expecting, but Richard? With a bouquet of flowers in his arms? He gives me a nod, and I nod back.

Oh boy.

I refocus on Donald Marks, the head of the visual arts department, who came over right away to congratulate me in person, but the urge to run over and tell James the news is almost overwhelming. I want to tackle him and kiss him right against the wall, but I'm sure that wouldn't be considered appropriate fancy art gallery behavior.

"He's an excellent contact to have," he continues, gesturing across the room. "I'll introduce you two later so you can talk more in depth about this. Are you considering a future in sports photography specifically?"

"Maybe," I say, and the best part is, I'm not lying at all. I could do that—or I could do anything in the world. For the first time since I was a little kid, the whole world is open to me; I don't have promises to worry about breaking. I'm free. "I really love the atmosphere of sporting events."

"That's important." He smiles, breaking eye contact to look over my photography again. "Truly excellent work. I'm sorry that we didn't have you in our department."

"I'm starting to realize what I really want."

He nods. "I'm glad, Ms. Wood. Do stay in touch."

The moment he wanders away, Izzy darts over to me, James on her heels. She has a cup of wine in her hand, which James deftly takes away before she can gulp it down.

"Hey," she protests, crossing her arms over her lilac velvet dress. "No fair."

He hands the wine to me instead. "After the stunt you pulled at that party last weekend? You're lucky Mom and Dad let you out of the house."

I take a sip, but I don't taste it. I'm practically vibrating with excitement. "Hey."

He kisses me quickly. "How's it going so far?"

"It's actually kind of amazing." I reach out and take his hand. "I have to talk to you."

Izzy looks between us, raising one dark eyebrow. "That sounds ominous."

"Why don't you go bother Coop?" James says dryly. "It looks like he's trying to chat up that poor girl over there."

Izzy looks over her shoulder. Cooper is leaning right next to a beautiful watercolor, gesturing with his wine cup as he talks to a young woman. She doesn't seem that interested anyway, but I have a feeling Cooper is about to strike out thanks to Hurricane Izzy.

"I'll bet I can make her think he has an STD," she declares.

"Wait," says James, but she's already striding across the room. He sighs, turning to me. "You look beautiful, by the way. Who are the flowers from?"

"My mother."

"That's sweet. My parents have a bouquet for you too."

"She's over there . . . talking to your mom," I say as I realize what I'm seeing. "Oh God. She works fast."

James glances over. "I think that was my mom, actually," he says. "She's been dying to meet her. But what's up?"

"My mom talked to me before the show started. She's selling the diner."

He pulls me into a hug so quickly I nearly spill the wine on the floor. "No fucking way!"

"Yes!" I hug him back, unable to keep myself from laughing. We probably look ridiculous, but right now, I don't care. The whole gallery could stare, and I wouldn't give a shit. All that matters right now is him. "Yes. She's selling it."

His grip on me tightens. "Princess. Please tell me that means what I think it means."

I pull back far enough to kiss him. Even in heels, I'm up on my toes, cupping his neck with my hand. I look into his ocean eyes, and I see a million possibilities. A future we can share. I see love and desire and everything I thought I couldn't have, in between shades of blue.

"Yes," I murmur against his mouth. I grin, feeling him smile in turn. "Wherever you go, I'm following."

James

April, Two Months Later

Bex kisses me again, panting softly against my mouth. "Wait, baby. Wait. When does the show start again?"

I keep fingering her, scissoring the two fingers inside her as I slip my thumb against her clit. She gasps, her next protests lost. She's right, we need to get back to the waiting area—the producer who came by before we slipped away warned us that it was almost time for the televised portion of the draft—but I can't help myself. I want her to come, I want us to be the only ones in the whole crowd who know what we just did. My family is probably wondering where we are, but whatever. They can wait.

What matters right now is making my girlfriend feel good.

She clutches at my arm, but doesn't try to move me away. I kiss her neck, resisting the urge to give her a visible love bite, and work in a third finger. I swallow her moans even though I wish I could make her scream; it's good enough to feel her clench around me, shaking as she comes. I ease out my fingers, letting her down from where I'd pushed her up on her tiptoes against the wall.

"Holy shit," she murmurs, looking a little dazed.

I kiss her again. "Fucking gorgeous."

She shakes her head as she rearranges her dress. "I can't believe you just did that. We're about to be on television!"

I lick her slick from my fingers, relishing in her taste. "I have it worse. I'm hard as hell and just have to live with it."

She shakes her head. "No way. You got yourself into this mess, I refuse to feel sympathetic."

When we look presentable again—although my shirt is a little wrinkled, and Bex insists her hair doesn't look the same—we peer out of the supply closet. The coast is clear, so we walk out, trying to look casual.

"I'll go around this way, you go around the other way," I say. "If anyone asks, I got caught up saying hello to some old teammates from LSU."

She rolls her eyes fondly. "I'm just going to say I was in the bathroom."

Ironically, I do run into a couple of people I know on my way back to the waiting area, so when I do manage to get back to my family, Bex is already there, deep in conversation with Sebastian. She's still a little flushed. I wink at her as I sit down.

She rolls her eyes, waving her hand at me.

"How are you feeling?" Dad asks.

We haven't gotten back to the place we were before, but things are a lot better than they were back in January. Even though we don't view football and this career exactly the same anymore, he's still my father, and I want him by my side for moments like this. He understands, better than anyone else, what I'm about to embark on.

In less than an hour, Bex and I will know where we're moving after graduation.

For a while, all the talk seemed to be about San Francisco, but there are rumors that Philadelphia might trade up to get a better first-round pick to take one of the three really good quarterbacks on the board—me, the guy from Alabama who beat me back in

January, and the QB from Duke. Back when I won the Heisman, there was no doubt I'd go first in the draft, but the loss in the championship game screwed with that certainty. I don't mind; there's no guarantee that where I start out will be where I spend the majority of my career, but the hope is that whichever team takes me is willing and ready to build a team around me that can win. I've tried not to think much about the specifics, because it's not like I can pick, but it would be great if we didn't have to be the only ones in either of our families to live all the way across the country.

"It's starting," a producer says, speaking to the room at large. "As a reminder, we'll be cutting between this backstage waiting area and the stage, so remember you're on camera. If you get the call, first and foremost congratulations. Remember to answer the call and then follow the green arrows to the stage to be introduced. The live feed will be played up front on the TVs."

I look at my dad, taking in a deep breath. "I'm ready."

He squeezes my shoulder, rocking me slightly. Honestly, I think he's more nervous than I am.

As the feed goes live, Bex holds onto my hand.

The San Francisco 49ers have the first pick. They take the quarterback from Alabama.

The New York Jets have the second pick, and they take the best tackle on the board.

With the third pick, things get interesting. Philly trades up from the slot at sixth, offering Houston a slew of picks in the later round.

I know, deep in my bones, the second they announce the pick is in, that they've chosen me.

My phone, resting on the table before us, rings. I'm frozen for half a second, but then I feel Bex dig her nails into my hand, and that prompts me into motion. I pick it up, clearing my throat as I say hello.

"James," my new coach says. "Welcome to the Philadelphia Eagles."

"Thank you, sir."

"You ready to work?"

I meet Bex's eyes. She has her hands clasped over her mouth, probably to keep from screaming while I'm on the phone. God, I love her.

Philadelphia. We can work with that.

I wink at her.

"Yes, sir."

Acknowledgements

My warmest thank you is for you, reader!

In all the years I spent writing to this moment, I never quite dared to dream so big. It's surreal to think of all you beautiful strangers taking a chance on this book. Thank you for spending some of your time with James, Bex, and the rest of the Callahans. I hope you loved experiencing their story as much as I loved writing it. And to everyone who has been here since my first faltering steps with this book in the fall of 2022, thank you for being on the journey. Please know that I see it, and that I appreciate it more than I can ever express in words.

Thank you to Claire, who encouraged me to finally put my sports fanaticism to good use and try my hand at a sports romance. To my parents and sister, my very first cheerleaders. Anna, I'm endlessly grateful that online fandom led me to you all those years ago! This book would not be finished, much less on this path, without your editorial thoughts and love. Thank you for holding my hand and letting me ramble as much as I need.

To Sylvan, and the entire team at Avon: thank you for believing in me and these books. I'm so thrilled to be on this journey!

TURN THE PAGE FOR AN EXCLUSIVE
EXTENDED EPILOGUE!

CHAPTER 1

Bex

June

I stare at the check on the countertop.

Twenty million dollars.

Only my boyfriend would bring home a twenty million dollar signing bonus like it's nothing, leave it on the counter, and disappear into the shower before even kissing his girlfriend hello.

I'm terrified of touching it, like if I do, it will crumble to dust.

Twenty. Million. Dollars. He told me that being the third pick in the NFL draft would come with a hefty price tag, but I never imagined it would be quite that much.

I can't believe he drove all the way home from Philadelphia without saying a word. We need to have a talk about the way I expect to receive big news, because this isn't going to cut it.

"He's back?"

I look over my shoulder. Cooper has been in a spectacularly bad mood recently. His team fell short of the Frozen Four, and even though he won't admit it, I know he's going to miss having James around. Soon, James and I are going to be living in Philly. I figured I'd live in the same town my whole life, so going even one state over is a big deal. Living with my boyfriend for real, instead of just hanging out in his off-campus house most nights. Since graduation came and went, I've been in a state of low-simmering excitement and panic.

Last fall, when my ex was harassing me and I made a deal with James that I'd tutor him if he pretended to be my boyfriend, I never expected it to blossom into this. This wild, weird life that's apparently mine. *He's* mine, for as long as I want him, which I already know will be forever. We're not engaged or anything yet, but knowing him, he's thought about how he's going to ask.

"Yeah," I tell Cooper. "Left this on the counter while I was cooking dinner and went to go shower. Without saying anything."

He raises an eyebrow. "Why do you sound upset?"

"Look at it!" I brandish the check at him. "Who doesn't talk about this?"

Cooper takes the check, glancing at it for half a second before setting it back on the counter. "I don't get it. This is awesome, you guys are set."

"He could have, I don't know, mentioned what his agent was negotiating for him."

Cooper rubs his beard. We all begged him to cut it after the hockey season ended, but he hasn't, so he looks like a lumberjack. If he's not careful, Sebastian is going to sneak into his room in the middle of the night with clippers. "You know him. He isn't really thinking about it. It's a means to an end."

"Only rich people talk like that."

He shrugs. "Might need to bump up your rent threshold. I saw your Zillow account."

I flush. It wasn't even a discussion that James and I would move to Philadelphia together, but despite starting to look, we haven't found a place yet. Cooper's right, though. The places I've been looking at us renting are laughable in the face of this check. He could buy an entire apartment building with money like this.

"I was being realistic."

He wanders over to the stove, peering underneath the lid of a pot. "There's realistic, and then there's depressing. What did you make for dinner?"

"Red sauce. And I made cheesecake." With the diner sold and school over, I've had free time on my hands for the first time since I was a little kid. It's weird, being in such a limbo. I've been looking for a job, but most of what I've done this June is work on a new photography series and cook up a storm. Sebastian has been helping—we're an awesome duo in the kitchen—but tonight he has an end-of-season thing with his baseball team.

"I love you," Cooper says fervently.

I roll my eyes fondly as I open the cabinet next to the stove. "I thought you didn't even like cheesecake."

"I like anything you make." He watches as I reach for the pasta bowls, which unfortunately elude me even on my tiptoes. I'm going to have to get the stepstool, which I hate doing because it makes the Callahan brothers—even my boyfriend—hoot with laughter.

"Here, princess," I hear James say. He comes up behind me, wrapping an arm around my waist and grabbing the bowls with ease. He winks as he sets them on the counter, apparently completely unfazed by my very best glare.

I cross my arms over my chest. James's hair is damp from the shower, and he smells like his woodsy aftershave. The Eagles sent him a ton of gear after the draft to welcome him to the organization, so he's wearing one of a dozen deep green T-shirts. The color looks especially nice against his summer tan. "I'm mad at you, you know."

He glances at his brother, who retreats to the kitchen table. "Why?"

"This!" I say, grabbing the check and waving it in his face. "What if I spilled tomato sauce on it or threw it out? Who brings home this kind of money and just leaves it on the counter?"

He blinks. "We're having pasta for dinner?"

"That's not the point."

"It smells good. I'm starving."

"James."

"What?" He wraps his arms around me, bending to kiss my neck. "This is a good thing, honey. We'll get set up in our new place and put the rest away in the trust. Besides, the check is just for show, the money is already in the account."

I pull back to look at him. "When were you going to, I don't know, mention the fact they were going to give you this money?"

"I thought you'd be excited."

"I am." My stomach pinches in on itself. I set the check down carefully, even if it doesn't matter, and turn to the stove, putting spaghetti into the pot of water I have going and giving the sauce a stir. Perhaps a tad too aggressively, because sauce splatters everywhere. I wipe it away from my cheek. "It's just . . . that's a lot of money."

"I know. It's great. Even if something horrible happens and I don't play—"

I make a soft noise. "Don't talk like that."

"It's not going to happen. But we're set, princess. I wanted to surprise you. When Jessica gave me the news, I couldn't believe it either."

"Bullshit," I say. James has never had an issue knowing what he's worth. I admire that confidence, but I haven't quite been able to emulate it yet. Even with our plans for the future solidifying day by day, it's hard to really imagine that I'm going to have a career in the field I want. A future like the kind I dreamed.

His expression falters at the clipped tone of my voice.

"Are you really mad?" he asks.

Out of the corner of my eye, I see Cooper slip out of the room. I almost call for him to stay, but that would be cowardly. I know we already annoy him when things are good and we can't keep our hands off each other; I can't beg him to stick around for our fights, too.

I give the pasta a stir. We have about nine minutes until it's ready, and pasta isn't the sort of thing you can let go unattended and still expect to taste the same. Nine minutes to blow up before we need to simmer back down.

"No," I say. I swallow the lump in my throat. "I just don't want you to surprise me. What's next? Did you already buy us a house?"

"I wouldn't do that."

"You did this."

"Beckett," he starts.

I bite my lip. Sometimes he'll call me Beckett in bed if he's feeling serious. Usually, he doesn't bother with it when we're arguing. Instead of deferential, it feels like a reprimand, like a parent calling their child by their full name.

"What?" I snap. "We've spoken about this before, and you went and did it anyway."

"I wasn't trying to keep anything from you."

"But you did!" I try to keep my voice down, but it rises anyway, sounding crude in the small kitchen. I roughly wipe at the corners of my eyes. "James, we've talked about this. I don't need you to keep saving me."

Here's the problem with that: he did save me. I don't regret it, but sometimes it feels embarrassing, knowing my boyfriend stole me away from a life where I felt trapped. If he had his way, he'd take care of me without expecting anything in return forever.

It's what he does, it's who he is—yet if we're going to build a life together, he can't do this over and over without me giving him anything back. He says my support is enough, but what's support in the face of the most concrete thing of all, money? Whatever job I get, it's not going to hold a candle to his. I promised I'd come with him to Philadelphia, but I didn't consider what that truly meant until I saw the check on the counter.

It's too much. Too much money. Too many implications.

"Is this about the diner?"

"No."

"Because I've apologized for that about a million times."

"I know."

"And this is for both of us." He gestures between us. "You think I didn't tell my agent to get the best contract possible for both of us? For our futures? I thought we agreed we were moving forward together. I'm not saving you; I'm just helping."

"We are."

"So why are you looking at me like I did something horrible?"

He takes a step forward, but I sidestep. I'm not hungry anymore. "The pasta will be ready in two minutes. I'm going upstairs."

"You need to eat."

I bite my lip. "I'll eat later."

When I'm in our room—James's room—I shut the door, slumping against it. All around me, I see evidence of not just his life, but mine—ours. Especially now that college is over, most of my things are here. My camera is on his desk. Our clothes are mixed in the closet. Half of the bathroom counter is covered in my skincare products, which drives him nuts. He added another nightstand; on his side, there's an alarm clock shaped like a football and the Gillian Flynn book he's reading, and on mine, my journal and the photography book his siblings gave me last Christmas. Our diplomas, framed but not hung, lean against the wall.

I gave Izzy my camera for graduation day, and she took dozens of photos of us in our caps and gowns. My favorite is of us on McKee's football field together. I'm hitching a ride on James's back, my cap knocked askew as we laugh. It's the one we've discussed printing and hanging up in our new place.

When we've spoken about Philadelphia, it's always been with the assumption that we'll be there together. That this room of ours can exist there. I want it, I truly do—but it's hard not to feel strange when he's a millionaire and I'm jobless. I love him and I know he loves me, but if we start a life together and it doesn't work out, what will I do then?

CHAPTER 2

James

I watch as Bex turns on her heel and heads upstairs.

What the fuck just happened?

You'd think she would be happy that once we get to Philly, we'll be set. I haven't bought a house, wouldn't do it without making sure she loves it, but I've been looking in the neighborhoods where my new teammates live, and I've found a few options for us to consider. I didn't keep the bonus from her because of some fucked up reason; I wanted to surprise her with a gift.

Cooper pokes his head into the room. "Coast clear?"

I scowl at him. "Set the table."

He watches as I drain the pasta and dump it into the pot with the sauce. "She didn't like your surprise?"

I serve two bowls, putting the lid over the pot so it'll be warm in case she decides to come downstairs. If she doesn't, I'll bring her a bowl later. Cooper brings silverware over to the table. He's still looking at me as we sit down; I can't tell whether he's about to commiserate with me or tell me I fucked up.

"No," I admit, after a couple minutes of silence. "But what did she expect, you know? It comes with the territory."

"We know this, but maybe she doesn't yet."

I stab my fork through my pasta and take a bite. I can tell instantly that she made the red sauce from scratch. It's delicious; she never does anything halfway. We're the same like that, and usually it makes us a good team, but right now, I'm resenting her stubbornness.

"I just want to take care of her."

"And you do." Cooper settles back in his chair, water glass in hand. "But you saw how she reacted when you found a buyer for the diner. You shouldn't spring big things on her. She freaks out. For the record—"

"I know," I interrupt. Cooper and Seb told me I shouldn't surprise her with this, and I didn't listen.

He gives me a pitying look. "I can't decide which I'd rather have around, your relationship or Izzy."

"Definitely me."

"I don't know, Izzy might have a hot friend."

I'm shaking my head before he even finishes his sentence. "No way. If you hook up with one of Izzy's friends, you're dating her. Izzy won't let you ghost. Whoever she brings around is off-limits unless you suddenly like the idea of domesticity."

Cooper with a girlfriend? Our mother would love nothing more, she's constantly fretting over him, but when I try to imagine it, my mind goes blank. Sebastian? Sure, one day I'm sure he'll find someone he wants to go out with. But I can't even think of the type of woman who'd be able to tame Coop. Even in high school, he didn't date, which, as I understand it, was a tragic blow to the girls in his and Seb's class year.

He pushes his pasta around the bowl. He ought to be starving, we spent half the day in the gym together. He takes a sip of water. "You're right."

"I'm not going to be here to smooth things over if you fuck up."

"Gee, thanks for the vote of confidence."

I sigh. Why did Bex have to go upstairs? "I didn't mean it like that."

"It's cool," he says. "I know that Dad likes having you around to make sure I don't embarrass the family."

He stands, taking his bowl with him.

"Coop."

He shakes his head. "Why don't you go find your girlfriend?"

He goes upstairs too, leaving me alone at the kitchen table. I'm glad Sebastian's not here, because I'm sure he'd find some reason to get mad at me and leave as well. Izzy, on the other hand? When she's mad, she never backs down from the fight, so she'd still be here, telling me all the reasons why I'm being an idiot.

Maybe that's what makes me call her. I can't decide whether it would be smart to go find Bex and finish the conversation or if I should give her space. Talking to Izzy might not lead to good advice, necessarily, but it's not like I have any ideas myself.

Izzy picks up on the first ring. "Who died?"

"What? No one."

"Then why are you calling?"

"I don't know, maybe I wanted to hear my little sister's voice?"

"Aw," she says. "James, that's so weird."

"Weird?"

"You could have just texted." There's some background noise, like she's sitting, or more likely, flopping herself onto her bed. I think of that pink monstrosity and shudder. I'm surprised that her stuffed animal collection hasn't suffocated her yet. "Mom and Dad are excited that you signed your contract."

"I need to call them too."

"Or you could text like a normal person. We have a family group chat for a reason."

I blurt what I'm thinking before she can draw me into a conversation about our parents. "Bex is mad at me."

"Oh. What did you do?"

"Nothing," I say. "Nothing bad, anyway."

"Did you propose?"

"What? No. Why would she be mad about that?"

"Because she doesn't like surprises, and a proposal is like, the biggest surprise." She gasps. "If you proposed and didn't give her time to get her nails done first, I will drive to your house and murder you myself."

"Jesus, Iz."

"How else can you expect her to get good ring hand pictures? The proposal game has changed. It's not enough to just ask anymore, you need to go all out or it's like, did you even propose?"

"I don't—"

"And before you blow me off, may I remind you how many Instagram followers you have? You have to give your future fans what they want, James. Patrick Mahomes proposed to his wife at the Chiefs' stadium."

Frankly, I hate my Instagram account. The woman in charge of publicity for the Eagles is thrilled that I'm already growing such a following—and have a cute girlfriend to show off—but whenever I post about Bex, both of us get way more DMs from horny dudes asking about her tits than either of us are comfortable with. Despite what my family might think, proposing isn't the first thing on my mind, but the reminder that it's going to be a whole production is annoying. If I had my way, I'd just ask her in bed one morning and be done with it, and I know Bex would like something understated as well, but Izzy's right. We'll need someone on hand to take pictures, the whole nine yards.

"It was a surprise," I admit. "But not that."

"James!" she says. "Did you learn nothing after the diner?"

"She didn't react like that when I got her a camera last fall."

"That's different," she says. I can't see it, but I'm sure she's waving her hand dismissively. "That was just a gift, it wasn't like, a huge decision."

"I know the diner thing was bad."

"Extremely."

"But it all worked out."

She sighs. "What did you do this time, exactly?"

"I just brought home my signing bonus."

She gasps. "As a surprise? Dad told me how much it is."

"Yes, a surprise. But she knew I was getting a bonus."

"Twenty million dollars is not something that just happens. No wonder she flipped out."

I rub my temple. "Yeah, well, it's not like it changes anything. We were always going to buy a place together."

"Money is important in relationships," she says. "Keeping news about money from your girlfriend, even if it's good news, is probably not the best idea, you know?"

Sometimes, my sister talks for an hour and I have no idea what she's saying. Other times, like this? She gets through to me crystal clear.

"Shit."

To her credit, she doesn't gloat. "You should probably go tell her you fucked up."

"I love you, Iz."

"Love you too."

"Don't give Cooper too much hell this fall."

She giggles. "This fall? Wait until we go to OBX next month."

Bex

James knocks on his bedroom door instead of just opening it, which makes me flush with embarrassment. It's his room, after all; he should be able to go in whenever he wants. I call for him to come in, and he opens the door slowly. Cautiously. I curl into a tinier ball, feeling the guilt pinch my stomach.

He's carrying two bowls of pasta, a fork stuck in each, along with napkins. He hands one to me, then settles into bed beside me with the other one.

"Thanks," I say.

"It's too good to go to waste," he says. "Thanks again for making it."

I swallow past the lump in my throat. "You're welcome."

He sighs, dropping his hand to my knee. He rubs his thumb over my skin, making me shiver. "I'm sorry I didn't tell you how much the bonus would be."

I poke at my pasta. My stomach started grumbling the moment I ran upstairs, so I'm glad he made me a plate, but it's one of a million little things he does without asking that reminds me he's pretty much perfect, and right now, that makes me feel like the ass in comparison. "It's not like it's a bad thing."

"No," he says. "But it affects both of us, and I should have told you differently."

"Either we're in this together, or we're not, you know? Like the diner. I still can't believe you did that."

He runs his hand through his hair, looking down at his lap. I'm not that upset about the diner situation anymore, but at the time, it led to the biggest fight we've had so far—the mess of January aside, I suppose—and I'm glad that he has the decency to be ashamed about it. He used his family's connections to arrange a buyer behind my back, even after I told him I didn't want his help with it. In the end, my mother and I sold it to someone who promised to keep it a diner. The buyer James chose would have wanted to tear down the building entirely.

"I know," he says quietly.

"That didn't have anything to do with you, but you made it about you."

"I was trying to help."

"And you made it way more complicated than it needed to be!"

He withdraws his hand. I bite the inside of my cheek. Why does this have to be so hard? Why can't I just be grateful that he wants to help? Laura keeps telling me that James always has the best intentions, and I know that. I love that about him. But unlike the diner, this isn't just about helping. This is something that affects us both, not just for now, but for the future, too.

"And like I said, I've apologized and apologized. Are we good or not, Bex?"

"We're good."

His eyes tell me that he doesn't believe me. "Maybe about that, but not about this."

"You can't keep these things from me, especially if we're supposed to be moving in together." I blink back the tears that are burning in my eyes. "I can't handle surprises, James. Especially where money is concerned."

"We're never going to have to worry about money if we're smart."

I wipe away the tear that escapes down my cheek. "What if we break up?"

"Baby, we're not breaking up."

I press my lips together, shaking my head. "No, I know. But what if? What if suddenly, things just . . . fall apart?"

"Why would they fall apart?"

My mind eagerly offers up half a dozen reasons. It's not that I don't trust him, but what if he finds someone he likes better and decides he wants to be with her? He keeps telling me I'm enough for him, I'm who he wants, but it's one thing to hear it and another to internalize it. "I don't know, it's just . . . it's your money, but you're acting like it's not."

"The only thing I intend to use it for right now is to buy some-place for us to live."

I scramble out of bed, nearly spilling the pasta in my haste to set the bowl on the nightstand. I pace, because that's better than just sitting there under the scrutiny of his gaze. "And if it doesn't work out, it's your place, not mine."

"We're not breaking up," he says again. His voice has a firmer edge to it now, and I know without looking at him that he's start-ing to feel a little bit of fear. We've had good months since we de-cided to make this work, the issue with the diner aside, and here I am, throwing a grenade into everything. "We can talk about money, okay? No more secrets."

"I . . . I don't know if that's enough."

The admission startles me as well as him. I stop at the foot of the bed, accidentally banging my knee on the edge.

"Fuck," I gasp. James is there in a second, kneeling to examine my knee. I grind my teeth, clutching his shoulder.

"Let me get you some ice."

"It's fine."

"It's going to bruise."

"It's fine," I repeat, jerking away from him. "Just—stop, okay?"

He looks up at me. Normally when he's on his knees, that means something good is coming my way, but right now the sight makes me sad.

"Bex," he says. "Tell me what I'm doing wrong here. I thought I was just helping us get to where we decided we want to be."

"I think maybe we're moving too fast," I whisper. "I've been ignoring it, because we're not really living together for real right now, you know? But now I don't have the dorm, and you have all this money for a house, and it's not—we're not—I don't know, I feel like maybe we should live apart in Philly."

I keep looking at him, so I see the moment his expression shifts. The concern for me is still there, but he's guarded now, feeling out the situation. I set up a barrier between us—not impenetrable, but one that didn't exist until this moment. He stands, swallowing hard, his hands fluttering at his sides like he wants to gather me into his arms, but is afraid I'll jerk away.

I want nothing more than to be with him. To sleep beside him, even though he wakes me up way too early when he leaves for training. To keep up the life we've been building together, moment by moment. But up until a couple weeks ago, we were still in college. We don't live alone here; his brothers are always around. Without the diner, it's like I've been living in a dream version of real life, and now . . . now I need to think about getting a job, and paying off my student loans, and what if everything changes the moment we're true adults, living true adult lives? What if I need to do it on my own eventually, and I fail because I never learned how to begin with?

"I thought we were going together."

"We are," I say. "Just . . . maybe I'll get an apartment, once I have a job. And then we can . . . see."

"We can see," he repeats flatly. "Does this just apply to living together, or the whole thing?"

"Just living together." I shake my head. "You can't actually think I'm considering—"

"I don't know," he interrupts. "Because I thought things were fine, and now we're having a conversation where I had to use the phrase 'break up' twice, which feels pretty fucking awful, by the way."

"I don't want to break up."

"You sure about that, princess?"

"I don't want to break up!" I cross my arms over my chest, glaring at him because suddenly, he's acting impossible. "I didn't say that. Don't put words in my mouth."

"You just don't want to live with me."

"That's not—stop being so frustrating," I snap.

"That's not a real answer."

"I'm scared!" The words rip themselves from my throat, silencing whatever else he might've said. "I'm scared, okay? I don't want to live with you and get used to it and then suddenly, if it's gone . . . be alone again."

My face burns with the admission, and when I blink, I feel tears. I shake my head slightly, wiping at my cheeks with both my palms.

James gathers me into his arms gently, like he's worried I'm about to yell at him again, but I just sag against him. My knee is still throbbing, and I can't make myself stop crying. He cradles the back of my head with his hand, the other holding me to his chest firmly.

"We're fine," he says quietly. "If you need some space, you can have space. But you're not going to lose me, I'm right here."

"You are."

"Yes. I am." His lips press against the top of my head. "Now, can we have dinner?"

"I feel like we should be having something way fancier, since you're a millionaire and all."

He brushes my hair behind my ear. "Your cooking is all I ever want to eat."

I roll my eyes, unable to hold back my smile. "James?"

"Yeah, princess?"

"I love you."

He ducks down to kiss me before responding. "I love you, too."

James

Bex comes with a hoarse cry, curling up against me. I pull her closer, so her pillowy tits are pressed against my chest. I feel her heart racing. She kisses my shoulder, scratching her nails down my stomach, making me shiver pleasantly.

"Good?" she murmurs.

"Absolutely." We've had sex pretty much every way possible, but she always finds ways to surprise me. Before her, I had good sex, but not the kind that truly makes you feel connected to the other person. Now? Every time she kisses me, every time she looks into my eyes while I'm deep inside her, it loosens something in my chest that chants her name. She woke me this morning with a kiss, tits in my face, and what could I do but tease her beautiful breasts until she was begging me to fuck her?

I'm not done, though. I came inside her bare; we've mostly stopped using condoms since she has an IUD and we're monogamous, and I want to lick the come out of her. Whenever I coax her into sitting on my face, she blushes and gets shy, which is fucking adorable.

"Princess."

She looks up at me. "Mm?"

I pat her thigh. "Come sit on my face." It's cute to see how her eyes widen.

"Babe?"

I settle against the bed, urging her to sit over me. She's hesitant at first, but once my hands are on her ass, she scoots forward. I press my tongue against her cunt, relishing in the breathy moan she gives me, and find her clit, sensitive still from the first orgasm. I rock her forward slightly; she drops one hand to my hair, tugging sharply, making me smile. I could happily stay just like this, breathing against her, taking in her warmth and scent, but she squirms.

"James," she says, her voice high, ending on a question.

I turn my face to kiss her thigh. My hands press into her ass, kneading her firm skin. "Be a good girl and make a mess all over my face."

"James," she says with a moan. "James—fuck—"

I hum against her in response, and the vibrations make her moan, smacking her hand against the headboard. I don't tease, I suck on her clit until she's grinding down harder, then lick down her folds sloppily. I can taste my come mixing with her slick and groan; I love the way she tastes, the edge of salt and earthiness. She never lasts long like this, knowing I have her caught, ready to ravage, even though she's the one on top of me. I dig my nails into her ass hard enough she cries out, rocking forward, finally letting loose. I lick into her hole, and I think my nose bumps against her clit because she sobs, her breath catching in her throat. She keeps riding my face until something comes undone inside her, and the moment it happens, I feel warm wetness spread from my mouth down my chin.

I look up at her. Her cheeks are dark pink, her eyes screwed shut. Her chest, still reddened from my ministrations, heaves. She looks gorgeous, caught in a moment of ecstasy. Not for the first time, I wish I could capture this exact scene; her thick hair tossed over her shoulders, nipples stiff and deep pink, her mouth screwed into a sweet little pout, saying my name. Whenever she squirts, it brings out something primal in me, and this time is no exception. I lick and suck at her sensitive skin until she's begging me to let her go, my chest swelling with the knowledge of the trust she puts in me, to allow me to see her like this. To allow me to taste her, fucking worship her, especially when she's feeling so vulnerable.

When I finally switch our positions, she's like jelly, clinging to me as if afraid she's going to sink into the mattress. I smooth back her hair and kiss her on the mouth, letting her taste herself, and give her the praise she's waiting for. "Such a good girl."

She pulls me into another kiss. "Say it again."

"Good girl," I murmur against her mouth. "I fucking love you."

"I love you too," she says, stroking my hair. "Sure we have to go out?"

* * *

SEVERAL HOURS LATER, I turn my car onto a tree-lined street full of beautiful old houses. Most of them are set back from the road, hidden by bushes and gates. This neighborhood, Cherry Hill, is in South Jersey instead of Pennsylvania. The commute to the stadium is easier on this side of the Delaware River, so it's where a lot of my teammates and coaches live.

Beside me, Bex looks out the window. I wasn't sure she would come house hunting with me, after our conversation, so I'm grateful she's here, even though it seems like I'm going to be living alone and visiting my girlfriend in whatever apartment she rents, instead of living with her like we basically have for months. Training camp is looming, and with it, my permanent move to my new city, so I need to figure out a living situation. I could just rent something, but I'd rather buy and have the investment, and the thought of having privacy is appealing. Plus, a yard means plenty of room for a dog . . . or for kids, later down the line. Assuming talking about that doesn't make Bex shy away even more.

Bex takes her hair out of its ponytail, shaking it out. "This looks fancy."

"Definitely."

She glances over at me. "It's not actually in Philly."

"No." I see the realtor, Kerry, slow her car and head into a driveway, so I follow. "But it's only twenty minutes to the stadium, so I won't have much of a commute. And we can go into the city whenever we want."

She shrugs. "I guess."

"Keep an open mind, okay?"

She gets out of the car after I park, grabbing her purse. "Sure."

I thought maybe this morning erased some of the awkwardness we've been dealing with, but nope. I lock the car and follow her to the front door, where Kerry is waiting, clipboard tucked under her arm.

"Hi," Bex says, shaking her hand. "Thanks for taking us around to look at houses today."

"Of course." Kerry shakes my hand too. She's around my mother's age, dressed in a navy pantsuit accessorized with a sleek pearl necklace. The team set me up with her; apparently, she's a go-to for athletes in the area. "If you're looking for privacy, this is an excellent option. Many other Eagles players live in the area, as I'm sure James has told you. And the schools are wonderful in this district, if you're considering children right now."

Bex smiles at me. "Maybe one day, but we're not even engaged yet."

"Of course." Kerry unlocks the door. "Everything is updated

and upscale, so if it's to your liking, you won't have to do anything but move in."

The entryway reminds me a little of my parents' house; the cathedral ceiling opens to the second floor. Everything is a warm white, with gorgeous hardwood floors that shine. Kerry's heels echo as she takes us through the rooms on the first floor. This is definitely more than we need right now, but it's beautiful, from the butcher block kitchen island to the stone fireplace in the living room to the original crystal doorknobs, polished and refurbished so they look brand new. I already studied the house online, though, so mostly, I look at Bex, cataloging her reactions.

She likes it, I can tell. When we get to the guest room that Kerry points out has excellent natural light—and could make a wonderful photography studio—her smile relaxes, taking on the genuineness I'm used to seeing.

"It would be beautiful," she says. She looks over at me. "Did you notice this when you looked at the listing?"

"Of course," I say. "I told Kerry we needed somewhere with plenty of space for your art."

"It was very sweet," Kerry adds.

She tucks her hair back, flushing lightly. "Thank you."

"Why don't you go explore upstairs?" Kerry says. "I'll be in the backyard when you're ready to look at the pool."

We wander to the owner's suite, which is enormous . . . and currently filled with the ugliest bedroom set I've ever seen. Bex evidently agrees with me, because she snorts, clasping her hand over her mouth.

"Oh my *God*. Who staged this?"

"A time traveler?" I can't hold back my laughter. "Why does it look so . . . Victorian? I don't even know."

"Maybe it was an alien," she says. "No human would think a bed this . . . opulent . . . is tasteful."

"Are those carved doves on the headboard? And . . . pineapples? Pomegranates?"

She nods, her shoulders shaking with silent laughter. I peer into the bathroom, which is not much better. Who remodels a bathroom and keeps the red toilet?

"So, we'd need to change this."

She wipes at her eyes as she peeks in, succumbing to laughter once more. I love her when she's like this, silly and loose; I pull her into a kiss just because I can. She indulges me for a minute before pulling away. "Definitely would need to do some remodeling."

"I don't even know what decade that's supposed to be from."

"We should ask Kerry if the furniture is for sale too."

"Absolutely not." I pull her into my arms again, rocking us from side to side. "But I don't know. It doesn't feel quite right."

She looks at me. "It would be a big place for just you."

I swallow my protests. If we find the perfect home, she'll have to move in; she'll see it's meant to be for us both. I need to let the space itself do the talking. "It would be nice to spend more time in the city, but I'll probably get recognized a lot, especially if the Nike sponsorship works out."

She shrugs. "That's happened already, and it's been fine. Weird, but fine."

She's right; we spent the weekend in New York City last month, and I got stopped on the street a couple times for autographs and pictures. (And one Giants fan who wanted to heckle me.) It felt weird, because up until this point, whenever it's happened it's been because I'm with my father. And when we went to Carbone for dinner with my parents? I felt more eyes on us than any other time in recent memory that Dad and I have been in the same public place.

Bex, for her part, was really sweet about it. I'd have preferred to be left alone for a romantic weekend with my girl, but you don't go third in the draft in a visible position like quarterback and not gain a certain level of visibility, especially in the age of social media.

She smooths my hair back. "Does Kerry have anything else on the docket?"

CHAPTER 5

Bex

As we crossed the Benjamin Franklin bridge into Philadelphia, something shifts in my chest. As lovely as Cherry Hill is—and I could definitely see it being a beautiful place to raise a family—it doesn't feel right for right now. We're only twenty-two, and don't know anyone in Philly aside from James's new teammates. Whether we live together or apart, being close to the culture of the city feels important. Aside from a tour of Lincoln Financial Field, I haven't been to Philly, and I want to be close to whatever job I end up starting, and near museums and restaurants and nightlife.

James slows the car for a red light, drumming his fingers on the wheel. "Bit of a different feel, huh?"

"This could be really nice."

"Definitely. There's a lot more energy."

"This is a seriously expensive neighborhood, right?"

"Rittenhouse Square? I won't lie, this listing is even more expensive than the house."

I work to keep my mouth from dropping open. The house in Cherry Hill is listed at 1.7 million, and when I heard that, I felt my heart drop like a stone into my stomach. James, meanwhile, was totally at ease as he spoke about it with Kerry. Usually, I don't think too much about how differently we grew up, but over the past few days, I've felt it more keenly. How can I live in a multimillion-dollar home, all thanks to my boyfriend's money, without feeling out of place? "How much more?"

"About 4 million."

"Holy shit."

He looks over, a grin on his face. "It's really fucking nice."

"It better be a castle."

"There's a rooftop patio."

I sigh. "Don't tempt me."

His smile just gets wider, more self-assured. "That's exactly what I'm doing, princess."

Of course. I shake my head. "The light's green."

The townhouse is, predictably, gorgeous from the outside. The stone facade and cheerful yellow door make me smile, despite my hesitation to go inside. Kerry unlocks the door with a flourish, though, and I have no choice but to follow her into an upscale, modern entryway. "This was built in 1800, if you can believe it. But everything is completely redone, no issues at all, and gorgeous to boot."

"1800?" I repeat. "That's incredible."

She gives us a smile. "It would be a wonderful investment. Philadelphia has many historical homes like this, and this is one of the nicest I've come across. Very lucky that it's on the market, given the street, and at such a reasonable price point, too. Why don't you explore on your own and let me know what you think? Make sure you check out the rooftop patio, the views are just lovely."

She walks down the hall into what looks like a sitting room, her heels clacking loudly on the hardwood floor. James turns to me, eyes bright; I can tell that he loves it already.

"What do you think?"

I trail my fingers along the sleek banister. "Let's check out the kitchen first."

The kitchen is devastatingly pretty. I don't know what I love more, the white quartz countertops paired with bold navy cabinets, the modern gold finishes, or the pristine Viking range that nearly has me salivating. Perhaps it's the long, gorgeous island perfect for everything from hosting a party spread to baking. James doesn't even walk around; he just leans against the doorway and watches me open the cabinets and peer in the drawers. Someone must have tried to make this floor feel more open concept, because the kitchen opens to a beautiful dining room, and beyond that, a cozy living room with a gas fireplace.

We move through the rest of the rooms slowly. There's a room with plenty of light that James mentions could work for my photography studio, and I do see possibilities in the white walls and big windows overlooking the houses across the street. Guest bedrooms, in case my mother or any of his family comes to visit. An owner's suite that fortunately is beautiful and not crammed full of hideous furniture, plus a bathroom with the biggest tub I've ever seen; even James, as broad-shouldered as he is, would be able to sit in it with me.

By the time we reach the rooftop patio, my heart is beating faster. There's history in this house, and room for a future, too. Maybe not a forever future, because having a yard would be nice, but for now? I could see us here, making it our own. The walls are ready for new art. The kitchen, clearly brand-new, needs someone to cook in it. The owner's suite could be a beautiful sanctuary, a place to block out the rest of the world. Every inch of it has charm and character, thanks to its history. I like the idea of not being the first ones to live here.

The stager knew what they were doing for the outdoor patio. Strategically placed plants make it feel private, almost like a garden, rather than a roof. The view shows off the city, streets of old houses like this and newer, taller buildings several blocks down. I peer over the railing at the street below and see someone walking a pair of dogs. Right now, in late June, this is lovely, but I'm thinking of fall evenings as well. A little fire pit and blankets to keep us warm, music playing softly in the background.

"Bex," James says, tugging me into his arms. His chest is solid and warm. I melt into him, despite the heat, and tilt my chin up to look at him.

"Hey."

"Houses like these are hard to come by."

"It's perfect." I turn in his arms so I'm meeting his gaze. "You should buy it."

He shakes his head. "I don't want to live in it alone."

"I looked at more apartments," I say. "I could get something nice. I'm not sure how close it would be to this neighborhood, but it wouldn't be too far."

"But you don't need to."

"I know. But I can't just be this . . . freeloader in your house. Not contributing anything."

"You're going to get a job, but money isn't the only way to contribute."

I pull away, giving us a couple feet of distance. "But it's important that I do. Maybe if we were married already, it would be different, but we're not there yet. I'll feel weird living someplace I could never afford to be in without you."

"But that's the whole point. You're not without me."

I shake my head. "I'll spend time here, I'm sure, but . . ."

"Space."

"Yeah."

His jaw takes on a harder line. I hold my ground, crossing my arms over my chest. "It wouldn't be forever."

"I thought that maybe once you saw somewhere you loved, you'd realize . . ." He trails off, running a hand through his hair. "It's fine. I told you I wouldn't push."

"Thank you."

"But you do love it?"

I nod. "It's beautiful, and not too far from the stadium, and a good investment, like you keep saying. Why not go for it?"

I know why he doesn't want to pull the trigger. I can see the hesitation, plain as day, on his face. I bite my lip. I just can't shake the horrible image of myself—now in even greater detail, if this house is the backdrop—packing my things and leaving the home I shared with him, just to be back where I started, all alone. If I'm going to move in with him, I want it to be forever, and I need it to feel like the playing field is at least a little equal. Maybe I wouldn't be able to contribute to a mortgage payment on a place like this, but groceries? The phone bills? I can't keep cooking him dinner and dessert and pretend it's an equal exchange.

"I'll think about it," he says, after a moment. "I want you to be happy."

"I am happy." I cup his jaw, rubbing my thumb over his smooth-shaven cheek. "I'm happy, and I don't want to break up. If you want the house, buy it."

He snorts out a laugh, but the amusement doesn't quite reach his serious eyes. He takes my hand away from his face and kisses the palm.

"What if we were engaged?"

"What?"

"If we got engaged, would that be enough to convince you? You said it'd be different if we were married, but what about an engagement?"

Before I can reply, he leans in and kisses me on the forehead. Feather-light, the way he does sometimes when we're in public.

I see why when I notice Kerry waiting by the door to the roof. I swallow, trying to keep a friendly look on my face, like James didn't just rock my whole world. I've assumed, for a while now, that we'll get married one day, but that's always felt like something we'd talk about far into the future. Marriage isn't just dating, it's a commitment I only intend to make once. With James, of course. But now? Does he really want that, or does he just want us to live together, and this is how he thinks he'll get me to agree?

If he got down on one knee right now, what would I say?

"What do you think?" Kerry says, hands clasped in front of her. "Sold?"

James smiles, all at once apologetic and charming. "Not quite. We'd like to keep looking." He glances at me, wrapping his arm around my shoulders. "And there's another investment I want to make first."

CHAPTER 6

James

July

"Are any of these to your liking, sir?"

The attendant, Erin, unveils a velvet-lined box of rings, each more sparkly than the next. With the promise of lunch at Gramercy Tavern, Cooper and Sebastian took the train to the city with me today, and we went straight from Grand Central to Tiffany's. Bex knows I'm in the city, but she thinks I'm just spending some time with my brothers before we move. Fortunately, she has a job interview today, so she didn't ask too many questions.

A couple days ago, I made an appointment at the 5th Avenue location that left no questions about who I am and what I'm looking for. It's a shame that Izzy isn't here, because it's how she prefers to shop: in a private room, refreshments in hand, with an attendant ready to offer more selections on demand. It's a little over the top, but I'm not interested in dragging my feet. I'm going to propose to Bex soon, and before that happens, I need a ring. Despite the slight embarrassment at the red-carpet service, it's nice to have the privacy to consider my options, especially for such an expensive purchase. I'm not looking for just any ring. I need one worthy of a princess. *My* princess. It needs to be the perfect assurance for Bex that we're in this together, for the long haul.

Cooper sets his glass down on a coaster and leans forward.

The room we're in is filled with Tiffany blue accents, and the couch looks delicate compared to my rough-and-tumble brother. "Yellow diamond?"

I shake my head. "That's not her. She'd think it's too flashy."

"The circular diamond is pretty," Seb offers. "It feels classic, like her."

Sebastian, perceptive as always. "Yes," I say. "I like the circular cut."

"I'll go fetch some more circular options," Erin says, tucking her deep red hair behind her ear. She gives Sebastian a flirty little grin. "I like a man who knows his jewels."

"Oh, come on," Cooper says the second the door shuts behind her. "You don't even like gingers!"

Seb laughs. "Maybe you're trying too hard. You made eyes at her the moment we walked into the store."

"And I was expecting an invite back to her apartment, which hopefully she shares with an equally hot roommate, but instead, she's going to extend you that honor."

"She's a little old for you," I say with amusement. "Either of you."

"I can dig maturity," Cooper says.

"Because you have none, so it's a novelty to you," Seb shoots back.

Cooper blinks, then bursts out laughing. I duck my head to hide my shit-eating grin. I'm going to miss this so much when I start my job. Teammates and friends are one thing, but nothing beats brothers.

"I'm still curious to see how you're going to sell this to Dad," Cooper says.

"Yes, I'm sure Richard will be thrilled," Seb says, his tone a touch dry.

I just roll my eyes. Dad's been a lot better about Bex, the more he's gotten to know her, but they have a point. I'm sure he's expecting us to date for a while longer before committing to each other. "He likes her a lot more now. He watched this photography documentary the other day and called her to talk about it."

Seb settles against the couch, crossing his ankle over his knee. "It is soon for an engagement."

Cooper nods as he takes a long sip of his drink. "I know we're here and everything, but are you sure? It hasn't even been a year."

I just shrug. "Hey, when you know, you know."

"Can't imagine."

"One day you will."

Cooper sighs and helps himself to more bourbon. "Ever since you fell in love, you sound like Mom."

"I love our mother, and therefore don't see it as an insult."

Erin sweeps back into the room, another case in her hands. "Forgive me," she says. "But you did say that the budget is . . . flexible, so I had a bit of fun."

She unveils another set of gorgeous rings, each with a big, circular cut diamond in the center. They're all perfect in different ways, but my eye is drawn to one in the upper right corner—a big, but not flashy, flawless diamond, flanked on either side by sapphires.

"I'd like to see that one, please."

Erin puts on gloves and carefully takes out the ring, holding it underneath a lamp so I see it catch the light. "It's a gorgeous 2.5 carat, so it's big without being too flashy, and the sapphires are of equal quality."

"It's beautiful." I can imagine it on Bex's finger. The diamond is classy, and the sapphires add a pop of color that reminds me of her. It's fancy and special and exactly what she deserves. I'm sure it's expensive as hell, but it's money I'd be glad to spend. She doesn't like when I spoil her too much, but I can afford it, and who wants their fiancé to skimp on their engagement ring? "What do you think, guys?"

Erin shows Sebastian and Cooper the ring. She has that sultry smile on her face again as she addresses Seb. "Yes, what does our resident jewel expert think?"

"It's stunning," Cooper says, but he's not looking at the ring. I nudge him apologetically. It's true that he's always had a weakness for gingers; he always stops when he's channel surfing and spots an Isla Fisher movie. An overnight with a hot older redhead would be perfect to get him out of the funk he's been in, but it seems like that's not meant to be. The one consolation is that Seb would never sleep with a woman that Cooper is interested in.

"Very nice," says Seb. "What's the band? Platinum?"

Erin leans forward, clasping her free hand on Sebastian's knee. "Yes. You know, most of the guys who come in here don't know a thing about jewelry."

"You sure she won't think the sapphires are too much?" Seb asks me, politely moving her hand off his knee.

"I think it's just indulgent enough I can get her to accept it, but not so much that she'll think she doesn't deserve it," I say.

Erin settles the ring back into the case, seemingly unruffled by Seb's subtle rejection. "You are the sweetest. My dad is a huge Eagles fan, he's going to flip when he hears I helped you out today."

I shoot my most charming smile in her direction. "Would you mind keeping what I'm actually buying a secret? Wouldn't want the news to reach my girl before I manage to pop the question, even accidentally."

She winks at me. "A jeweler never spills client secrets. So, is this the one?"

I look at it again, waiting to see if any part of me feels hesitation, but that doesn't happen. I just feel steady, with excitement starting to build in my stomach. I haven't worked out yet how I'm actually going to ask Bex, but it feels right to do it soon. It's not just that I want her to live with me, although of course I hope she decides this is enough to convince her. Kerry is letting me know if anyone else offers on the house, even though it's not the house I care about; I just want to go to sleep at night—every night—beside Bex. I've known since last Christmas that she's the one for me, that I'll accept no one else as my wife. The stability of an engagement, especially heading into our post-grad careers, would settle the knot of worry that we might not be forever that I can't quite untie, and I hope she'll feel the same.

"Yes," I say. "It's perfect."

"Congratulations." She peels off her gloves, fixing me with a smile. "Let's talk price and payment."

I take out my wallet and hand her my card. "Gladly."

CHAPTER 7

Bex

B ex, hey," Laura says as soon as I pick up the phone. "How did the job interview go?"

I make a face, even though she can't see me. It sounds like she's walking somewhere in public; a car honks in the background, nearly drowning out the end of her sentence. Almost immediately after our graduation ceremony, she went back to New York City, moving in with Barry instead of her parents—not that her parents are there much right now anyway, they've been preferring Florida lately. I haven't had a chance to see their apartment yet, but knowing Laura, it's a classy space, perfect for her to come home to after her classes at Columbia Law. Not for the first time, I'm glad that James was drafted by a team in the Northeast. It would suck to be preparing to move to California or Texas right now. We'll still be close to his family, I can see Mom and Aunt Nicole whenever I need to, and I'm sure that soon Laura will be luring me to the city with promises of fancy dinner and an evening spent clubbing.

"It was a disaster."

"What? No way."

"Yes," I say miserably. I'm alone in the house, since James and his brothers went to the city for the day, and at the time I thought I didn't care, but now I wish James was around so he could console me. "It was just a mess. They hate my work; they kept talking about the energy being wrong."

"It was a gallery position, right?"

"Yes, but they like their staff to also be artists. Apparently, I'm not the right kind of artist."

Laura sighs. "Well, boo. They sound like jerks and you're better off without them anyway."

"Bedford is the most prestigious gallery in Philadelphia."

"And there's your problem. Ugh. Philadelphia."

I laugh despite myself. "That's our new fanbase that you're talking about."

"I know James needs to be a man of the people, but do you? Everyone knows the art scene in New York is the best." The background noise cuts off abruptly, like she just walked inside a building. "If you're not going to be living with him . . ."

"No. I'm not moving to New York."

"You could."

"Definitely not. I want to be close to him."

She sighs again, more for the dramatics of it this time than genuine exasperation. I know what that sounds like very well. "Then you should just move in with him. What's the point of being alone in Philadelphia?"

"Or South Jersey. Apparently, a lot of the guys from the team live there instead, because the stadium is just across the Delaware River."

"You are not making any of this sound appealing. Wait one second." She switches the call to video so I can see her face. She smiles, giving me a wave as she flops back against a pink velvet couch. "That's better. I'll bet those guys who live in South Jersey have kids, so they need to be near the nice school districts. If you're moving anywhere, it should be to the city. I haven't been to Philly all that much—"

"And yet you're judging it," I interject.

"—and yet, excuse you, I'm sure there's culture. Somewhere. It is one of the most historical cities in the country, after all. And you'll find a gallery that recognizes your genius."

"I don't even know if I want to work at a gallery," I admit. "I don't know what I want to do at all. That's part of the problem. Before, I had the diner, and now I know I can do anything, and that's . . ."

"Kind of freaking you out?"

"Possibly."

"You have a rich boyfriend who wants you to move in. You don't have to do anything right away."

I groan. "I can't feel like I'm taking advantage of him, Laura! It's not like we're married, although . . ."

Laura's mouth drops open, correctly interpreting my silence. "Really? How do you know?"

"When we went to look at this townhouse in Philly—which was gorgeous, by the way—he asked if I'd change my mind about moving in together if we were engaged."

"Holy crap."

"I know."

"This is amazing!" She sits up, practically bouncing, making the phone freeze as it tries to catch up with her movements. "He's totally going to propose. You're so lucky, I can already tell that convincing Barry to pop the question is going to be more work than torts."

"What's torts?"

"A law thing. Do you think he's made plans yet? Where is he right now?"

"In the city with his brothers," I say. I can see the exact moment the gears start working in Laura's head. He told me he was going to lunch, and didn't seem weird at all, although to be fair, I was distracted with interview prep. "But I'm sure he's not . . ."

"Why not?" she says. "Want me to go see if I can spy on him?"

I shake my head. "Please no."

"You're going to say yes, right?"

I don't answer. I do know the answer; I want to marry him—eventually—and if he asks, there's no way I'm saying no. But it feels difficult to imagine being engaged. Having a fancy ring on my finger. Promising to have a future with someone, even if that someone is the man I love.

"Bex?"

I bite my lip. "I'll say yes."

She breathes out a sigh of relief. "I was worried for a moment there. I'm going to be the maid of honor, right? Or will that be Izzy? I totally understand if it has to be her, but then I definitely want to be a bridesmaid."

"Even if we get engaged, I don't think we'll be getting married anytime soon," I say, trying not to think too hard about what it would be like to actually plan my wedding. When James and I spoke about it on the way home from Philadelphia, he assured me that we're on the same page about having a long engagement. "We're not ready for that, this would be more about . . . assurance. Being on the same page about our future."

"I'll bet he's buying the rock right now." Laura raises an eyebrow. "Which means you'll be living in that gorgeous townhouse and considering your future career options without feeling so stressed out, right?"

"You make it sound so easy."

"I think you're the one making it too difficult."

I flop against the bed and drag my hand over my face. I'm still wearing my interview makeup, which I'm sure is smearing. As soon as I get off the phone with Laura, I'm hopping into the shower to try to wash away the nervous sweat and stink of absolute failure. Somehow, the fact it was a Zoom interview made things worse. "I don't know, Laura."

"There's no shame in being with someone who wants to take care of you. In fact, that's what most people want. If you truly love James and want this future with him, I think you need to give yourself permission for it to start now."

When I don't say anything, Laura makes a worried sound. "I thought that was pretty awesome advice, if you ask me. What's wrong?"

"Nothing."

"Bex, come on. I know you."

I blink. Now I'm going to cry, and in addition to smeared makeup, I'll have mascara stains on my cheeks. Just great. I shake my head, suddenly unable to speak through the knot in my throat.

Laura is quiet for a moment, letting me breathe, but eventually she tries again. "Let's talk about this. You're going to be engaged soon! You should be excited."

"I am excited," I say thickly. "It's just . . . I'm scared, too."

"You said yourself that it's not like you're actually getting married right away."

"No, I know, but . . . what if it doesn't last? What if I move in and get used to this whole life, and then we break up and I'm alone? And all the way back at square one?"

"You wouldn't be at square one, for one thing."

I just shake my head.

"You wouldn't," she says firmly. "The diner was square one.

You've moved on from that. And if you do break up and need to move out—which isn't going to happen, because you're madly in love and I know he is too—then you come straight to me. You'll stay with me and Barry, we'll cry enough to fill the bathtub, and then I'll help you figure out the next steps."

I smile despite myself. "Really?"

"Of course. You think I won't be there for you? Please. You're stuck with me, even if you're moving to an inferior city."

"I love you," I say helplessly. Laura always knows what to say. She's going to make an excellent lawyer—and if I told her that, she'd just say, "I know."

"I love you too," she says. "And I wish I could hug you right now, as always. But Bex? You're not going to break up with him. You two are forever, and you know it. Why torture yourself, and him, when you can be happy? You don't have to have everything figured out to enjoy it."

I sit up. "You're right."

"Of course I'm right. Do you have pictures of the townhouse? Send them to me so we can start decorating."

I smile. "You're going to love the rooftop patio. Just let me jump in the shower first."

CHAPTER 8

James

Bex bounces on the edge of the bed as she watches me change into my bathing suit. "What do you want to do first? Ocean or pool?"

We've been at the rental house for about half an hour, and in that time, Izzy went to sunbathe, Seb and Coop argued over which of them the flight attendant flirted with, Dad mapped out the restaurant schedule, and the housekeeper dropped off enough groceries to feed an army. You'd think we were settling in for the month, rather than just the week.

I pull off my shirt, leaning over for a kiss when she reaches for me.

"Ocean," I say, kissing both her cheeks before brushing my lips against hers. "Because someone's never been. And somehow, I've never seen you in a bathing suit."

Bex bites her lip. "You'll hold onto me?"

"Of course, baby."

She slides off the bed and goes to her suitcase, pulling out something that will no doubt look hot as hell on her. While I would like the show, I don't mind when she disappears into the bathroom. I check the side pocket of my backpack yet again, making sure that the little square box is still tucked inside.

I've gone on family vacations to Kitty Hawk for years, but never with a girlfriend . . . and especially not with an engagement ring in hand. I've thought about how to propose for the better part of two weeks, and when it came down to it, I couldn't think of a better way than somewhere private and beautiful, with my family on hand to celebrate. It's not a proposal in my future football stadium, but Bex wouldn't want that anyway.

I tuck the box into my pocket and knock on the bathroom door. "I'm going to talk to my parents, okay? See you down at the beach."

While I'm not about to ask my parents' permission to propose, I don't want to surprise them when I get down on one knee. Mom will be thrilled, but I'm not sure about Dad. Even with the ring in my pocket, my conversation with Cooper and Sebastian echoes in my head.

I find my parents in the kitchen. I knock on the doorframe, interrupting their quiet conversation. They're officially in vacation mode; my mother is in a bathing suit and lacy coverup, big sunglasses perched atop her head, and it looks like my father has broken out the Hawaiian shirts.

"Hey."

Mom looks up. "Hi, sweetie. What are you and Bex up to this afternoon? Cooper and Sebastian are at the beach with Izzy."

"I think that's what we're going to do too," I say. I lean over the kitchen island. "I just . . . had something I wanted to talk about with you first."

Dad looks up from his phone. "What's up?"

I run my hand through my hair, scratching the nape of my neck. My heart jumps with nervousness, but I push forward anyway. "I wanted to let you know that . . . I'm going to propose. This week."

Mom puts her hand over her mouth to muffle her cry of excitement. She turns to Dad, her eyes shining, as she grabs his arm. "Oh, James! That's wonderful. Isn't it wonderful, Richard?"

Dad taps his phone against the table, pursing his lips. "It hasn't even been a year."

"Oh, don't be hypocritical," Mom says. "We barely dated for a month before you proposed."

I raise my eyebrows. "Seriously? I thought it was a couple years."

"That was the official proposal." She smiles at my dad, who sighs, shaking his head. At least the expression on his face is fond. "We discussed it very soon after we started to date. What did you say again?"

Dad kisses her cheek. "I said that I was going to marry you one day."

"And you were quite determined, I remember."

"I knew what I wanted."

"And I know what I want," I say. "We're not going to get married right away, but we know we're it for each other, so why not make it official?"

Mom sighs happily. "You've always had a romantic side."

I take a seat at the kitchen table. Dad doesn't look horrified, or anything, but it would be nice if he stopped looking at me like he's expecting me to backtrack and say I was just joking. Mom reaches over and squeezes my hand. "How are you going to do it? Do you need a ring? You could use my mother's ring; the emerald is just gorgeous. I always planned to offer it to you, or perhaps Cooper, when you were ready."

Dad snorts. "You'll be waiting quite a while if you're hoping Cooper will take it."

"Oh, shush," Mom tells him. "Cooper will find his way eventually."

I pull out the ring box and set it on the table. "Save Grandmother's ring for Cooper. He'll appreciate it. I picked something out for Bex before we came down."

Mom opens the box, gasping when she sees the ring. Dad raises an eyebrow after taking a peek.

"That's quite the ring," he says. "Tiffany's?"

"What, the box didn't give it away?"

"She's going to love it," Mom says. "A circular diamond works perfectly for her."

"It's a bit close to the start of the season to propose, don't you think?" Dad says. "You need to be focused."

"I thought we agreed that you'd let me handle my work-life balance myself," I say.

It's taken us a while to get to this point, and I'll admit that I am still nervous about making my NFL career work alongside a fulfilled personal life, but at the end of the day, I need to work on it myself, in my own way. I know that the steadiness of my relationship—a fiancée, a house together—will help remind me what I'm working for every day, but given my track record, I don't blame my father's hesitation.

Dad, for his part, leans back in his chair. "Just make sure you feel good about it."

"I do."

"Then I'm happy for—oh, Bex, hello."

I grab the ring box and shove it into my pocket as Bex walks into the room. She's in the middle of putting her hair into a ponytail, and her blue and white tie dye bikini shows off her curves beautifully. She's going to look amazing with my ring on her finger, but it's not time yet. When I propose, it's going to be special, not while we're standing in little more than underwear in a kitchen with my parents.

"Hey," she says, cocking her head to the side. "Am I interrupting?"

"Nope." I stand and kiss her cheek. "I just realized I forgot my sunglasses upstairs. I'll go grab those and meet you on the beach."

I bound upstairs before she can say anything else and hide the ring. By the time I actually find my sunglasses and grab sandals and a towel, Bex is sunbathing next to Izzy. The two dots floating in the ocean way out from the shore are Seb and Coop, I assume.

She shades her eyes as she looks up at me. "Hey, babe. There you are."

I pull her up. "Come swim with me."

Izzy turns the page of the magazine she's reading. "You were too slow. We're hanging out. I need her advice now that there's finally another girl around."

Bex stands, hanging on to my hand. "Want to swim with us? We can talk about Christian there."

"Who's Christian?" I ask.

"A server at the club," Izzy says. "Not that it's any of your business."

"And how old is Christian?"

She tosses her magazine to the side and sits up with a sigh. "See, Bex? Any mention of a boy and he decides it's his business."

"It's my business if it's Christian Rozzi, who, last I remembered, is my age."

"And last *I* remembered, you're only four years older than me," she shoots back. "Not everyone finds love in their class year, James."

Bex looks at me, squinting against the sun. "She likes him. He's doing a masters in the city, so he won't be far from McKee."

"Oh, joy."

"If I had a little sibling, I'd rather they date someone I already know," she adds, her voice teasing now. She pokes my stomach. "Take me swimming. Iz, come on, I've never been in the ocean before."

"What?" Izzy says, scrambling to her feet. "Do you know how to swim?"

"Thanks to the pool at the Y, yes."

"Don't let any of my idiot brothers dunk you under. But if they do, I'll pull on their hair."

They high-five. "Solid plan," says Bex, giggling when she sees the stony expression on my face.

She takes off running in the direction of the ocean. Izzy sticks her tongue out at me and follows. I give them a few seconds head start, watching Bex's ass in that cute little bikini bottom, but I catch up when she wades into the water, laughing as she hops around.

"It's cold!" she says.

"You'll get used to it."

"Carry me in?"

I lift her into my arms, and she steadies herself by wrapping her arms around my neck. She shivers, pressing her face against my chest, as I wade into the surf. It's calm today, good conditions for someone who has never been in the ocean before, but she's right, it's a little chilly. Eventually, it gets deep enough I have to let her down, and she splashes around, shaking but smiling, as I tread water next to her.

Cooper and Seb swim over. Seb looks like a seal, his dark blond hair plastered to his forehead. Cooper has on a pair of sunglasses that are definitely too expensive to risk losing in the water, but he's never worried about things like that. Izzy swims next to us, wrapping her arm around Cooper's to steady herself.

"How's it going?" Seb asks.

"This is Bex's first time in the ocean," Izzy says.

Cooper gestures to Bex with his free hand. "Enjoying it?"

Bex's lips are looking a bit blue, but she smiles. "I thought there would be seaweed and I'm happy I was wrong."

Seb laughs. "It's really calm and clean today. But I like when the surf is rough, it's great for body surfing."

She makes a face. "Maybe I'll watch that from the shore."

"You're going to love this whole trip," Izzy says. "We're having dinner at the club tonight, but I always make us go to get ice cream at Big Bucks after. And when the boys go golfing tomorrow, we're going to the spa with Mom. Think about what color you want for your nails."

"Oh, that's so sweet," Bex says. "Did you already make reservations? How much is it?"

"Don't worry about it," Izzy says. "It's a welcome to the fa— welcome to OBX gift."

She shoots me a guilty look, but if Bex puts the dots together, she doesn't say anything. Since we've talked about it, it's not a surprise that I'll be proposing soon, but it's fun for there to be at least some anticipation.

I just hope Bex doesn't surprise me with her answer.

CHAPTER 9

Bex

I set my empty wineglass on the coffee table, tucking my feet up underneath me as I nestle against James's side. He puts his arm around me, pressing a kiss to my forehead before going back to his conversation with his father. I tuned it out a while ago, but last I heard, they were discussing the upcoming training camp, James's first real time practicing with his new team ahead of the season opener in September. On my other side, I hear Izzy teasing Seb about the girl at the ice cream shop who flirted with him shamelessly while we waited for our sundaes. It sounds like the hot streak he's been on is continuing, much to the chagrin of Cooper.

I look up. We're outside on the patio, sitting in a circle around the low light of the fire pit. The sky is so clear out here, dotted with tiny stars, and the moon, nearly full, hangs like a perfect pendant. In the background, an Allman Brothers record plays. The wine is making me warm in a pleasant way. This is the furthest south I've ever been, and I like it; the salty ocean air feels fresh, even in the humidity.

"Bex."

I lift my head up at the sound of Richard's voice. "Yeah?"

"I've been meaning to mention that I was talking to an old friend the other day, and his husband works for Temple University. He's going to pass along your information."

"Oh." I glance at James, who shrugs. "Um, cool? What does he do?"

"He works for their football team. Which plays home games at Lincoln Financial."

"Seriously?"

"Yes. He said his husband might be able to put in a good word with their media department." He settles back in his chair, swirling around his glass of whiskey. "Of course, it might not interest you, but if it works out, you could work as a photographer for Temple."

James's face breaks into a smile. "Wow, Dad."

"Yeah, thank you." I sit up properly, James's arm still around me, and smile at his father. Working at another university would be awesome, and I know I have the portfolio to back it up if they do end up taking a look. Maybe it's a better bet than trying to get into the fine arts scene through a gallery, or news photography with a magazine. "But Temple would play on Saturdays mostly, right?"

"We'd both be spending a lot of time at the stadium," James agrees.

"I'll give you his contact information tomorrow," Richard says. "It could be a possibility."

"Definitely, thank you." If it does work out, it would feel weird to get my first job thanks to Richard Callahan's connections, but at least I know I have the talent to handle it. "I've been applying mostly to galleries and magazines, but I like the idea of staying in the sports world. I've also been floating around the idea of freelance photography, rather than a staff job."

"The senior portrait you took of Izzy is just lovely," Sandra cuts in. "You'd be excellent at that kind of work."

"You'll be wonderful at whatever you do," James says, squeezing my shoulder.

"Thanks." The praise on top of the lingering warmth from my glass of wine is making me blush. I reach for James's hand, squeezing lightly. "I'm feeling pretty tired, I think I'm going to head upstairs."

"I'll go with you," James says as I stand.

I can tell why the moment we're inside the house. He pushes me against the kitchen counter and kisses me, his hands finding the fabric of my dress and bunching it up. I kiss back, moaning quietly when he nips at my bottom lip. I nearly take it a step further by cupping his crotch so I can massage him over his pants, but I remember his whole family is right outside. Upstairs, in the bedroom we're sharing, we'll have a greater chance at privacy. It's not foolproof, but at least we won't be giving his parents a show on purpose.

I whisper in his ear, "Come up in a few minutes." Then I kiss his cheek and saunter out of the room—but not before letting the straps of my dress fall down my shoulders. I look at him, pleased to see the heat in his gaze, and bite my lip.

He takes a step forward, but stops when I shake my head. "Wait. I'll make it worth your while."

I head upstairs slowly, knowing he's listening for each of my footsteps. At the door to our room, I slip out of my dress entirely, letting it pool on the floor like it's made of liquid. I leave it there for him to find and do the same with my bra once I'm in the room, and then my panties, leaving a trail to the ensuite bathroom.

I turn on the shower and let the spray warm up, rooting around in the cabinet for the aromatics I bought at an outdoor market this afternoon. Soon the bathroom is filled with steam and smells like rosewater, and I'm soaking wet—both from the shower and from the way I'm touching myself, imagining the expression on James's face when he finds me.

I'm starting to get antsy with anticipation when the door opens. James walks in, my panties in hand. When he spots me through the swirl of steam, he stops.

I drag slick hands up to my breasts, playing with my hard nipples. If there's one thing he's never been able to resist, it's my tits. He licks his upper lip, shaking his head in disbelief . . . and brings my panties to his nose, breathing in deeply, before dropping them to the floor. I squeeze my legs together as a white-hot pulse of heat shoots through me. He takes a step closer, undoing the buttons on his shirt. He takes off each layer slowly, keeping his gaze on me. I'm aching to scratch my nails against his taut stomach, kiss the sensitive place underneath his ear, and play with his gorgeous, thick cock that's currently getting harder by the moment from the teasing, but I wait for him to come to me. Slowly. Carefully. Like a predator about to catch prey that he's been hunting for miles.

He finally gets close enough to touch, but I wait, letting the water fall over us both as he looks at me. When he reaches out, it's my chin he grasps firmly. He tilts my head up, almost as if he's examining me, and finally leans in, brushing his lips against mine.

I whimper against his mouth, bringing my arms around his neck. He puts his hands on my hips, squeezing tightly, and kisses me until I'm forced to break away for air. He moves his hands, cupping my ass instead, and drops his head to my breasts, kissing each one before taking a nipple into his mouth. I gasp, because his warm mouth around the tight little bud is enough to make my belly tighten with want. Whatever we do, I won't last long, and I know that just means he'll bring me to a couple of climaxes instead of one. We know each other's bodies well by now. I know exactly how to get him to come down my throat, and he knows where to find that little spot inside me that makes me come messily, whether it's on his fingers or cock or thanks to his mouth. He continues to suck on my breasts, scraping his teeth along the sensitive underside of one, as he massages my bottom, but eventually he groans and drops to his knees.

I blink down at him, shivering as he drags his hands up my thighs, nudging them apart. He kisses my belly, resting his chin against it so he can look up at me.

"You're so beautiful."

I run my hand through his soaking wet hair. "You are."

"You know I want to devour every inch of you, always." His fingers trace patterns into my inner thighs, teasingly light. "You're my princess. And princesses always get what they deserve."

I tug on his hair, and he responds by nipping at the skin of my belly.

"And what do I deserve?" I ask. It's a game we've played before, but the answer never fails to leave me breathless.

He waits a moment before answering, drawing out the anticipation. I want his mouth on my cunt so badly I can hardly stand it, but I don't press. Not when I'm this close to being rewarded.

"Princesses deserve to be spoiled." He punctuates that by pressing his mouth to my folds, kissing and sucking, before he looks back up. "You deserve to be spoiled."

Bex

I gasp. I press forward, urging him to get his mouth back on my skin. Like this, it's easy to take his affections. What woman doesn't want to be spoiled in bed? It's the rest I have trouble with. I shove the thought out of my mind, determined to focus on this perfect moment, and like he can tell, he finds my clit, sucking on it in that way that never fails to make my nails dig into his shoulders. He eats me out until I'm begging him for his fingers, his cock, anything more to tip me over the edge. He drags it out, though, getting me close only to back away, forcing me to beg for it.

Instead of rising, pulling me into a proper kiss, and giving me his cock, he turns me around, his big hands keeping me steady. Before I can react, he slides two fingers into my cunt—and presses his tongue against my asshole.

I cry out against the slick shower tile. I should have known that getting him into this mood would lead to trouble. I may have started out in control, but he's wrested it from me deftly, making me weak with his talented tongue. He keeps his fingers inside me, moving them lazily, as he spreads my ass with his other hand, licking me out until I don't know whether to press back against him for more or try to get him to finger-fuck me properly. My toes curl against the tile and the shower pours down on my head, adding to the dizzying sensations running through me.

He bites my ass gently, his thumb on my clit once more, and

I moan his name as the orgasm rushes through me. My eyes squeeze shut, tiny dots of light dancing on the edges of my vision. I clench my pussy around his fingers, pleased to hear his groan, but rather than working up to another round, he withdraws them entirely.

My eyes fly open; I look back at him in outrage. He strokes my cheek as he reaches over to shut off the shower spray. "Don't worry, sweetheart. You're going to get my cock."

He wraps me in a soft, fluffy towel, but my skin is so hot and sensitive that it feels like sandpaper. I let it fall off me as he lifts me into his arms. He walks us back to the bed, even though we're dripping wet, and lays me out—on my hands and knees.

I shiver as he strokes a hand down my back. He moves my hair over one shoulder, pressing an open-mouthed kiss to my skin. "How should I spoil you?" he murmurs. "Fill your aching pussy while I spank the tease out of you? Make you come again while my cock is buried inside your tight little ass? What did you imagine when you were touching yourself?"

"James," I gasp out. It's rare that he gets so dirty, speaking so plainly about the things he wants to do with me, and I can't believe he's willing to do it while his entire family is right downstairs. He's taken my flirting into the stratosphere. "Whatever you want."

"Not good enough," he says, still pressing kisses to my sensitive skin. I shiver as his teeth scrape against the nape of my neck; I'm cold everywhere except where he's touching, and of course between my legs, already aching for another orgasm. "Pick one."

While he's played with my ass a lot, we've never gone all the way when it comes to anal sex, and I know what he's really asking. Do I want to press forward and try it out, or have I reached my limit?

He's patient, continuing his stroking, the kisses, while I think. I swallow, turning my head so I can see him. "The second one."

I think he's surprised, because he ducks his head, hiding his smile. But when he looks up, his expression has turned wicked. "Which was the second one again?"

"James," I whine, blush erupting on my cheeks. He's going to make me say it. I should have realized; as much as he likes teasing me, he needs my definitive say-so to go forward, especially with something new.

"Tell me and I'll do it, princess. How do you want to be spoiled?"

I feel like I'm on fire—but the flames of desire outweigh the ones of embarrassment and nervousness. It's just James, after all. He might be acting like the devil, but underneath the facade, he's my devoted boyfriend, and he'd never hurt me.

I force myself to look at him as I say it. "I want you to fuck my ass."

"Good girl," he praises, cupping my cheek. "You're such a perfect girl for me, Beckett."

I turn my head into his hand, pressing a kiss to his palm. He gets off the bed. I can't see him, but I hear him unzip his suitcase. Another hot drip of desire settles low in my belly. The thought of him packing lube, maybe hoping this would happen, is both sweet and incredibly hot.

One hand settles on my lower back, and the other toys with my still-wet cunt. He slides in two fingers, curling them slightly. "Let me know if it's too much," he says. "We can stop whenever."

"I know." I squeeze around his fingers, pleased when that makes his breath stutter. "I trust you."

He pulls his fingers, now slick, out of me, and smacks my ass. I moan, dropping my head down low. He hits me again, harder, before trailing his fingers down to my asshole, rubbing against my skin. The heat of his hand combined with the coolness of the lubricant has me curling my toes.

He starts with one finger, allowing me to adjust. He's fingered me here before, so soon he moves on to two, stretching me gently. By the time he reaches three, I'm whimpering, pushing back against him. It's a strange sensation, almost like I'm feeling him in my ass and cunt all at once, but not unwelcome. He takes his time, kissing my neck all the while, murmuring encouragement against my skin.

Then he withdraws his fingers, and his much bigger cock, slick with lube, presses against my hole.

He groans; he must like the sight of the head of his cock rubbing against my skin, his hands spreading my ass wide. He presses in just slightly, but even that punches the breath out of me, and I moan.

"Good?" he checks.

I nod. "Keep going."

"Good girl," he says again. He steadies me with a hand on my hip while he presses forward. "Just relax, you can take it."

I take a deep breath. He pushes in another inch, his thumb rubbing against my upper thigh soothingly. I'm trembling by the time he's in all the way; I've always thought he felt big in my cunt, but that's nothing compared to this. He reaches around, rubbing my clit to spark more pleasure as he lets me adjust, and if the way he's shaking is any indication, it feels just as overwhelming to him. There's nothing I love more than the proof that he's as affected as I am by what we do together, and that, more than anything, makes me deliberately clench around him.

"Beckett," he says, his voice low and nearly shaking with desire. "Fuck, I love you."

He keeps his fingers on my clit as he thrusts, first shallow, experimental, but then with purpose once he's satisfied that the discomfort has faded and I'm not feeling anything but pleasure. I whimper, gasp, and cry out his name as he builds up a rhythm, dragging against places I've never felt before with each thrust. My second orgasm takes me by surprise; one moment I'm teetering on the edge, the next I'm falling, bunching my hands in the sheets and clenching around his cock so tightly he moans, biting my shoulder. I think distantly that it's going to leave a mark his family will see, but it doesn't bother me. I just hope no one is upstairs right now, because I'm sure they'd be able to hear the noises we're making.

The steady rhythm he built up begins to unravel as he gets close to coming himself. I reach back, looping our fingers together since I can't kiss him in this position, and squeeze. "Come," I urge. "Come, honey. Right inside me. I love you, I love you."

"You feel incredible," he says. "My perfect, perfect girl." He snaps his hips forward, pushing even deeper inside me, forcing a loud, but fortunately muffled, cry of pleasure from my throat. He curls over me as he comes, holding me tight to his chest; I hear his groan of pleasure right against my ear. He plays with my clit, his other hand squeezing one of my tits, until I come again with him still pressed deep inside me. It almost hurts, right on the edge of being too much, and when he finally slips out of me, I just melt against the bed, totally boneless and spent.

He pulls me into his arms, settling us both against the headboard. I'm covered in slick and lube, water and sweat, and my heart is beating like a drum, but I can't stop smiling. I reach up, winding my arms around him, and nuzzle his neck.

"Wow," he says.

I stretch luxuriously. "Seriously."

"That was amazing." He runs his hand down my side, settling on my upper thigh. "I was nervous."

I look at him, biting my lip. "I was too."

"You feel good, right? I didn't go too hard?"

"I feel like I won't be able to walk straight," I say, my voice mostly teasing. I'm not sure how much I'm going to be aching once the adrenaline fades. Even if that's the case, it was totally worth it. "But really good, yeah."

He brushes his lips against my forehead. "Good."

Our gazes meet. For a long moment, I just stare into his blue eyes, feeling myself settle down. I can never decide what his eyes remind me of more; right now, they seem like the ocean we swam in earlier, endlessly deep and passionate. Every wave like a beat of his heart.

"Beckett, will . . ."

My heart takes off sprinting, even though he lets the sentence hang in the air, unfinished.

He shakes his head slightly. Seems to reach a conclusion.

"Will you come back to the shower with me?" he says. "Let's clean up before we go to bed."

I shake off the disappointment. For a moment, I thought it was *the* moment, but I'm glad he didn't do it. When it happens, I'm going to want to share the news immediately, and after what we just did, I need more time alone to collect myself.

"Sure," I say, sliding off the bed and offering my hand. "But let's have a bath this time instead."

CHAPTER 11

James

For the first and only time in my life, I wake up knowing that by the time I head to sleep later, I'll be an engaged man.

After last night, which was unexpected, hot as hell, and made me fall in love with Bex all over again, it's hard to drag myself up and out for golf at the club with my father and brothers, but somehow I manage. When I'm dressed, I lean over to kiss Bex goodbye; she's still buried under the covers.

"I'll see you later," I say. "Enjoy the spa."

She mumbles out something I can't hear. Hopefully she isn't too sore. I fucked her hard last night. It felt incredible; she was impossibly tight and so sweet, a vixen turned princess in my arms. I can't help but kiss her hair again. "I love you."

"Love you," she says, eyes still closed. "I'll see you later."

I bring the ring box along with me. Maybe pulling it out from time to time today will settle my nerves.

Our round of golf is, predictably, a disaster. It's sort of hilarious, considering all four of us are or were athletes, but collectively, our golf game sucks. Dad curses up a storm at the 10th, 13th, and 17th holes, Cooper nearly throws his club into the brush, Sebastian gets his shoes soaking wet trying to fish for a ball in one of the ponds, and as for me? Halfway through, I give up and fill in random scores on our cards. By the time we make it back to the club and settle at a table, we're all sweaty and cranky. The only saving graces are the nice breeze off the water and our cold beers.

Dad mops his forehead with a handkerchief as he squints at his card. "You gave me a thumbs up as the final score?"

"You showed admirable restraint for the first nine," I say, grinning. "The back nine, I don't know."

"He gave me a smiley face," Seb says as he wrings out his socks.

Dad shakes his head as he sighs. "They've asked me to play at the Pro-Am this year, and clearly, I should save myself the embarrassment."

"Nah," Cooper says around a swig of beer. "It's fun even if you play horribly. A lot of NFL guys have been doing it."

Dad gives Cooper a look. "Sure," he says sarcastically. "A weekend watching Tony Romo charm everyone."

"You could own the awfulness," I offer.

"It's depressing, how shit my game is." Before he can go on, a pair of guys around his age walk over to the table. One of them is Bill Huxley, an old family friend. I remember going to dinner parties at his Nags Head mansion many times as a kid. The other guy I don't recognize, but he waves at the table, so I wave back.

"So, it *is* the Callahans," Bill says. "Hi, boys."

Dad stands, reaching out his hand for a shake. "Bill, Jordan. Nice to see you."

While Dad is preoccupied by his conversation, Cooper leans over. "Wait, so you brought the ring with you?"

I take it out of my pocket, lifting the lid to admire it. It's still pristine, the sapphires sparkling on either side of the diamond.

"You know how expensive it was. I didn't want to just leave it for anyone to find."

"Sure," Cooper says with a knowing look. "Is that why you're staring at it, too?"

"Is it happening today?" Seb asks.

I shut the box, turning it over in my hands. "I think so. I almost did it last night, but it wasn't the right time."

Bill's hand settles on my shoulder. "Your father just said you have a serious girlfriend."

"Yeah." I smile. "Her name's Bex. We met last year, at McKee."

"Pretty. Is that a ring I just saw?"

"He's proposing soon," Dad cuts in.

"Make sure she's the right one, kid," the other guy, Jordan, says. "Saves a lot of heartbreak."

I hold up the ring box. "I'm sure."

"Bex is wonderful," Dad says, looking right at me as he speaks. "We're all so thrilled for her to be part of the family."

I swallow the lump in my throat. We really have come a long way since last winter. I'm relieved as I realize that all over again, because choosing between Bex and my relationship with my father would have been painful. I'm lucky I didn't have to make that choice. "Thanks, Dad. I'm glad you think so."

"And no matter how you do it, I'm sure she'll love it, but care to fill us in?"

* * *

IN THE END, only one way seems perfect. When we get back from dinner that evening, the summer sun is just starting to set, sending tendrils of blue and purple across a gorgeous orange and yellow sky. All of us go barefoot onto the beach; Izzy's in a white dress and oversized sweater, her dark hair a tangle over her shoulders, my parents walk hand in hand, letting their feet get wet, Seb and Cooper skip rocks into the surf while the wind ruffles their hair. Bex looks stunning in a sleeveless cobalt blue sundress—something new she bought today, at Izzy's urging, she told me as we got ready earlier—but she's chilly, so she's wearing my suit jacket, the sleeves rolled up as she snaps a picture of the sunset with her camera. She has a gold chain around her neck, matching the earrings I bought her for Christmas. I walk alongside her, patiently waiting as she gets her fill of the moment. As soon as we arrived at the house, she dashed upstairs for her camera, shouting down to me about the perfect, clear dusk.

She steadies herself to take a picture of my parents. My dad is saying something, but whatever it is gets lost on the wind.

I see my mother's smile.

There are twenty-five years in that smile.

If someone could fast forward twenty-five years, where would they find me and Bex? I hope, more than anything, that they'd see love between us.

I hope we're still standing shoulder to shoulder, no matter what we've had to endure. I hope we have children with Bex's eyes and our shared determination. I hope we're walking together on the beach, talking about everything and nothing. I hope I'm privileged enough to say that even my most ordinary moments are special because I get to share them with her.

My wife.

I just have to take the first step.

I signal to my sister, who runs over and tugs on our brothers' sweater sleeves. I take the ring out of my pocket. In my palm, it looks so small and delicate. It's the strongest symbol I can think of to prove to Bex that our love is the forever kind.

"Hey, Bex."

"Yeah, honey?"

I sink onto one knee, holding out the ring. "Take a picture of me."

CHAPTER 12

Bex

For a moment, I just stare.

James. On one knee. Holding a ring.

I nearly drop my camera, but fortunately the strap saves it from hitting the sand. I clap a hand over my mouth, unable to look away from him. The pure love on his face makes my heart gallop. The reality of the moment hits me like a wave.

"Beckett," he begins.

"Yes." The word slips out before I can stop it. I fall to my knees on the sand, pulling him into a kiss, before he can get any further. "Yes, yes!"

He pulls away, laughing. "Wait. Let me ask the question."

I nearly tell him there's no need, but I stop myself. He brushes my hair behind my ear, his hand lingering, stroking my cheek. "Beckett. From the moment I first saw you, I wanted to know you. And when you kissed me—"

I can't hold back a little sob, half amused at the memory of kissing him at that stupid frat party, half so overwhelmed by love I can't stand it.

"—I knew where I wanted us to end up. It took a little while, but I wouldn't change the path for anything. Not when it led me to you."

"James," I whisper.

"I want every moment with you, good and bad. When I think of my future, you come to mind before anything else. I mean it."

"I know you do."

He holds out the ring. I glance down at it, taking in the gleam of the diamond and what looks like sapphires, before settling my gaze back on his face. He could propose with a piece of seaweed and my answer wouldn't change.

"Will you do me the honor of marrying me?"

"Yes." I pull him close, breathing in the smell of his cologne, digging my nails into his skin. We tip backward onto the sand; I kiss him like that while we both laugh. He slides the ring onto my finger, pressing his lips to my hand. I know that his family is right there, I can hear their exclamations and congratulations, but in this moment, the only living thing in the world I'm truly aware of is James.

No longer my boyfriend—my fiancé.

He helps me to our feet, picking me up and spinning me around. "I love you," he murmurs.

I cup his jaw with both hands, looking into his eyes. They're shining with tears. "I love you too."

He sets me down. Izzy engulfs me in a hug. Sandra asks if she can look at the ring. Cooper hugs me, then Sebastian, and Richard kisses me on the cheek as he pulls both of us into a hug.

"Congratulations, both of you," he says. "Bex, we're so happy to call you family."

"Yes," Sandra says, clapping her hands excitedly. "James already mentioned the wedding won't be for a while, but whenever you're ready, I know a few wedding planners."

"Want me to take photos?" Izzy says. "Like at graduation?"

It's nearly dark now, the nighttime chasing away the sun, but we still wade into the surf. It's too perfect a moment to worry about the cold. James holds onto me securely—not that I'm worried about him letting go. Not now and not ever. Izzy walks around us, snapping pictures with the flash on, while James admires the way the ring looks on my finger.

"Do you love it?" he asks.

The diamond takes my breath away, but the sapphires are just wonderful. I don't know if he did it on purpose, but they remind me of his eyes, and I like the thought of wearing something that feels like him every day. I'm sure it was expensive, but it's like last night: he spoils me because that's who he is, and he can.

I lean up, kissing him again, and murmur my answer against his mouth. "It's perfect."

"My brothers helped me pick it out."

"The day you went into the city?"

"Yep."

I shake my head as my smile widens. "Well, you all have excellent taste. I'm proud to wear it."

"And I meant it, there's no rush. We can stay engaged for as long as you want. I'm not quite ready to plan a wedding either." He picks me up unexpectedly, his hands secure underneath my thighs, leaving me no choice but to wrap my wet legs around his waist and my arms around his neck. I glance back at his family, but no one seems scandalized—just thrilled. I swear I see Cooper wiping at his eyes. I smack James's chest lightly anyway, making him laugh. The sound of it makes me laugh as well, and I have a feeling that's the best photograph Izzy takes.

"I have to call my mother. Oh, and Laura. She's going to flip out."

James just hums, hugging me closer.

"But actually . . . I think we ought to call Kerry first."

"You sure?" I hear the surprise in his voice. I'm sure he hoped I'd say that, but he didn't expect it—and it's one of the millions of reasons I love him.

I take a deep breath. Despite being in his arms, despite wearing his ring on my finger, it still scares me, thinking of living together, alone, in a new city. I hope we can handle it. I hope it's the beginning of something wonderful.

I think it will be.

I cup the nape of his neck as I murmur against his lips, "Yes."

* * *

August

A month later, Kerry meets us on the steps to the townhouse, a set of keys in hand. She drops them into my palm, a wide smile on her face. "Congratulations, both of you. I have champagne waiting."

My hands are shaking so badly I can barely turn the key. James pushes the door open as soon as the lock finally slides out of place. He takes my hand, and together, we step over the threshold.

Without anything in the house but the chandelier overhead, our footsteps echo. This is an old house, one that will make sounds as it settles. I don't know the history of this building yet, but I'd like to find out about it, if I can. I hope that this house was filled with love before, just like it will be now and in the future.

We walk slowly through the empty rooms, planning out where to put the furniture, where to hang art on the walls. When we eventually make our way to the kitchen, I see the promised bottle of champagne sitting in ice, along with two glasses.

James pours us each a glass. We clink them together and toast, but I only take a sip before I get distracted by the perfect kitchen once more. I'm peering into the pristine refrigerator, thinking about the old one at the diner that was always on the fritz, when James pulls me into his arms.

I look up at him. "Hey, you."

"Hey, yourself. Is it like you remembered?"

"Even better."

"Good." He drops a kiss to my hair, then walks me back to the island. He presses me against the edge as he kisses me, his knee spreading my legs as his tongue teases the seam of my lips.

"James," I gasp when we break apart.

He plays with the ends of my hair. "We need to christen it, you know. Our home."

I press my lips together to keep from smiling, shaking my head slightly. "Here in the kitchen?"

"I'm improvising."

"Clearly," I tease. I wind my arms around him, squeezing, and indulge him with another kiss, tasting the champagne on his tongue. "It's a good thing you have me. We have a rooftop patio, and I packed a blanket."

CHAPTER 13

James

I drag myself from the car to the front steps, bag drooping over my shoulder. Prior to training camp, I heard a lot of things about how much more intense the NFL is, but I didn't truly believe it until today. I'm sore all over, and my mind is still reeling from the amount of information I was expected to absorb. I'm going to have my work cut out for me if I'm going to be successful in the league. Trust me, I loved every moment—but I'm dying to be horizontal. Preferably next to my fiancée.

I find her in the kitchen, sitting at the island as she peers at her laptop. The whole room smells amazing, like some kind of casserole, but beyond that, I'm too tired to try to identify it. I drop my bag and hobble over to her, hooking my chin over her shoulder.

"Hey," she says. "You're later than I expected."

"It was . . . such a long day."

She looks at me, her brown eyes filled with concern. "In a good way?"

"Mostly. But it was intense. I'm going to be busy all season, but especially the next couple of weeks."

She strokes my face with her left hand—the one with her engagement ring. That never fails to make me smile. "We'll make it work. Are you hungry? It's ready, I was just keeping it hot in the warmer."

"What is it?"

"Meat lasagna," she says, kissing me before she slides off the stool and walks around the island. "I figured you could use something hearty after your first day."

"Holy shit, I love you."

She laughs as she pulls the dish out of the oven. "I love you too, babe. Do you want a plate or just a fork?"

My stomach grumbles. The lunch I had at the facility feels like it happened in another lifetime. "Eh, let's just eat from the pan."

I fill her in on all that went down during my day while we eat the lasagna, standing at the island, dueling with our forks for the best bits of cheese. She has this cute, serious expression on her face as she listens; I know she's determined to get to know all my new teammates and coaching staff. For our preseason game next week, she's planning on sitting with the girlfriends and wives of some of my teammates, and she's already made plans with my family to go to the home opener in September.

When I feel a little revived and stop rambling, I gesture to her computer. "What were you working on when I came in?"

"Remember how K'Andre's girlfriend is a graphic designer?"

"Yeah."

"Well, we're chatting about me hiring her to make a logo. For . . . me. If I open this business."

I let my fork drop. "No way! I thought you were still considering the offer from Temple."

"I was," she says. "And it was so sweet of your father to set that up. But if I do freelance photography, my schedule will be more flexible, so I can come to more of your games."

"You don't have to."

"I know," she says, wiping the corner of my mouth with her thumb. "But I want to. And I really like having creative freedom."

"Beckett Wood Photography."

She bites her lip. "Well, I was thinking . . . maybe Beckett Callahan Photography. Even though we're not getting married right away, I know I want your name, so why not use it now?"

"Really?" We haven't spoken about whether Bex would take my name, and if she didn't want to, I wouldn't have pushed, but hearing it aloud makes me love it immediately. I wind my arms around her, tucking my hand into her back jeans pocket and squeezing.

She pokes me in the chest. "Well, I'd much rather have my husband's name than my shitty absent dad's."

"Here's to that."

"Mom is changing her name back to her maiden name," she adds. "She's going to be Abby Clark again."

I hug her close. Things with her mom have been going well for the most part, fortunately, but she's always a little fragile when she brings her up. It was a relief to hear that she approved of our engagement, because if she hadn't, that would have been hard on Bex. "That sounds like an excellent idea. Did you start anything else for the business?"

"Not yet. I wanted to run it by you first." She runs her hand through her hair, tucking it behind her ear. "I know that we've worked out a money solution you can work with—"

I grumble a bit. It took a long conversation, but eventually we agreed that I'll take care of the big stuff like the mortgage, but Bex will help with things like groceries, as well as handle her own student loans. That, more than anything else, is frustrating to me, but I know it's important to her to feel like she's contributing, so it's a compromise I've reluctantly made.

"—but if I start this business," she continues, "my money situation will be pretty sparse for a while, at least until I build up a steady group of clients. I wanted to make sure you're okay with that."

"Of course," I say. It's not even a question; I'll support her no matter what she wants to do. "I want you to follow your dreams, princess. I'm with you."

She smiles, leaning up to peck me on the cheek. "Thank you. I was all nervous, but I don't know why."

"Taking the leap is always scary. I felt like I was going to puke for most of the day, and honestly, I'm absolutely terrified to actually play. But I did it, and you can do this." My eyes widen as I remember another detail of the day that I want to laugh about with her. It's nice to have these experiences, but having someone to share them with is even better. "Wait, I have the funniest story to tell you."

She takes my hand, giving me a look that I know all too well. As exhausted as I am, I perk up with interest.

She tugs me in the direction of the stairs. "Mind telling me in bed?"

About the Author

GRACE REILLY writes swoony, spicy contemporary romance with heart–and usually a healthy dose of sports. When she's not dreaming up stories, she can be found in the kitchen trying out a new recipe, cuddling her pack of dogs, or watching sports. Originally from New York, she now lives in Florida, which is troubling given her fear of alligators.